# EMBERS OF
# COURAGE

# EMBERS OF COURAGE

A NOVEL BY
## DIANE & DAVID MUNSON

MicahHouse
media

Grand Rapids, Michigan

# DEDICATION

In writing this thriller about persecution of Christians, we remember the many Christians who have been persecuted and even killed through the centuries since Christ taught that His believers would be hated for following Him. At a time when the world is increasingly hostile toward those who follow Christ's teachings, we dedicate this book to those who are next to be martyred, and they may be people we know.

# ACKNOWLEDGMENTS

Many thanks to Micah House Media and those supporting them for this story of faith and courage, which we hope you will enjoy reading. We give a special thanks to Pamela Guerrieri-Cangioli for her expertise in editing and great support for our endeavor. Jeremy Culp has our heartfelt thanks for his excellent interior design and splendid cover that artistically reveals how human weapons turn to ashes as well conveying the key theme that spans our pages of history.

# ABOUT THE AUTHORS

**ExFeds**, Diane and David Munson write *High Velocity Suspense* novels that reviewers compare to John Grisham. The Munsons call their novels "factional fiction" because they write books based on their exciting and dangerous careers.

**Diane Munson** has been an attorney for more than thirty years. She has served as a Federal Prosecutor in Washington, D.C., and with the Reagan Administration, appointed by Attorney General Edwin Meese, as Deputy Administrator/Acting Administrator of the Office of Juvenile Justice and Delinquency Prevention. She worked with the Justice Department, U.S. Congress, and White House on policy and legal issues. More recently she has been in a general law practice.

**David Munson** served as a Special Agent with the Naval Investigative Service (now NCIS), and U.S. Drug Enforcement Administration over a twenty-seven year career. As an undercover agent, he infiltrated international drug smuggling organizations, and traveled with drug dealers. He met their suppliers in foreign countries, helped fly their drugs to the U.S., feigning surprise when shipments were seized by law enforcement. Later his true identity was revealed when he testified against group members in court. While assigned to DEA headquarters in Washington, D.C., David served two years as a Congressional Fellow with the Senate Permanent Subcommittee on Investigations.

As Diane and David research and write, they thank the Lord for the blessings of faith and family. They are busy collaborating on their next novel, and traveling the country speaking/appearing at various venues. Check out their critiques of the popular TV show found on their NCIS blog at their website below.

## WWW.DIANEANDDAVIDMUNSON.COM

# CAST OF CHARACTERS

(Alphabetical) *Indicates Real Historical Figures

**Alphonso de Alvarado** – The count's son

**Aneka Vander Goes** – Pieter Vander Goes' wife

**Andrei Enescu** – Romanian terrorist and fugitive, aka Francois Petit

**Andy Montanna** – Eva's fifteen-year-old son

**Archbishop of Canterbury, Henry Chicesley***

**Bishop Alnwick***

**Bo Rider** – CIA agent

**Brandon Tate** – Professor at International Christian College

**Butrus** – Member of Coptic Church in Egypt

**Captain Van Ritter** – River/sea captain

**Count de Alvarado** – Pieter's nemesis

**Dirck Vander Goes** – Pieter Vander Goes' oldest son

**Duke Charles the Bold***

**Duke Philip the Good***

**Eva Montanna** – ICE special agent on Staff of Joint Terrorism Task Force

**Father Angus** – Pieter's cousin and Lollard preacher

**Father Maxim** – Abbot of Middleburg abbey and Pieter's friend

**Fiona Billingham** – Journalism student

**Griff Topping** – FBI agent and Eva's partner on Task Force

**Hamadi Von Bilgon** – Egyptian (Coptic) Christian and Priest

**Heather Pentu** – Wife of NCIS agent Raj Pentu

**Ishaq** – Weapons buyer for Egyptian Brotherhood and terrorist

**Jenny Vander Goes** – Pieter's daughter

**Johann Fust*** – Financier of Gutenberg

**Johann Gutenberg*** – Inventor of the printing press who printed the first Bible

**John Wycliffe*** – Reformer; first to translate the first Bible into English

**Julia Rider** – Bo's wife

**Justinus Vander Goes** – Pieter's son

**Kaley Montanna** – Eva's seventeen-year-old daughter

**Karl Badger** – Kaley's government teacher

**King Edward IV***

**Lexi Dawson** – Kaley's friend

**Marcia Vander Goes** – Eva's mother
**Margaret of York**\* – Jenny's friend and sister to King Edward the IV
**Marty** – Martin Vander Goes, Eva's grandfather
**Olivia Badger** – Karl Badger's daughter
**Pieter Vander Goes** – Magistrate for Duke Philip and Eva's ancestor
**Raj Pentu** – NCIS agent and Eva's colleague
**Reverend William White**\* – Christian martyr
**Scott Montanna** – Eva's husband and press secretary for the house speaker
**Trish Dawson** – Owns Wholly Ground coffee shop; Lexi's mom
**Yakov Gusev** – Russian arms dealer

# TERMS

**Abbey** – Christian cathedral in Middleburg, the Netherlands
**AK-47** – Russian-made selective-fire/automatic assault rifle
**Asset** – Term for CIA informant/spy
**BOLO** – Law enforcement warning to "Be On The Lookout"
**Bucar** – Griff's FBI car
**CIA** – America's Central Intelligence Agency
**Cog** – Captain Van Ritter's boat
**Coptic Christian** – Egyptian Christian, also known as Copts
**EB/Egyptian Brotherhood** – Islamic terror group in Egypt, linked to IS
**G-car** – Government issued vehicle
**HQ** – Headquarters
**ICE/Immigration Customs Enforcement** – Eva's federal agency
**IS** – Islamic State, militant terrorist group linked to Egyptian Brotherhood
**MI 5** – British Domestic Intelligence Agency (their version of our FBI)
**Mossad** – Israeli Intelligence Agency
**RPG** – Rocket-Propelled Grenade and Launcher
**SCIF** – Sensitive Compartmented Information Facility
**"The Agency"** and **"The Company"** – Insider's terms for the CIA

"Be strong and courageous. Do not be terrified;
do not be discouraged, for the LORD your God
will be with you wherever you go."

Joshua 1:6 (NIV)

# CHAPTER 1

## APRIL IN FAIRFAX COUNTY, VIRGINIA

Federal Agent Eva Montanna hadn't been home from church more than five minutes before her husband Scott and their three kids became glued to the TV. A roar coming from an auto race was so thunderous, it shook the plates she'd set on the dining room table. How could she ever tune out such earsplitting noise?

Her job as a special agent with the Immigration Customs Enforcement (ICE) was hectic, and often carried over into the weekend. But this Sunday she had off. An idea spun in Eva's mind as she hustled to the raucous family room.

"Let's all head to the exhibit for veterans at Patriot Park," she announced.

It was as if her clan hadn't heard a word. They were hooting too loudly. Her son Andy tore open a bag of chips and plopped next to Scott, who reached in the bag.

"Thanks, buddy."

As Scott shoved a fistful of chips in his mouth, Eva left the room to Scott's cries, "His tire's goin' down!"

Eva opened the fridge, noticing a leftover chicken casserole among the purple containers. Her family didn't act as if they wanted to sit around the table, so she took down five bamboo trays. She would go support the local veterans by herself after lunch. Because of their sacrifice, she and her family could live and worship freely.

Another idea gripped her. She and the kids could help the church youth group place American flags on graves of fallen soldiers. She turned back toward the race zone.

"He hit the wall!" Andy blurted.

At fifteen, he loved all kinds of action. Dutch, their youngest, sat on Scott's other side, and Kaley, her seventeen-year-old daughter, looked precious wearing a cap from her favorite driver. Eva left them to enjoy their fun time, and sped to the small antique desk in the far corner of the living room. She wrote a quick note to the pastor. On the way back to the kitchen, something sparkling on the mantelpiece caught her eye.

The sun shone through the picture window, its rays brightening an ornate metal container. Eva did a double take. Inside that round container rested a pouch of unexplained ashes. Up until now, she'd blocked those ashes from her memory. How come?

Last summer, she and Grandpa Marty found a deerskin pouch at his farm in Zeeland, Michigan. All he could remember was that his Dutch aunt had given it to him at WWII's end. Eva had secured the pouch in the container several months ago. The ashes had apparently rested undisturbed for centuries. She now traced the filigree with her finger.

"Who are you?"

Her whispered question drifted away amid gleeful shouts from the family room. Their din deepened her resolve to renew her search. She grabbed the cordless phone and before she could punch in her aging grandfather's number, her phone rang. It was Tim, the watch officer at HQ.

"I've been trying to reach you," he complained.

"My phone never rang." Then she saw a flashing red light on the phone base. "Sorry, I didn't check when I got home from church. My cell is still on silent."

"I first called an hour ago," Tim said. "One of your BOLOs has a hit."

"I haven't posted any new 'be on the lookouts.'"

"It's an older case. A guy escaped from federal prison. Andrei Enescu mean anything?"

Her heart flipped. "Yes! What's happening?"

Tim's keyboard clattered in her ear before he told her about receiving an alert from Global Worldwide, the contractor that monitored anti-terrorism video feeds. Global ran images through facial recognition software to spot terrorists and fugitives.

"Tim, this is critical," Eva said seriously. "Agent Topping and I arrested Enescu, but he slithered away from the U.S. Marshals after being sentenced. We've been after him ever since. Where is he now?"

"They spotted him at the mall in Fairfax. They claim it's a perfect match."

Eva's breath came in short bursts. She was minutes away from grabbing the felon who'd escaped after her testimony convicted him of passport fraud. Enescu's passport scam helped deadly terrorists. She was taking no chances that he would slip away again.

"Tim, keep Global on the line. Ask them to follow protocols and notify local police and mall security. See if other cameras in the area can isolate him."

"He's already been detained. I promised to send you on your way."

"Agent Topping and I should be there within thirty minutes."

Eva disconnected the call and hit speed dial for Griff Topping, the FBI agent assigned to her task force. He answered on the first ring.

"Hey, Eva. Why are you calling me on Sunday?"

"I have important news."

"You're inviting me over for Scott's famous Texas burgers?"

"Wait a sec."

Eva hustled past her family whooping in the den. There was no way they could hear what she told Griff, but she stuck to the rules. She blasted down the hall with the cell phone tucked against her shoulder. Eva shut her bedroom door and told Griff of the stunning phone call from ICE HQ.

"What are the odds it's really Enescu?" Griff scoffed. "Right under our noses."

Eva pushed back. "It's him. I'm leaving home now. You joining me?"

"Okay, I'm twenty-five minutes away from the mall. I'll catch you on the radio."

Eva hung up, yanking jeans from a hanger. It didn't take her longer than thirty seconds to change. She slipped on the shoulder holster holding her semi-automatic Glock and handcuffs. Then she thrust on a light jacket, which covered her weapon.

"Scott, I'm called out," she said, striding into the family room. "You're on your own for lunch."

She turned and headed for the garage. Behind her the kids were cheering and laughing. No one said good-bye, but she tried not to take it personally. Scott soon caught up to her.

He pulled her into his arms, and with an exaggerated wink he said, "I'll take the kids out for tacos later."

"So that's why they're cheering."

"Eva, where are you going?"

She told him about her fugitive and how Griff would meet her at the mall. Eva kissed his cheek and opened the door to the garage. As the overhead door rattled, he gently tugged her back for a better kiss.

He released her with a whispered, "Be careful."

"I always am, honey. Bring me home a chicken burrito for later."

He promised he would. Eva blew him another kiss and hopped into her G-car. She backed down the driveway, doubt sweeping over her. This government-issued Ford Fusion had left her stranded on the roadside last week. The mechanics replaced the fuel pump. Had they found the real problem?

To her neighbors, her vehicle looked like any family sedan. That was far from the truth. Eva sat ensconced in her mobile command center. Her emergency flashers were hidden above the sun visor. With deft movements, she opened the glove box, exposing two hidden radio systems. Each radio boasted tiny green lights and microphones attached to curling cords. Eva rolled through the neighborhood, stretching her arm to change her radio's channel.

She eased onto the ramp of westbound I-66 before tromping on the accelerator. The six hundred horsepower pursuit engine catapulted her back into her seat.

"Okay then."

Eva laughed, gripping the wheel, ready for the power under the hood to rocket her to nab Enescu ASAP. She veered left into the passing lane, switching on her high beams. Although equipped with flashing lights, she didn't use them for fear of attracting media or thrill seekers hoping to capture video on their smart phones. The last thing she needed was some wannabe uploading her face and G-car on social media.

She checked in with the base radio operator. "I'm en route to a mall in Fairfax County. Details should be on your console."

"Ten four. One other unit is on the air and en route."

"Any new developments?" Eva glued her eyes to heavy traffic snarling around her.

"The subject should still be in custody at the security office, waiting for your arrival."

"Ten four."

Eva flashed her lights at a slow-moving car ahead of her in the passing lane. The driver glanced into his mirror—she saw his eyes moving—but his red sedan stayed put. Eva backed off the accelerator, fuming. Whenever she had to be somewhere quickly, why did some slowpoke foil her?

Griff's voice burst from the radio speaker, "It's me on air. I'm twenty minutes out."

"Ten four."

Eva flashed her high beams again. Though the slow driver glanced in his rearview mirror, he refused to budge. Eva had encountered this kind of self-appointed traffic monitor before. Well, she'd teach him a thing or two.

She pulled down the passenger sun visor, and flipped a switch mounted by the steering column. Flashing LED red lights reflected off his red car. She toggled another switch and pressed her horn rim. At the sound of her screeching siren, the driver's eyes flew to his mirror. He swerved erratically into the middle lane.

Eva zoomed by him, snapping off her switches and raising the sun visor. Once again her super-fast G-car resembled a family sedan. Minutes later, she wheeled into a parking space near the security office. A familiar figure was entering the mall entrance and she ran to catch up. She arrived at the security office the precise moment Griff opened the door.

He wore a friendly grin. "Looks like this time I beat you."

"Some maniac driver nearly wiped me out." Eva wagged a finger at him. "You should be thankful I made it alive."

The reception desk was empty, so they strode toward a corridor of doorways looking for the guard. A large man in uniform finally emerged from another doorway. Griff held up his leather credential case. Eva shoved hers in front of Griff's.

"Our fugitive is being held here," she said, angling past Griff. "Where is he?"

The uniformed guard extended a smooth hand. "I'm Director of Security Rob Swift. Come to my office."

Eva didn't like Swift ignoring her question. She followed him into an austere office with two chairs placed in front of a cheap desk. Eva wasn't about to sit and chat.

Before she questioned him further, Swift asked, "You weren't notified?"

"Yes, that's why we're here," she shot back.

"No, I mean … ah …"

Eva glowered at the security director. Griff gaped at Eva and shook his head.

"Your partner was already here." Swift folded his arms across his massive chest. "The guy we cuffed and dragged in here wasn't your fugitive."

Eva's hands flew to her hips. "What do you mean our 'partner'? We've no other partners."

Griff thrust his FBI identification in Swift's face for a second time.

Swift nodded his round head. "Yessir! His badge and ID looked just like yours."

"What was his name?" Eva's blood pressure was climbing.

"Ah," Swift stammered. "I don't know your names either. The badge speaks for itself."

"Where is our suspect?" Griff stepped toward Swift.

Meanwhile, Eva thrust a photo of Enescu in his face.

"Did you cuff this guy?"

Swift studied the photo before covering Enescu's moustache and chin with his fingers.

"Yup. He's not sporting a moustache now, but that's Francois Petit." He handed Eva the photo. "Your partner checked the guy's identification."

"Quit calling him our partner," Eva barked. "We already told you we have no partner. You didn't even get the guy's name."

"Well, the other FBI agent told me the guy I cuffed wasn't a fugitive. I don't need a false arrest lawsuit, so I released him. He beat feet in a hurry. In fact, so did your FBI agent. I needed info for my report, but the agent followed the guy right out the door."

"Did you let Francois Petit make any phone calls?" Eva demanded.

Swift shrugged his shoulders. "He phoned his wife, who was somewhere in the mall on her cell phone. He knew she'd be afraid if she couldn't find him."

"And did Mrs. Petit come to the security office to comfort her husband?"

A look of enlightenment passed over Swift's face. "Nope, she didn't."

"That's because there is no Mrs. Petit, just like there is no Francois Petit. He's our fugitive, Andrei Enescu. You probably let him phone an accomplice posing as an FBI agent."

"Well, that stinks," Swift grumbled.

Eva walked to the doorway, looked into the hall, and then told Swift she spotted a surveillance camera. "Can you call up the data so we can see who the FBI agent was?"

Swift smiled sheepishly. "That's a good idea."

He jerked toward the door. Whirling around, he faced Eva with a frown. "It's no good. I turned it off."

"You did what?" Griff bellowed. "Did the other FBI agent instruct you to do that?"

Swift shrugged. "Management's worried about being sued. Whenever we're about to arrest someone, we arrange for the video system to malfunction. You know, turn it off-like."

"How idiotic!" Eva blared.

Swift shrugged his shoulders. "Camera's off, but I know what the FBI agent looked like."

"We might as well sit, Griff."

She dropped into the closest chair, her adrenaline spiking. She needed to calm down and make Swift spill everything he knew about the bogus FBI agent. For the next hour, she and Griff took copious notes about Enescu's arrest and escape. Swift's description of the counterfeit FBI guy sounded like too many male FBI agents. After they'd combed through Rob Swift's memory bank a second time, Griff pocketed his notes.

He handed Swift his card. "If you recall any detail, no matter how small, call me."

"Sir, I will. I've always wanted to work with the Bureau." Swift lowered his voice. "In fact, my application is pending. If you could check for me, I'd appreciate it."

Eva took the director's card and with an anemic salute, strode from his office.

Griff caught up to her and sighed. "Another wannabe. I can't believe we were this close and Enescu disappears once again. Who's the pretend agent?"

"When we find out, he is toast," Eva promised. "We'll charge him with obstruction of justice. We should interview the clerk at the computer store."

They walked into the mall with Eva looking over her shoulder. Was Enescu hovering down a side aisle, wearing a disguise, and monitoring them? She shook off the creepy sensation and strode with Griff into the computer store. The sales rep talked a mile a minute as he claimed the man in the picture had been looking at hard drives.

"Only he didn't have a moustache," he insisted.

Armed with video copies of Enescu's actions in the mall prior to his arrest, Eva and Griff left the mall, licking their wounds.

Eva stopped by her car. "This is terrible. Enescu's in league with violent

terrorists. He's not some felon who will disappear and make a nice life somewhere else."

"Head home and I'll comb the videos. If you don't hear back, it means
I found zip."

"We should pray. God knows where he is and what that creep is up to."

"Amen to that, Eva." Griff sprinted to his bucar carrying videos in one hand.

She trusted him to leave no stone unturned. Still, she steeled herself for
what might be ahead. Her job could be mundane for days and then a crisis
leapt at her like a snarling lion. Today was a perfect example. Eva hopped into
her G-car, vowing to slap handcuffs on Enescu. Only this time she hoped it
would be for good. She refused to let some lousy criminal defeat her.

# CHAPTER 2

That night and the next, Eva dreamed she was after Andrei Enescu, chasing him from Fairfax, to London, and then Moscow. She awoke exhausted. Tuesday morning, she sped to the office where she downed mega-cups of coffee. So did Griff. Finishing another cup, he ambled to her desk.

"Eva," he said ominously. "Enescu was on a private jet departing Syria for Moscow."

Her blue eyes rounded. "I dreamed he was in Moscow."

"Uh oh, not your uncanny dreams again."

"When was he there?"

"Four months ago. The FBI analyst on our Russian desk just phoned me on the QT."

"What do you make of the news?" she asked him.

His smile grew wider. "A former Syrian Army general was on the same flight."

"So where's Enescu now? He can't just drop off the grid."

"Unless he's no longer living. That's what our analyst thinks."

Eva didn't buy that possibility for one minute.

"Unless he's living as Francois Petit," she quipped.

Eva pressed her lips and spent time reviewing reports for her grand jury testimony next week on a different case. On the drive home, she focused on Enescu, who had slipped her net again. She couldn't even savor the pizza she fixed for supper. Nor did she concentrate on Scott's take about his new position as press secretary for the speaker of the house.

Her mind replayed her disappointing race to the mall. She slammed dishes into the dishwasher, all the while plotting how to outwit the Romanian felon who had outfoxed her.

After she tidied the kitchen, and the kids were doing homework, she sat beside Scott on the sofa watching a DVD of their trip last year to the Netherlands and England. That reminded her of what Griff found out as she left the office—three months ago Enescu had been spotted in Amsterdam. She leaned back against the sofa. So he'd flown from Moscow to Holland. Then he must have come to the U.S. where she and Griff nearly caught him.

But "nearly" was unacceptable. What if she went abroad and searched for the elusive Enescu herself?

"You're too quiet," Scott probed. "What's bothering you?"

"Work."

"That's my sweetheart, committed and courageous. Tell me more after we're ready for bed."

Eva turned off the lights and locked the back door. She set the new alarm system. The kids were all asleep in their rooms and everything *seemed* secure. Was it really?

Anxiety pelted her mind. If only she'd listened sooner to that message from HQ. Enescu's evading her for a second time cast doubts on her family's safety. The moment she joined Scott in their master bedroom, he spun around from the bay window looking tense.

"Kill the lights," he ordered. "I heard something out there."

Panic seized Eva. She snapped off the lights and closed the bedroom door with her foot. Scott pulled back the curtain. They stood at the window, seeing nothing, hearing nothing.

"I sounded a false alarm. It's probably the raccoon I found raiding our bird feeder."

"I'm not sure." Eva kept her voice low. "What if he's out there?"

Scott took her hands in his. "We shouldn't live our lives in constant fear."

"This guy is a Romanian intelligence officer, left over from the Soviet system. He's a mercenary who sells his knowledge and wares to the highest bidder, including terrorist organizations. Is it just coincidence he turns up at the mall a few miles from our house?"

"Don't the marshals search for fugitives?"

"They send out alerts." She withdrew her hand and stared out the window. "They see him here, they see him there, but he's never anywhere!"

"Sshh, you'll wake the kids. There's one thing we can do besides wait on the marshals."

"What's that?"

"Trust in God. He has not failed us and won't this time."

"Yes. It's easy to say but hard to do when an escaped felon is out there somewhere. I'm not afraid for myself. It's you and the kids …"

Her words fell away. Scott put his hands on her upper arms.

"You're paranoid because of what happened last year. But that worked out okay, right?"

Eva had to admit it did. As she readied for bed, she became calmer. Unfortunately, her sense of peace didn't last. She fell into a restless sleep.

Hours later she awoke trembling. She'd been racing after Enescu on Germany's Autobahn when his car careened off the shoulder. His BMW flipped end over end and landed on its roof. In her dream, she heard his screams.

Eva sat up in bed and listened. Outside the window, an owl screeched. Her heart fluttered and she sank to the bed beside Scott. His steady breathing meant he was asleep. She glanced at the lighted digital clock on her bedside table.

It was five a.m. and Eva was wide-awake. For another hour she plotted her next move on the chessboard. Enescu must be caught no matter what. An hour later, the sun lit the sky. Eva eased from bed. She left a note for Scott by the coffee carafe. After ordering hot java and a bagel at the Wholly Ground, she goosed her Ford to the office. There she checked her messages and e-mails.

Nothing urgent required her attention, so she completed her fugitive report. Her sole fugitive should be in prison, but because he'd escaped, she had to write these quarterly reports, which only made her more annoyed. Normally, the U.S. Marshals Service would track him down, but neither they nor the FBI took any interest in Andrei Enescu.

Because the Romanian spy threatened Eva when she'd arrested him years ago, she took his recapture personally. She began another computer search.

Griff sauntered by with a wave. "I spent last evening flying—tried to clear my mind."

"Did it work?"

"The sunset was beautiful. Otherwise, no."

Eva could relate. Griff had a pilot's license and she sought other ways to relax. Only nothing worked for her either. She told Griff of her search for Enescu's name in public and social media records.

"Check Petit too," he reminded, telling her of a lead he received yesterday. "We may have to drop everything and go after these Chechen terrorists. I'll let you know."

"I could use the distraction," she replied, returning to her computer.

While she didn't expect to find Enescu using his real name, she tried even the most rudimentary methods. No doubt he was using a well-documented alias. She searched the database for recent sightings of Enescu or the mystifying Francois Petit. Mid-morning, she stumbled on a possible alert from the ICE office in El Paso. Could he be the same Petit?

Eva called El Paso, only to find the resident agent was gone, meeting with the Texas governor about the border crisis. She left a message and updated the BOLO advising law enforcement agencies that Enescu should be held and Eva notified.

After she finalized the entry, her cell phone rang. The LED screen flashed *Marty Vander Goes.*

Her grandpa sounded out of breath. "When are you visiting? I miss you guys."

"We miss you too," Eva said tenderly. "Are you all right?"

"Busy with a new painting. I'd love you to see it."

All the work Eva had yet to accomplish for the grand jury buzzed through her mind like angry bees. Summer vacation seemed far off. Still, she wanted to be encouraging and said she hoped to visit soon.

"Oh goody," he chirped. "I'm judging at the 4-H fair."

"Are they hosting artists these days?"

Marty laughed, a lilt in his voice. "I'm deciding the best-tasting canned tomatoes. Oh, I had a surprise phone call this morning."

Worry flitted through Eva's mind as she recalled the scary episode from last year.

"Do you mean you heard from Brittney Condover?"

"No, something enjoyable. Your father is coming to see me for a week. That's why I'm calling. I envisioned us being together for once."

Eva forced out a sigh. "I can't come next week. You two need to spend time with each other anyway. God may have a special purpose in his visit. Don't you think so?"

"Miracles are occurring, I agree. Clifford driving here is one. After you and I returned from England, I told your dad how the local Dutch museum is showcasing my WWII drawings. He's helping me assemble my sketches and paintings."

Eva asked him the date and made a note on her smart phone. "We'll try to come for your showing. Dutch talks nonstop of your Army days."

"I love how my great-grandson loves all things Dutch," Marty said, chuckling.

Another idea crept into her mind. "Will you send the other journals Aunt Deane gave you? You know, the ones telling of the earlier Vander Goes family."

"You took them with you. Aren't you still writing my memoirs?"

Eva did a quick mental assessment and told him the one she needed was about Pieter Vander Goes, the judge in the fifteenth century. She heard her grandpa opening and closing a drawer, and visualized him sitting at the old dining room desk.

"Here's the one," he said. "It's pretty old and worn."

Marveling at how well he still got around, she advised him to insure and register it at the post office so it didn't get lost. Her vibrating cell phone interrupted her train of thought. Her mother was calling. Eva's pulse raced. She hoped nothing was wrong. Mom rarely phoned.

"Grandpa, Mom's on my other line," she said. "Is she coming with Dad to see you?"

"I don't think so, but she's welcome. Stay in touch, Eva."

"Watch your mailbox for cute photos of the kids. Gotta go."

Eva ended one call and took the other one on her cell phone, asking her mom if everything was okay.

"I wanted to talk with my daughter," Marcia said. "Do you have time?"

"Grandpa just phoned, so this is my day to talk with family. I'm pretty busy though."

"That's too bad. Any chance you can meet for lunch? We need to talk."

Eva detected a note of stress in her voice and instantly agreed. Her mom suggested the Wholly Ground coffee shop, which meant she'd do most of the driving. Eva arranged to meet at noon. As she hung up, her mind pulsed with possibilities.

A sharp wedge had come between Eva and her mother after Eva's twin sister Jillie lost her life in the terror attack on the Pentagon. The time since 9/11 had taken a toll on Eva's parents. They traveled the globe searching for a new beginning. Well, Mom was reaching out and Eva would be there for her.

The search for Enescu could wait a few hours anyway.

# CHAPTER 3

With the sun sending cheery rays on the spring day, Eva pulled into the café's parking lot. She'd taken her parents here last fall to meet Eva's pastor. They had a wonderful time talking about what it meant to leave a legacy for Christ. She spotted her mom's white car under a large shade tree. Eva hopped out of her G-car filled with anxiety. What did her mother have to say? Did one of her folks have an illness Mom couldn't admit over the phone?

Marcia waved at her from a bench in the side garden. Eva dashed over, embracing her mother with a loving hug. Marcia returned the hug before pulling back.

"What have you done differently with your hair? I like the way your ends curl."

Eva touched her hair self-consciously. "They do that naturally. What's so urgent?"

"I am sorry, Eva Marie."

"Why apologize? It's okay calling me away from work, though my case could erupt any moment."

Marcia swept her shoulder-length blond hair away from her forehead. Eva liked how her mom now wore her hair exactly like Eva's.

"I'm famished." Marcia lifted the handle of a small suitcase. "Let's go in."

"What's with the luggage, Mom?"

Marcia simply rolled the suitcase in behind her. Her cryptic manner gave Eva a start. She went inside wondering what was going on.

A teenager from Eva's church seated them at a corner table adorned with daisies. Eva was glad Kaley and Lexi Dawson were close friends. Lexi had pulled her brown hair into a ponytail, which showed her toothy smile. She produced menus, telling them the special was chicken salad with strawberries.

"Is your chicken organic?" Marcia asked.

Lexi nodded, tapping her pencil on her small pad.

"And the strawberries?"

"Organic." Lexi fiddled with her tiny pencil.

Marcia ordered the special with a tall glass of sweet tea, and gave Lexi the menu. Eva wanted the same salad with plenty of hot coffee. Lexi left with her pad and pencil, allowing Eva to give her mother a brief update on her three grandchildren. Marcia seemed distracted as she drummed her fingers on the table.

"What's up with you and Dad?" Eva probed, dreading what Mom might reveal.

Marcia spread her fingers apart. "Your father is planning to see your Grandpa Marty."

"Grandpa told me. You're staying home alone?"

"Ye-es," Marcia replied slowly. "Clifford's helping him prepare for his art showing. I have other things to see to."

"Such as?"

Marcia stared at Eva. "Family matters."

Before Eva could ask her to explain, Lexi delivered a carafe of iced tea and glass brimming with crushed ice. She spun around and quickly returned with a cup of coffee.

She set this in front of Eva, blurting, "I hope Kaley recovered from what Mr. Badger did. He's a total jerk."

"What happened to Kaley?" Eva demanded. "She mentioned nothing to me."

Lexi's brown eyes widened. "I shouldn't have said anything. Sorry."

She sped away, plunging Eva into concern over why—and what—Kaley hadn't told her.

Marcia gripped her glass. "There's no easy way to say this. If only your father were here."

Uneasiness pummeled Eva's stomach. She glanced at her mother's suitcase. "You look miserable," Eva said. "Tell me, please."

"Ah … your father and I are—"

Eva interjected, "You and he are … okay, right?"

Marcia's eyes glistened. Eva plunked down her cup. Reaching out a hand, she asked her mother how she could help.

"I don't know why I'm acting like a big baby. I'll just say it. We're selling the house."

Eva inhaled sharply. "Is this your idea or Dad's?"

Marcia yanked a tissue from her pocket. Lexi brought two large plates heaped with chicken salad, fruit, and cheese bread.

"Enjoy, ladies. Let me know if you need anything. And Mrs. Montanna, forget what I said about Kaley. She must not want you to know."

The teen sauntered to the kitchen humming a praise song. Eva shook her head. This day was throwing her one curve after another.

"I haven't a clue what's going on with Kaley, but I'll find out later. This salad is monstrous."

"Mercy me." Marcia sighed. "I'll never eat it all. My appetite has shrunk over our move."

"May I say grace, Mom?"

Marcia nodded and held her fork in mid-air. Eva prayed softly, thanking God for the food and asking Him to bless her parents.

She opened her eyes, saying, "Tell me everything. When and where are you moving?"

"Your dad's retirement is official. He, I mean we, both want to start fresh." Marcia dabbed her eyes with a tissue. "Each day we wake up haunted by memories of you girls growing up in the house. The pain never leaves. Jillie won't step through our front door again."

Sorrow flooded Eva's heart. She missed her sister, although the throbbing ache had dulled with time. She had no words to ease her mother's grief. Eva couldn't imagine coping with losing one of her dear children.

She lightly touched her mom's arm. "Each September eleventh, with all the news coverage, I watch the Pentagon ablaze again. It's like a knife stabbing my heart."

Marcia silently wiped her eyes. For the next few minutes they were content to nibble their salads. Then Eva picked up the earlier thread.

"By all means, you and Dad deserve something new. You haven't said where you're going. Are you keeping secrets from me like Kaley is?"

Marcia pierced a strawberry with her fork. The way she looked up at Eva with glittering eyes, it seemed as if she was looking forward to the change.

"We will have fun. First, we'll tour the Dutch villages where Grandpa Marty lived. Your father regrets not going with you both on the excursion last year. Then we head to Scotland and England, where I believe my family is from."

"We'll miss you terribly! How long will you be traveling?"

"For several months I should think. You gave me the idea, Eva."

Eva sat back, stunned. "No. I never wanted you and Dad to move away!"

She understood nothing of this conversation. What on earth had she done?

"Darling daughter." Marcia cracked a tiny smile. "Let me begin again. Your search for your father's family and what you found prompts me to search for my ancestors. My parents told me nothing of my heritage. This may sound strange, but I won't have rest for the future until I learn about my past."

Eva sipped her coffee. "Your people came from Scotland? I never knew."

"Me neither. Then I found this buried beneath a pile of old newspapers."

Marcia zipped open a flap on the carry-on and removed a book with a flag on the front. This she handed to Eva, who read aloud the inside inscription:

"To Callum, our son. Be brave as you are strong. Happy eighteenth birthday. Mum and Daddy."

The book was handwritten in pen. Eva couldn't make out any of the words, and she told her Mom so. Marcia took back her Scottish book.

With a comical tone in her voice, she said, "I've been clearin' out the spare room. Dad found the family Bible and wants you to have it for your family history."

She reached into the suitcase and tugged out an old volume, followed by another. Eva touched one of the tooled leather covers. A sacred moment washed over her.

"Mom, these look ancient."

"I believe they are. Your dad says they're in Latin, but other than that I know nothing about them."

Eva turned to the first page with care and ran a finger across blue and gold filigree. Line after line contained the Vander Goes family name.

She thanked her mother. "Grandpa Marty's bravery in WWII makes me want to learn all I can about our family. He's sending me Aunt Deane's journal about the earlier history. I want to see how far back we can trace our Christian heritage."

Eva's mind returned to the ashes on her mantel. She kept being distracted from checking into them. Her cell phone vibrated, and she snatched it from her waist. Griff was calling. She didn't want Mom knowing about her case, so she let his call go to voice mail. She'd phone him when she was back in the car.

"Mom, whatever you and Dad decide, I support you. We'll all miss you."

Marcia laid down her fork. "We found a buyer for the house. A couple from our small church wants to bring up their five children where we raised you and Jillie."

Eva blinked back tears, inviting her mom and dad for dinner and to stay the night. She wanted their grandchildren to have a special time before they began traveling. They settled on the coming weekend, with her dad driving to Michigan from there in his car.

"Just know how much I love you," Eva said.

"Oh sweetheart, me too."

Mother and daughter wiped their eyes, paid their bills, and shared another hug. Eva waved as her mom went to her car. Eva stood alone with the old Bibles under her arm. A myriad of questions rolled around in her mind. Had her folks lost their senses? Why not keep their house and just travel abroad?

Possibly she could talk sense into Dad when they came to visit. Eva put Mom's suitcase in the trunk before zipping in the Bibles. Once inside her car, Eva wasted no time dialing Griff. She reached his voice mail. She raced back to the office, only he wasn't there. She listened to his earlier message on her voice mail, and all he said was he'd be out the rest of the afternoon.

Eva logged onto her computer to see if she had any responses to Enescu's BOLO. There was nothing. After three hours of reviewing files, she locked her desk and stopped on the way home at a local deli, where she picked up chicken strips and mashed potatoes for supper. She wondered what, if anything, Kaley would say about her teacher's conduct.

Eva dropped large take-out bags on the counter. Andy and Dutch were playing with a miniature race set Dutch received last Christmas.

"I'm home," Eva chirped. "Kaley, the table's not set."

"She's moping in her room," Andy called from the living room.

Eva went straight to Kaley's room. Her door closed, Eva knocked softly.

"Andy, I said leave me alone," Kaley grumbled.

"It's Mom. Will you help me put supper on the table?"

Silence. Eva rapped again. More silence, so she spoke from behind the door.

"I met with your grandmother at the Wholly Ground for lunch. Lexi served us and said you had difficulties. Want to talk about it?"

Eva heard a thump. The door cracked open. Kaley dropped down on the bed, her eyes red. Eva sat beside her and waited. She'd learned Kaley needed to be the one bringing up what troubled her. Her daughter clammed up whenever Eva pushed.

Kaley pounded her feather pillow. Still Eva waited.

"It's my dumb government class," Kaley admitted. "The teacher barks at us."

"To everyone or just you?"

"Today it was me. He doesn't approve of me speaking against his beliefs."

"His beliefs in what?" Eva forced herself not to overreact.

"Mr. Badger insists God does not exist. He blames Christians for chaos around the world. He's making us write how our country will be better without Jesus followers."

Blood pounded against Eva's ears. She compressed her fists.

"He said that in class?" she asked through clenched teeth.

"Oh, yeah. And much worse."

Kaley jumped off the bed. Eva could tell from her blazing red cheeks that she was deeply conflicted. She should be having the time of her life in her junior year. Eva wanted to remove her angst and not light a fuse. She chose her words carefully.

"You are not alone in this."

Her seventeen-year-old daughter paced her neatly kept room. She picked up her earbuds and twirled them in the air.

"We can pick one of five topics for our paper. Get this, Mom—taking God off our money, forbidding anyone to speak of Jesus in public, not allowing kids in school to pray, forbidding us to bring Bibles on school property, and removing every cross from the national cemeteries."

Eva blew out her breath. "What will you do?"

"I raised my hand, asking what if I didn't believe as he did. I asked him to let me write on another topic. He yelled, saying I was insubordinate. Kids in class snickered and told me to shut up."

Tears flooded her eyes. Eva folded her into her arms and soothed her hurting daughter. This was no time for a lecture on religious liberty.

"You treated him with respect. Tell me about Mr. Badger."

"He's new since January, and is arrogant. His first name is Karl, like Karl Marx, if that tells you anything."

Eva leaned against the headboard. "What else does he talk about in class?"

"Oh, stuff." Kaley whisked tears from her eyes.

"Does he talk about the three branches of the federal government?"

Kaley sniffled again. "No. A few times we have a substitute."

"Do you know why?"

"Yup." Kaley giggled. "He brags about getting drunk and blasted after alleys and gutters."

"What's alleys and gutters? Some kind of new booze and pot combo?"

Kaley howled in laughter. "Mom, it's a bowling alley on Route Seven. He's in a league and sometimes gets home too late."

"It's terrific hearing you laugh." Eva rose from the bed. "I'll contact your principal about your teacher's bullying."

"Please don't! You'll make things worse."

Kaley's bottom lip trembled, causing Eva to rethink her strategy. She patted her hand.

"We'll talk to your dad after supper and see what he thinks."

Eva set the table and called everyone to eat. Dutch asked her to tell stories about dangers Grandpa Marty faced in the Dutch Resistance.

"Is that where my nickname comes from?" he wanted to know.

Without waiting for an answer, he spooned a second helping of mashed potatoes on his plate. Scott lifted up his plate so Dutch could give him more potatoes.

"You're called Dutch because your name is Martin, the same as your grandfather's," he explained. "Should we call you something different?"

"Nah, but I wanna see Grandpa Marty before I forget him."

Eva traded glances with Scott. "Okay, I get the hint. We'll make plans for our summer vacation when school's out in June."

"Goody," Dutch said.

Eva recalled with amusement that Grandpa Marty had used the same term earlier in the day. She smiled and ate her chicken.

"Hey, Dad, let's try out the stunt kite you gave me for Christmas," Andy said, shoving food in his mouth.

Kaley didn't join in their banter. She picked at her food and asked to be excused. As soon as supper was over, Eva nudged Scott into their room, quickly telling him of Kaley's dilemma. He agreed with Eva. The government teacher must be called out. She went to tell Kaley. Upon learning of her father's reaction, she raised a fuss.

"Let me handle it, Mom. I wish Lexi had done what I'd asked and kept quiet."

Eva relented. "Dad and I will give you some leeway, and ask God to guide you."

She cleaned up the dishes, not at all content to remain in the background. Yet Kaley was about to enter adulthood. She'd give her space, for now anyway.

# CHAPTER 4

The rest of the week passed in a blur. Eva helped Griff conduct surveillance on the Chechens. So far, they committed no crimes. On Saturday, they'd all enjoyed going to Arlington National Cemetery with Eva's folks. Although Kaley had acted glum, Andy and Dutch were mesmerized by the changing of the guard at the Tomb of the Unknown Soldier.

Eva had also spoken to the youth pastor and he liked her idea of placing flags in the cemeteries for Memorial Day. Of course, that was still weeks away. Sunday evening ended with the grandparents giving presents to the kids to be opened on their birthdays.

Monday morning, Eva's parents left before breakfast in a great flurry of hugs and kisses. Their departure left her wondering when she'd see them again. She whirled green smoothies in a high-tech blender, the concoction mirroring her turmoil over Kaley's being bullied by Mr. Badger. His name fit his character, but his antics were anything but funny.

After Kaley had rushed home in tears last Thursday, Eva arranged to meet the principal this morning. Mr. Troop had come into his position this term after the previous principal retired unexpectedly for health reasons. Strange things were happening at the school.

Where were the kids, anyway? Scott slipped out minutes ago, claiming an early meeting. No doubt he stopped at a fast-food joint for one of his favorite greasy breakfast sandwiches. Eva turned off the blender. In thirty minutes she needed to drive Kaley to school, where she'd confront the principal.

She yelled down the hall, "The smoothies are ready."

A ringing startled her and she lunged for the phone.

"Sorry to bother you so early," the female caller said.

Eva's mind churned. She couldn't place the voice, so she asked, "How may I help you?"

"This is Heather, Raj Pentu's wife."

"I haven't seen you since the office Christmas party."

"Eva, I realize you must abide by secrecy, but do you know where I can find Raj?"

Eva swallowed. "I can't tell you a thing."

"I was afraid you'd say that." Heather coughed a sigh. "Have you heard from him at all?"

"No, which isn't unusual. We're on the same task force, yet he's often out of contact."

"Raj promised to text me when he reached a secure location. We had our one-year anniversary three days ago. I'm worried because ..." Her voice broke.

"Your husband is reliable." Eva couldn't say more on the unsecured phone. "Perhaps he has no access."

"I saw on the news that several Americans are being held hostage in Iraq. Oh, Eva, that terror group is killing them and posting online! Perhaps you'll understand when I say in my spirit, I'm sure something is wrong!"

Eva briefly shut her eyes. She'd seen the same news reports and had no way of knowing if Raj was one of the captives.

"I don't always know what Raj is working on," Eva replied.

Heather sighed into the phone. "He's on loan to your task force, so I didn't call his boss at NCIS. He'd just tell me to call your office, wouldn't he?"

"Yes. NCIS won't have a clue."

Eva checked the clock. She must get a move on. Still, Heather's concerns gave her pause. Raj often went undercover for the task force, and Eva would expect Griff to help Scott if he worried about her safety.

Heather interrupted Eva's train of thought. "I wouldn't compromise you or what Raj is doing. Can you help me?"

There was someone Eva could call. "I'll try checking at the office. We could meet at the Wholly Ground café after work to discuss things."

Heather gushed, "Thanks ever so much. Is that the café near Pal's Furniture Mart?"

"Yes. I know the owners. They serve great coffee and salads."

They agreed to aim for 5:30 p.m., with Eva next phoning Bo Rider on his cell. Too bad her friend and CIA agent didn't answer. Eva left a message on his voice mail.

"Bo, call me ASAP. Your package appears to be missing. I need to know if you have a way of tracking when it will be delivered."

She hit the "OFF" button on her cordless phone. If Bo was overseas, it might be hours before he received her message. Raj had previously disappeared from the task force while helping Bo Rider and the CIA.

Eva toasted wheat bread, deep in thought. Perhaps Raj was really a CIA agent working on the task force. Though he'd been a special agent with NCIS (Naval Criminal Investigative Service) for several years, his birth and early years in Egypt made the Arabic speaker especially attractive to Bo's "Company."

She stepped in the hallway and called, "Okay, get in here and eat breakfast."

Eva drank her smoothie and ate her toast. When no kids wandered in, she suspected they were hiding in their rooms until it was time to leave. Did they hate her green smoothies that much?

She rounded up the kids, and it was too late to make something else, so she gave them each a granola bar to eat on the way to school. Fifteen minutes later, Eva shut off their new SUV. Kaley clutched her backpack with something akin to fear in her eyes.

"Mom, I know how you are when someone is unjust. Promise me you won't cause trouble." Kaley's eyes began tearing up.

"Mr. Badger said cruel things about your Christians beliefs. How will my ignoring his actions make things better for you?"

Kaley twisted a strand of her blond hair. Eva inhaled. This was going to be harder than she thought.

"Okay, we talked with your dad about this last night, and he agreed," Eva said, fighting to stay calm. "If we allow bullies to flourish, there's no end to their tyranny. Look at Russia."

"Mr. Badger isn't that mean. He's nice sometimes."

Eva reached for Kaley's hand. "Christians are being killed in places like Iraq and Egypt for daring to believe in Jesus. We should challenge him now, before things get out of hand."

Kaley gave a tiny shrug and twirled her hair.

"What do you want me to do, Kaley? I respect your judgment. That's how Dad and I have raised you."

"I wish Dad were here. He's not so … um … confrontational."

"Oh. I see."

Eva's mind reeled. Her own daughter thought she was over-the-top.

"All right, Kaley. I'll change my appointment with the principal until your dad can come along. How does that sound?"

"You always tell us to forgive. Mr. Badger might apologize."

Kaley practically flew from the car. Eva grabbed her keys, emerging slowly. Her daughter had poise and sense, for which Eva was grateful. She rescheduled the meeting with Mr. Troop with no trouble. Then Eva went home and switched vehicles. Her G-car could be used for official purposes only.

In the Ford, she hit the accelerator to make up for lost time. Every other team member was in the office when she arrived, except for Raj. In response to discreet questions, she learned no one had heard from him. Griff shook his head, typing furiously on his computer. She was about to ask if he'd heard anything new on Enescu or the Chechens when her cell rang.

The moment she answered, Bo Rider barked, "Get to secure, pronto."

Eva checked her watch. "It takes thirty minutes to reach ICE HQ."

"Works for me."

Bo gave her the secure number to call in thirty-five minutes. Eva pocketed her cell, telling Griff what was happening.

"Raj's wife reached out to me this morning. He's been out of touch with her for days."

Griff looked up from his keyboard. "You know better than anyone that going dark is not unusual when we're undercover."

"He missed a scheduled connection point with Heather."

"Before Raj left a week ago, he said something strange. Now I wonder."

Time was ticking down for her phone call, and she fired back, "Get to the point."

Griff stood, facing her with a scowl. "He told me, 'I hope I'm back by the World Series. You know how I love baseball.' Course Raj laughed. I took it as a big joke."

"He played baseball in college," she answered with a shrug.

"The World Series is months away. What could he have meant?"

"Maybe he was passing you a code." Eva shoved her Glock in her purse. "You and Bo stay calm and collected. Me, I trounce on everyone. Ask my daughter."

"Sounding bitter isn't like you. What's up?"

She locked her desk. "Tell ya later. Heather is afraid, so I hope to pry something out of Bo to reassure her, but I doubt it. Our CIA colleague has stiffed me more than once."

"Me too," Griff called as Eva strode out the door.

She headed for the freeway in her G-car, realizing Bo might not know Raj's whereabouts. But then, why tempt Eva with a secure phone conference? Nothing added up, especially her earlier conversation with Kaley. Her daughter's truthfulness burned a hole in her heart bigger than her parents moving away. Eva would ask Scott later if she was being difficult. Just now, she had fifteen minutes to cut through this traffic and reach a secure phone.

# CHAPTER 5

Eva's drive to ICE's headquarters was plagued by unmercifully heavy traffic. She swerved in and out of the passing lane, and shot past a lumbering garbage truck, nearly missing her exit. There were no empty meters near the building. She circled the block a few times. Finally, she spied a car pulling away.

She fed the meter and ran full speed to the security post, where she flashed her badge. Against all odds, Eva reached the booth with one minute to spare. She and Bo Rider were soon conversing on a secure connection.

"Eva, I don't have long. Your request sounded urgent."

"Raj Pentu's wife called. He hasn't been in touch as promised. And with Americans being captured in Iraq, she's worried he is one of the victims. Can you shed any light?"

"Why should I know?"

Eva pushed back. She was in no mood to play games.

"Raj and I work on the same task force. He's loaned out for his language skills. Are you involved, Bo?"

"Not directly."

She seized on that tiny clue. "So maybe indirectly?"

Bo chuckled and said with grit in his voice, "Don't get carried away. I saw him yesterday. He looked healthy, wealthy, and wise. Well, maybe not wealthy. Can't say more."

"You've told me enough," Eva said with relief. "If you see him, say Heather was asking."

"Sorry, Eva. He doesn't need any distractions right now."

Eva balled her fists. "Still, I can tell her not to worry."

"Right. No more than that, Eva."

"How could I tell her more? I don't know anything."

"Right," he said again as if reinforcing she shouldn't read too much into his pathetic clues. "How are Scott and the kids?"

"We're fine." While Eva hadn't called to chitchat, she felt obliged to ask, "And your family?"

"Julia and I won't be able to meet you for dinner tonight. Will you call her and say you and I spoke about finding another time? Maybe next week. She'll understand. I have to run."

Static buzzed in her ears. She stared at the receiver. Had Bo lost his senses? The Montannas and the Riders had no dinner plans. Then she realized Bo was doing what Raj should have done. He intended to contact his wife through Eva.

Once outside HQ, Eva phoned Julia using her cell phone, intending to convey what Bo asked without giving anything away on the unsecured line.

"I spoke with Bo. He suggested I pick a date for a barbeque next week since he can't make it tonight."

Julia gasped. "He called you?"

"We talked about a mutual case. I was on a secure line."

"Oh, Eva. My mind is racing. He's been out of touch for days. I'm not sure Bo wants a barbeque. He must be coming home by the weekend. Thanks for letting me know."

"Happy to be of service. Julia, call me when he's back if you want to get together."

"Okay." She let out a ragged sigh. "My kids miss seeing yours, now that we've moved."

"Don't let too much time pass by."

The two women said their good-byes and soon Eva was back in her G-car heading to the task force office in Virginia. She would need to be careful talking with Heather at the Wholly Ground. Perhaps Bo would have Raj call her, letting Eva off the hook.

Eva found the office empty, save for Griff.

"Where is everyone?" she asked, dumping her purse on the desk.

Griff swiveled his chair around. "Serving a search warrant on an export company in Anacostia. I waited for you. Did Bo come through?"

"Yes and no."

"Let me guess. He phoned, saying zip. Am I right?" Griff raised his bushy eyebrows in expectation.

"Bo did see Raj yesterday, so I conclude he's not one of the American captives. I'll convince Heather to be patient."

"You may have your hands full. She called twice while you were gone."

"You're kidding. Is she canceling?"

"Nope. I suspect she and Raj haven't been married long enough for her to know the drill."

"It took Scott a couple years to adjust to my crazy schedule."

Griff handed Eva a glossy sheet of paper. She gazed at it and snapped up her head.

"Where'd you get this?"

"From my State Department contact who shall remain nameless." He flashed a grin. "The features are grainy, but that's a photo of Andrei Enescu going through security at Montreal's International Airport. His passport had the same name as the guy at the mall, Francois Petit."

"When was it taken?"

"After he slipped away from us at the mall."

Eva slumped in her chair. "Will we ever catch him?"

"Being defeated reaps just that—defeat. We keep digging."

Enescu's easy movements had Eva stumped. She went on her computer and typed in a request for the ICE agent assigned at State to send her a copy of Francois Petit's passport application. She had no concrete proof, but she suspected there would be no such application.

Meanwhile, Eva regretted having to meet Heather. She should get home and talk with Scott and Kaley about seeing the principal in the morning. Sensing Griff hovering by her shoulder, she sent the passport request to State, then swiveled her head.

"Thanks for the pep talk, but my day has turned out nothing like I wanted it to. I've accomplished nothing."

"Give your trusty partner credit for sniffing out a new lead on Enescu. That's something."

Eva nodded. "Sure is, and you're the greatest partner I've ever had. Truth is, Kaley's teacher is a knucklehead, and my daughter is rejecting my help."

"Welcome to her soon-to-be adult world." Griff waved his hand. "The son I adopted lives his life with his bride, and I see little of him. Yet my love for Wally is always there."

Eva's heart surged. Griff had it right. She rapped her hand on the desk. "And with love comes trust. I'll back off and let her handle it."

"Sounds like a plan. Kaley is what, seventeen?"

"Yes, and old enough to take on more responsibility. It's time she found a job."

Eva started humming, anxious to put her new ideas for Kaley in place. She also plotted how to nab Enescu. In a few days, Eva should hear from the ICE agent at State. If there was no passport application for Francois Petit, she'd ramp up the search. Griff might lose interest, but Eva intended to hound him forever.

A FEW HOURS LATER, Eva strode into the café, spotting a woman resembling Heather Pentu. Only her hair was a lighter brown from when Eva last saw her. Heather didn't look up from her smart phone. Eva pulled out a chair, scraping the legs on the tile.

"Sorry it's after five thirty. You know how snarled traffic is during rush hour."

Heather thrust her phone into a pocket. "I was checking to see if Raj texted me."

"Did he?" Eva hoped Bo had come through.

"Not yet." Heather sipped a drink in a frosty mug. "Want something? This fruit smoothie is excellent."

"Nothing for me, thanks. I must hurry home. My crew will be waiting for their supper."

"With Raj away, my time after work passes slowly."

Eva dropped her voice. "I understand your anxiety, and reached out to a colleague. Your husband is fine. I put out the word asking him to call you soon."

"You're the greatest!" Heather's smile brightened her hazel eyes. "I feel silly asking you."

Eva told Heather she understood, adding, "Scott worries when I'm on assignment. Our kids keep him busy, though."

"We hope to start a family soon. I'm more ready than Raj. Being an attorney in a mega- law firm is pretty boring. I may look for a new position."

Eva took the car keys from her purse. A thought pushed forward and she wondered if Heather would be open to the idea. She broached the subject lightly, wearing a grin.

"Are you good at crafts?"

"Such as sewing or painting? Not really. Why?"

"A week from this Saturday, our church is holding a craft fair. We're raising money for Transitions, a local agency that helps special needs kids. I'm running the 'Snack Shack,' making smoothies."

Heather sat back as if astonished. "I was just asked to sit on Transitions Board of Directors. How is that for a coincidence?"

"Then you'll help us?" Eva asked, certain Heather's call had been no accident.

"I bake cookies. My grandmother owns a bakery in Paris. She taught me how to bake."

"My, you have excellent credentials. French pastry chefs are famous."

Heather burst into giggles. "Granny lives in Paris, Virginia. Do you know it?"

"There's a wonderful inn we drive to sometimes." Eva gave Heather a card with her email address. "Send a message so I have yours and we'll make arrangements for the fair."

One obligation complete, Eva hurried home to find out how Kaley's day had gone. Her daughter sat hunched over the computer at the small kitchen desk, typing intently.

Eva stopped long enough to ask, "Did Mr. Badger apologize as you hoped?"

"Not even close."

Kaley pushed back her chair and faced Eva with a puckered brow. "He was horrid."

"What did he do this time?"

"He issued a decree. Whoever fails to finish his assignment, you know the one I told you about, flunks the class. I stood up and said he had no right to push his humanistic beliefs on Christians. He pounced on me something fierce."

"That sounds challenging. You did the right thing."

Kaley's lips drooped. "Mom, you won't believe what happened after I said that."

Of course, Eva imagined the worst. She wished now she hadn't delayed meeting the principal. It was too late to second-guess things.

"Do you want to hold me in suspense?" Eva pressed.

"He wrote Jesus' name on a piece of paper, which he tore into tiny pieces, mocking me and saying, 'I dare you to resist.'"

Eva leaned against the counter. How much latitude should she give Kaley to handle this thorny issue?

"I'm reading an interesting book about Lord Acton," Eva said. "He lived more than a hundred years ago and what he said then applies today: 'Power tends to corrupt and absolute power corrupts absolutely.' Mr. Badger is power mad."

Kaley chewed on her bottom lip. "After class, I talked things over with Lexi. She reminded me of Jesus saying, 'Give to Caesar what is Caesar's and to God what is God's.'"

"Jesus did encourage people to be good citizens and respect the government God had put into place. Yet, Kaley, Jesus would never condone your turning your back on God."

"I know. Jesus teaches I should love God with my whole heart, and I want to." Kaley sat down with a mournful sigh. "It's all so complicated that I don't know what to do."

Andy burst into the kitchen and rummaged in the fridge. "What's to eat? I'm hungry enough to gobble a horse."

"No horses, but supper is in one hour. Find a cheese stick and bring one to Dutch. Kaley and I will get things started."

Andy grabbed two cheese sticks, waving them in the air like a trophy. Eva smiled at her son's pure innocence. She patted Kaley's back.

"This calls for my special spaghetti. We'll talk while we cook. Let's wash up first."

After cleaning her hands, Eva pulled out jars of marinara sauce from the cupboard. She simmered it in a pan, while Kaley chopped a small onion. After putting the onion into another saucepan, Eva tossed in ground beef.

She glanced at Kaley. "So far, you've respectfully disagreed and asked your teacher to respect your conscience. He isn't doing so. Rather, he wants you to violate your religious beliefs. If we put up with it, who knows how far he will push his tyranny."

Kaley used a wooden spoon to break the meat into pieces. Eva watched her eyes flicker with concern. It was not easy becoming an adult. Eva desired to be the most loving and supportive parent she could be. Her parents hadn't always been there for her.

Some time passed before Kaley said, "This may shock you, but I think you're right. Will you and Dad meet with the principal? I was wrong to think I could handle Mr. Badger's bullying on my own."

"You standing up for yourself makes me proud," Eva replied earnestly. "Dad and I may have more clout with the principal. We'll see him tomorrow as planned."

Kaley's lower lip trembled. "Why is there so much hate, Mom? I despise conflict. You face it every day on your job."

"Sure I do. Maybe that's why it's easier for me to handle. Do you want to fix the salad?"

"I really should finish my paper. Will you read it after I'm done and see what you think?"

"Is it for Mr. Badger's government class?"

Kaley set down the wooden spoon with a thump. "Yes. I came up with a new take on his assignment. My teacher may not be happy, but at least I will turn in something."

At the unwavering look in Kaley's eyes and set of her chin, Eva recognized her own tenacity that had propelled her to where she was in her career. Her daughter also showed Scott's gentler approach to life. Eva patted Kaley's shoulder.

"Spend the time you need. I'll ask Andy to set the table. It must be his turn."

Kaley whirled around and typed with purpose. After supper, the family watched a funny movie on TV while Eva read Kaley's first draft. She approved of the logic her daughter used to support her conclusions. During a commercial break, she sat beside her.

"If this doesn't score you an A, I will be surprised," Eva whispered. "Let Dad go over it too, just to be sure. Better wait until his movie is over."

Kaley beamed and Eva washed the dishes, trusting her daughter would be a winner no matter how Mr. Badger reacted. She jammed a plate in the dishwasher, thinking of her pursuit of Enescu. She didn't exhibit as much grace under fire as Kaley did. Rather, she continually mulled over catching him.

Straightening her back, Eva realized why his escape bothered her to such a degree. She wasn't letting God do the search, but labored in her own steam, which could end in disaster. Eva slipped to her bedroom and prayed to God, asking Him to help her face this wall.

"I haven't let You take over and I'm sorry," she whispered.

She spent time opening her heart and talking with her Heavenly Father. He must have heard because when she joined Scott on the sofa to watch the last minutes of the movie, the churning in her stomach was replaced with peace in her spirit. She watched pretend secret agents sparring with each other on screen and laughed out loud.

"That's what I like to hear," Scott said. "We need more fun around here."

"Do you mean that?"

He nodded and Eva dug her fingers in his ribs. He howled and tickled her back.

Kaley picked up a throw pillow and smiled. "Oh, they're gettin' mushy again."

She tossed the pillow at Andy, hitting Dutch. He chased her out of the room giggling. Seconds later, Dutch returned to jump on Andy as they tussled on the floor. As if enjoying the relief from tension, Scott grabbed one of Dutch's racing cars and sat down by the small track. Soon he, Andy, and Dutch were re-enacting Sunday's race.

Eva wiped tears of joy from her eyes. Why couldn't every day end with such happiness?

# CHAPTER 6

The delight Eva experienced the previous evening soon evaporated in the small confines of the principal's office. She and Scott sat across from Mr. Troop, who glowered from behind his desk, looking agitated as he stared over the top of his half-glasses. Worse than his scowl, he seemed indifferent in Kaley's plight.

"Your daughter chose to take government," he intoned. "We at Washington High teach our students to think for themselves."

Scott leaned forward. "I think not, Mr. Troop. Our daughter thinks for herself. When she verbalizes thoughts of her faith, she's condemned by your teacher."

"I talked with Karl Badger after you phoned last week, Mrs. Montanna." Mr. Troop flung off his glasses in an irritated manner. "Your daughter was out of line, refusing to participate in the assignment. Perhaps you give her the impression she should challenge those in authority."

His insinuation made Eva's jaw drop.

"How dare you make such a claim?" Eva demanded.

Scott quickly interceded, his voice rising, "Has Mr. Badger told you how he wrote Jesus' name on a piece of paper and tore it to shreds, all to demonstrate Christ isn't real?"

"I doubt he'd do anything so childish. He comes to Washington High with years of teaching experience in Seattle."

"Kaley wouldn't lie to us." Eva folded her arms and glared.

Troop held his ground. "All parents think their children are angels. Anyway, I fail to see the relevance of what the teacher did in class. It's simple. Your daughter either completes the project, or risks flunking the class."

Eva gripped Scott's arm. If she showed how furious she was, she would enflame matters for Kaley. Her mind flashed to her interrogation techniques. Troop was one of those people who wouldn't know the truth if it bit him on the ankle. Perhaps she should try an indirect approach.

She smiled. "You have so many students under your wing. I know my father came home from teaching with similar concerns. He just retired after thirty-five years of teaching."

"Oh? Who is your father?" Troop's mouth formed into a tight smile.

"Clifford Vander Goes. He began his career teaching high school biology and then went on for degrees to become a professor at Virginia Commonwealth University."

Troop shot up in his chair. "Do you mean Dr. Clifford Vander Goes, *the* expert on research on the James River in southern Virginia?"

"Yes." Eva was uncomfortable with the way this conversation was going. "My father just retired from the Inger and Walter Rice Center."

"My, my. This is a stroke of luck." Troop rubbed his hands together. "I'd like to invite him to speak at our science fair. Several large corporations are offering scholarships to the winners. Is it too much to ask if you would put me in contact with him?"

Eva hid a smile. Only God could have turned the tables like this.

"I'm happy to talk with my father. His schedule is extremely complicated right now; however, I know he loves the students. And now, perhaps, you will take a moment to read my daughter's paper, which she completed last night for Mr. Badger's class."

She handed the principal a three-page document, stapled together at the top left corner.

"Certainly. Let me see."

Troop replaced his glasses at the end of his nose and began reading aloud from Kaley's paper, "Many in our community spend time strategizing how our lives would be better without the Christian faith. I would rather enunciate three ways in which society benefits from Christian people and Christian charity. First, some of our finest colleges were established by those of faith. Many pilgrims were abused for their faith in Europe and immigrated to America. By 1636, more than 1700 Puritans resided in New

England, prompting a group of ministers to start a church in the wilderness. You may recognize the name Harvard University."

He looked up and smiled. He handed Eva his card.

"There is no doubt Kaley Montanna is an excellent writer. It is my pleasure to speak with Mr. Badger at once to straighten out any misunderstanding."

"Thank you." Eva stood and offered her hand. "You should expect my father's call soon." She and Scott left the windowed office. Neither said a word until they reached their SUV. Scott opened the doors with his key fob. Once inside, he let out a whoop.

"Unbelievable! We were getting nowhere until you mentioned your father. What made you do that?"

"I can only say the idea came from above." Eva pointed toward heaven.

LATE IN THE AFTERNOON EVA'S BOSS walked up and dropped a package on her desk. He stalked off, and Griff sauntered over, acting curious.

"Has Jeff given you a new case?" he asked, palming his moustache.

"There's one way to find out."

Eva tore open an envelope addressed to Special Agent Eva Montanna, and tugged out a single sheet of paper. On it was typed:

*Eva,*

*It's been a while since you heard from me, but not to worry. You soon will. My sentence is nearly up. Then I'll be on special parole. Don't take this as a threat. But know this: I'm a much smarter lady since you put me away. Have a happy day, Special Agent Montanna.*

"She didn't sign it." Eva thrust the paper into Griff's hands.

He read it and shook his head. "How do you know who it's from?"

"Guess work. I assume Brittney, my incarcerated cousin, wrote it, but I suppose this piece of trash could be from anyone."

Eva launched to her feet. Annoyance—rather, anger—besieged her mind. She turned over the envelope. It bore no return address.

"Whoever wrote this note had someone smuggle it out of federal prison," she said. "The postmark is smudged. Does it look like Atlanta?"

Griff removed a large magnifying glass from his top drawer. "This proves my motto, never go anywhere without a magnifier."

His comical face, squinting at the postmark with that large magnifier, made Eva chortle. "Okay, Sherlock, what's your diagnosis?"

"It looks like Atlanta," Griff responded, standing tall.

His desk phone rang and he dashed to grab it. He paused and said, "Okay, Brent, give it to me hard-boiled."

Griff glanced at Eva with a shake of his head.

"Thanks, Brent. Don't cancel the lookout until we grab him. We'll make sure the U.S. Marshals handle things from here."

Griff jammed down the receiver. "Okay, it's definite. Enescu has been found."

"What are we waiting for?"

She yanked open her drawer, snatched out her Glock, and grabbed her big purse.

"Eva, stop."

"No way. I heard you say the marshals can take over, but we're the ones to ensure he doesn't escape again. And Griff, I mean never."

She shoved her powerful gun into her purse. Griff walked over and laid a hand on her shoulder.

"Nope. He's in Ukraine, or what's left of it. We are *not* heading into a fire zone to retrieve him. Jeff won't sign off on our going there, not with Raj still gone."

Eva's shoulders sagged. She imagined steam blowing out of her ears. She was that riled. She forced herself to admit Griff had a point. Running around the world chasing after one crazy felon was insane. Besides, her family needed her. Eva dropped into her chair.

"It stinks. Who gave you the tip?"

"My FBI contact. He's been right so far. Forget Enescu. You've got bigger problems."

"The letter," Eva said, reaching for it.

"Hold it! Get your head on straight. Don't touch it again."

Eva balled her fists. "Correct again. We need to check it for prints."

With Griff's help, she secured the unsigned letter in a plastic envelope and copied it. Eva faced Griff with determination.

"It's ironic this note arrives the moment you tell me Enescu is found. I need to move on and quit living in the past. You follow up on the letter, will you?"

Griff took the envelope into his capable hands. "Count on me. I don't subscribe to the idea that the past determines our futures, but I've learned our future is incomplete without our past."

"My mother said something similar recently." Eva locked her desk drawer. "I have to decide what's important. I function best when I'm solving a major case. Maybe I should think about changing agencies."

"Are you kidding me?"

She tugged at her hair. "Maybe, maybe not. I need a change."

"If you leave the task force, would you join me at the FBI?"

"Raj hinted NCIS has openings. Of course, that was before he left on his undercover assignment. They might be filled in DC and I don't want to move to New Orleans or LA."

"Speaking of Raj, did he ever contact Heather?"

"Not yet." Eva picked up her purse. "Don't stay too late."

On the way home, Eva stopped for pizzas and a salad. When she came in through the back door, she called, "I'm home, and the pizza is hot."

Silence greeted her, magnifying Eva's turmoil about the cryptic letter she'd received. She strode into the kitchen. Kaley shuffled around the dining room table, plunking down forks with a loud wallop.

"What's wrong?" Eva asked, taking the salad from the bag.

Kaley tossed down paper napkins. Her cheeks blazed.

"Mr. Badger accepted my paper."

"That's good, isn't it?"

"Mom, *please* wait. As I was leaving class, he called me to his desk. The other students were already gone."

Eva's heart thudded in her chest. "What did he do?"

"He glared with pure hate in his eyes. He didn't appreciate you and Dad going behind his back. When I insisted you are my parents and care for me, he spewed a sinister laugh …"

Kaley's words fell away. Eva waited a moment before drawing her into a hug.

After releasing her, she said, "Your teacher has probably traveled a long and hard road. We should pray for him, which is something I haven't been doing."

"Me either." Kaley stood by the table looking forlorn. "Then he hissed, 'You haven't heard the last from me. Your parents are brainwashing you.' He threatened to notify Child Protective Services and start a case on you. I ran out, Mom. He's a complete weirdo."

Eva's jaw dropped. Badger had the audacity to accuse her and Scott of abusing their daughter? She looked into Kaley's tortured eyes, and gripped her sweaty hands with hers.

"Jesus teaches us to love our enemies. It's hard to do. We should pray for Mr. Badger, so he doesn't carry out his threat."

"Okay," Kaley said. "I'll think about it. He's the last person I want to help."

She trudged off to her room. Eva was proud of her maturing daughter, but also scared. How could she continue to protect her children from life's savage moments? Her parents raised her to be strong. Oops. Eva recalled her promise to Mr. Troop about calling her father. She snatched the phone and dialed Grandpa Marty's number in Michigan.

Her grandfather answered, trilling, "Eva, how nice to hear from you. Your dad and I are having fun. Is everyone well?"

"Yes, we have some issues with school, but hope to see you soon. Can I talk to Dad?"

"He's in the garage, collecting my artwork. Oh, here he is. Cliff, Eva is calling."

She imagined Grandpa Marty thrusting the handheld phone into her dad's big hands. When he came on, Eva told him about Mr. Troop's invitation and the science fair.

"We went to see him about Kaley's disagreement with a teacher. Your name came up in a roundabout way, and Mr. Troop went from glum to smiles in a heartbeat. You helped your granddaughter, just by being you."

Clifford rumbled into the phone, "Stuff and nonsense. I've never done anything as important as you, Eva."

She smiled. That was her humble dad.

"This time you did. I hope you contact Mr. Troop."

"Your mother phoned me earlier. Our house may sell faster than we thought. If so, we may be in the Netherlands before long."

"I made no promises," Eva assured. "Yet, if the timing works out, you and Mom could drive up for the fair and spend time with us. Come see us before your European adventure."

Clifford cleared his throat. "Since you brought my father to Middleburg where he saved many Jewish families in WWII, I have a great desire to trace Marty's footsteps over there."

"Dad, I begin to understand the circles our lives take. From my reading the journals about Grandpa Marty and Aunt Deane, I'm eager to know more about what they lived through."

"Yes, and Eva, there's something else. I never felt God ordering my profession. It was what I selected for myself. These last few months, the

Lord is compelling me to act. Sell the house; go to the Netherlands, and then England. Your mom feels the same. We don't know the results, but we trust Him to show us."

Tears pricked Eva's eyes. She swiped them away.

"Splendid. Mom gave me the old Vander Goes family Bible. I haven't yet compared family names in it with what Aunt Deane wrote."

"I never once opened those old volumes, much to Marty's disappointment. I may yet live to give him joy."

"Grandpa loves you, Dad," Eva said softly.

"His love is unconditional and I have not repaid it well."

Eva wished she was having this conversation with her father in person. Talking over the telephone was too impersonal.

"You will," she told her father. "Grandpa just said what a nice time you're both having."

"It's the least I can do after so many years of neglect. I'm ashamed of myself, Eva."

"Let us know when we can see you again," Eva said. "Don't fly off in the night."

# CHAPTER 7

## DAHAB, EGYPT, THE SINAI DESERT

Morning dawned with perplexities for Raj Pentu, Eva's colleague on the Terrorism Task Force. He lounged on a deck chair aboard a sleek yacht, the rising sun painting the lagoon bright blue. Raj popped on a pair of dark sunglasses to ward off the sun's intense rays. Dressed in a khaki shirt and shorts, this was no vacation.

In fact, his undercover assignment was going sideways. His unsavory companion irritated him to no end. No doubt Yakov Gusev's booming Russian voice could be heard for miles down the sandy beach. Raj struggled to ignore Yakov's outburst over his lousy breakfast, and instead, he cast his dark brown eyes across the water at Dahab's skyline.

The tourist town sat perched on the southeast coast of Egypt's Sinai, along the shore of the Gulf of Aqaba. Its pristine waters served as a magnet for windsurfers and divers. A rider galloping down the beach on a camel grabbed Raj's attention. Soon, the odd pair disappeared into far rugged hills, and he relaxed.

The American special agent rubbed his one-day growth of beard. He longed to cover his ears at Yakov's new round of badgering the yacht's chef for burning his pancakes. The Russian informant hadn't figured out that mixing his fractured Arabic with the Jordanian chef's broken Russian would never bring him a better meal.

Raj sipped his orange juice, mulling over what he hoped to achieve here in Egypt. His last several cases had turned out well, which must be a good omen. So must be the fact that he was Egyptian born. He'd lived in Cairo with his parents and sister until he turned fourteen. Because of his father's cooperation with the United Nations (UN), the family had moved unexpectedly to New York. Raj had adapted smoothly to the language and customs of his new homeland. He considered himself a proud American patriot.

After graduating from George Mason University with an advanced degree, Raj obtained U.S. citizenship and became a special agent with the NCIS. So far, his chosen career brought excitement and plenty of rewards. These upbeat thoughts were interrupted by Yakov flopping in a chair next to him.

Yakov's shoulder-length graying hair quivered as he growled, "Tell dat chef we starve."

"What do you mean *we*?" Raj shot back. "I'm not starving."

"You too hate dis slop."

Raj waved a hand. "Hate's a strong word. I've had better, I've had worse. It's a small inconvenience."

"Oh, blast you."

Yakov laid back on the recliner, giving Raj another chance to scan the shoreline. He spotted nothing unusual. Still, something besides crummy food gnawed at his stomach. This Russian snitch bothered him. Besides Yakov's constant complaints and tendency to mumble, he bore every hallmark of a traitor. Of course, what criminal was trustworthy?

The director of NCIS had sent Raj to work with the Joint Terrorism Task Force because he was familiar with Middle Eastern culture and spoke Arabic fluently. Before this assignment, Raj had been loaned to the FBI, ICE, and CIA to act as interpreter and assist cases involving Arabic speakers. A sour thought pierced his mind.

NCIS must think he was of little help to them; Raj was always being sent to other federal agencies. It all started when he'd transferred from NCIS Norfolk to NCIS DC. Raj liked being helpful, but he missed the day-to-day camaraderie with other NCIS agents.

Here he was in the harsh Egyptian heat with Yakov, one of the CIA's volatile assets. He was also a reprehensible weapons dealer who sold arms to the highest bidder. This time it was the Egyptian Brotherhood (EB). Raj suspected CIA Agent Bo Rider didn't trust Yakov either, and so needed Raj to spy on his asset. Raj would never choose to go cruising with Yakov.

Raj mulled over the briefing he'd gotten before leaving for Israel. Bo had sworn Raj to such secrecy that he'd been forced to avoid Eva, Griff, and other agents at the task force. Raj shifted his eyes from the shoreline to Yakov.

"You comfortable with our story?" he asked.

"Story?" Yakov looked puzzled.

"How we met," Raj snapped, rolling his eyes. "I've not been your interpreter on previous deals, and they'll be suspicious of you bringing me along, a person they don't know."

"Oh, da last time I don't talk so good. You make it better."

Raj sighed inwardly. Three days ago, the unlikely pair met with Bo and Judah Levitt, an Israeli Mossad agent. Their meeting place, the Israeli town of Eliat, also on the Gulf of Aqaba, had been crawling with Israeli Defense Forces. Raj could tell Bo and Judah were fast friends by their references to past excursions together.

Judah arranged for this yacht and crew to bring Raj and Yakov to Dahab. Moments from now, the NCIS agent and Russian arms dealer would tangle with the EB, ostensibly to broker another delivery of mortars. EB's aim was to smuggle these rocket-launched explosives into Gaza, where their comrades in arms would fire them into Israel. Raj's mission was to help Mossad and the "Agency" track EB's movements of the weapons. He assumed the mortars would be seized or that they were defective.

Yakov was nodding fiercely. Raj snapped his eyes to a fast approaching Land Rover.

"In da last meeting," Yakov mumbled, "da buyers drove such a vehicle."

The Rover screeched to a stop near the dock. A dark-haired driver dressed in camo stepped out and wildly gestured for Yakov to approach the car.

"Remember, we don't go with them," Raj cautioned. "We talk here on the boat."

Yakov shrugged and climbed down onto the aft deck. Raj followed at a safe distance. Before stepping from the yacht onto the dock, he gazed down into the galley. The chef was busy preparing a meal. Would their guests stay for lunch? He didn't know.

The driver swung open the Rover's rear door, and out stepped a trim man with a youthful face. He wore all black with a green headband and checkered scarf around his neck.

Yakov shook his hand before turning to Raj. "Dis man my assistant."

"I am Ishaq," the Arab man said in English. He pointed to the rear seat. "Get in."

Raj responded in Arabic, "Yakov prefers to talk here. Our chef has lunch ready."

Ishaq flinched, presumably at Raj's Arabic. Ishaq flexed his hands and opened the door more widely. That's when Raj spotted another Arab guy sitting against the far window. Dressed in black, he aimed a semi-automatic pistol at Raj's eyes.

"Yakov should not be alive," Ishaq hissed. "We decide where to talk."

The Russian shifted frightened eyes from Raj to Ishaq, then back to Raj. His fearfulness prompted Raj to push himself forward.

He swung his arms easily at his side. "I know nothing of your relationship with Yakov of whom you are displeased. I'm simply his translator."

"You may assist, but get in the Rover with him. Now!" Ishaq insisted.

Raj turned to Yakov, telling him in English they were being taken elsewhere. Yakov shrugged as if there was nothing to do but comply. The gunman hustled out of the backseat and plunged into the front seat. Yakov and Raj were forced to squish next to Ishaq in the rear. The doors locked with a loud click.

Raj was a prisoner of the violent rebel group, the Egyptian Brotherhood. Dryness clutched at his throat. He willed himself to stay sharp and alive. This was more perilous than working undercover at home. No fellow agents were on surveillance. No friendly agents watched his backside. Here in Egypt, he was totally helpless. He clenched his fists, aching to fight. Yet his judgment told him to remain calm and form a plan.

The gunman up front shifted in his seat, keeping his pistol pointed over his shoulder at Yakov and Raj. This rebel was careful not to extend the powerful weapon within arm's reach of either man. The Rover swerved off the main road and began a steep climb into the mountains.

Yakov sniped, "Let me go. Der's no reason to treat me so."

Ishaq stared straight ahead, making no reply. Yakov rammed his elbow into Raj's side.

"Maybe he talks to you."

Raj had no respect for the turncoat snitch and wanted his captors to know he wasn't Yakov's good buddy. Still, it was worth a try. He moistened his lips and leaned forward.

"I'm confused," Raj told Ishaq in Arabic. "Are there ill feelings between you and the man that I help transact business with you? Can I assist in achieving peace?"

Ishaq gave Raj an icy glare. "Shut up. You will learn soon enough."

Raj said nothing else. He stared out the window, memorizing the landscape as they bumped along the mountainous road. The driver eventually wheeled into an inclining driveway. Raj spotted a church adorned with a Coptic cross. The Arabic sign in front heralded this was Saint Mark's Coptic Church. Tremendous relief surged through him. Could he be in the protective custody of local Christians? They were often persecuted by the Brotherhood.

The driver skidded to a stop and stepped out. He flung open the rear doors. The armed guard exited the front seat, ordering them outside by waving his gun. Camo-driver herded them to the church. Raj strode to the door, anxiety building in his chest. Spray paint in Arabic proclaimed: *Death to Christians*.

Yakov sauntered along as if he had no cares in the world. The door banged shut behind them. A muscular man leapt at them from the shadows. He grabbed Yakov's long hair, thrust a large knife at his throat, and dragged him into the sanctuary.

A thug grabbed Raj in a choke hold.

"Wait a min …" he gurgled.

The beefy militant pressed a sharp object into Raj's spine, then yanked him to a chair alongside the wall. Raj struggled to get free, but it was no use. Another EB rebel pointed an AK-47 assault rifle, while two others bound him and Yakov with ropes. Ishaq hauled a chair in front of them and sat down. He tugged on his neck scarf, fixing an evil eye on Yakov.

Ishaq bellowed at Raj, "Yakov knows why we take him. I demand he tell you why."

"Spill what you know or we're goners," Raj shouted to Yakov.

"*Nyet*. I know nothing."

As Yakov shook his shaggy head, the man from the shadows hit Yakov's head so hard his chair tipped over backwards. The Russian's head bounced off the wall before the chair dumped sideways. He lay unconscious on the floor.

"He lies!" Ishaq spat. He stared defiantly at Raj. "You know what he did to us!"

"No, no, no. He paid me only to interpret. I too think he is a dog."

It was obvious these men understood Yakov's Russian-English. Raj strained to recall the bogus story he'd concocted with Bo and Judah. For the next few minutes, Ishaq shot questions at Raj about his background and where he'd met Yakov. Certain facts flowed from Raj's lips as though true. Ishaq appeared to believe him. Raj realized most of his claims about growing up in Cairo and living as a merchant in London would be hard for Ishaq to verify.

Yakov thrashed his legs and moaned on the floor. Two thugs raised his chair back to its four legs. Bound with ropes, Yakov's head hung limply to the side. The guard slapped his face and shouted.

Raj, too, yelled at him, "Sit up and pay attention."

Yakov's head tilted slightly toward Ishaq. His eyes remained shut. Raj wondered if he was conscious. Ishaq paced the floor, throwing his arms around madly.

"Yakov, you miserable toad," he spat. "Those mortars we bought from you last time were stolen in two days. You're in league with the Cairo regime or the Jews."

Raj did some fast figuring. The CIA must have placed a tracking device in the earlier mortar shipment and then stolen the load to protect innocents. If only Bo had shared that crucial tidbit with Raj. But he hadn't. And Raj found himself in a precarious situation.

He whirled on Yakov and said slowly in English, "Do you understand what he's saying?"

Yakov's head bobbed once.

"Did you steal their mortars?"

Raj needed to uncover what happened to those stolen weapons or his life was worth nothing. Heather's mournful eyes darted through his mind. No! He couldn't allow her to invade his thoughts. He must focus like a laser on getting free.

"I brought dem," Yakov slurred. "Don't know more."

Raj shared his response with Ishaq, who in turn nodded at the gunman standing by Yakov. With the quickness of a cat, he slapped Yakov's face. His head bounced toward Raj.

"Do you work for our Cairo oppressors or the pig Jews in Israel?" Ishaq bellowed.

Raj translated Ishaq's demand, but Yakov didn't answer. His entire body shook.

Ishaq crept up to the Russian on the balls of his feet and pounced like a tiger. "You helped them track our mortars so they could find our hiding spot and steal them back. Now you try to sell them back to us again. Do you think we're stupid?"

Raj repeated Ishaq's accusations in English, which gave him time to memorize the terrorist's intelligence for later. If he lived long enough. And that was a big if.

"*Nyet! Nyet!*" Yakov denied knowing of the theft.

"Enough!" screamed Ishaq. "We take our revenge."

Before Raj could react, a slender man stalked in carrying a rocket-propelled grenade (RPG) launcher on his shoulder. He and Ishaq's gunman wasted no time dragging a table to the middle of the mostly-empty sanctuary. Another giant of a man hefted in two sandbags, placing one on the table with a loud bang.

Sweat poured down Raj's armpits. He feared what was coming.

The EB rebels laid the launching tube over this sandbag, aiming it right at Raj and Yakov. Raj fought against the ropes. Adrenaline pumped through his body. His mind was ablaze with one thing: He must find a way out before it was too late.

"Wait!" he screamed in Arabic.

The rebels placed another sandbag atop the launcher.

How could Raj make Ishaq see reason?

He swallowed. "You have badly injured this man. Let him regain consciousness, and he can help you."

Ishaq compressed a two-inch spring. He quickly wrapped the spring with twine, which he inserted inside the trigger guard. When the twine broke, the spring would expand, activating the trigger. Raj watched in dismay at what Ishaq did next.

He slid a candle next to the RPG and wrapped the other end of the twine around the top edge of a candle. He lit the wick. Smoke rippled toward the ceiling. Raj gaped at melting wax saturating the twine. His life was about to turn to ashes. *God help me!*

# CHAPTER 8

Raj lurched against the tight ropes. His eyes rounded in horror. Ishaq flung his arms toward his loyal men. They fled the church amidst much sick laughter.

"They leave us to die!" Yakov cried.

"Hush!" Raj shot back. "I need to think."

That was difficult. His mind convulsed with dozens of scenarios, all bad. Car doors slammed. He heard the Rover start. Its droning engine sound quickly disappeared.

"The Brotherhood's gone," he hissed.

While that might be good, panic threatened to engulf Raj. He flailed against the ropes, but they didn't budge. His eyes locked onto the burning candle. He swiftly calculated. Within minutes, the flame would burn across the twine. When the twine burned to the compressed spring, it would expand and press the trigger.

Heather would be a widow after their brief one year of marriage.

Yakov fidgeted like a whirlwind next to him, to no avail.

"Cut the noise," Raj ordered. "We've two minutes to escape, or we're toast."

"You genius, what's da plan? We're tied and already toast."

Raj glared at the RPG as if the force of his eyes could disarm the weapon. With his feet bound, he leaned forward with tremendous strain. Yes!

He shifted more weight to his feet … leaned farther and … surprise, surprise. Raj was standing.

He bent forward with the chair roped to his body. Relief flooded over him. Even if he fell over, he'd escaped the direct line of fire.

An intense desire to live smoldered within him, propelling him to use every bit of his strength to hop like a kangaroo. Sweat, dripping in pools from his brow, sprayed outward with each leap he took. In this strange fashion, he managed to leap twelve inches.

*Boom!*

Raj snapped his head around. There lay Yakov sprawled on the floor, still tied to his chair. He'd apparently tried copying Raj's success, only to fail miserably. Yakov groaned. Raj ignored his pleas for help and focused on the RPG, which could explode in a minute or less. Pushing against the ropes, he chanced another hop.

If he landed in a heap like Yakov, all would be over. But Raj refused to give up. With a burst of willpower, he hopped twice more. He closed the gap. Over and over again, he leapt until he reached the table.

He inhaled deeply, bent forward, and blew on the candle flame. It was extinguished.

"Yes!" Raj cried.

He eased back into the chair for a moment. Still tied tightly to its legs, he struggled against the cords, causing excruciating pain to his hands. Yakov's head lay awkwardly against the floor as he frantically tried to free himself.

Raj whispered harshly, "They may be nearby, waiting for the explosion. We don't have much—"

He stopped talking. Up in front of the church, a wall with an oasis mural swung into the room like a swinging door. From behind, a human hand gripped the painted tree trunk at the edge. It moved about a foot and from the darkness two eyes peered at Raj. His pulse skyrocketed. He quit breathing. By now their captors could see the candle was not lit.

In one swift move the wall opened fully into the room. A small man dressed in a linen robe hustled forward. He advanced on Raj, demanding in Arabic, "Who are you?"

Raj tried clearing his mind. If this man was from the Brotherhood, he would know who Raj was. So he answered truthfully, also in Arabic.

"The Brotherhood captured us, bringing us here." He nodded at the RPG. "They meant to kill us with that device. It is safe now."

The man scurried over to Yakov and lifted him so his chair was again upright.

"I am called Hamadi," he said. "We must hurry. They might return."

He untied Yakov before coming to Raj's aid. As he freed Raj, Hamadi explained he was a priest of St. Mark's Coptic Church. "The Brotherhood hates us Christians. They forced us from the church and killed a fellow priest. They are treacherous people."

"How did you get in here from behind the wall?" Raj asked.

A slight smile graced Hamadi's aged features. "We have long been persecuted by these people who do not condone our faith. Years ago we built a tunnel for escape."

Raj smoothed his stinging wrists. Some of his skin was rubbed raw. He surveyed the room. They dared not leave by the church door. He doubted he and Yakov could find their way off this mountain. But did Hamadi trust them enough to save them? Should Raj trust him?

Raj offered an olive branch by saying forcefully, "I, too, am a fisher of men."

"You are a Christian?" Hamadi asked, spinning around.

"Yes. I was born in Egypt, but live and worship in America."

"Come." Hamadi's voice remained low. "We must get you to safety."

The Coptic Christian lunged toward the false wall. Then instead, he dashed to unlock the window. He slid it up half an inch. "Let your captors think you escaped out the window."

Raj quickly removed the spring from the trigger guard. He flung off the top sandbag and grabbed the RPG. The trio scooted behind the wall. Hamadi then returned it to its original position. They headed for the trap door and stood before a two-foot-wide compartment, the open trap door leading to a tunnel. A ladder beckoned from the dark unknown.

Yakov wasted no time fleeing down the ladder. Hamadi pointed for Raj to hurry down.

"This RPG might be of use to us," Raj reckoned, so he carried it to the bottom where he stooped beside Yakov in the diffused light.

Hamadi stood above on the rickety ladder, his teeth gripping a tiny flashlight. He slid the cement trap door closed, and fastened a small-gauged wire to an electrical connection before climbing down.

"We take ladder so the Brotherhood can't come after us," Hamadi said.

He squeezed past Yakov and Raj, dragging the ladder with one hand, and giving Raj the flashlight with his other.

"Grab my hand," Hamadi whispered. "It becomes very dark. Hold your friend's hand, or he might become lost."

After Raj repeated this to Yakov, he let him carry the RPG with his free hand. Aiming the flashlight, Raj awkwardly pulled Yakov along, proceeding slowly. They hobbled in the tunnel for a while until Hamadi set the ladder against the cement wall.

"Why do they want to kill you?" he asked Raj.

"Yakov's past dealings with the rebels turned out badly."

"They used force to expel us from our church. They take over our beloved building for their evil purposes. Surely God will judge them."

Raj tried to get his bearings. "Where are we heading?"

"To a shelter. This tunnel hasn't yet been discovered by the rebels," came Hamadi's quiet answer in the flickering light.

They plunged forward in silence. Hamadi stopped them with a caution. "Prepare your eyes. I turn on the light. We have arrived."

Raj released Yakov's hand saying, "Where we are, I know not."

The light from a low watt bulb blinded Raj. He blinked rapidly. Hamadi rushed up a different ladder to pound against a cement trap door. This slid open above his head. He scrambled up to the floor and reached back a hand. With his help, Raj hoisted himself through the opening, landing on his feet in a compact warehouse.

A lone light bulb burned. Raj bent down and grabbed the RPG from Yakov, who came up through the opening grunting and groaning. The sound of clicking metal caused Raj to whirl around. Two men raised automatic rifles, pointing them at Raj's head.

"Why do you have a grenade launcher?" one of them demanded in Arabic.

Hamadi lifted a hand. "It is no problem. The Brotherhood captured these men and tried killing them by using RPG. I save them."

"I'm American and a Christian," Raj said, gathering his wits.

These men were with Hamadi, and posed no threat. At least he hoped not. His sharp instincts were wearing down.

Hamadi commanded his men to lower their weapons. He drew everyone close, explaining the church was equipped with a sensor and door alarm.

"So we know if they find the tunnel," Hamadi said. "We help you leave Egypt."

Raj told Yakov they were going to be safely taken out of the country. The Russian grinned profusely. "*Da*. I thought we would die."

Raj didn't have a clue what to do next. He looked at his ragged wrists. This was the most dangerous case he'd ever been thrust into. He was rattled.

Was Hamadi for real? Or was Raj about to enter something even more deadly?

# CHAPTER 9

## NORTHERN VIRGINIA

On a stormy Sunday morning, Eva entered the sprawling gatheria outside of her church's sanctuary. She had no idea of the ordeal Raj was enduring in the Middle East. With as little sleep as she'd had recently, she headed straight for the café, needing a large cup of her steaming morning joe. This coffee was steaming all right; it was too hot to drink. She had only one option, and that was to wait in line for ice.

The problem was the folks ahead of her took their time tearing open little packets, dumping the contents in their cups, and mixing their coffee with plastic stirs. Eva fumed. At this rate, she'd miss the opening worship. Why didn't everyone drink coffee like she did—black? At last, she reached the ice decanter and dropped in three cubes. She popped on the lid and turned.

Trish Dawson, Lexi's mother from the Wholly Ground, tugged on Eva's sleeve.

"Eva, do you have a minute?"

"Sure, I have a few seconds."

Trish fumbled in her purse. "Lexi told you about their disturbing teacher, Mr. Badger."

"Lexi felt she spoke to me out of turn." Eva gripped her cup. "But I asked Kaley about it."

"Oh good. Well, he's outdone himself this time. Did you receive his letter?"

"A letter? No."

"Then read this right away." Trish handed her a folded piece of paper. "If he didn't send you one, I think he means Kaley is the problem student."

A mother's outrage flooded Eva. She sped from the café to find Scott and the kids. They were perusing summer youth camp brochures in the gatheria.

On tiptoe, she whispered in Scott's ear, "Go on in. I have something to do."

"We'll wait."

"Nope," Eva objected. "I'll join you soon."

Scott raised his brows, but must have recognized the determined look in her eyes. He rounded up the kids, and headed for the sanctuary. Eva perched on a small chair. She forgot about her coffee and opened the letter, her heart pounding as she read Badger's disgusting words:

*Dear Parents:*

*At Washington High, we provide a safe place for your children to learn. We want to ensure classrooms are free from anyone establishing religion in violation of our Constitution. I write to warn parents of a student in my second-hour government class who insists on exercising her freedom to speak of her religion to the point of proselytizing. I understand each of you wants your student not to be unduly influenced so they may choose to be free from religion, if they wish.*

*Because of this student's perverted sense of social norms, she is often overbearing with enthusiasm for her religion. Since we educators aren't permitted to constrain her free expression, you might caution your children that they can choose not to listen to her unwanted comments and not associate with her.*

*Sincerely,*
*Karl Badger, teacher of government*

Shock waves thundered through Eva. She was stunned. What a diabolical schemer!

Badger had branded Kaley a social outcast. Bullying was a huge problem for teens, and here he was showing them how. Eva pitched her coffee in the trash and walked into the sanctuary, the letter crushed in her hand.

A thousand happy worshipers were on their feet, singing. The happy melody only made Eva more discouraged. She eased alongside Scott in the pew. A weasel named Badger had stolen her desire to sing. He'd robbed her of all joy.

Eva heard little of the pastor's message as she plotted how to stop the teacher from harming her beautiful daughter. On the way up the aisle after the service, she noticed Heather Pentu looking forlorn. She approached Eva with fear in her eyes.

"You said Raj was okay, but I've heard nothing from him."

"I'm glad to see you here," Eva replied warmly. "But you probably didn't get much from the service."

Heather's shoulders drooped. "You invited me and I'd like to help with Saturday's craft fair. I wish Raj was here too."

Eva drew Heather's arm into hers. They walked together toward the exit where Scott waited with the kids.

"Heather, when we're undercover, especially in foreign locales, it's impossible to contact family. Someone had seen Raj and he was fine. I'm sure he'll contact you soon."

Heather tilted her chin at Scott. "I see your family needs you. Let me know if you hear anything."

She turned and left the church. Eva ached for her, but what could she do? She rejoined Scott and the kids, two matters weighing on her. She wanted to show Scott the hate-filled letter from Badger as soon as possible. Also, she needed to phone Bo Rider. But she would do neither of these around the children. Life sure was proving difficult.

The ride home from church was unpleasant. Kaley grumbled at Andy, Andy grumbled at Dutch, and Dutch kicked the seat behind Eva. Scott acted gloomy as he sharply changed lanes on the slippery road. Most Sundays, Eva enjoyed discussing the teaching and worship with her family. With a dark cloud of worry hanging over her head, she was scarcely aware of their presence. Sundays should be God-filled and better than this.

They reached home with the kids still at each other's throats. Eva breezed through the kitchen, smelling pot roast cooking in the Crock-Pot.

She zoomed straight to her office and shut the door. Though Bo hadn't admitted it, Raj was most likely overseas. Eva knew the Agency had no authority to work within the U.S.

As Bo's home phone began to ring, Scott cracked open the door. "Have you defected from your family for good?"

Eva shook her head and held up a finger. "I'll be—"

"Hello," Bo said in her ear.

Eva didn't bother with a greeting. "Bo, can we meet tomorrow?"

After a long pause, he said, "Is it about work? Because we aren't secure."

"I know we're not. This morning in church I saw the wife of someone you and I spoke of recently. She's heard zilch. I thought if we met, you might have news."

"No need. I have no news."

Anxiety swept over Eva. "Really? Aren't you concerned, Bo?"

"Yes," he said abruptly.

"Then we should meet."

"Eva, I have nothing to say."

"Then maybe you need to speak to the wife. You owe it to her."

"Not an option."

Eva's eyes searched the ceiling. "What should I tell her? She's worried sick."

"Lie, or use your wily ways to assuage her fears."

"Like you do? Thanks for nothing, Bo."

Eva prepared to hang up, when he added, "Hey, Eva, pray. Just pray."

With a click, he was gone. Eva set the phone in its cradle. Cupboards banging in the kitchen burst her concentration. She hurried to find Scott and Kaley busy shuffling dishes to the table. Eva snatched her apron off its hook and washed her hands.

"Sorry for the delay. I had an urgent call to make."

Scott retrieved their large meat platter from the high shelf. "But everything's okay, right? Or are you leaving us again this Sunday too?"

Eva's lips quivered and Scott's look became tender. He pulled her to him. "What can I do?"

Eva hugged him back. "Work won't take me away. We need to talk about Kaley."

"Now?"

"Let's have a wonderful dinner together first. There's time later for bad news."

Scott stared at her. A baffled expression blazed across his handsome face. She shook her head, dishing roast and trimmings onto the platter. This was Scott's favorite meal; if only he could enjoy the food.

After they all sat around the table, he prayed the blessing to scents of cooked meat and vegetables hovering above the table. Eva spooned helpings for everyone, with Dutch bubbling over about his chance to play soccer on the summer team.

Andy rapped the table with his index fingers as if playing the drums. "Are you guys coming to my final concert?"

"That's the first I heard of it," Eva replied. "When does the junior band perform?"

"My teacher gave me a note. I'll see." Andy leapt from his chair.

Scott passed the potatoes, asking Kaley, "What's your next week like?"

She simply grimaced. Eva surmised Kaley knew about the letter. Andy scurried in with his note, so they talked of his concert. After the delicious Sunday dinner, the kids settled into their homework and Scott picked up the TV remote. Eva asked him to come with her to the pharmacy. Instead, he plopped on the couch.

"Please, that TV will always be there," she said, her voice laced with distress.

"I want to watch the race."

At her intense stare, Scott tossed down the remote. They drove two blocks when Eva pulled to the curb and jammed the car into park.

"Why are we stopping here? Are you ill?" Scott asked.

"I'm furious!"

She yanked Badger's letter from her purse and gave it to Scott. He read it, shaking his head from side to side. Meanwhile, she tried getting a grip on how to proceed. Scott raised a fist.

"Does Karl Badger think he's in some third world country where parents don't know the law?" he seethed. "The school administration must not know about this."

"You think so?" Eva countered. "He must know they'll back him up."

Scott fluttered the letter. "You realize he's referring to our sweet Kaley, don't you?"

"Yes, and Kaley knows it too. She's hardly said a word. The other kids are probably treating her like she has leprosy."

Scott grabbed her hand. "Eva, there is one thing to do."

"I know, but my first reaction is to fight."

Then she sighed and closed her eyes. Together there, on the side of the street, they reached out for God to help Kaley, give them courage, and prevent Mr. Badger from ruining their lives. Eva's heart overflowed with emotion as Scott paused to clear his throat.

"Father, our daughter is attacked for believing in You. Your Son, Jesus, suffered in dying for our sins, but never sinned. Thank you that Kaley loves You as she does. Give us wisdom to defend our freedom to believe in You and share our beliefs with hurting people. We ask in Jesus' name, amen."

Eva squeezed his hand as she prayed for Raj and Heather. "Father, You know their needs better than I do. Please keep Raj safe."

She drove home with Scott reading the horrid letter again. When they reached their driveway, he told Eva that he would spend time with Kaley.

"My lovely daughter is more important than a crazy race. Maybe I'll challenge her to a chess game."

"I love your idea." Eva pulled into the garage. "And teach her strategy to defeat enemies while you're at it."

SAFELY BACK HOME, Eva perused the living room shelves, desperate for a good book to take her mind off their difficulties. She was amazed at how quickly Scott cajoled Kaley into playing chess. Guess their teenage daughter needed more quality time with her upbeat dad. Their banter echoing from the den put a smile on Eva's face.

She leafed through a devotional by a retired FBI agent, and sitting on the footstool, she read the last chapter. The theme of his book was thanks for God's protection as he worked undercover against the mob in the seventies. Eva returned the slim book to the shelf.

Then she spotted the tooled leather cover of her two-volume family Bible and wondered. What did her ancestors know about Jesus? How had this Bible come to their family? She stepped back when Scott ambled by. He whistled a merry tune, carrying a bowl of frozen yogurt topped with fruit.

"What happened to your chess match with Kaley?"

Scott grinned playfully. "Oh, she beat me and is talking to Lexi on the phone."

"Did you bring me a treat?" she asked, wanting to be as happy as he sounded.

"No. You said you're skipping snacks 'cause your jeans are too snug."

Eva's heart sank. "Are you implying I should lose weight?"

"Don't put words in my mouth. To me, you are perfect and always will be."

"You had me worried there for a second."

Eva took out another book and leaned back on the sofa, ready to enjoy a suspense novel.

"Want a bite?" she heard Scott offer. He held up a spoon of the creamy confection. His eyes gleamed.

"Okay," she relented. "With some strawberries."

The icy yogurt mixed with berries tasted delicious on her tongue. She fought the urge to go dish up a bowl of her own. To help her family eat healthier, she struggled to remain a good example. Eva opted for water and went to pour herself a glass. When she returned to the living room, Scott was scraping the bowl clean with his spoon.

"You wasted no time," she said. "I wasn't going to beg for more."

Scott licked the spoon. "I didn't want to tempt you."

He took his empty bowl to the kitchen, returning with a serious question. "So do we confront this Mr. Badger?"

Eva gripped the glass in her hands. The cold penetrated her skin.

"Kaley will be a senior next year. After this dreadful experience, I know why Julia Rider is homeschooling her kids. Has Kaley mentioned transferring to the charter school?"

"No." Scott returned to his chair. "She has time to decide. Summer may perk her up."

Eva put down her water and rubbed her clammy hands. "Mom and Dad's house sold."

"Your parents are starting afresh. Good for them."

"The moving estimators come tomorrow. I can't believe they're moving away."

"Eva, you've hardly gone to Richmond in the last ten years. Why make an issue of it?"

"Because all my childhood ties are ending," she said, surprised how much it hurt to say it.

Scott came over to sit beside her. "You still have Grandpa Marty's farm. Call him tomorrow. Let him know when we're coming to visit."

Her husband was a sweetie. Eva kissed him lightly and told him Marty wanted them to come for his art show when the kids were done with school. Scott's brow creased.

"With my new job, that's a bit soon for me, but you have unused vacation. In fact—"

He jumped up and walked to the bookcase, pulling something out. He flipped through Aunt Deane's journal that Grandpa Marty had sent recently. He turned it toward her.

"Eva, take a look at this. Your aunt wrote a cryptic note on the final page."

She zeroed in on Deane's handwritten words. Though in English, the tiny curved letters were hard to decipher.

"Do we have a magnifying glass?"

He shrugged, prompting Eva to add, "Griff never goes anywhere without one, which seems odd in this technological age. But I see his point."

Scott sped from the room while Eva struggled to read Aunt Deane's writing. He came back in, waving his prize in the air. Eva snatched the large glass. She placed the magnifier against Deane's words and read aloud:

"'The Lord bless and keep the Vander Goes family. May the Vander Goes family always honor Him and proclaim His name no matter the trying circumstances. May the Vander Goes family always keep this Bible and our hero's ashes. Romans 12 tells us to feed our enemy when he is hungry, give him drink when he is thirsty. Thus, we will heap on his head burning embers.'"

She sat against the sofa. "Her words are visionary."

"Indeed. She must have had incredible faith to outlive the Nazis."

Scott removed one of the Bible volumes Eva's mom had given her, looking for Romans. His face fell. "I can't read this ornate script."

"Mom says it's in Latin." Eva ran a finger down the page. "Let's check our Bible."

They did and Eva read some other verses in Romans 12.

"The Apostle Paul teaches we shouldn't repay evil for evil. He says, 'Be careful to do what is right in the eyes of everybody. If it is possible, as far as it depends on you, live at peace with everyone.'"

Scott's eyebrows shot up. "Your family must have had enemies, perhaps by the name of Badger."

"Enemies, embers, and ashes," Eva said thoughtfully. "Deane wrote those verses for a reason. Maybe if I dig into her journals, I'll discover who 'the hero's ashes' belong to."

Eva skipped the first pages until she found a reference to Pieter Vander Goes. Grandpa Marty had once explained that he'd been a judge for Duke Philip in 1455. Aunt Deane's letters were tiny, yet her intriguing way of telling a story made Pieter come alive for Eva. He and his wife Aneka raised two sons and a daughter, just like Eva. She became so engrossed in the lives of Dirck, Justinus, and Jenny that she never heard Scott say goodnight and head for bed.

Pieter ran a large estate in Middleburg, the same historic city Eva had visited with her family last year in the Netherlands. It was also where Grandpa Marty rescued Jewish families from the grip of the Gestapo. The town had to be largely rebuilt after Germany's bombs demolished it at the start of WWII.

With great interest and a pillow stuffed behind her back, Eva returned to page one. What she read rattled her to the core. Could this be whose ashes she had in the leather pouch?

Eva couldn't wait to find out. She kept reading...

*Jesus comforted His disciples by teaching, "Do not let your hearts be troubled. Trust in God; trust also in me... For I am the way and the truth and the life. No one comes to the Father except through me."*

John 14: 1, 6 (NIV)

# CHAPTER 10

## SEPTEMBER 1428, NORWICH, ENGLAND

Father Angus dabbed the last bit of gold paint onto Christ's crown. Angus had been chosen from all the priests at the monastery to illustrate this Latin Bible. Another honor was about to be bestowed on him: Henry Chicesley, the Archbishop of Canterbury, and Bishop Alnwick invited him, a Scottish priest, to the harvest luncheon. Angus decided to bring the holy archbishop one of his rare beauties.

So he stowed his paints and bustled to the flower garden near the western wall of the stone edifice. Roses were his special domain. The autumn air stayed mild, so his bushes were bursting with delicate flowers of varying hues. He snapped off a mature blossom of milky white and deep burgundy. As he reached for a matching bud, a shrill uproar reached his ears.

*Ach no!*

The archbishop must have arrived early. Angus' mouth watered, imagining aromatic lamb awaiting them, roasted and juicy with spices. Before long, he'd be spooning delicious mint sauce over his peas. The clamorous tumult from the village grew louder.

A dark sense of foreboding enveloped him. Angus looked upward, and despite a blue sky with wispy clouds streaking past, the air felt heavy with pending rain. He sniffed his prize rose. Rather than a wondrous fragrance, a putrid smell reached his nose.

"Thomas burns the lamb!" he cried, running toward the kitchen.

Suddenly Angus stopped. The smell came not from the kitchen, but the opposite direction. He turned abruptly and headed to town. A woman's cry shattered the air. Someone must be hurt. Angus gathered his thick brown robe above his knees and ran mightily, coming upon a woman sobbing beneath a hedgerow. Her red hair streamed in clumps around her shoulders. Her hands covered her face, and she wore no shoes.

Angus bent down. "Are ye in pain?"

His compassion fueled her sorrow. She wept fiercely. When he reached a hand to her, anger burned in her red-rimmed eyes.

"It's you and your kind what's killed him!" she wailed, tugging on his brown robe.

He dropped his hands to his side. "I hurt no one, madam. What's amiss?"

"My husband was a Lollard preacher," she whispered as if in pain. "You can't save him."

She slumped to the ground. Angus' knees quaked. Plumes of smoke rose above the trees, blackening the heavens. In his concern for the distraught woman, he'd forgotten the foul smell until now. It assaulted his nose and burned his lungs. Picking up his robe, he ran over the bridge, reaching the village. A revolting scene unfolded before his eyes.

The charred remains of a human form were bound in chains, wrapped to a scorched log. The figure stood in a barrel. Flames leapt in great arcs around the blackened head, void of hair. Angus stared, stupidly blinking his eyes.

"Why's that person bein' burnt?" he asked in anguish.

"Are you blind or dumb?" a villager asked. "Your archbishop just killed Reverend White, the greatest teacher who showed me the true Christ and no false religion. He taught me to seek forgiveness of the Heavenly God. We don't need priests interceding for us. Your Pope's no friend of Christ, with his wicked living."

Angus couldn't fathom Archbishop Chicesley burning a man of God!

This same villager shouted into the unruly crowd, "Reverend White is no heretic!"

He seemed not to care who heard; he kept yelling. Angus' heart nearly failed him. He began to flee this gruesome, violent scene. Then Bishop Alnwick rose, gesturing wildly, and Angus stopped to listen.

"Who dares proclaim this enemy of Christ is not a heretic? He is condemned for over thirty acts of heresy against the Church. Show yourself and you too will burn."

The Archbishop of Canterbury's eyes searched the crowd, and locking onto Henry's, he roared above the flames, "If you do not believe the Church's true teaching, go to your priest and confess your sin of disobedience. If you reject the Latin Bible as the true word of God and defile your soul by reading tracts written by a convicted heretic—this Reverend White, or the Bible written by John Wycliffe—you will burn."

At the archbishop's dire warning, murmurs spread like wildfire through the crowd.

He wasn't finished ranting. "Anyone who defies the king's edict not to own or read the Scriptures in any language but Latin will burn twice. Your bodies will burn on the earth and your soul will burn forever in eternity."

A gust of air swept through the crowd. Flames erupted, devouring what remained of poor Reverend White. Angus felt sick. Chills of horror ran down his spine. It was appalling, ghastly, and terrible all at once, witnessing a person burned alive. What kind of church did this?

His eyes wet with tears, he darted into the crowd. Some villagers stood silent while others chanted support for the Archbishop of Canterbury. Fear clutched Angus' heart like some ferocious beast threatening to rip him apart.

Why did the archbishop stare at him? Did he know Angus read Wycliffe's Bible?

Angus scurried back over the bridge, his lungs heaving. At least his Wycliffe Bible, written in English, was now safely in the hands of his cousin, Lady Jane Vander Goes, who lived in the Netherlands. He'd sent it to her hidden in a feed sack. His mind taunted him. Then why run? He knew the answer.

The Church of England forbade anyone from following John Wycliffe. It also prohibited priests from using or even speaking of his English Bible. Angus ran to the countryside, undergoing a drastic change at the core of his being.

Never would he be the same. Never would he return to the monastery. Never would he go back to what he was.

In his quaking heart, Angus knew what God wanted him to do: become a Lollard, and proclaim the blood of the Lamb without fear. He would be a beacon of light to a lost world.

# CHAPTER 11

## TWENTY-SIX YEARS LATER, MAY 1454, MIDDLEBURG, THE NETHERLANDS

ord Pieter Vander Goes tethered his horse outside the courthouse, his heart heavy as a stone. Although he was honored by Duke Philip appointing him as *grietmannen* a month ago, Pieter now wished he hadn't accepted the judicial post. Was it too late to resign and return to his simpler life on his estate?

In minutes, he would have to decide a lawsuit filed against his childhood friend, Harmon Van Fleet. Count de Alvarado, a wealthy officer in the duchy court whom Pieter had never met, was suing Harmon for a great deal of money. Harmon wasn't dripping in money and jewels as was the count. While Pieter had ignored gossip about the count's ruthless reputation, last week Duke Philip had confirmed those very rumors to Pieter in a letter.

Pieter patted his trusty horse with fresh resolve. He must be fair and fulfill his duty.

A hand grabbed his arm and a raspy voice hissed, "Duke Philip follows this case."

Pieter flinched and shook off the offending hand. He straightened his six-foot frame.

"Who are you, sir?"

"Count Juan de Alvarado at your service."

"You of all people know I am sworn to uphold justice in Burgundy. I weigh all evidence fairly."

"Even if my opponent is as close to you as a brother?"

Pieter's temper flared. "Harmon Van Fleet is a friend and no more."

He stared defiantly at the elegantly dressed man until Duke Philip's letter swirled in Pieter's mind: *Count de Alvarado often lends to those unable to pay. When they default, he and I are the beneficiaries of rich farmland. I trust you to decide correctly.*

To think Duke Philip approved of de Alvarado's heartless scheme disgusted Pieter, and he vowed to avoid being drawn into the fiendish plot.

"Land next to yours will be up for sale," de Alvarado said, fingering his ermine cloak.

"And I suppose you're offering the farmland to me at a reasonable price."

The count snickered. "Duke Philip had informed me of your impressive intellect."

"And I am his busy servant."

Pieter shrugged off the count's insincere flattery and hurried into the duchy court. The suggestion he could be bribed revolted him. More disturbing was that de Alvarado had even tried. Pieter saw Harmon standing off to the side, wringing his hands, and looking fearful.

As the bailiff gaveled Pieter's court to order, in slipped the haughty count with his eighteen-year-old son, Alphonso. Pieter called the legal combatants forward. The count satisfied onlookers as he sauntered with great flair. He bowed upon reaching Pieter's ornate wooded carved desk, a gift from Duke Philip.

Pieter growled at de Alvarado, "You say Harmon Van Fleet borrowed five thousand *vierlander* from you a year ago. You claim he owes the principal, plus twenty percent interest, or forfeits his farmland. Where's your proof?"

"Simply this." With his jeweled hand, he passed Pieter a folded parchment. "Van Fleet agreed to it, and you must enforce the law."

"Twenty percent interest is exorbitant," Pieter countered.

A fierce look erupted in the count's eyes. "Did you read what he signed?"

Pieter's own eyes flickered to the unfair terms. It was no use; he must enforce the law, unless … He might find another way.

"Harmon, did he force you to sign the loan?"

The pudgy man twisted his hands. "Pieter, I mean, Your Honor, I need more time."

Harmon was a kindly man. However, his reputation for making unwise business decisions was widely known. Pieter grasped for a way to help him.

"Did he threaten you or obtain your signature under false pretenses?"

"No."

Pieter fixed a cold gaze on the count. "Will you extend Harmon thirty days?"

"Absolutely not."

Alphonso said loudly, "Father, you said more time is no problem."

"Be quiet!" Count de Alvarado thrust an elbow into his son's ribs.

Harmon snapped his head upward. "He's already taken my wife's inherited house in town and her silver and gold plate for last year's harvest loan. Now he wants our farmland and house. My harvest is almost complete. What I receive for my wheat should satisfy him in full."

Pieter perused the loan papers again. His eyes rested briefly on the date, then flew to his calendar. The truth sparked within him. He smiled gleefully at Count de Alvarado.

"Sir, you are here too early. The one-year period concludes at today's end."

The count snatched the parchment from Pieter's hand. He struck Alphonso's chest.

"You stupid fool. You told me it came due yesterday."

Pieter held firmly to his decision. "In two hours, Harmon will pay the sum you demand."

Harmon protested, "But I have no way."

"You hear for yourself," the count intoned. "He admits defeat."

Pieter raised a hand. "Harmon, I will loan you the money."

"No!" The count slammed the table. "You must not take sides."

"My ruling stands."

Pieter swiftly collected his files as Harmon hastened forward.

Pieter stepped from behind his desk. "Friend, you try my patience. Come to my home and settle matters. Then return here and pay de Alvarado what you owe."

"How will I ever repay you?"

"Finish your harvest and sell your livestock. Never sign such an unfair agreement again."

"That thieving count wants all my farmland. He seeks to ruin me!"

Harmon fled the court, and Pieter faced de Alvarado with a grave look. "Waiting a week or two wouldn't have worsened your position."

"It is a question of law, not my position."

How quickly de Alvarado had morphed from offering Pieter a bribe to a shining example of virtue. Pieter stiffened. A stinging rebuke rolled off his tongue.

"You incorrectly calculated the due date, which gives Harmon grace for today. That's the law."

"I will ensure Duke Philip learns of this," the count warned.

"Justice without mercy is hollow indeed. Harmon's wife is dangerously ill."

"She is not my concern."

Alphonso stepped near. "*Padre,* do you forget my own *madre* lies dying?"

"Be quiet," the irate father snapped, handing his son a stack of papers.

Pieter noticed Alphonso wore a dazed expression. Eying the boy, Pieter told the count, "I wonder at the example you give your son."

The elder man turned, rebuffing Pieter. His expensive robe and silent son trailed behind him. After they climbed into a litter, four horses with a gold braid carried them away. Pieter hopped onto Willow and rode to his estate left to him by his father. He chastised himself for agreeing to hear Harmon's case.

Still, he had no choice—he was the only judge in this southern part of the Netherlands. Pieter urged Willow into a gallop up the long, tree-lined drive. He quickly spotted his beleaguered friend pacing by the large elm tree. Restlessness settled into Pieter's bones. Surely life held more than broken promises and greed.

MANY HOURS LATER AT HIS MANOR HOUSE, PIETER SURVEYED THE TABLE. It fairly groaned with five giant platters of meat and vegetables for their dinner. A comforting fire blazed in the fireplace, yet a chill seized him. He pushed aside his trencher of pork in disgust.

Had he made things worse for his friend? Harmon had taken Pieter's *vierlander* all right, but with a cry, "Treachery! The count will try any trick to seize my land."

At least Pieter had given Harmon more time to sell his farm and keep the excess profit. He looked up to see everyone staring at him.

"Will you, my dear?" Aneka's question floated lightly in the air like a butterfly.

His wife's lovely smile from across the table gave him pause. Pieter stirred in his chair.

"I'm sorry. My mind was elsewhere."

"Justinus, ask Papa again."

His twelve-year-old son peppered him. "Will you read from the Wycliffe Bible? It has marvelous drawings. My friends don't own Bibles. I dared open it, but Mama says you must read it to us."

Nine-year-old Jenny stuck out her lower lip and refused to eat.

"Finish your cabbage, or no apple tart," Aneka scolded. "Mollie made the sweet especially for Papa's birthday."

Jenny shoved her tiny hands firmly on her hips. "Only if you make Papa eat too."

"Go upstairs to your room," Aneka commanded.

Jenny bounced from her chair and ran out.

Dirck, their oldest son, shook his head. "Correct her or you will be sorry. Did the duke pay another visit, Papa?"

Duke Philip was the last person Pieter wanted to speak of. He would certainly hear from him once he learned of Pieter outmaneuvering Count de Alvarado.

"Papa, it's your birthday," Justinus pressed. "Will you tell us about Grandpapa? You say he's a hero, but never tell us why."

Aneka interceded by reminding the boys of Pieter's obligations. "He oversees our farms here in Middleburg and in Goes. Someday you boys will understand what it means to be a man of position. Until then, finish your studies. Neither of you is proficient in Latin."

Pieter mouthed "thank you" to his wife of sixteen years, and found solace in his library where he began working on the harvest figures. Deep into adding up bushels of barley and oats, Harmon's earlier cry flashed through his mind, "He's trying to ruin me!"

Pieter tossed down his quill, which spilled ink on his ledger. Aneka was right about his responsibilities weighing on him. Acres of land needed tilling before he could plant. He should hire a steward as she often urged him to do.

A knock sounded at the door. He opened it, ready to implore Aneka to leave him be. A woman of short stature peered in. A shiny black cap covered her hair. Her eyes were shielded, as if holding a mystery.

"A message just coom," she said in her thick Scottish brogue.

Pieter thrust out a large hand. Mollie gave him a folded piece of paper, which he brought to a flickering candle. His heart raced at the urgent words:

*Harmon collapsed. You're needed at once. Doctor Van Kalk*

Pieter swung into action, telling Mollie to have Fitch saddle his horse. Aneka had retreated to her sewing room. When he burst in, she shoved her needle in the fabric and glided over to him.

"Harmon's life hangs in the balance," he snapped. "It's my fault."

Her eyes clouded over. "Surely not. What happened to him?"

"I dare not lose one second."

Pieter escaped the house, desperate to reach Harmon in time. He rode Willow hard, showing the horse no mercy in the fast-darkening night. A maid showed him to Harmon's room. His friend lay with eyes closed on a bed jutting from the wall. Pieter plunged toward the bed, drawing back when a scrawny dog bared its teeth.

Doctor Van Kalk swept in, cautioning, "Do not stay long. I will find his wife."

"Promise me," Harmon said, clawing Pieter's arm, "my wife will receive the harvest proceeds. Other debts … save this farm."

He slumped against the bed. Mrs. Van Fleet entered slowly, leaning on the doctor's arm.

"Lord Vander Goes, why are you here?" she asked with frightened eyes.

Harmon rasped, "He makes my last will and testament."

She began to weep. The doctor slipped from the dimly lit room, quickly returning with a quill and ink. Pieter dragged a wooden chair to the bed.

"How do you want your goods and property distributed?"

"Please don't leave me!" Harmon's wife wailed. She collapsed onto the floor.

Harmon struggled to lift his head, and with great effort, croaked, "Write this: My farmhouse, crop proceeds, horses, and cattle go to my wife. My dear, I lost your home in town, and the silver plate and knives. The gold ones too!"

"Money means nothing. I want you to live!" she beseeched him.

Harmon's reddened eyes rolled toward Pieter. "Give to the poor one hundred *vierlander*. Two hundred for a requiem mass at the abbey. Is that sufficient to atone for my sins?"

"You should ask the priest," Pieter replied softly.

Doctor Van Kalk guided Harmon's sobbing wife from the room. Once she left, Harmon rallied, "If she remarries, this house and land go to my daughter."

Pieter looked at him skeptically, pen in the air.

"Write it," Harmon commanded. "My enemies will not succeed upon my death."

Pieter wrote the requested provisions. Harmon had one final bequest: His dog would go to his grandson. A tear escaped from Harmon's eye. Wind whistled down the chimney, rattling the parchment Pieter held. Though an icy cold breeze tore through him, he read aloud the will he'd just written. Harmon scrawled his name at the bottom.

Pieter clutched the parchment. "Try to triumph over your weakness."

Harmon moaned in reply. The whimpering dog shoved its nose under its master's hand. Dismay gripping him, Pieter rushed to find the doctor to witness the testator's signature. The legal formalities finished, Pieter tucked the will in his cloak.

"I will secure this in my office, and see to your harvest."

Harmon nodded weakly. The doctor stopped Pieter on the way out, asking him to send for a priest. "He won't last the night," was his gloomy proclamation.

Pieter rejected the notion that life or death was in his hands. With long strides, he went to the barn where the groom instantly set off for Father Maxim. Regret clinging to him, Pieter returned to Harmon. He stayed at his friend's side until Father Maxim came.

It was a torturous night of waiting. In the wee hours, Harmon breathed his last, his earthly presence no more. His widow was left to cope with the aftermath of her husband's imprudent business decisions.

Pieter rode home beneath a multitude of stars, his thoughts a tangle. Count de Alvarado had finagled Harmon's other home in town. Alphonso had said his mother was dying. Could it be Harmon wrote his will to prevent the count from getting the land if he married his widow?

After handing his horse over to Fitch, Pieter hurried inside the brick home built by his father years ago. He wanted to throw himself on the bed and rest his weary mind. He passed the sitting room and saw Aneka asleep by the fire. His heart leapt.

Her loose hair nearly touched the coals!

Pieter swept her into his strong arms, and carried her upstairs to their sleeping chamber. There, he placed her upon the plush bed. A hush fell over him. She looked so serene.

"Is Harmon all right?" she whispered in the dark.

Pieter perched beside her on the bed. "I'll tell you in the morning. Go back to sleep."

He rose, but Aneka caught his arm. "Pieter, please tell me."

"I can't, not now. I must be alone."

He fled downstairs to his library where he tossed a log on the embers. Sparks curled in the air. Pieter dropped to a chair. Someone touched his shoulder. He jerked his arm upward, jarring a goblet. He sprung to his feet, sorry to see cider dripping down Aneka's robe.

He towered over her, demanding, "Didn't you hear? Leave me alone."

Her bottom lip trembled, and she spun toward the door. Pieter reached for her arm.

"I'm sorry to speak gruffly. It's not your fault."

He took the goblet and downed the cider. With a deft movement, he set the goblet on the mantel before pulling Aneka to him.

"I'm covered in cider," she protested.

He held her tightly in his arms.

"How is Harmon?" she asked.

"Dead!"

Grief pummeled against Pieter's heart. Aneka's cold fingers dug into his arm.

"It's true," he said. "Yesterday, I loaned him money. Now he is gone."

He pulled away from her painful grip. How to voice the turmoil swirling inside of him? Pieter swallowed and gaped at Aneka. In her white dressing robe and golden hair, she looked like a heavenly being come to chastise him. Was he losing his sanity?

She extended her arms. "Let me help you."

"Life must have more meaning," he muttered, pressing his hands against his temples.

"Do you want Count de Alvarado to win every time?"

Pieter narrowed his eyes. "Hardly, but I no longer wish to decide. I quit. I shall write the duke immediately."

"He appointed you because of your fairness. We were proud when Duke Philip placed the gold chain of office around your shoulders."

Aneka swirled away, leaving her sweet fragrance behind. Pieter scrambled for parchment and ink. He couldn't remain as judge following Harmon's death mere hours after appearing in his court. Quill in hand, Pieter's mind veered to something more troubling. His life had no meaning.

So what if he met his family's needs and gave alms to the poor? What did it matter if he brought his family to Mass on Sundays? He managed his estate competently, but an appalling thought blazed into a consuming fire. Pieter was unworthy of all God had bestowed on him.

He put down his quill to hunt for the Wycliffe Bible his mother had given him on his twelfth birthday. His search proved futile. It wasn't on the usual table, nor anywhere in his library. He nudged Aneka awake in their sleeping chamber.

"Did you or the children take my Bible? I need it and can't find it."

She leaned on one elbow, suggesting Justinus might have the Bible. Pieter reluctantly postponed his search, and fell into an agitated slumber.

# CHAPTER 12

Before the sun's rays lit the sky, Pieter charged out of bed and shook his sons awake.

"Did you take my mother's Bible?" he asked, frustration rising in his chest.

They knew nothing of its whereabouts. Mollie helped him search the house. Pieter questioned Fitch, who sleepily replied, "I don't read, yer lordship."

Of course, Pieter knew that. He apologized for waking the groom, and then sheepishly asked if he'd heard any strange noises after Pieter left for Harmon's last night.

"Nothing, my lord," Fitch answered with a scratch of his chin.

"I believe my family Bible was stolen while I was away."

Fitch scowled, looking distressed. Pieter asked him to saddle the gray mare. Then he barged into the house, informing Aneka he was leaving. He dashed outside, and hopped onto Star, his younger and rested horse.

Pieter reached the abbey in time to hear six bells. His emotions boiled over as he strode down the great hall. Sunlight streamed through a stained glass window, and he noticed three splendid tapestries hanging on the far wall. In one, baby Jesus lay in Mary's arms while His earthly father Joseph looked on.

Hundreds of Flemish weavers had woven threads of lapis blue with burgundy and silver threads. Such impressive tapestries cost the equivalent of thirty years' wages for a worker, a staggering amount of money. Though these splendid works of art proclaimed the message of salvation in Christ, they left Pieter more bereft. His life would never count for anything as important.

Approaching footsteps made Pieter spin around. Maxim stretched out a hand in greeting with a congenial smile on his round face.

"Have you finished morning prayers?" Pieter asked the abbot.

"Yes. I see you admire the tapestries commissioned by your parents. Their patronage also helped us to complete the abbey."

Pieter turned his face away. "Need you remind me of my own failings?"

"You need cheering up. Come join me in my study."

They retreated out a back door. Pieter struggled with how to tell Maxim of his deep pain. It was Father Maxim, and not Harmon Van Fleet, who was as close to Pieter as a brother. Maxim opened the door to the chapter house where he kept a study and sleeping room. Pieter took a chair, well worn from those who had sought Maxim's attentive ear over the years. Stacks of illuminated manuscripts in French, Latin, and Dutch were spread across a table and multiple shelves.

Pieter mindlessly leafed through one.

Maxim offered him a cup of mead. "I spooned in your honey, the sweetest this side of the sea. I would turn down breakfast for a mouthful, but that isn't why you're here at dawn."

Pieter sipped the warm drink before confiding, "My life is a hollow shell."

"Be careful," Maxim warned. "You are close to blasphemy. Do not mock anyone God has created, including yourself."

"You know as well as I that Harmon's demise is my fault."

"That also is near blasphemous. Our lives are in the hands of God."

Pieter bolted up from his chair. Could he admit God seemed as far away as a distant star?

"Maxim, I work two estates for my sons and heirs. Our dairy herds are the most successful in the Netherlands. Our sheep produce the finest wool to compete with Flanders."

"Pieter, I know this."

"Do you know what my inheritance means if I die tomorrow?"

Maxim surprised Pieter by saying, "Remember your twelfth birthday?"

"Of course, but why should that matter?"

"Your gravely ill mother urged me to help you study Scripture and give you proper instruction. I promised I would. On that day, she gave you a Wycliffe Bible."

"It has been stolen."

Shock rippled through Maxim's eyes. "That could be dangerous for you."

"How so?"

"Much unrest in the church is because people like John Wycliffe brought God's word to the common man. Those in power object to Wycliffe translating the Bible into English."

"You think whoever stole it means to cause me difficulty?"

A sharp knock sounded on Maxim's door. He opened it and introduced Pieter to Father Cornelius. He and Maxim briefly discussed taking food to needy villagers after a recent flood. Pieter expressed willingness to have Aneka prepare baskets of bread and cheese.

"That would be most appreciated," Cornelius said before he withdrew.

Maxim closed the door and tapped a finger to his temple. "Where were we? Oh, I was about to ask if your mother also gave you a family scroll."

"Yes, she sewed one with Scottish thistles along the border. Why?"

"I remind you because your mother lived with purpose each day of her life. She clothed the poor, and cared for the sick. Her unselfish acts give the Vander Goes name respect."

"If only she was still here." Pieter sighed. "I need her advice."

"Her dreams live on in you."

Pieter didn't know how to respond, so instead he walked to a square window and watched black crows gathering in the courtyard.

From over his shoulder, he heard Maxim say, "I see it is I who has failed you."

"No!" Pieter turned, pounding his chest. "Something is wrong with me!"

"Not so, my friend."

"If I do not use knowledge for good, it is without value. So is my life."

"I may have a new quest for you," Maxim said, joining him by the window.

Intrigued, Pieter pressed him to say more. Maxim refused, telling Pieter to call back in a week. Meanwhile, he would make inquiries into the lost Bible.

Pieter grabbed onto Maxim's hand. "I appreciate your caution. Something so prized will have few buyers."

On the ride home, his spirit revived. He neared the enormous elm, planted by his mother when she'd traveled from Scotland to marry his father. Powerful memories assailed him. The night she had lain so ill, he'd

snuck in and kissed her cheek. In a faint whisper, she had told Pieter the
Holy Bible would protect him from the thorns of life.

Her eyes fluttered as she had said, "Son, remember your heritage from
Scotland to the Netherlands. Most importantly, know you are a child of
God. Never forget I love you. You might be in danger for having this Bible,
but stay strong and courageous."

Now her Bible was gone. Pieter hadn't bothered to even look at it. Her
sudden death had wounded him too deeply. To avoid speaking to anyone,
he took the long way home, riding into the village to see firsthand the
squalor Cornelius had described. The many women and children needing
clothes and nourishment weighted his shoulders.

He traveled home along the river, mulling over his frank talk with
Maxim. What did he mean that Pieter's mother's dream lived on? In his
heart he knew whatever hopes she once had for Pieter were gone forever.

PEITER COMPLETED TOURING HIS ESTATE drained of energy. Failure dogged
his steps as he left the sweaty mare with Fitch and trudged up the gravel
drive to the manor house. He stopped to look at a carved stone placed
among the brick doorpost. His father had been proud of their family's motto: *LUCTOR ET EMERGO.*

"I struggle but arise," a voice chimed behind Pieter.

He whirled his head. A stranger smiled at him. The strong way in which
this man spoke these words lit a spark within Pieter's dry soul. Could he too
arise from the dust of disappointment?

"Do I know you, sir?"

"Laddie, I ken it's many a year since I came to yer dear mother's funeral ..."

"Cousin Angus!" Pieter welcomed him with a hearty handshake. "I
didn't recognize your face, but your Scottish burr I can't ever forget.'

Angus' eyes shone. "Much has happened. I didna' mean to surprise
ye so."

"Your Latin is up to the mark," Pieter said, grinning. "Come inside.
Let me introduce you to my wife and two sons. We also have a young
daughter. And Mollie's still here. She came from your home in Perth with
my mother."

"I see with me own eyes God has blessed ye."

Angus' open gaze marveled Pieter. Though his cousin had traveled a
far distance, he seemed like a man at peace with his Maker and the world,
something that had escaped Pieter all these years.

"I shouldna keep it from ye." Angus tapped Pieter's arm. "England is unsafe fer me. I'm a Lollard noo."

Pieter ushered him inside, saying, "I've heard of Christians being persecuted. You're welcome to stay with us as long as you'd like."

Pieter settled Angus into the study, urging him to rest. Angus sank into a comfortable chair, and picked up a manuscript from Thomas a' Kempis. Pieter raced out to find Dirck and Justinus, who were in the barn talking of the sea. He quickly brought them to meet Cousin Angus. Both boys greeted the Scot with good humor. Angus' first question, if they knew the game of chess, pleased them both.

Pieter poked his head into the kitchen. "Mollie, bring refreshments into the study. Your old friend is here, from Perth."

"Ye don't mean Angus?"

Pieter nodded with a grin. "Look lively. The man must be famished, although I must say he's a sight for sore eyes."

He left her to whip up a feast fit for a king and climbed the stairs two at a time. Amplified voices spilled from Aneka's side room.

"Mama, look at this lovely scroll!" Jenny cried.

Pieter gasped. There was Jenny, crushing beneath her fingers the very scroll Maxim had asked him about earlier. He plied it away from her clutches.

"Be careful! Your Grandmamma sewed this delicate scroll for me."

A pink blush erupted across Jenny's fair cheeks. She gazed at Pieter with hurt in her emerald green eyes. Then she tossed her curls and probed deeper into the trunk, pulling out a bulging reddish brown pouch.

"This looks special."

"Give it to me," Pieter said. "I warned you both, *never* touch my mother's trunk."

He seized the deerskin pouch, and respecting his bittersweet memories, wrapped the heirlooms in the trunk. He snapped the lid shut.

Jenny drew her lips into a pout. "You are mean."

"Your mama and I have business."

"You always send me away." Jenny stomped her foot. "Can I help it I'm not your son?"

Her words stung Pieter and he softened his tone. "We'll have a nice talk at supper. How would you like me to tell a story about your Grandpapa?"

Jenny was all smiles and skipped from the room. Pieter reached down a hand to help Aneka to her feet. As she rose, her lace cap slipped, covering her eyes.

"Keep the children from this trunk," Pieter reminded gruffly. "It holds much regret."

Even opening it had stirred fresh concern over his missing Bible. Thoughts of Angus waiting downstairs disappeared from his muddled mind.

"What is so valuable about that deerskin pouch?" Aneka asked.

"My mother prized it." Pieter propelled her toward the stairs.

"Did you see a well-dressed young man around here?"

Aneka shook her head. "Is he the reason we had to eat luncheon without you?"

"Not at all. My ride on the estate took forever. I'm sorry."

"Who is the young man you're asking me about?"

"I still don't know where my mother's Bible went."

"If you think it was stolen, then you must think it's by 'a well-dressed young man.' A poorly dressed young man can't read." She tilted her head. "Might it be a well-dressed old man?"

"Why do you question me?" Pieter objected.

Aneka's bottom lip drooped. "You said you have business with me."

The way she stared with her grave blue eyes touched Pieter deeply. He wrapped his arms around her. With one hand, he removed the errant cap from her head, freeing her blond hair to fall across her shoulders and down her back.

Aneka rested in his arms. "Pieter, I sense you're not telling me something important."

He thumped his forehead. "I nearly forgot! Cousin Angus is downstairs."

"Oh, I look a fright," Aneka declared, straightening her hair.

Pieter went downstairs ready to implement a new plan—Angus would make a perfect tutor for his sons.

# CHAPTER 13

Pieter ate his creamed herring across the table from Angus. Mollie hovered nearby, filling goblets with cider and replenishing platters of bread and cheese. She hadn't stopped smiling since Angus arrived. Pieter too appreciated his cousin's presence. His chest swelled with pride recalling Angus' earlier response to Pieter's proposal to tutor Dirck and Justinus.

"It's an honor to teach 'em. The brawny lads have keen minds."

A momentary snag surfaced when Angus refused to accept wages. After much back and forth, he finally agreed to a small stipend, along with his room and food.

"More onions?" Aneka asked, puncturing Pieter's mental wanderings.

Angus nodded, and she passed him the dish.

"Papa," Jenny interrupted. "Remember the scroll and special pouch?"

She grabbed a wrapped parcel from beneath her chair and ran to his lap. Pieter fought rising ire at her disobeying him once again. Angus wore a bemused look, prompting Pieter to set down his knife. He took out the pouch.

"What's in that? Did Grandpapa put seeds in it?" Justinus asked.

Dirck shook his head. "No, he probably hid gold in it."

"It could have held Judas' thirty pieces of silver," Pieter replied.

"Ach." Angus put a finger to his lips. "Yer pouch is dear, and holds a great mystery."

Before Pieter could open it to see what was inside, he caught sight of his mother's scroll. Along the top she'd sewn *Jesus amor meus.* His mind tumbled.

"Sons, do you know what these words mean?"

They both shrugged.

"May I see?" Aneka shyly glanced at Angus.

Justinus handed her the long piece of linen and she smiled. "Your mother wrote, 'Jesus is my eternal love.'"

"Why is your Latin so much better than mine?" Pieter complained.

"Do you forget I've been teaching Latin to our sons?"

Pieter took the scroll from her. "From now on, Angus takes over those duties."

Aneka lowered her eyes. Pieter ignored the tension in the air. His mother's faint, ragged breath pounded in his ears from many years ago.

"I was twelve when your Grandmamma made this scroll," he said with reverence. "See? She sewed names of my grandparents and great-grandparents along this tree."

"What are those ugly flowers, Papa?" Jenny asked bluntly.

He rubbed the purple threads along the bottom edge.

"May I?" Angus reached for the scroll.

"By all means," Pieter said. "I've never set foot in Scotland, your homeland."

Angus' lean face crinkled in a smile. The children listened with rapt attention as he wove a story about the thistle being the national emblem of their grandmother's homeland. Legend held that the "ugly" thistle protected Scottish fighting men from Vikings. The fierce invaders stepped on them with bare feet in the darkness. Thorns tore their flesh to pieces.

"Who are the Vik—?" Jenny started to ask, but Dirck interrupted by declaring, "I want to go to Scotland!"

"Me too!" Justinus chimed.

Pieter lifted his chin. He and Angus traded knowing looks. A trip to Scotland might be possible if it was safe for Angus. A sudden desire to visit his mother's birthplace cascaded over Pieter. Mollie hustled in with a message for him. He seized the parchment with one hand, gathering the scroll and pouch in his other. Then he nudged Jenny from his lap.

"You promised to tell a story," she protested.

Pieter strode from the room. "Angus just did."

In his library, Pieter secured his mother's scroll and pouch in a large box with blue stones on top. The parchment unrolled with a snap. He could hardly believe his eyes. The duke's chastising words leapt from the page:

*Lord Vander Goes,*

*The report of your ruling against Count de Alvarado is most disturbing. I do not condone injustice. Your immediate explanation is required.*

*Duke Philip*

Pieter stalked the room. So it had come to this. His Sovereign was telling him how to rule. He tossed a dry log on the smoldering fire. As flames consumed the fresh fuel, so a realization spread within him. He must act to save his conscience. He scribbled with his quill:

*Your Excellency Duke Philip:*

*Count de Alvarado mistakenly demanded payment from Harmon Van Fleet on the same day the loan was due, instead of the next day. I ruled as I thought proper, giving Harmon the day's balance to pay his debt. He has since left the earth. Since I failed you and what you expect of me, I beg you to release me as your magistrate.*

Pieter signed the missive. He released his indignation like steam escaping from a covered boiling pot. He sealed the parchment, and pressed his ring into the hot wax. Then he decided. Rather than go to Scotland, he would take Maxim up on his proposed quest, whatever it was.

A FEW DAYS AFTER MEETING WITH MAXIM, Pieter brought his sons into town, letting Dirck drive the wagon to Middleburg's center. After praising his fine efforts, Pieter jumped from the wagon, instructing the boys to stay with the horses. He walked with purpose into the market bustling with tradesmen hawking their wares.

Pieter didn't focus on stacks of cloth or barrels of fish. His mind was all business. He passed the fishmonger's stall so quickly he didn't notice a young man lurking in the shadows. Instead, Pieter spotted the man he'd come to interview, his rough features befitting a life at sea. So did the sharp barbs he traded with men clustered around him.

The hearty ship captain let out a guffaw. "I'll handle cargo for half the fare. My barge is the best on the river. The Rhine isn't in disrepair like these roads. It remains as God made it, constantly moving you to your destination."

Several men strode away, but most in the crowd roared in laughter, stirring the seafarer to a greater passion. He pumped his fist in the air.

"Duke Philip fails to improve these wretched roads since the Romans were here six hundred years ago!"

Pieter cringed inwardly. It was dangerous to disparage the duke in public. Conniving ears were everywhere. He waited for the rowdy men to disperse before greeting Captain Van Ritter.

"Lord Vander Goes, you're better suited to travel as other nobles, in a gold litter."

"Perhaps your barge is not fast enough," Pieter fired back. "I need to reach Mainz quickly."

He stepped away, shrugging off the captain's continual boasting of his "able craft." Pieter's eyes locked onto those of Alphonso de Alvarado. Pieter wondered if he'd overheard his conversation with Van Ritter.

So he asked Alphonso, "What are you doing in town? Buying fresh trout?"

His dark eyes surveyed Pieter with contempt. "I could ask you the same. Why are you here, listening to criticism of Duke Philip?"

No longer an awkward young man, Alphonso's surly air brought Pieter unwanted memories of the duke's stinging letter. Would this family always be a thorn in his side?

Rather than issuing a rebuke, Pieter approached Van Ritter, who looked contrite.

"Lord Vander Goes, forgive my weak humor. I'm a commoner, unused to transporting nobility. My craft is simple, and your travel companions will be crates and barrels."

Pieter nodded toward Alphonso who was walking a few paces away.

"Captain, I appreciate an honest man more than riches. My title doesn't make me who I am. Important business calls me to Germany and I will pay you well for the voyage."

"Then I am at your service." Van Ritter removed his cap.

"Is your vessel ready for a hasty voyage?"

"She's swift and sturdy, if small. I'll safely take you to the Rhine River and on to Mainz."

"Where are you traveling to, Papa?" Dirck asked, suddenly appearing in the mix.

"I told you to watch the horses."

"We tied them up. See?" Dirck pointed behind him.

"My directions are the same. Wait for me at the wagon."

"Come on, Justinus," Dirck groused. "We aren't wanted."

Pieter hastily grabbed Dirck's arm. He glanced back at Alphonso, and whispered, "Have you seen that young man near our estate?"

"No, Papa. Should I have?"

"Avoid him always and advise me the moment he comes near," Pieter warned.

He released Dirck's arm to Van Ritter's chuckle. "Your sons are feisty like me. Will they journey with you? I could use extra hands."

"No."

They proceeded to discuss the trip to Mainz, and what provisions Pieter should bring. The brawny captain stroked his full beard, suggesting Pieter could journey back with him if his stay was short. Then he peered into the shadows where Alphonso had vanished.

"I'm eager to leave town," Van Ritter said, keeping his voice low. "A spy for Duke Philip sneaks around, and can't be trusted. Another captain's boat was confiscated for unpaid taxes."

"We shouldn't discuss such things in public."

"Right you are. Want to inspect my vessel?"

They walked to the waterfront, but stopped abruptly. Men and women ran in all directions to escape advancing, snorting horses. The sleek horses pranced in formation, ridden by heavily armed soldiers wearing chainmail battle suits. At least a dozen of these riders swarmed the little village. Swords dangled at their sides. They gazed sternly at watching villagers, their horses splattering mud as they pranced past.

Dirck grabbed onto Pieter's coat. "Father, who are those men?"

"Duke Philip's knights. They are of the Order of the Golden Fleece."

"Why are they here, Father?"

Pieter ignored his son's barrage of questions and pushed him toward the boat. Dirck took off running as two muscular deckhands raised a tall, round wooden mast.

"I could do that," he bragged.

Shielding his eyes from the bright sun, Pieter replied, "Watch and see."

The deckhands dropped the mast and its square base into a wooden box, which held it upright. Such was Pieter's fascination that he forgot to scold Dirck for leaving his brother with the horses.

"If only I could travel the river with the captain to new places," Dirck said.

"Van Ritter, as you see, my fifteen-year-old son, Dirck, is keenly interested in your boat."

"He is welcome to come aboard with you." Van Ritter pointed in the direction of the knights. "I see the duke's thugs dashing by. Do they search for Count de Alvarado?"

"Do they have business with him?" Pieter wondered aloud.

"I'm told the count seeks a commission as a knight. Then he can steal even more."

Pieter addressed him severely. "Captain, be more cautious. He's already a powerful man."

As Van Ritter's eyes followed the disappearing knights, Pieter lowered his voice. "If what I hear is true, the count may change his desire to join the Golden Fleece."

"Oh?" Van Ritter raised his shaggy eyebrows. "You've heard gossip of your own?"

In hushed tones, Pieter explained that Duke Philip vowed to send his knights to fight the marauding Ottoman Turks. He looked the captain square in the eye.

"Can you see the elegant count on horseback fighting Turks?"

Van Ritter let out a hefty belly laugh. His merry eyes twinkled. He invited Pieter and Dirck onto the deck where he pointed out his ship's many attributes. Dirck stooped to grab an oar. Struggling to lift it to his chest, he let it go with a bang. Pieter noted with approval the craft had ample room for his supplies, and concluded his arrangements with the captain, asking if he had room for another. He did.

Pieter turned to his watchful son. "Your mama doesn't know yet of my trip."

"Count on me to keep a secret, Papa."

Pieter clapped him on the back. He then thanked Van Ritter, and bought Aneka's trout. Stopping to haggle over a piece of blue cloth, he saw Alphonso watching from a window across the street. As Pieter went to join Justinus by the wagon, he looked over his shoulder. Justinus wasn't pleased at waiting so long.

"I'm parched," he growled.

"Your brother helped me with some purchases. Your turn will come."

Pieter was pleased with Dirck's helpful attitude. "Go ahead and drive the wagon home. While I'm away, I expect you to keep a watch on your mother and siblings."

Dirck nodded and Pieter added sternly, "Alphonso seemed occupied with mischief in town. Don't let him at the manor house for any reason."

"I can spot troublemakers, Papa. Just yesterday I shooed a fox from our henhouse."

"You're maturing into a fine young man. I will involve you in more estate matters."

Dirck slapped the horses with the reins. Pieter sat back, satisfied all was in order for his excursion to Mainz. Reaching the barn, Pieter climbed from the wagon.

Justinus did too, but then ran off, giving Dirck a chance to ask, "May I go along on the trip?"

Pieter thought of the implications. "I can't take you to Mainz."

"Let me go to Mainz!" Justinus sprinted up, clutching a kitten. "Where is it?"

"I should be the one, Papa." Dirck glared at his brother.

Pieter held up his hands with a determined set to his chin. "Enough arguing."

The kitten wriggled free and Justinus sped after the tiny creature.

"Papa, the captain said I could—"

Pieter dismissed Dirck's appeal. "We are late for dinner. Today is Jenny's birthday."

"Who cares," Dirck shot back.

"I do. Please give these to your mother."

Pieter handed him the cloth, and picked up the package of fish. He held the door open for his son, who stomped inside. Pieter gave Mollie the trout before heading to his library. When they last talked, Maxim had stressed how urgent it was for his inventor friend to receive Pieter's aid. So, for the next ten minutes, Pieter reviewed every angle of the trip.

Aneka came in and said, "Dinner is ready."

Her voice sounded dull, and he noticed her tired eyes. Was it wise leaving her? Then he recalled Angus would be here, tutoring Dirck and Justinus. Perhaps Pieter's rash decision to hire him would bring further benefits.

He broached the subject casually. "Maxim asked me to help his friend in Germany."

"So that's why you eagerly bought my cloth in town, to speed your getting away!"

Guilt pierced Pieter like a sharp arrow. He should stop keeping things from her. Aneka's lower lip trembled, and he recognized signs of her fear. Rather than discuss the inevitable, he tried lightening her mood.

"When Jenny was born, we were so happy." He grabbed her hands in his. "And still are."

She squeezed his fingers and smiled. They walked from his library together.

"Look what Mama made me." Jenny twirled, showing off her new gown.

Aneka beckoned everyone to the large oak table where beeswax candles glowed brightly. Mollie sliced rye bread and passed chunks of freshly churned butter. The spicy aroma of lamb and caraway pleased Pieter's senses. His concerns disappeared. He happily gave the blessing, and Angus shared snippets of his journeys throughout England as a Lollard preacher.

"Can we ever go to England, Father?" Dirck asked.

A worried look flashed across Angus' face. "Wait fer things to settle doon. King Henry's goin' mad, and the Duke of York's power mad. There's talk of war."

"Uncle Douglas and Aunt Emilee live in York," Pieter reminded Angus. "Are they safe?"

"Only God knows."

Pieter ate his meal, succumbing to second thoughts. Should he evaluate a business venture in Germany? Duke Philip still hadn't answered his message asking to be relieved of his duties. Upcoming cases needed to be put on hold.

Jenny tossed her red curls and said sweetly, "Papa, it's time for a story."

With Angus here, it was a perfect time to tell about Pieter's mother, the Scottish princess who left her homeland to marry. Yet, Pieter hesitated. He wanted to leave a lasting impression. An episode involving his father shot into his memory. Years shed themselves and he saw himself as an awkward nineteen-year-old.

"My father refused to let me attend Strasbourg University." Pieter nodded grimly at Dirck. "So I stayed at the Goes farm studying under my tutor."

"But he did take you to Bruges," Aneka reminded him crisply.

"Yes. And there I met a great painter."

Angus lifted his goblet asking, "Ach, who did ye meet?"

"Jan van Eyck, the court painter for Duke Philip. He later gave me one of his drawings. And now I must leave to aid a remarkable inventor."

His sons began squabbling in front of their new tutor and Pieter realized his mistake in mentioning his trip. He changed the subject. "Let me explain what happened in the barn."

"Did the cows run away, Papa?" Justinus asked, his blue eyes shining.

"No. Father joined me among the animals, and I braced myself for bad news. I didn't think I'd be allowed on the trip to Bruges. Guess what Grandpapa told me."

"He was giving you a cow as a present," Jenny chirped.

Justinus smirked at his young sister, and Dirck said, "You weren't going after all."

"He surprised me by saying, 'Pieter, you were unhappy not studying abroad, but never complained. You applied yourself to the farm and studies, rising above your disappointment.'"

"You really didn't complain?" Dirck pressed.

The way his son leaned forward, acting interested, made Pieter pause. He must remember to honor Dirck for staying home from Mainz.

"I was upset, so imagine my shock when my father forgave me," Pieter added.

Angus looked pleased. "The true forgiveness of Jesus is our subject on the morrow."

Dirck rolled his eyes. Aneka rose, telling her daughter it was time for bed. Jenny padded over, hugging Pieter's neck so hard he let out a sharp cry.

"Jenny, I am only human, you know." He unwound her arms from around his neck. "I'll be home a week yet. Listen to your mama, and I will tuck you in."

Jenny eased down from his lap, but not before planting a desperate kiss on his cheek. Pieter rubbed his face. His sons had left the table.

Pieter faced Angus. "I hope my boys understand. In the barn with my father, midst smells of cattle mingled with seasoned hay, I learned he loved me."

"Ye are blessed with a fine family," Angus replied.

"After our trip, Father went on a covert trip for Duke Philip involving a possible marriage to Princess Isabella. He was in Lisbon with Jan van Eyck when he died of a seizure."

Pieter went on to confide that in Mainz he would meet the inventor, Johann Gutenberg. He also shared his misgivings. Angus prayed aloud for him, asking God to give Pieter courage for the future and to show him if this was His plan. The way his cousin talked to the Heavenly Father, it was as if the Lord was right beside Pieter, and when he went to bed, his soul rested in peace.

He sensed Aneka slept fitfully. However, before long Pieter dreamed of sailing on a fast-moving river, and making a huge difference with his life.

# CHAPTER 14

The more Pieter prepared for the trip, the more Aneka's eyes flared with tormented looks. He could stand her turmoil no longer, and urged her to ride with him to see Maxim. Pieter reached the abbey first. When she arrived, he hoisted her down.

"You should ride more often, my dear. You were sorely outmatched."

"I did not realize we were in a race. My mistake," she huffed.

"You will find what Maxim has to say worth the ride."

He tied the horses to a post, and on long legs, he strode to the abbey with Aneka running to keep pace. Maxim was seated in the chapel house. A hot blaze burned. Pieter asked the abbot to tell his wife why he must be away.

Maxim rose, asking Aneka, "Have you read your husband's Wycliffe Bible?"

"How can she? Our Bible is gone," Pieter retorted.

"My point exactly."

Aneka folded her hands. "Maxim, I did read Scripture to my sons. Am I doing right?"

"Absolutely. Jesus taught both men and women when he walked the earth." Maxim stepped near to her. "Now your husband accompanies me to rescue an inventor who created a special duplicating device to produce hundreds of Bibles. If Pieter doesn't help, the Bibles may never be made."

"Oh, Pieter, is this true?" Aneka's blue eyes sparkled. "Why didn't you tell me?"

Maxim answered for him. "We must keep the truth from prying ears."

"So his trip *is* dangerous!" she cried, her hands flying to her cheeks.

"We go under God's protection, which should comfort you."

Aneka's watery eyes sought Pieter's. "Yes, but won't such a task take years?"

"My friend isn't using the ancient way of transcribing by hand," Maxim explained. "And now, Aneka, your husband and I must discuss the message I sent him."

She dipped her head and left them alone. Pieter knew nothing of his message.

Maxim's gray eyes clouded. "You received no word to come here?"

"No," Pieter insisted. "Have you found my Wycliffe Bible?"

Maxim hadn't. "A messenger surprised me at midnight, bringing an urgent letter from the Bishop of Mainz who is concerned for his parishioner, Johann Gutenberg."

"I brought Aneka here because she has an inkling we're heading into danger." Pieter rubbed his jaw. "Is there fresh trouble?"

"It seems so. Gutenberg's financial difficulties have become severe. Johann Fust lent him money and threatens to halt the project if Gutenberg fails to raise enough gold. Your investment means the Bibles will be finished. Any delay ..."

An ominous silence hung in the air. A burning desire to help Gutenberg gripped Pieter. The words, "He needs friends," just left his lips when Cornelius burst through the door.

"Father Terrance was attacked on the far side of the abbey!"

Maxim flinched, staring at Pieter. "I sent him to your home with the message about Gutenberg."

"He's in my room, bleeding profusely," Cornelius said.

Maxim darted away, returning soon to advise that Terrance was badly injured. "The good news is he will live. The bad news is his purse was taken."

"Do priests carry coin in their purses?" Pieter asked, frowning.

"I fear he had my careless note about Gutenberg's device. Terrance knew he carried a secret."

"Did he see the attacker?"

"He was struck from behind."

Pieter clenched his fists. "Alphonso skulked around when I inspected Van Ritter's vessel. The captain warned me that he was a spy. Is he capable of violence?"

"Spies against Gutenberg are everywhere." Maxim pressed a finger to his lips. "Even within the church, men strive to keep power. They resist the Bible being read by the masses."

Pieter drew his cloak around him, his mind assessing the risks if he supported the great inventor. And while he would ask Captain Van Ritter to leave sooner, a pivotal question remained. Was Alphonso in league with Gutenberg's detractors?

"Say nothing of the attack to Aneka," Pieter warned.

PIETER ARRANGED WITH THE CAPTAIN TO SET SAIL ON THE MORROW. When he returned home to finish packing his supplies, Aneka met him near the barn. She rested a quivering hand on his arm.

"How long will you be investigating the 'duplicating device'?"

"Weeks. Will your prayers go with me for the invention that will make many Bibles?"

As he stroked her cheek, Aneka smiled. The tender look she gave him smote his heart.

"I will buy you something special."

"I will be kept busy seeing that our sons pass their exams." Her voice shook.

At least she tried to sound brave. With much to do, Pieter promised to spend time with her after he saw Angus. He bustled to the study where Dirck and Justinus clustered around their tutor at a table. Pieter drew near, looking closely.

"You found my Wycliffe Bible!"

"Ach, no!"

Angus told him Maxim sent it until Pieter's or a replacement could be found. He mopped his brow, explaining he'd excused Jenny because their lesson turned gruesome.

Dirck pointed to John Wycliffe's Bible. "I wondered why he translated a Bible into English when the Church of England forbids it in any language but Latin. Angus was answering when you came in."

"Go on," Pieter urged. "I want to know about the troubles you've hinted at."

"Ay. Years ago, before I left the priesthood, I saw a right awful sight. May yer sons hear?"

"If I may stay and listen," Pieter replied.

"They burned William White alive, fer bein' a follower of Wycliffe." Tears ran down Angus' cheeks. "I will na' forget it. I too follow Wycliffe."

Dirck ran a hand through his thick hair. "Wycliffe was English. His Bible is written in English. Why do the English burn people? I don't understand."

Angus wiped his eyes. With grit in his voice, he explained many people had been killed for believing as Wycliffe did, that the Bible alone and not church doctrine was the true authority for Christians. The bishops of England considered his teachings heresy, and urged King Henry IV to decree owning Wycliffe's writings meant death. He was the first English king to kill a person for their Christian faith.

"Death by fire," Angus whispered.

Pieter touched the Bible. "No one in the Netherlands has died for believing in Jesus."

"The day may coom. May I tell ye about deaths of other believers?"

Angus pulled a small manuscript from his case. His somber gaze prompted Pieter to listen most carefully. During his life, Wycliffe had powerful people protecting him. It was years after his death, because he still had so many followers, that the Church of England declared him a heretic. Thereafter, Sir William Sautre, a priest, refused to worship the image of the cross. He believed as Wycliffe—that communion bread wasn't the actual physical body of Christ, but bread to remember His sacrifice on the cross.

"The king ordered Sautre burnt alive." Angus seemed to tremble as he spoke the words.

Justinus' hands flew to his face. "I do not like that king."

"Ach, he's long dead."

"Are you sure there are no burnings in Zeeland?" Fear flashed through Justinus' eyes.

Pieter assured his sons that so far there were none. Duke Philip was content for people in the Burgundian Netherlands to follow their consciences so long as they obeyed the laws.

Angus clutched the manuscript to his chest, telling them Jan Hus had been burned in Bohemia for preaching true authority of Scriptures.

"I never heard of that," Pieter said with growing alarm.

Angus opened the manuscript, his eyes flickering with sorrow. "A student drew Hus burnin' in the flames."

"Father!" Dirck gasped in horror. "Will such wickedness happen here?"

"People are evil!" Justinus cried.

Pieter gaped at the drawing of the burning man. What if Duke Philip ordered him to kill a man for his faith? Should he warn his sons of recent violence?

He swallowed. "The duke's knights used the sword against men to the south in Ghent who refused to obey. You saw them yesterday in Middleburg."

"God Almighty says, 'Thou shall not kill,'" Angus reminded.

Pieter was sorry he'd opened this complex discussion. He recoiled from damaging their young minds, but they must know the truth of the evil world.

"Duke Philip used violence to subjugate his people for our stability. I wished he had used other means. But if lawbreakers continue hurting others, our lives are in constant danger. The men in Ghent were defeated after years of rebellion and not for their faith."

Angus slid the manuscript into his case. He urged his three students to sit as he had more to tell. After Hus was martyred, Jerome of Prague refused to recant his belief that Christ alone could save. While he was burned, he sang. His final words were, "What I have just sung I believe. This creed is my whole faith, but I'm dying today because I refuse to deny that Jan Hus was a true preacher of the gospel of Jesus Christ."

Dirck stared at Pieter with a question in his eyes. "Do you know anyone of such faith?"

"I think we sit among one here," Pieter said, looking toward Angus.

Angus merely shook his graying head.

"I will write my uncle in England," Pieter declared, "and find out what is happening."

A knock interrupted them. Mollie entered with a tray of food and water.

"Yer steward wants a word with ye," she told Pieter.

It appeared their study of the persecuted was over for the time being. Pieter motioned for Dirck to join him, and they both went outside. Dirck faced him eagerly.

"Father, will you tell me about the duplicating device?"

Pieter stopped walking. "How do you know of the device?"

"I heard you and Mama talking outside," he admitted with reddening cheeks.

"Son, mention it to no one. I hold the matter in great confidence."

"Could you at least explain what it is?"

"Remember Mollie's ire when you tracked cow manure on her kitchen floor?"

Dirck shrugged his shoulders, looking perplexed.

"Herr Johann Gutenberg makes alphabet letters from metal. Ink sticks on the letters' smooth surface as the manure stuck to your boot." Pieter laughed at the mental picture. "I am anxious to meet the inventor and see for myself how it works."

"People suffer for owning a Wycliffe Bible. I want to see his invention."

"Yes, but I need you here. Let's find out what the steward wants."

Pieter sought to smooth over hard feelings before he left. Perhaps when he returned, he would buy Dirck a horse of his own.

# CHAPTER 15

A rooster crowing loudly woke Pieter with a start. He reached for Aneka. She wasn't beside him. He splashed cold water from a bowl on his face and went to find her. In the dining room, she held up a new pleated surcoat she'd made for him.

"It's lined with ermine to keep you warm." Aneka lifted her pretty chin.

His smile reflected his thanks. "You have given me a nice surprise. Be sure to rely on Angus and Dirck to help you."

"So you return by May's end?"

"I promise."

Her smile, though uneven, gave Pieter confidence. She helped him slip into his coat, then he went to check the wagon. In the thick fog, it was hard to see. Pieter felt the supplies beneath the tarp, trusting the barrels of salted fish, fresh ale, and baskets of cheese and bread were in order. He secured the money belt under his green wool shirt when Aneka appeared at his side.

As he locked her in a firm embrace, she rested her head against his shoulder. A voice in his head cautioned that if he didn't leave soon, she would soon be in tears.

"Remember me, Aneka."

He touched her lips with his. Seconds later, Pieter hopped onto the wagon's seat next to Fitch, who drove the team of horses. Dense fog swirled around them. Pieter could not see his wife waving good-bye.

The fog worsened as they neared the river. By the landing, he spotted a dark figure and jumped down. He steeled himself for an attack. When the man called to him, Pieter relaxed his fists. "Maxim, you surprised me."

"I came early to help you with the cargo."

They unloaded several crates with Fitch's help. The abbot's newfound vigor astonished Pieter.

"You are much thinner, which I failed to notice before. Have you been working in the fields?"

"Not wanting my former appetite to burden you, I fasted. Is it a great difference?"

"Van Ritter may put you to work yet."

The captain must have heard them, because he shouted from the bow, "When the fog clears, we will load your cargo. Go stretch your legs."

Pieter nodded and told Fitch to wait for the captain. They set off for a short walk along the riverbank. Maxim acted tense.

"Are you sorry we are embarking on this adventure?" Pieter asked lightly.

"I'm nervous. This is from Gutenberg himself."

Maxim thrust a parchment into Pieter's hands. He scanned the short message. Gutenberg wrote to say lack of funds, deceiving friends, and scheming enemies would not hinder him.

"He mentions unrest, but that should not worry us," Pieter replied.

"But Pieter, if anything happens to you, I will not forgive myself. You have a wife and three children to look after."

"As you said days ago, this is God's plan to further His word."

"Eating my own words should be sweet. You are right to refresh my memory."

With renewed purpose, they returned to the cog. All supplies had been loaded, and Fitch was gone. They stepped aboard. Van Ritter ordered his crew to cast off the lines. Pieter helped hoist the sail, which billowed in the rising wind. He filled his lungs with cool, damp air. He had grown up near the sea and loved the water's constant motion. Its unpredictable character was part of him.

After a successful day of sailing, breezes stirred by the heat faded as the sun dipped in the west. Pieter settled on a rope coil to watch the passing windmills.

Maxim leaned on an adjacent coil. "I hope our trip isn't too late."

"You don't like traveling in the dark?"

"I refer to Gutenberg's heroic project. More than money threatens to shutter him."

Maxim spoke with such fervor that Pieter's mind veered to Harmon's sudden demise due to Count de Alvarado's lawsuit.

"Who tries to stop him and why?" he snapped.

Maxim was unsure of any names. "I know opposition to making Bibles is why he keeps his works such a secret."

Pieter fell silent, trying to put a voice to his inner confusion.

"I find it hard to trust God in trouble," he confided at length. "I prayed for my mother and she died."

"Christ Himself bears our burdens. If we are part of God's plan to further His Holy Word, you shouldn't allow past grief to stop you."

"When I hear of people being killed for their faith, it doesn't help my quest to trust in God."

"We must separate the character of God from men, and have courage of our convictions."

"Here's what I wonder." Pieter gazed at the slow-moving river. "Those who demand only bishops and priests read Scripture are burning Christians for following Wycliffe. Are they behind Gutenberg's troubles?"

Maxim nodded at the crew lowering a sail. "It doesn't take much to be declared a heretic. Be wise and proceed cautiously."

"We stop for the night," Van Ritter shouted from the stern.

The crew rigged the cog to a piling near the riverbank. Pieter and Maxim ate pickled herring in darkness falling like a curtain. Unable to sleep on coiled rope, Pieter watched moonlight dance upon the water. At least traveling by river was saving him much money, which meant more gold for Gutenberg. Finally, he slumbered until he felt a tug on his sleeve.

Where was he? Water lapping against the hull brought him to his senses. Someone shoved a lamp in his eyes. Pieter blinked as the first mate gaped down at him.

"Ah … do you need help with the rigging?" Pieter stammered.

"You need to follow me, sir."

Pieter scrambled to join the sailor at the stern, his mind a blur. He spotted a trim figure sitting on a crate near the gangplank. Fear welled in Pieter's throat. He recognized his son.

"Dirck, is something amiss with your mother? How did you find us in the wilderness?"

The first mate leaned in. "The deck beneath me began to rise. I thought we were sinking. I grabbed this boy's hair as he raised the deck boards."

Dirck kept his head bowed as the mate went on, "Thinking him a rascal, I was gonna heave him overboard. When he claimed he was your son, I recalled seein' him with you."

"Sorry he disturbed your sleep."

Anger replaced Pieter's panic. He took Dirck by the arm to the other side of the vessel. They stumbled, groping about in the black night.

"Dirck, how did you get on board?"

"From the wagon. I hid beneath the tarp when you and Mama said good-bye. Later, you and Maxim walked away, so I scurried below. The hands were busy."

"It will take days to notify your mother that you're safe."

"She knows I am here."

"What? Aneka gave you permission and never told me?"

"No! I left Justinus a note to find."

Pieter fumbled for an apt reply. How should he discipline Dirck for sneaking aboard? Maxim's loud snoring convinced Pieter the punishment could wait for morning. They sat on the coils. Pieter shut his eyes, only to be awakened by mates hustling about. He pushed to his feet and went to tell the captain of Dirck's unruly behavior.

Van Ritter stroked his beard. "Don't trouble yourself."

"You take his sudden appearance more calmly than I do."

"Perhaps God has a plan we know nothing about."

Van Ritter unexpectedly turned. Pieter threw up his hands, and found Maxim and Dirck in a deep conversation. His son faced him with glistening blue eyes.

"Please forgive me. Your father forgave you."

Pieter gazed at Maxim, who shrugged as if to say, *He is your son.*

"Dirck, I see you are sorry and I forgive you. When we disembark, stay by my side. Understood?"

Dirck's lean faced ringed with a smile. "Papa, can you imagine the mystery of transcribing God's sacred texts?"

"I do." Pieter forced a smile. "And I can't wait to see how Herr Gutenberg achieves that."

The remaining days passed quickly on the Rhine. Dirck did some last-minute fishing as they neared the outskirts of Mainz. Maxim drew their attention to a high castle. "The Romans kept a military post here before Christ's birth."

Pieter pulled on Dirck's empty net. "That rugged bluff is something to tell your mama about when you return home."

"I have no fish stories to tell her," Dirck complained with a shrug.

He gave up trying to catch a "whale" of a fish and put away his net. Van Ritter soon docked the boat, and issued instructions for the return trip in three days. Pieter counted out a sum for this leg of the voyage, including extra for Dirck.

The captain held up a calloused hand. "You owe nothing else. I once had a son close in age to yours. My first mate will bring your cargo to Gutenberg's shop after his duties are done. Mainz is unfriendly. I should have said so, but you know your business."

With a nod, Pieter secured his money belt, eager to discover the adventure awaiting them up the steep flight of stone steps.

# CHAPTER 16

## MAINZ, GERMANY

Pieter walked with Maxim and Dirck straight to the market, teeming with merchants and shoppers. Pieter was jostled by men of all sizes and shapes rushing at them.

"Buy my spices! Ours is the freshest fish!"

He stepped away, his eyes leaping from brilliant cloth, to piles of wool, and on to glittering jewelry. He spotted a stunning small cross encrusted with jewels. On a whim, he pulled gold coins from his pouch and bought the piece for Aneka. Smells of plucked chickens roasting on spits tickled his nose.

Across the square, he saw two lads lobbing rocks. Their victim, a man with one foot, struggled to walk. He leaned awkwardly on a stick, which the hooligans kicked with glee. The man fell on his face. Pieter hurried to help, but he whacked Pieter with his stick. Maxim bent down to lift him up. The man smacked his hand.

"Back off, you."

"Do as he says," Pieter ordered.

They fled the chaotic scene. Pieter tried to get his bearings, all the while keeping Dirck close. He prodded his two charges up a long and narrow street. They wandered around the city a good hour. Pieter finally pulled out his own message from Gutenberg: *Lord Vander Goes, your upcoming visit overwhelms me. I will see to your every need. Go to the Ale House Inn. Around the corner, at Liebfrauenplatz, is my shop. God's servant, Johann*

Though the message contained no mention of Gutenberg's scripting device, all had been arranged between Maxim and Bishop Francis for Pieter's inspection. He directed the others around the corner, and upon seeing the Ale House Inn, he concluded the shop was nearby.

Pieter scanned the square, pointing at the half-timbered buildings. "Aneka would love this splendid architecture."

"The upper stories might be for lodging," Maxim guessed.

Dirck glanced upward. "The way the upper stories protrude over the shops below, looking down the street is like looking through an upsidedown keyhole."

"You are astute," Pieter said. "But hurry before we meet more ruffians. Light grows dim."

They picked up the pace. Heavy footsteps beat along the stone street. Men raised their fists at a couple of figures dashing by in black capes and hoods. Doors slammed. Crashing sounds reverberated along the narrow street.

"You cheat!" someone yelled. "You die!"

A small wagon rumbled straight toward them.

"Maxim, look out!"

Pieter snatched him out of the way. The wagon veered into cans of milk, and they stepped carefully over spilt milk. Because Mainz was governed by the archbishop, Pieter had expected a peaceful city. Such acrimony surprised him. No wonder Herr Gutenberg found difficulties here.

"I think we're here." Dirck gestured. "See? His windows are covered."

Pieter's eyes shot to the high glass windows. These were uncovered, but the ones at street level were shrouded in heavy drapery. No doubt, they kept onlookers from guessing the secret operation Gutenberg waged inside. That is, if they were at the right address.

Pieter banged the brass knocker. After what seemed an eternity, the wooden door opened. Pieter's nose was instantly assailed by a pungent odor. They must be at the inventor's abode. A young man blocked the doorway, looking puzzled.

"Yes?"

"I am Lord Vander Goes here to see Johann Gutenberg. We are expected."

"There should be two, not three of you." The nervous man shifted his eyes to and fro. "Wait by this door. I will announce your presence."

Considering the draped windows and the youth's admonition, Pieter decided they should be safe in Gutenberg's house. Moments later, the aide returned, followed by a man plainly dressed. His hair was graying as was his flowing beard. Yet for all his simplicity, Johann Gutenberg was an imposing figure.

He ushered them inside his home and softly closed the door behind him. Herr Gutenberg welcomed Pieter and introduced his apprentice, Wilhelm. Pieter shook their hands, and in turn introduced Dirck and Maxim.

"What a noisy, hectic scene we encountered outside," he said, hoping things would be calmer on this side of the door.

"The citizens argue with the guilds and the archbishop." Gutenberg fingered his beard. "Come to my study. I prepared oranges, a sweet fruit. Once you have rested, you will see my shop. Is one-half hour sufficient time?"

Pieter nodded as Dirck edged past him. Gutenberg took them to a comfortable room with gold and red tapestries obscuring the windows. A small feast awaited them. Their host bowed and left them to sample the food.

Dirck whirled around. "His beard grows nearly as long as my arm!"

"So it does." Pieter smiled, reaching for a meat tart. "He is gracious yet ready for business. We will see many amazing things, I imagine."

Maxim sought out Pieter. "I am troubled by the threats outside. Be careful with Dirck."

"I will talk to Gutenberg about safety precautions." Pieter tapped his money belt. He carried much gold coin. "Yet our host seems untroubled."

A noisy clamor erupted outside. Dirck sped to the window, pulling back the heavy curtain. Pieter ordered him to come away.

"We came all the way to Mainz to eat an orange. We may never have one again."

Pieter ate a piece, enjoying its sweet nectar. He sampled another when Gutenberg returned. After wiping his hands on a cloth, Pieter followed him toward the workroom.

"You are about to enter my print shop." Gutenberg stopped walking. "May I have a private word, Lord Vander Goes?"

"Of course, but will I see your scribing invention?"

"My invention replaces the scribes. I call it my *kunst und aventur.*"

"Very clever," Maxim intoned. "Your art and enterprise."

"Others refer to my enterprise as print and a printing press. Either way, I must speak to Lord Vander Goes before we proceed."

He took Pieter to a hallway adjacent to the workroom entrance. Gutenberg fidgeted with his cloak. "Please forgive my impertinence, but I have been deceived and cheated by longtime acquaintances. Many have tried to relieve me of my print machine."

Glancing at the shrouded door, Pieter replied, "Is that why you keep the shop in virtual darkness?"

"I want no one learning how I print documents. I am about to reveal my dearest trade secret. Are you truly prepared to invest?"

Pieter understood. He removed his surcoat, unbuttoned his outer shirt, and opened his leather pouch. "Herr Gutenberg, upon agreement, I'll contribute gold florin to your Bible duplicating project."

"Please refer to me as Johann. You and I have developed a trust."

"Yes, we have, or I wouldn't have traveled all this way. And call me Pieter."

With a puckered brow, he then confessed that Dirck had stowed away on the boat, as he was so eager to see the duplicating device.

"I do not encourage his behavior. Are there chores he could perform while we are here?"

"Ah, it is my turn to be perceptive." Johann tugged on his beard. "I have a notion. But come see my reason for living."

He guided Pieter, his would-be benefactor, into the print shop. The strong smell of ink stung Pieter's nose. His pulse quickened at what he was about to learn. Dirck and Maxim crowded behind him into the large room crammed full of tables and enormous devices. Men bustled about carrying paper and ink. Oil lamps burned at multiple workstations. Though crowded, everything was neat and orderly.

Johann showed them a shallow cabinet consisting of two sections, with both an upper case and a lower case he had created. Each case was divided into thirty separate small compartments. He lifted a slender piece of metal half the length of his thumb.

Pieter guessed it was a nail.

"No, this strip is an uppercase 'R,' which begins a sentence."

Then Johann removed a lower case piece, explaining the smaller "r" went within the body of the sentence. It had taken a day and a half to carve each of the metal-type letters.

"But your letters face backwards," Dirck objected, tilting his head.

"Each one will soon be in the correct direction. Watch."

Johann dipped his fingertip in black ink, which he spread on the backward letter. He pressed the letter against a tiny scrap of paper. As though he'd performed a magic trick, there was the uppercase R, facing the right direction.

Pieter's imagination whirled. "How did you invent such a wondrous thing?"

"My father and I worked in the mint for the Archbishop of Mainz. There I learned to cast and stamp gold and silver. Harder metals cause the type to break. Others are too soft and easily melt."

Dirck piped in, "So your father invented the printing machine?"

"No, lad. After years of toil, I invented this myself!" Johann glanced at Pieter. "The process of making coins is similar, such as weighing, pressing, and polishing metals. Helping my father helped me develop movable type. Would you like to see its precise movements?"

"I am greatly interested," Pieter replied airily.

Captivated by the possibility to print Bibles, he had another inkling. But he would not divulge it now. Johann poised a metal strip in the air. His guests gathered round him in a tight circle as he explained how hot, liquid metal was poured into a mold for each letter.

"I invented special molds and created letters in different widths to fit various page sizes. My Bible has two columns of forty-two lines per page."

He waved them to another area. Pieter was astounded by the sheer number of hammers, punches, and every kind of metal stacked neatly on wooden tables. A balding man sat on a stool heating metal.

"Is he making a mold?" Pieter asked.

Johann nodded so vigorously, his beard trembled. "It took me years to perfect the blend of lead, tin, and antimony. Of course, the exact quantities are secret. I have cast 290 different letters, numbers, and symbols."

"This is beyond what I imagined," Dirck chimed. "Are they all used for the Bible?"

"I prefer not to discuss that yet."

Pieter lifted a finger to his lips. Dirck nodded in understanding. Johann walked them throughout the shop, stopping at a workstation containing more print cases. He selected a long, grooved piece of wood.

"I created a composing stick the same width as a page."

After placing several backward letters into the long groove, he strode to one of six wooden winepresses. Each press stood one and a half times as tall as Pieter, and he was six feet tall.

Maxim whispered to Pieter, "I once saw such a press used to squeeze juice from grapes."

"I adapted the winepress into my printing machine." Johann's face glowed. A new world opened before Pieter's eyes. Johann put the composing stick on a smooth, flat stone, slid letters into a wooden frame above the stone, and inserted metal spacers between each letter. Johann tightened the frame to keep the letters in place. How he remembered all the steps, Pieter could not fathom. Respect for the inventor grew by the second.

"The forms are ready to be put to bed," Johann announced.

Dirck's face fell. "Must we go to bed already?"

"Stay alert, lad." Johann handed Dirck a round apparatus with a wooden handle.

"It's an upside-down mushroom, Papa!"

Johann chuckled, resuming his tutorial. He showed Dirck how to apply ink with the leather pad he was holding. The round section turned out to be a mass of horsehair covered with dog skin so the surface didn't crack. He instructed Dirck to carefully dip his "upside-down mushroom" in black pasty ink.

"Watch you do not apply too much ink, or the parchment will smudge."

"Yes, sir."

With a hand placed over his, Johann guided Dirck to the type, and helped him dab ink on the precise spot. He set the parchment on top before sliding the entire frame beneath the former winepress.

With a grin, he ordered Pieter to pull the press' handle. "Pretend you're hauling out a tree stump. The center worm gear lowers the platen and pushes the parchment against the type."

Pieter breathed in deep, expanding his chest. He yanked the large wooden handle toward him. The collar traveled down the worm gear and lowered the press onto the parchment.

"Tug harder," Johann commanded. "Use all your strength."

"What do you think I am doing?" Pieter puffed.

"Put your foot on the table for leverage. The more pressure, the better the print."

Pieter gave the handle a mighty tug, pushing against the table with his leg. Sounds of creaking made him wonder if that was his bones or wood against wood. Exhausted, he dropped the handle. Johann pushed the worm gear handle back to the beginning point. The group gathered around as he lifted out the parchment.

Beautiful black letters read: *Dirck Vander Goes is my special guest.*

Johan handed Dirck the special parchment to keep. "Do not roll it up until dry. How would you like to assist Wilhelm tomorrow?"

"Oh yes!" Then he flashed Pieter a sheepish look. "Will I print like Papa just did?"

"That is only for experienced printers. Tomorrow, Wilhelm needs a helper to obtain raw materials for my ink. You will learn to print from the bottom up."

A clock struck four bells and Johann's hand flew to his cheek.

"We should be at the cathedral."

"To meet with the bishop, I imagine," Pieter mumbled.

The delay bothered him. He had more interest in learning about printing than Mass. Still, Johann was his host. Pieter was anxious to show him a manuscript he hoped the inventor would print. He doubted two days would be sufficient time to spend with such a learned man.

# CHAPTER 17

As they made their way to the Mainz Cathedral, shadows played across its ornate front facade. Six imposing towers reached into the heavens like massive fingers. A priest led them through the four-hundred-year-old structure to Bishop Francis' study. Along the way, no one uttered a word. Conversation seemed out of place.

Bishop Francis was effusive in his praise. "Lord Vander Goes, your arrival is timely. Johann endures obstacles building a duplicating machine for God's Holy Word. He must preserve his idea from those who would steal it before the work is complete."

Johann pulled on his beard and examined the toe of his pointed shoe sticking out beneath his cloak.

"I want to hear of his difficulties," Dirck blurted.

Pieter cast a disapproving eye on his son. Meanwhile, the bishop apologized.

"Please excuse me. An important man died this morning, and I must oversee the arrangements. Perhaps tomorrow we can talk at greater length. God bless you all."

With these warm words, he swept from the room. A blush crept across Johann's face. He stared in seeming disbelief as his patron's red mantle swished away.

"He was expecting us," Johann sputtered. "Lord Vander Goes, I do not understand."

Pieter clapped a hand on Johann's shoulder. "First, you agreed to call me Pieter. Secondly, his departure means nothing to me. Your printing press is extraordinary. Perhaps it does Bishop Francis good to meet your other supporters, even if briefly."

"An excellent point," Maxim said. "Johann, our time here in Mainz is short. Do you have any Bibles printed yet?"

"I had hoped to share the good news with Bishop Francis who strongly supports the work. Each page requires three thousand pieces of type!"

"Each page?" Pieter was dumbfounded. "It will take ages to finish."

Johann simply led them away. Beyond the door, he revealed his plan to print three hundred Bibles. Each one comprised six hundred forty pages, with the first fifty pages already printed.

"With your help, we could print more than three hundred."

Pieter admired Johann's commitment to excellence. He had seen enough.

"Your suggestion mirrors my thinking. I will give you sufficient gold for another ten Bibles. I will keep one for my family and give one to the King of England. I believe that country needs reforming."

Johann pumped Pieter's hand vigorously. "Much work waits to be done."

"I am famished." Maxim sighed, holding his stomach.

Pieter couldn't help laughing. "Your fasting comes to an end, I see."

As they left the enormous cathedral and walked down its many stone steps, Pieter grew alarmed by the long shadows. Torches burning by its door failed to reach the street below.

Johann peered down the street. "I didn't think to bring a candle."

As they rounded the corner, not a ray of light could be seen. Pieter seized Dirck's shoulder, his other hand clutching a brown leather case with the manuscript. He hoped the case concealed his money belt fastened beneath his cloak.

A scream pierced the night. Pieter strained to see, but it was too dark.

"Hurry," he said. "I have a bad feeling about this place."

A body slammed against his back, thrusting Pieter forward. He crashed chest first into a stone building. The very essence of his life seemed to leave his body. He tried sucking in air, but couldn't breathe. In the pitch-black, bright lights splintered behind his eyes. Was he dying?

His chest ached greatly, as if Willow stomped on him. He doubled over in pain.

"Help me!" someone cried beyond him.

Adrenaline burst through Pieter. He groped along the ground to find who was hurt. His breath came now in short bursts. Something wet collided against his head. Pieter's leather case and the manuscript spun beyond his grasp. He lunged for it, but a boot crashed upon his hand.

"Grab his bag," a man growled. "Run for it."

The booted creature snatched his case and sped away, leaving Johann and the others sprawled on the street. Pieter's back throbbed. He shook off the pain and crawled along the cobblestones searching for Dirck. His fingers touched a body. The curly hair felt like Dirck's.

Pieter lifted his limp son into his arms. "We must take Dirck to the shop right away!"

"I'm stunned, but can walk," came Maxim's reply along the murky street.

Johann grabbed Pieter's cape and led the way as Pieter carried his unconscious son. Inside, the parlor was lit with candles. In the soft light, he gently laid Dirck on a pallet covered with a rug. A welt as big as a coin spread across his check. He didn't open his eyes.

Maxim slipped out to pray. Johann retrieved warm water and dipped in a clean cloth, which he pressed on Dirck's forehead.

"I will find my physician," he said. "I hope he doesn't refuse for fear of the night."

Left alone, Pieter soothed his son's brow with water. He touched Dirck's arm, willing him to stay alive.

"Please do not die like my mother!"

Tears flooded his eyes. If only he'd stayed home, Dirck would be safe. His son was at death's door because Pieter wanted to be great like his father. What a mistake! How wrong!

Dirck's pale face pierced his heart. Pieter crushed his face into his hands and wept. If only Aneka was here. In time, his tears spent themselves. He clasped Dirck's hands and tried warming them in his own. A thought penetrated his mind.

*What if I ask God to spare Dirck's life?*

Pieter shook his head. He could make no contract with Almighty God. A hand gripped his shoulder, and a voice behind him whispered, "Pieter, let not your heart be troubled. Trust in God, trust also in Me."

Pieter whirled around to face Maxim. No one was behind him. Dirck remained still, his blue eyes hidden behind closed lids. Pieter tried grasping the truth. Had a real voice spoken to him? He dropped to his knees by his son's pallet.

For the first time since his mother had died, Pieter talked to God from his heart.

"Lord, forgive my stubborn doubt. You brought me to Mainz to see how much I need You. Teach me to love You with my whole being. Father in heaven, You gave Your Son for me and I long to be Your servant. I trust You with the life of my precious son."

PIETER CONTINUED PRAYING. Johann returned with his physician, who examined Dirck with speed. He straightened his back and gave Pieter good news.

"Your son has no fever. His pulse is nearly normal. Spoon him water when he revives."

"Will he regain consciousness soon?" Pieter asked, sponging water on Dirck's brow.

The doctor picked up his medical case. "Keep him still through the night."

"Ah, then I am free to check on progress in my print shop."

Johann spun around. The doctor left too. Pieter leaned over Dirck. "Son, I don't blame you for stealing away on the boat. Your zest for life is contagious, and I need you!"

He closed his eyes and thought he heard a moan. Pieter's eyes flew open. Dirck groaned and this time Pieter lifted a cup to his lips.

"Slowly," he cautioned. "A small sip will do."

Dirck drank some. As he sat up, Maxim returned. Moments later, so did Johann, who asked if Dirck was well enough to conduct a printing assignment.

Pieter reacted swiftly. "That's unthinkable."

"Father," Dirck said, trying to stand. "I want to help."

His breathing was labored, so Pieter tried to end further talk.

Johann raised a hand. "Wilhelm comes from a cautious family. Let the young men work in the morning until the noon meal. If Dirck wants, and you agree, he can finish out the day."

"He must rest," Pieter said. "I'll interview Wilhelm in the morning and see if I trust him."

# CHAPTER 18

Pieter had given his permission, and by mid-morning, Dirck found himself in the middle of a very dirty job. He examined his grimy hands.

"When Herr Gutenberg asked for my help, I had no idea I'd be so filthy. Scraping soot from chimneys is worse than cleaning our stables."

Wilhelm roared in laughter. "Wait 'til we mix soot with egg whites and linseed oil."

"I am tired. Let me sit a moment."

"No. We need more soot for the ink to mix properly. It's the most important ingredient." Wilhelm snapped his fingers. "If we fail, no Bible."

"I don't see you scraping," Dirck fired back.

"You'll scrape for one day, but I'm apprenticed for years, until I complete the Bibles."

"All right." Dirck wiped his forehead, leaving a black smudge.

Wilhelm handed him a metal scraping bar, coaxing him to crawl deeper into the fireplace to reach more soot. Dirck scraped and scraped, saving as much as he could. When he backed out, his hair, face, and arms were streaked with the black stuff.

"We need to scrape you off," Wilhelm said in jest.

"Like this, you mean?"

Dirck raked the metal tool across his arm, laughing heartily.

Wilhelm ended his antics. "We need more soot before the next phase."

"Which is?"

"You'll see soon enough, my friend."

Dirck did not enjoy being a printer's apprentice, yet he kept at it. By morning's end, his leather bags were brimming with black soot.

Wilhelm snickered. "You can back out by telling Herr Gutenberg your head aches."

"I'd rather see every phase of the printing. I am famished though."

"Me too. I hope we haven't missed lunch."

They trudged inside the shop where Herr Gutenberg gladly accepted their pouches.

"You look worse than when you left, lad. Perhaps it is fortunate your father meets with the bishop. Are you strong enough to continue?"

Dirck nodded. "I have learned so much about chimneys already."

"The lesson is written all over your face." Herr Gutenberg's smile was jovial. "And your arms and legs."

Wilhelm grinned. "With Dirck's small size, he crawled in farther. It was proper for him to scrape and I supervise."

"That's precisely how I thought the work would progress," Herr Gutenberg said, placing a hand on Dirck's shoulder. "Go wash in the courtyard before the noon meal. You need time to finish the next task before dusk."

Dirck felt ashamed at getting so dirty. He cleaned his hands, and then sat across from Gutenberg at the table. Wilhelm introduced a new assistant named Schöffer. They ate a delicious meal of sausages, pickled cabbage, bread, and almond cheese shaped like a swan. Dirck relished every morsel despite Schöffer's repeated vexed glances.

Gutenberg waited for the new aide to excuse himself before telling Wilhelm to drive the wagon to his parent's farm for the egg whites. He stared at Dirck. "Talk only to Wilhelm's parents. Understand?"

Dirck did. After promising to be quick about the work, Wilhelm and Dirck stepped out in the gloomy courtyard. Dark clouds swirled overhead. Wilhelm jumped up onto the cart, and Dirck squeezed beside him on the board.

"Why did Herr Gutenberg lecture me about secrets? Does he think me a child?"

"It's his way. He protects his invention like a mother goose does her goslings."

Wilhelm guided the horse down a narrow lane into tall woods. Dirck shivered, finding the dense forest rather eerie with its strange sounds. Thunder rumbled overhead, prompting Wilhelm to drive the horse faster.

"If we're caught in a storm, we might not make it back before nightfall."

"Hurry then," Dirck implored.

Last night's assault taunted him, and he shuddered. He was no coward, but he'd promised his father to be careful. They reached the farm before any rain fell. Dirck leaped off the wagon, eager to discover everything about making ink. Frau Brueger folded her son Wilhelm into her arms before bustling to the henhouse.

She gave them baskets for collecting eggs. Dirck marveled at seeing more than one hundred fowl. Once they found every small treasure, she showed them how to crack an egg.

"With the yolks, I make delicious cakes," Frau Brueger said. "Save the whites as I showed you."

Wilhelm leaned back against the wall. "Go ahead, Dirck."

Before he was finished, Dirck's shirt was covered with a mass of sticky eggs. Many of the whites floated inside clean clay pots, and Frau Brueger announced they had enough. Wilhelm took Dirck behind a stone house. A brook bubbled over a churning wooden wheel. Dirck spotted a tall man hanging something onto a frame.

"That's my papa," Wilhelm said, grinning.

Herr Brueger talked in rush, never stopping his work. "The water turns the wheel, which turns the hammers inside the barn. Trip-hammers pound linen rags into pulp. Wilhelm's brother is in the barn straining pulp through a sieve. We form that into sheets of paper, which I hang to dry."

Then Herr Brueger tied animal skins around the paper to keep it dry, telling Dirck that Gutenberg would stretch and cure the skins to make vellum.

"That is an alternate to paper for the Bibles," he added knowingly.

"I will tell my brother Just—" Dirck stopped. "I forgot, I will tell no one."

He sped to help Wilhelm load the paper onto the wagon. He began to see the pure genius of Herr Gutenberg and his invention. Frau Brueger hustled out with a basket of onions, a fresh pike wrapped in leaves, and two nut cakes.

"Do not stop on the road," Herr Brueger warned. "My neighbor was robbed earlier."

He slapped the horse, which Wilhelm steered down the narrow lane. Soon, they were back in the cool forest. In the wind, trees creaked and groaned. Still, rain didn't fall.

"Papa worries," Wilhelm said. "But I make this trip dozens of times with no trouble."

"I am ready for the feast your mother packed."

"Her apple strudel is delicious."

Dirck's mouth watered, and he could almost taste it. Still, he felt compelled to brag, "Her strudel can't be as good as my mama's fritters."

"We shall see whose mother is the best baker."

Wilhelm jerked the reins, stopping the horse and wagon. Dirck took hold of the reins while his friend jumped into the wagon's bed. He broke one cake in half, and Dirck reached for the forbidden treat, letting go of the reins. Sensing freedom, the horse lurched forward.

Wilhelm lost his balance. He crashed onto a crate. Chunks of cake flew into the road.

A gruff voice demanded, "Get out of the wagon!"

Dirck spun his head around and gasped. A monstrous man wielded an enormous stick with a metal hook. He blocked the lane. Two eyes bulged above a scarf tied over the man's face.

He raised his weapon. "Do as I say! Or you'll be hurt!"

"Robbers!" Wilhelm yelled.

Dirck scooted forward to grab the reins. He slapped them across the horse's haunches.

"Ga weg!"

The horse obeyed, overturning the highwayman in its wake and trampling the cake to crumbs. Wilhelm bounced in the wagon. His feet jarred the pots, and the egg whites spilled in the dirt. Dirck drove the horse fiercely, the remaining miles to Mainz sheer torture.

When they at last reached the city gate, he pulled the mare to a stop. "Surely we are safe here. Wilhelm, are you all right?"

"Losing the egg whites is an awful setback. That hurts more than my head right now."

"My father will be upset we risked our lives for scrambled eggs."

Wilhelm climbed up to sit beside Dirck. "I can tell you this. Problems follow Herr Gutenberg everywhere. When the guilds revolted, he was forced to leave Mainz and open a shop in Strasbourg. He cut jewels hoping to make a printing press. He found trouble instead."

"Like the robber we just met?"

"Enemies try to stop Gutenberg. A wealthy man named Johann Fust

sued him before finally giving him the guilders. Then Fust brought in
Schöffer as calligrapher. I can't say more."

"Why not, Wilhelm? Don't you trust me?"

Wilhelm looked perturbed. "Please don't tell your father about those
trying to stop the printing of Bibles."

"I wonder if Gutenberg's enemies knocked us down last night and stole
my father's manuscript?"

"Most people fight Gutenberg in court without resorting to violence.
You should never go out at night."

"My father needs to know. He's a magistrate for Duke Philip."

"So? Your duke is powerless in Germany. Let's get this food inside before it rains. Gutenberg and your father won't be happy."

"Surely lost eggs can be replaced."

Wilhelm whistled through his teeth. "Gutenberg and Schöffer seek
perfection. If a single letter is blurry, they toss an entire page. With no egg
whites, we've no ink for tomorrow."

"What can we do?"

"Break it to them gently," Wilhelm responded.

He took the reins and guided the wagon behind the shop. Dirck removed the horse's harness before taking her to a trough for a drink of water.
Wilhelm opened the back door with a key. Dirck hauled in the supplies,
minus egg whites. When his father stopped him in the back hall asking
how his day had gone, Dirck shook his head. He was mortified his teasing
caused such a disaster.

PIETER NOTICED DIRCK'S SHOULDERS SLUMPED as he sat down for the evening meal. Johann took his place at the head of the table, and Maxim asked
a blessing. A steward poured ale into goblets for each guest, and spooned
generous portions of fish and vegetables onto pewter plates. Pieter studied
Dirck's darting eyes and glum expression. Something must have gone seriously wrong.

Gutenberg selected a slice of bread. "Pieter, was your meeting with
Bishop Francis a success? I remained here to ensure we had no delays."

"The bishop expressed thanks for my investment in your project."
Pieter buttered his bread, noting the two boys exchanged worried looks.

Maxim picked bones from his trout. "He asked lay leaders to watch for
Pieter's manuscript, which is probably long gone."

"God's will is sovereign and best," Pieter replied. "I want to hear about Dirck's day."

His son stole a glance at Wilhelm, who focused his eyes on his plate of fish bones.

"Printing is complex. It takes a determined person to complete it," Dirck replied.

Johann beamed at the young man. "Scraping chimneys did not dissuade you? Surely you could avoid the tiresome tasks of collecting eggs and separating the whites."

"Papa taught me to tell the absolute truth." Dirck's eyes locked onto Wilhelm's.

Pieter squared his shoulders. "What's it all about?"

"We collected eggs, saving out the liquid white part," Dirck replied. "Frau Brueger gave us apple cake. Wilhelm's father made paper, which we brought back."

This was good to hear because Pieter planned to give Johann the gold after the meal.

Then Dirck added ominously, "Everything went well until the ride home."

Wilhelm coughed as if a bone lodged in his throat, leaving Dirck to tell the regrettable tale. "A robber jumped us. I drove the wagon too fast, and the egg whites smashed into the road. Can Wilhelm and I replace them tomorrow?"

"No," Pieter snapped.

"Sir, don't blame Dirck." Wilhelm's eyes were downcast. "Papa warned me not to stop because of an earlier robbery. I went for my mother's cake, which is why Dirck drove the team."

"That's one too many close calls for my son. We start for home in the morning."

Johann wiped his hands and face with a cloth. His lips turned into a smile.

"All is not lost. We have extra ink. Pieter, you said moments ago the Almighty's plans are best. Perhaps I should move operations closer to the shop."

He rang for the steward, who brought steaming cups of strong tea and apple strudel. Pieter asked Johann how long his printing would be delayed.

"In the short run, we are behind. In the long view, it makes little difference. Dirck and Wilhelm, you may be excused."

Dirck shoved cake in his mouth and sprang to his feet. Wilhelm was fast on his heels.

Johann waited for the steward to clear the dishes, then said, "Now, I confide in you."

"Should I leave you alone with Maxim?"

"It is not for the confessional, but business. Pieter, please remain."

Johann shared of his failing business relationship with Fust, to whom he owed a great deal of money. "With your financial support, I should complete three hundred Bibles and your additional ten. But there is not much time. The loan is coming due."

"And if I withhold my support?"

"Fust takes all my equipment and I am ruined."

Maxim folded his hands. "Bishop Francis mentioned your hardships."

"It's as if some force tries to prevent me from printing the Bible. When my mother died in Strasbourg, the Mainz town clerk refused to hand over my inheritance unless I moved here. I was to be married and did not want to stop work on my invention."

"Did you marry?" Pieter asked.

"Well, no. Other complications occurred."

The printer, looking uncomfortable, told all. Johann had threatened to arrest the Mainz clerk. When he finally agreed to pay the inheritance, Johann had him released. But the clerk returned to Mainz, sending a mere pittance at a time. Johann was forced to move to Mainz for the balance.

"By that time, I changed my mind about matrimony. The woman sued me for breach of promise and I won, even though her shoemaker testified against me."

"Her shoemaker?" Pieter was incredulous at the twists and turns of Johann's life.

"It was my fault. During the court case, I called the woman's shoemaker a miserable wretch who lived by cheating and lying. Alas, he sued me too."

"For slander," Pieter said. "Why do I think the court was not as kind to you there?"

"Correct. However, I came to Mainz and started afresh."

Pieter's hand went to his gold purse. "You are clever, Johann, but not in business."

"When I approached Fust for the loan, I tried learning from my past mistake." Johann wiped his brow. "A former partner retained some of my molds. His relatives sued me upon his death. I destroyed every mold and letter, putting my press behind. So when Fust made the loan, I forbade him from working on machines or entering the shop. It is strictly a paper transaction."

With all these complications, Pieter's mind turned. Was his support of Johann foolhardy? Then he thought of God's Holy Word being spread throughout the land, changing lives. An inner peace swept over him. He knew without any doubt what he would do next.

"It is imperative you finish the Bibles," Pieter said earnestly. "You shall have my gold."

"I bless you from the bottom of my heart. May Dirck stay as my apprentice? I trust you both."

"First, I must seek God's plan about my son's future."

# CHAPTER 19

## MIDDLEBURG, THE NETHERLANDS

A brutal wind blew in from the north, sweeping away the mild morning. Rain lashed Justinus as he fumbled with the barn door latch. His wet fingers slid on the metal clasp before it gave way. He scurried into the barn where he was greeted by anxious whinnies. Wind whistling through cracks in the wood made him jumpy.

He approached his father's great horse, Willow. The mare reared on powerful hind legs, her large hoofs crashing down near his feet. Justinus stroked her thick mane. He spoke in low tones, hoping to soothe the nervous animal.

"Angus went to the abbey. Mama left me in charge. She took Mollie and Jennie to help villagers. Eat or she'll blame me for not caring for you."

His favorite horse still refused to eat. Justinus thrust a hand into the trough and dug out a large portion of oats. Nostrils flaring, Willow finally ate the proffered treat from the palm of his open hand. Justinus fed the other animals before tightly bolting the door.

Outside, he fought to stand against the wind, which blew fiercely. Treetops blew parallel to the ground. A terrific gust stripped his wool cap from his head, tossing it into the air. One huge limb ripped from an old poplar tree right over his head. Rain fell in torrents. Squawking chickens and honking geese fled from the destroyed coop, wings flapping.

Justinus ran in the pouring rain trying to round up the frightened birds. It took him an hour to corral them into an old hut behind the barn. His growling stomach was a painful reminder he'd eaten nothing since breakfast. He threw stale bread to the birds, tempted to eat the bits himself.

Justinus thought to count the hens. Two were missing. So was the rooster. He sped to the collapsed coop where he searched among piles of broken timber. Lifting up a jagged piece of wood, he saw drops of blood under his wooden shoe. A faint sound of water rushing reached his ears, growing louder by the second.

The dike! Would it hold?

He ran up the rise, beyond his boyhood tree home. He saw a stunning sight. The river had swollen to the top of the dike. Boiling waves lapped over the edge. Trees planted by his father along the top were washing away and cascading down toward the riverbed. A sheep whirled by in the churning water so fast he couldn't tell if it was alive or dead. Howling winds stoked his fears. If the dike failed, rushing water would obliterate their home.

Lightning flashed in the distance and he cringed. Never had he been so fearful of a raging storm. Mesmerized, he watched the swelling river, his woolen breeches sticking to his skin. Suddenly, a bolt of lightning struck a tree near shore. The giant split down the middle, its trunk smoldering.

"God, save me! Save my family!" he yelled.

No living soul could hear his anguished cry. The biting wind hurled his words back into his face, mocking him. His resolve melted away. Justinus ran back up the rise and to the barn, where he sheltered under an eave. He gaped at the gushing water, unsure what to do. Eventually, the rain subsided and he fled into the house, cold and soaking wet. He slammed the wooden door behind him, finding momentary peace until gusts of wind rattled the glass windows. What if the glass crashed in on him?

Justinus shook his fist at the fierce storm. "You'll not get the better of me!"

His mother could walk in at any moment. He should light a fire. After changing into dry clothes, he heaped dry wood in the stone fireplace. The act of stoking the fire took his mind off the chaos outside. He searched for another chore. Because he'd seen Mollie make pottage before, he imitated her movements. Pouring water into her iron pot, and measuring oats in a tin cup, he tossed these in a pot with dried fruit. Then he swung the pot over the flames.

Peeking beneath a piece of linen, he found the rye bread Mollie had baked the previous evening. His mouth watered at the taste of toasted caraway. He lit candles, and put butter in the bowl Papa had bought Mama at the fair. He carved chunks from a wheel of cheese, and sampled a sliver.

Still the wind blew, and he was alone. A grim thought gnawed at him. What if Mama's cart had turned over?

The cheese he'd eaten left a sour taste in his mouth. He paced by the window, glancing outside every few seconds for sight of his family. Darkness would fall soon, bringing more danger with high winds. He'd saddle Willow and go look for them.

Justinus pulled open the door. Streaks of white and purple lightning split the sky.

*Boom!*

Loud thunder shook the house. Justinus slammed the door with a bang. Branches from a falling tree broke the window glass. He fell to his knees by his father's chair near the fire, his emotions red-hot. Tears sprang to his eyes. He wiped his cheeks with his wet palms.

"My life is in Your hands! Almighty God, please save everyone I love."

Then he heard his name. "Justinus!"

"I'm here, Lord," he croaked, still on his knees.

He heard pounding at the door, and jumped to open it. Mama stood there dripping wet, holding a baby. Mollie pushed Jenny and a village lady inside, right up to the fire.

"Yer mama's all in," she said. "She found a wee bairn by the river."

Angus charged in behind them, drenched with water. The baby began howling. As Aneka cradled the babe, Angus and Justinus peppered her with questions. Mollie led Aneka and baby from the room, the village lady following. Jenny trailed behind, silent for once in her life.

Justinus turned to Angus. "Mama found the babe in the storm. I can't believe something so small could survive. I was scared out of my wits."

"Ay, laddie." Angus wiped his face. "'Tis a miracle yer all safe. I ran all the way here."

Justinus set about preparing a hot meal. A whistle sprang from his lips. He'd been afraid, but why? Hadn't God protected even a tiny baby from the raging storm?

PIETER ARRIVED HOME THE NEXT WEEK. He started unloading the cart in the pouring rain. Mollie scooted outside to greet him, water running down her weary face.

"Tis good yer home. Much happened while ye've been away."

"Mollie, go indoors," he commanded. "You look like a drenched hen."

She tossed her head. "Yer good lady willna' tell ye how tired she is."

"I'll speak to Aneka once I get these things out of the rain."

Mollie touched his sleeve. "I'm hopin' ye willna' delay."

Pieter saw trouble in her brown eyes. He dropped the barrel back into the cart, ordering Fitch to unhook the horses and finish unloading. Pieter dashed up the stairs. Aneka was resting on their bed with her eyes closed. A shawl was bunched beneath her head.

"Dearest wife, I am home."

"Pieter … lovely dream," she murmured, pulling the coverlet to her chin.

Pieter whisked damp hair from her forehead. "It is me. Wake up, and let me hold you."

She remained still. He pulled off his leather boots and wet cloak. Then he propped himself on the bed to wait. He was drifting off to sleep when a sharp cry shattered the quiet.

Aneka's eyes flew open and she threw off the blanket.

"The baby!"

"What baby?" he asked in confusion.

The crying stopped as soon as it started.

"Ah, Roos must be here." Aneka slumped beside him.

He gently rubbed her upper arms. Her eyes rounded and she clung to his neck. After holding each other, she eventually pulled back.

"You really are home. Please ask Mollie to bring me something to eat, then I'll tell you a story."

Pieter hurried to the kitchen, demanding Mollie tell him why Aneka had a baby in the house. The Scottish housekeeper stirred the black pot over the fire, never looking up.

"Mollie, I insist on knowing about this babe. And who is Roos?"

"Nay. Yer good lady will tell ye."

He asked her to bring up some bread and cheese, and spun on his heel. This mystery better be solved soon. Aneka reclined on the bed, and as he sat beside her, everything spilled out. How she had taken Mollie and Jenny to the village. How the wild storm caught them by the river.

Her eyes held sorrow. "We received word of a suffering lady. It was ghastly."

Tears spilled down her cheeks. He wiped them away with his hand, sorry he had ever left.

"She died after giving birth to a baby boy," Aneka whispered. "Justinus and Angus buried her. Mollie found Roos, a new mother from the village. She nurses him here. Did I do right?"

He kissed her hand. "You are amazing. Let me tell you about my trip."

"Pieter, I'm so tired. When the baby cries, I jump up. I just moved his cradle into Mollie's room to sleep. But with him gone, I worry more. I need you and our children near me."

Pieter quietly soothed, "I will take care of everything."

Doubts washed over him. How would she react when she discovered Dirck was still in Mainz?

# CHAPTER 20

On the first dry morning since he returned home, Pieter excused himself from breakfast. Aneka stayed in her room, upset at him for allowing Dirck to remain in Mainz. Angus, too, had raised a critical eyebrow, or so it seemed. Pieter needed fresh air to clear his mind. He donned a wool hat and cloak, promising to return by dark.

Mollie ambled up, handing him a package of cheese and bread. She shook her head vigorously. A strand of gray hair fell from her cap.

"Yer wife's plannin' a party. But ye didna' hear of it from me."

"There are many needed repairs," he objected.

"Doves are roastin' as we speak. Justinus is tryin' to catch a fresh trout fer steamin' with leeks. It's in yer honor."

She turned her back to poke the fire. Pieter laughed at Mollie's good-natured ribbing, which she'd dished out since he was a small lad. He agreed to be home when the sun was overhead, giving Aneka time to fashion a proper surprise feast. Pieter strode to the barn where Fitch had readied Willow. A second horse stomped next to his mount.

"Why is Star out?" Pieter asked.

Justinus stepped forward. "Papa, may I ride with you? Mama said I should."

"I thought you were fishing."

"Oh, I caught a few trout hours ago."

Pieter swallowed a biting retort. Truth hit him between the eyes. He did not deserve Aneka. His wonderful wife was caring for the babe as if he was her own son. She also considered Justinus more than Pieter did. At the serious glint in his younger son's eyes, Pieter realized it was time Justinus filled Dirck's shoes.

"Yes, son. We have much to attend to."

He lifted his slight shoulders. "Papa, I won't let you down."

"I'm proud you helped your mother after the storm. Let's be off."

Father and son rode along the receding river and to rye fields turning green. Pieter checked on one of his many *standaardmolens* recently built. The windmills had done their job superbly in the storm.

"Before I built this mill, the adjoining field was a lake." Pieter pointed to the fertile soil. "Now we have more land to plant rye, and the mill grinds more grain for our family and tenants."

Justinus held the reins of his horse. "During the storm, I inspected this mill. I was afraid the wind would tear off her sails."

Pieter eyed his son sitting atop Star. He had grown up quickly and was almost a man.

"Well done."

A smile flew across Justinus' lean face, lighting his bright blue eyes.

"We ride to the dikes."

Pieter nudged Willow with his heels. Though he galloped away from Star, Justinus kept up a good pace. They inspected the dikes and Pieter noted sections needing urgent repairs to ward off further breeches. They rode side by side along the riverbank until Justinus pulled his horse to a stop.

"Papa, something else happened while you were gone."

"What is it, son?"

Pieter drew his horse alongside Justinus, noticing a faint blush on his cheeks.

"Being alone in the storm frightened me. Sheep drowned. Our hens died from falling trees. A huge limb crashed in the glass window, and I dropped to my knees asking God to save everyone. He did, including me."

Pieter's mind recalled Dirck's injury, and he drew in a sharp breath. "I had a similar fright in Mainz, only circumstances were different."

"Papa, I'd like to tell you what's been on my mind ever since."

"You want to be more involved in the farm, is that it?"

Justinus' face shone. "I want to become a Lollard preacher like Cousin Angus."

"What?" Pieter exploded. "It's too dangerous. The church is convinced Lollards preach heresy. They would seek your death."

"Is it wrong to believe strongly in Jesus?"

"Absolutely not. While we have freedoms here in the Low Countries, that may not always be so. Powerful men want to control others, including their thoughts and worship."

Justinus yanked on the reins. Star whinnied, leaving her clump of grass.

"Papa, no one knows of my decision except you and God. Not Mama or even Angus."

Pieter lifted his eyes skyward. He refused to break his son's spirit as his father had done to him. But there was much he wanted to tell Justinus. Then he spied the sun breaking through heavy clouds, moving westward. His promise to Mollie sparked in his mind.

"I'll think on it, son. We must return to the house."

Pieter spurred on his mount, galloping back to the barn. His son raced after him.

Reaching the corral, an out-of-breath Justinus asked, "Is what I said so terrible?"

"No," Pieter puffed. "I promised Mollie to be home when the sun was directly overhead. You and I will ride to the abbey in the morning. Maxim may have sound advice."

Justinus smiled broadly. "Then I may tell Angus to begin my studies?"

"First, your mama and I must discuss such a change."

Pieter was certain his wife wouldn't take the news well. Then he recalled she was caught up caring for the baby. Perhaps the infant was part of God's plan for their lives. He stopped at the front door with a disturbing question. Should he be trying to find the babe's family?

MORNING DAWNED COLD AND WET. Pieter went to the abbey, taking Justinus and Angus with him. The baskets of food he brought for the needy proved timely as scores of men, women, and children huddled by the abbey's front door. Their grimy faces bore marks of hardship. None of them wore shoes.

Justinus nodded to his left, and Pieter saw a girl sitting in the dirt. She held an infant wrapped in nothing but a feed sack. She was sixteen years of age at most. When her baby began whimpering, she cuddled him close, lifting a song heavenward. Her clear, unwavering voice sent chills through Pieter.

He drew near to Justinus. "Her praise puts me to shame. She rejoices because the Lord doesn't forsake those who seek Him. We have much, and this desperate woman has nothing."

"Ye'll see many a poor folk in yer travels," Angus said, flashing Justinus a probing look.

Pieter nodded in approval. His cousin put Justinus on guard about the despair he'd encounter as an itinerate preacher. Pieter was grateful he'd come along. He wanted Justinus to realize what a difficult path he was choosing. They stepped past men and women staring blankly. With a heavy heart, Pieter entered the nave. All was quiet except for Maxim leading priests in a morning prayer, asking the Lord to help those hurt in the flood.

"Heavenly Father, may our love flow out beyond these walls. May we shower blessings upon the needy. In the name of our blessed Lord Jesus, amen."

Twenty robed men rose in unison to do their duty. Pieter's heart was filled with pity for those who lost their huts from wind and rain. He heard no sound, save his own breathing.

Maxim passed quietly by their pew. Pieter nudged Justinus, who quickly gave Maxim a basket, telling him that his mother had packed baby clothes, shawls, and cheese. Angus handed over another basket filled with fish.

Pieter thrust a pouch into Maxim's free hand, saying, "It's for those in most want."

"Your generosity provides for many who are struggling. Will you join me in my study?"

"I hoped to ask you something important," Pieter replied, glancing at Justinus.

Before long, they were ensconced in Maxim's study. Angus and Justinus spoke in low tones by the window. Before Pieter could discern what they were discussing, he observed a silver object on Maxim's desk and asked about it.

Maxim's brow flexed. "The deceased mother had it in her woven bag. Read the inscription."

It was inscribed: *From the Bishop of Utrecht to Father Gerard of Saint Barnabas*

He straightened his back. "Do you know this Father Gerard? Aneka sorely needs answers about the child."

"Only by name," Maxim said. "He's the prior at Saint Barnabas, selected by the Bishop of Utrecht. As you know, the bishop is Duke Philip's son born to a woman not his wife."

"I have a young man in mind who could have fathered the orphan child," Pieter snapped. "He and his father are without scruples. He may also have stolen the chalice. I should travel to St. Barnabas at once. Will you go with me?"

Maxim cleared his throat. "We could leave in a few days and meet Father Gerard directly. I thought perhaps he would gladly receive you, Duke Philip's judicial representative. My friend, Thomas a' Kempis, whose manuscript was stolen from you, wrote a letter introducing us. He lives near St. Barnabas."

Pieter and Maxim began discussing details for their journey when Justinus walked over and interrupted, "Papa, will you tell him or shall I?"

At Angus' sharp nod, Pieter looked at Maxim.

With reluctance he said, "My son wants to become a Lollard like Angus. We value your honest opinion of the life Justinus will lead as a traveling preacher."

"Have you thought this through, young man?" Maxim asked. "You will be loved by some and considered an outcast by others. You might lose your life."

Angus wiped his eyes. "Tis true. They burned Rev'rend White."

The young man never flinched. Rather, Justinus set his chin. "God changed my heart during the storm. I must reach people like the woman who died bearing her baby. Seeing the lost who know not the love of Jesus, I must act before it is too late. My life belongs to Him."

"Ach!" Angus raised his hands. "Tis the Spirit of God movin' in the lad."

Maxim stepped to the window, pointing at a large shade tree. He motioned for Pieter to join him. "Out there, among the giants of God's creations, I achieve a proper perspective of myself. Our Lord sent His Son to die an excruciating death, not just for me or for you, Pieter."

Pieter didn't respond, thinking of the tree's deep roots. How many storms had it survived?

"God's Word *is* for everyone, not just priests," he said. "That makes Gutenberg's printing of the Bible so crucial. But for Justinus to travel the country tempting laymen to read the Bible is filled with risks. Laymen who read the Bible in their language are considered heretics."

A look of compassion crossed Maxim's face. "I understand your concern. Yet every soul must know of Christ and His life everlasting. Jesus is the way, the truth, and the life."

"That's what I truly believe, Papa!"

Pieter was torn, but in the face of his son's honest commitment to serve God, how could he resist? Wouldn't he be tempting God's condemnation? He rested an affectionate hand on Justinus' shoulders. "Then you have my blessing."

After agreeing to their plans, Pieter voiced another decision. A grin stayed on Justinus' face all the way home. As Pieter rode up the drive, Mollie ran out waving a letter.

Pieter dismounted and tore off the seal.

*Dear Father:*

*Things are different since you left. Herr Gutenberg is gone! His assistant Schöffer is in charge. I will stay until every Bible is finished.*

*Your loving son, Dirck.*

*P.S. Schöffer calls again!*

Pieter tapped the letter on his palm. He didn't like Dirck staying in Mainz without Johann's guidance. Perhaps it was time to collect his son. But Pieter had just promised to help Maxim locate the irresponsible man who fathered the baby.

He would tell Aneka, but then what?

# CHAPTER 21

## SAINT BARNABAS, THE NETHERLANDS

Pieter was weary from the arduous ride. He pounded off his mud-caked cloak. Hens pecked beneath a tree, and a dog barked as if only to be heard. Maxim rested on a stump, while Pieter went into an inn for travelers. He ordered food and water to be brought outside. Pieter removed his heavy cloak, spread it on the ground, and sat down.

When a young boy brought trenchers for them both, Pieter paid him, offering him more if he placed a note in the hands of Father Gerard at Saint Barnabas.

"Will you?"

The youngster bobbed his blond head, snatched the letter in one hand, and the coin with the other. He flew down the dirt lane, his bare feet rising up and down like hungry seabirds.

"We should eat," Pieter said. "Father Gerard may be away from St. Barnabas."

They ate and rested, talking little. It was hot and Pieter was tired. Within the hour, the boy thrust a reply letter into Pieter's hand. After paying the extra coin, he tore off an official-looking wax seal. The creamy parchment bore a gold embossed crest.

"We have received a formal invitation," he told Maxim. "It says, 'Lord Pieter Vander Goes and guest, your presence is requested at the rectory of Father Gerard of Saint Barnabas. A dinner is given in your honor. Please arrive at four bells.'"

"Sounds as if Father Gerard does esteem your rank," Maxim quipped.

Pieter couldn't resist getting up and performing a mock bow. "Highly, Your Lordship."

"All well to jest, Pieter. But do you suppose Gerard will shed light on the dead woman who had the silver chalice?"

"If not, we take our search where the evidence leads us. Aneka is anxious to learn if we find the babe's family."

"I suppose you'll snatch the boy right out of your wife's arms?"

"What do you imply?" Pieter stiffened. "That Aneka wants to raise another child?"

Maxim fluffed his cloak. "Stranger things have happened."

"God leads our steps. We cannot go astray."

Having said as much, Pieter went to ensure the horses had been fed and watered. On the way to the dilapidated barn, his mind whirled at Maxim's suggestion. Did Aneka want to raise the boy to adulthood? Easy for Pieter to say he believed in God, but did he trust God with the future?

The horses were readied for another ride, and Pieter and Maxim wasted no time reaching Saint Barnabas. The vast stone cathedral towered above them on a steep knoll. A sullen groom took their horses, while a pock-faced steward carrying a torch brought them up a weedy incline. Though Pieter matched him step for step, Maxim lagged behind, struggling for breath. They reached the crest some minutes later.

Pieter gazed down with foreboding upon a watery moat. Something seemed amiss here among the high stones. The steward's fierce glower fueled Pieter's angst, though he followed him through a complex maze of iron and wooden gates. At its end, a guard held a long spear across his body. He looked more fashionable than strong in his red hat, gold doublet, and red breeches.

The steward spoke to the guard, giving Maxim a chance to tell Pieter, "The pontiff employs similar guards in Rome."

"Happily, I've never been to Rome," Pieter replied with a playful grin.

"It is nothing to laugh at. Priests there are mired in corruption, unlike our simple abbey."

"Corruption has seeped into the church. I hope we find nothing like that here."

Pieter was prevented from sharing his misgivings with Maxim because the guard raised the gate, then lowered the drawbridge over the moat. The trio traversed across. They entered a confined hallway at Saint Barnabas. In the dim light, Pieter walked by animal skins, swords, and small tapestries. They were shown to a plush banquet hall. The spacious room boasted fires blazing at both ends, a massive wooden table spanning the distance.

When the steward left, Pieter quickly examined four place settings.

"Do you see what I see?" His words echoed off the high ceiling.

Before Maxim could reply, someone said, "I hope you have not waited long."

Pieter tore his eyes from a silver chalice to a man extending his hand. His hair was cut as if he'd used a bowl for a pattern. He wore a friendly smile.

They shook hands, with Pieter intoning, "Thank you, Father Gerard, for inviting us."

"Father Gerard is with his clothier from the valley," he coughed. "I am Steven, his assistant. Allow me to pour out some wine."

Impatient to examine the chalice, Pieter accepted the wine. Drawing the cup to his lips, he saw it bore the same inscription as the deceased woman's chalice, which was safely tucked in his leather bag. Pieter narrowed his eyes at Maxim, who returned a knowing look.

"Steven," Pieter began. "Does the Bishop of Utrecht reside nearby?"

"He visits frequently."

Steven leaned forward to adjust the gold plate, stifling a cough.

Meanwhile, Pieter put his finger over the inscription on the cup he held, and said, "No doubt, Father Gerard and the bishop are close friends. These silver goblets and gold plate are magnificent. As is this dining hall."

"What an honor to be invited by your master to dine," Maxim gushed.

The more prolific their praise, the more unsettled Steven became. He had a coughing spasm and excused himself, supposedly to check on Father Gerard.

"Pieter, your speech was most impressive," Maxim remarked.

"And ineffective. We learn nothing."

Maxim placed a hand on Pieter's forearm. "The chalices are the same. Steven seems ill at ease among the splendid silver and gold."

A sudden, cold breeze stopped their conversation. Footsteps echoed out in the hall. Pieter strained to hear muffled voices. "Sshh." He pressed a finger to his lips.

He recognized Steven's voice declaring, "I've told you many times be-fore, Father Gerard will do what he can. You keep coming and asking, but you do not bring his new robe."

Mere scraps of a soft, wavering voice reached Pieter's ears. "She is gone … months. My daughter …"

The voices faded, and Steven returned, covering his mouth to mask his violent cough.

"Father Gerard is called away on an emergency. He instructs me to convey his apologies and asks you to dine with me."

After a light soup of fish and onions, course after course was brought in until Pieter could eat no more. Steven rang a silver bell signaling dessert was to be brought in.

"Do you dine like this every day?" Pieter patted his too-full stomach.

"Father Gerard wants his guests to have every comfort."

Maxim set down his spoon. "I could feed half of my parish."

A servant brought four individual fruit pies, topped with almond milk and spices. Pieter dipped a tiny spoon into the aromatic pastry.

Steven didn't touch his, but offered to inform Father Gerard that they were pleased, adding, "When he returns."

"We had hoped to discuss urgent business with him," Pieter said, dis-appointment lacing his words.

"He will be gone some time. May I help?"

Pieter quickly told Steven of the woman who died in childbirth.

A bewildered expression clouded Steven's eyes. "No women live here at the monastery."

"I know that," Pieter shot back. "Isn't there a family whose daughter left home?"

Maxim picked up the silver chalice in front of him. "She had one of these in her sack."

"Such goblets are created by many tinkers," Steven replied, seized by a choking fit.

"Not with the identical inscription."

Steven leapt from his chair. "No!"

"I assure you, yes." Pieter drew the chalice from his leather bag, lifting it high.

Steven's eyes scanned the table. He must have seen four chalices in their proper places because he slouched down on the embroidered chair.

"It's true," Pieter insisted, explaining he carried the chalice from

Middleburg. "It's not left my sight. You should know I overheard a man say his daughter was gone."

Steven hung his head. "I must unburden myself. You seem to be honorable men. You must agree to take me away from this place. I am ill."

"We will," Pieter assured. "Just waste no more time."

"After I gather my belongings, I will take you to the man you heard. He searches for his daughter. I had so hoped—" Steven coughed again.

"What did you hope?" Pieter prompted.

"That she would be found. Speaking with her father, I despaired she was gone forever."

Steven went to grab a valise with his clothing. They followed him out of the maze of gates and into a thriving shop district. Pieter sensed someone following them. Looking back, he saw Maxim on horseback, pulling Willow behind him. Everything was as it should be.

Why were Pieter's nerves on edge? Maybe he dreaded telling a father that his daughter had died. Steven took Pieter to a building with a hand-carved sign: *Wolfgang Halsma, Tailor.* Though the shop was dark, Pieter pounded on the door. He wasn't surprised when no one answered.

Maxim dismounted, tying the horses to a post. "Perhaps he looks for his daughter."

"Which will be futile."

Sorrow for the man welled in Pieter's heart. Suggesting they wait next door, Steven led them to be a smelly tavern. The patrons were imbibing too much ale and wine. Pieter downed a cup of bitter cider.

The innkeeper walked up, his eyes shifting from side to side. "Be careful. Two ruffians just left. I overheard them comment on your mounts outside."

A horse's whinny brought Pieter to his feet. He darted outside. Willow nervously stomped her great hoof and twitched her tail. Pieter's favorite mare was still tied to the post, but Star was gone.

"Stop, thief!" Pieter yelled into the black night.

Maxim and Steven hustled outside with the innkeeper.

"Do you know these ruffians?" Pieter asked the innkeeper, who shone a lamp down the dark street.

"One-eyed Jack and Toady are a father and son who rob rich and poor alike. The bailiff knows them two highway robbers well."

"What is that?" Pieter seized the lamp and walked over to something glittering. With one swipe, he plucked the silver chalice from a pool of water.

"That was inside with me, in my leather pouch!" he exclaimed.

"Wanna swear out a complaint to the bailiff?"

"Consider our other business," Maxim said, caution in his tone.

Pieter dried the chalice on the edge of his cloak. "The thieves are long gone."

"The bailiff is my brother," the innkeeper told them. "You have means and must stop them robbers from preyin' on innocents. Many around here are too afraid."

Pieter swung the lamp around, seeing no one else on the streets. He must do his duty.

"As magistrate for Duke Philip, perhaps your brother and I can see justice done. Maxim, wait with Steven in case the tailor returns."

He handed the innkeeper back his lamp, and the man pointed over his shoulder. "If you want Wolfgang Halsma, he's at the Church of Saint Mark, visiting the relic."

"What relic?" Pieter asked.

"Wolfgang is superstitious." The innkeeper tapped his forehead with his finger. "He thinks his daughter left home because he quit attending church. Ever since, he visits the wooden manger Christ slept in as a babe. It came from Bethlehem."

Pieter's head spun with robbers, relics, and now a manger. What did it all mean? Standing there in the street, he silently prayed, *Please God, direct and light our path.*

The innkeeper said to him, "Take my lamp, and I will get another."

"That's a good beginning." Pieter chuckled, taking the lamp.

He and the innkeeper hastened to the bailiff. Within minutes, the complaint was made. The bailiff promised to dispatch a contingent of Duke Philip's men to locate the bandits. The tailor hadn't returned, so Pieter and Steven went to Saint Mark's cathedral. Maxim stayed at the inn, keeping an eye on Willow.

An old man lied prostrate before a marble altar. His white hair fluffed around his head like the sun's rays. A blackened piece of wood, covered with glass, was set atop the altar. Two candles in brass holders burned alongside the relic. Steven quietly approached. He whispered in the man's ear.

Wolfgang Halsma scrambled to his feet, asking Pieter, "What do you know of my daughter?"

"A woman was found in childbirth near my home. Only the babe lived. He is strong. My wife cares for him along with a woman who recently had a baby of her own." Pieter pulled out a brown woven bag. "In her bag, your daughter carried this chalice."

"Becca made such a bag," the old man said, tracing words on the goblet. "Why did she have a chalice from Saint Barnabas?"

Pieter told him how Aneka had stayed by her side. "Becca said nothing until the baby was born. When my wife found this cup and read the words aloud, your daughter cried, 'Never let him have my baby! My little Wolfie.' Those were her last words."

Halsma's legs gave out. Steven helped him to a pew. Pieter wondered, did the dying mother mean her father Wolfgang? Yet his judicial experience pushed another thought forward. The tailor must have cared for his daughter. Hadn't he been desperate to find her?

Ten minutes later, the entire group, including Maxim, assembled in Wolfgang's room above his shop. A single candle lit the sparsely furnished room.

"Please, tell me everything," Wolfgang said from the shadows.

At these words, Steven plunged into a coughing fit. His pale features looked garish in the dim light. His sorrowful eyes locked onto the candle flame. Then, he began the heartrending tale.

His parents had died when he was a baby. Father Gerard's mother, a true saint, knew Steven's mother, so she looked after Steven as a child. His schooling ended, and Father Gerard offered him a position as secretary at Saint Barnabas.

"Father Gerard's mother died last year. If she was still alive, I'd never tell what I know."

A coughing spasm ensued, and Pieter waited for Steven to regain his breath. Then he urged him to continue. Steven wiped his mouth.

"From the moment I crossed his drawbridge, I noticed things I did not approve of." He turned to Wolfgang. "Becca accompanied you when you came with Father Gerard's robes. She reminded me of a fawn with large, brown eyes."

"I wanted her to learn my trade." Wolfgang choked back tears. "I'm old and won't live much longer. My wife, her mother, is gone. I didn't want Becca fading away in a nunnery."

Steven went on, explaining how Becca came to St. Barnabas with Gerard's new linen robe. "He instructed me to pour her wine. I did, in a silver goblet, like that one."

He pointed at the chalice in Maxim's hand. "She said she received great satisfaction in working with her father."

The old man gripped the wooden arms of his chair. His knuckles turned white.

"What else happened?" Pieter asked.

"Father Gerard swept in, ordering me to take a message to town. I saw them through the hall window in the outside garden. Becca carried the silver chalice. Father Gerard pulled her other hand. I heard him say he wished to show her a rose."

Wolfgang's face beamed red. "Is he the father of her child?"

"I should have gone to her, but I was afraid to confront him. I was alone, you see."

Steven covered his face with his hands and sobbed. Maxim lightly patted his shoulder, prompting the young man to lift his face.

"I am in agony over what must have happened. Before I turned from the window, I saw him drag her by the hand into his garden. Then, I fled."

Steven dropped his eyes. A tortured look crossed his face. "I should have protected her!"

The old man yanked the chalice from Maxim's hand and threw it on the floor.

"No! It's my fault! I should never have let her go to the monastery alone."

Pieter walked over to the grieving father. "Sir, anger will not bring her back."

He led Wolfgang to a chair. When the elderly man composed himself, Pieter brought up the babe's future. "He is your grandson."

Wolfgang's hands shook. "How can so old and feeble a man care for an infant?"

"I have a plan if you agree. Will you listen?"

BACK IN MAINZ, DIRCK DARED NOT READ THE LETTER he received by special messenger. Schöffer was always nosing around. Dirck's day had been full of inking and printing the Bible, with Schöffer supervising him nearly minute by minute. Dirck felt tremendous strain. He neared exhaustion.

With the parchment crinkling inside his cloak, Dirck focused on the inked page in front of him. His eyes scanned the verse in the Gospel of Saint John. Of all the pages he had printed for Gutenberg's new Bible, this was his favorite: *For God so loved the world that he gave His only begotten son. That whosoever believeth in Him shall not perish, but have everlasting life.*

"I see you admire your work," a deep voice rumbled.

Dirck snapped to attention.

"Yes. I mean, no," he stammered. "I should return to my printing."

"Your papa will be proud of you and your hard work." Herr Gutenberg smiled at him.

"You will see him?"

The inventor tugged at his beard. "I will write Pieter and say how his son and his gold are helping me print God's word so others may know the truth."

The great man's kind words soothed Dirck's ruffled mind, and his innermost thoughts gushed forth. "Back in Middleburg, something pressed me to adventure. I was wrong to disobey my father, but I want to become a printer like you, Herr Gutenberg. I mean to see the Bibles finished."

Gutenberg's eyes sparkled. "I understand your determination. I have worked twenty years to create a machine to print one Bible. Now we print not just one, but ten times twenty. Someday, I envision thousands of Bibles will be printed for thousands to read. It is my hope to remain part of the printing until I die."

"Why would you not, sir?"

"Tis a subject for another time. We shall talk again soon."

His long beard flowing, Gutenberg left as quietly as he had come. Dirck did not comprehend his many disappearances. The opportunity to speak with him for even the briefest moment spurred Dirck to work harder printing the Gospel of John.

Schöffer strutted in with his usual scowl.

"Who were you talking to?" he demanded to know.

Dirck shrugged and set the parchment to dry. The supervisor inspected his final page and pronounced it acceptable.

"Do not cross me, Vander Goes," Schöffer added. "You work at my pleasure."

Dirck bit his lip. He wouldn't dishonor Gutenberg by being disrespectful. He also dreaded moving his arms for fear of crinkling the hidden parchment. It would be just like Schöffer to seize Dirck's message and refuse to give it back.

"Yes, sir," was his curt reply.

He dropped his arms to his sides, making a rustling sound. Schöffer narrowed his eyes to slits and paused. Dirck felt sweat bead on his forehead. He willed Schöffer to leave him alone. Eventually the despised supervisor turned away. Dirck's shoulders sagged in relief.

Schöffer went to scold a new apprentice, saying, "See this smudge? Be more careful if you want to keep your position."

Dirck cleaned up his work area. Tired to the bone, he crept up to his attic garret, eager to read his message. He lit a candle stub, which he held above the parchment.

*Yer father's lookin' fer the family of a lassie who died. Her bairn lives with us. Yer sister runs wild, climbin' trees. She fell on her head. A strange man haunts the farm. Justinus visits a school with Angus. Will ye coom home?*

*Yer faithful servant, Mollie*

Dirck's heart raced. Mollie's words shook him. How he wished Wilhelm was here to talk over the letter. But he had gone to his parents' house for paper.

Deep in his heart, Dirck knew he should be home helping. But hours ago he'd promised Herr Gutenberg to see the Bibles were finished. They still had to print three hundred and ten copies from Saint John to The Revelation. The flickering light prompted him to write his mother, asking if he should come home. Her answer would dictate his future steps.

*"If you are insulted for the name of Christ, you are blessed, because the Spirit of glory and of God rests upon you."*

1 Peter 4: 14 (NIV)

# CHAPTER 22

## FAIRFAX COUNTY, VIRGINIA

E va tore her eyes from the journal. The bravery and honor Pieter and his family showed in difficult times made her want to keep reading. She knew something else. Mr. Badger harassing Kaley for her faith paled in comparison to Bible-believing Christians being burned alive in the fifteenth century. But didn't such verbal attacks lead to outright persecution?

Eva glanced at her watch. It was nearly two o'clock in the morning. Yikes! Work called in less than four hours. She scurried to bed without brushing her teeth, and slipped next to Scott.

"You okay?" he mumbled.

"Yes, love. Go back to sleep."

Yet Eva had difficulty releasing her ancestors. Pieter and his son's printing of the Gutenberg Bible intrigued her. So did Aneka's love for her family and the baby born by a flooding river. Their faith in God's goodness stayed strong despite being unable to read their Wycliffe Bible, which had been stolen.

She rolled to her side. Guilt prodded her to confess her weak faith. Her daughter was being pressured to keep quiet at school about believing in Jesus. Was Eva doing enough to encourage Kaley and her sons to stand strong? Yes, she was a federal agent who went after the bad guys. Yes, she took her kids to church and supported their involvement in youth group. But she had some of the same questions of her life's purpose that Pieter did. Maxim had suggested Pieter travel to meet Johann Gutenberg and invest in printing God's Word.

Though Eva knew she should go to sleep, she kept thinking of her own Bibles. On her shelves and tables were four or five different versions. How often did she seek guidance in them, wanting to know what God thought of mercy and justice? She squeezed her eyes shut. Tomorrow, after work, she'd investigate the Bible her mother had given her.

Vows made in the heart of the night often slip away come morning. This time, Eva kept her promise.

Come morning, she did phone the Smithsonian, and then Kaley's principal. Sadly, Mr. Troop was gone all week at a conference. Eva plunged into work for the next several days. She also reached out to Heather Pentu, who still hadn't heard from Raj. Eva wondered how long the NCIS agent would be working undercover, wherever he was in the world.

Thursday evening after dinner, she prayed for his safety and asked God to strengthen her faith. She cracked open her newest Bible, and turning to Genesis, she read of the creatures God had made in the beginning, including man and woman. Her eyelids grew heavy as she reached the terrible flood Noah survived with his family in the ark.

In the morning, Eva battled a howling gale of her own. Traffic congealed on the rain-soaked highway, nearly making her late. She dodged buckets of rain and sped into the Smithsonian, where she shook off her umbrella. The foul weather hadn't deterred dozens of visitors. They milled in a long line waiting to be cleared through security. Eva pulled her mother's little suitcase behind her, and strode right to the uniformed guard.

A man with a Boston accent called, "Hey, lady, we were here first."

She ignored his outburst, and handed over her credentials, complete with her sparkling gold badge. "I'm Special Agent Eva Montanna. Director Cecil Prescott and I are meeting in the Preservation Center."

Officer Brian O'Shea, according to his name badge, opened Eva's pocket-sized leather credential case. He scrutinized her picture.

"So, you're with Immigration Customs Enforcement. Lookin' for undocumented visitors in the Smithsonian?" His green eyes held a cheery twinkle.

Eva laughed. "I'm part of a security review to see if Officer O'Shea is doing his job."

"In that case, I'd better ask if you're armed."

"Yes." She patted the suitcase handle. "And I have a questionable document in here."

"Then I won't wand you. Screamin' beepers will scare the tourists." O'Shea gave her a clipboard. "Sign in and indicate you're headin' to Director Prescott's office."

Eva did so, handing him the board. He directed her to a double set of glass doors, which she went through wheeling her case. Her sturdy heels clicked on the polished hardwood floors. At the Preservation Center, she approached the receptionist, giving her name. The young man in a business suit consulted his computer screen and told her to take a seat.

She'd barely gotten comfortable when a middle-aged woman in a white lab coat rushed up. "I am Dr. Gretchen Wiles. Director Prescott has a conflict."

Disappointed, Eva rose to greet Dr. Wiles, who wore her hair drawn in a ponytail. She edged so near Eva that her arm collided against hers. Eva stepped back. The doctor's deep-set eyes locked onto her suitcase.

"I'm the Center's visiting scholar and will analyze your Bible. Is it in there?"

"Ah … yes," Eva replied cautiously, bothered by those glittering eyes.

Or did her second thoughts stem from Wiles' invasion of Eva's personal space? Either way, she disapproved of her. Was Eva being fair?

She shoved aside her federal agent instincts and lifted her pert chin. "I trust my case has kept everything dry."

"We'll see, won't we? Follow me."

The scholar stalked away on rubber-soled shoes. She took Eva to a vast room, which Eva recognized. She'd sat by this long mahogany table before. The room's splendor still impressed her. After opening her case, she hefted the two-volume heirloom onto the table.

"Everything is nice and dry," she quipped.

In reply, Wiles tapped aqua-colored fingernails on the table. Eva removed a plastic bag from around the volumes and displayed her exquisite family Bible. Wiles drew her hands together and leaned forward to inspect the two-volume set.

Eva fixed a stony gaze on the doctor's keen face. "Family records indicate my ancestors helped Johann Gutenberg. This may be one of his Bibles."

"I very much doubt it," Dr. Wiles snapped.

"You haven't even examined my volumes."

"Gutenberg created the first movable type. His Bibles are extremely rare. They are the first important books printed in the West."

Eva regretted having done no research on Gutenberg, but it was too late now. Wiles opened the heavy cover of the first volume, and ran a hand along the binding. She turned a page.

"I can give no opinion without knowing more of the background."

"Fair enough." Eva folded her arms. "This complete Bible appears to be in Latin. It's been in the Vander Goes family, my family, as far back as I can document. My great-grandparents emigrated from the Netherlands. My Grandpa Martin lived in Zeeland, Netherlands, and survived WWII. His Aunt Deane gave him these volumes."

"I suppose this *might* be an early Gutenberg, but counterfeit pieces abound."

The scholar went on to tell how she'd seen similar looking pieces for which dealers paid a fortune, only to discover they had a fraud on their hands.

"We at the Smithsonian do not like being duped."

Eva rejected her implication. "Our Bible contains multiple Vander Goes names in front. I find it hard to believe my ancestors purchased it. At least, not in the last couple of centuries."

"You may leave it for me to analyze the contents. Come, I'll show you out."

Eva balked at leaving without her Bible. Hadn't Aunt Deane written, cautioning the Vander Goes family to never part with this Bible?

"Is there anything you can tell me right now?"

Once again Dr. Wiles tapped her fingernails on the table. "You feel confident it's a priceless original and I appear to be suspicious. If it helps your trust level, I have ten years experience in my field. Recently, I was presented with what was considered an early Egyptian parchment. I proved it was 'The Great Hymn to the Aten,' which had been stolen from the Museum of Egyptian Antiquities. The museum was ecstatic when I returned it to them."

Dr. Wiles smiled widely, as if proud of her accomplishment. Eva wasn't so sure.

"I will have a receipt prepared for you," Dr. Wiles urged. "It is your choice."

Eva's mind pulsed with the possibilities. This hyper-confident "expert" might find the Gutenberg genuine, but stolen. She might take it upon herself to return it to some German museum. But wouldn't God want Eva to authenticate this Bible for purposes of His own?

Dr. Wiles walked to the door, resting a hand on the knob. "Well?"

"How long will you have it?"

"It's impossible to predict, perhaps several weeks or more."

"All right. You have three weeks."

Dr. Wiles enthusiastically agreed to her terms. Eva placed the two-volume set into the small suitcase and zipped it shut. In return, Wiles gave her a receipt with a confirmation number. Eva collected the plastic wrapping and left the Smithsonian. A peculiar feeling about Dr. Wiles gnawed at her on the drive back to the office. She wished she could put her finger on the problem.

Later that afternoon, she and Griff tracked down other Chechen suspects and scheduled a cursory interview. On the way home, she stopped at the library to check out a few books. Dinner was hurried, and then Scott drove the kids to church for their youth group sleepover.

He returned whistling a happy tune. Eva plumped the cushion, and Scott sat beside her on the sofa. She leaned her head on his shoulder, telling him of Dr. Wiles' doubts.

He smoothed her hair. "Did you tell her about your family journal?"

"No. Maybe I should have. Her motives seem suspect. She reminds me of a greedy doctor of archaeology I once arrested."

"What will you do about your misgivings?"

"I checked out some library books to investigate." She straightened and leafed through a book about Gutenberg. "It says he died broke. Maybe his enemies finally got to him."

Scott selected a book about Christianity in the Middle Ages. "This records Christians with Wycliffe Bibles being killed as heretics. Many were burned at the stake, bound in chains."

"Oooh!" Eva's arms covered in gooseflesh. "Aunt Deane wrote of William White's burning. My ancestor Angus witnessed his awful death."

Scott told her about his challenging new job. "My boss, the speaker of the house, left me a message on my phone. He's concerned about massive armaments our government sent to Qatar, such as air defense systems, and Apache helicopters. Yet the administration turns its back on Egypt's new government."

"Scott, will the speaker call for hearings?"

He yawned. "Probably, but that won't stop the terrible killings and beheadings of Americans."

Eva fought a yawn of her own. She closed her book and brushed her teeth. Scott turned out the light. As she snuggled in beside him, she shivered.

"Brrr. I wished we'd watched a funny movie instead of talking about martyrs and the mess the world's in."

"Do you need an extra blanket?" he whispered in the dark.

"No. Sweetheart, you are all I need."

In that moment, Eva realized how true that was. Scott meant the world to her.

EVA WALKED BEHIND AN OLD BRICK CHURCH. What she saw rocked her to the core. Powerful men were wrapping a man in chains. Ruffians hauled him to a large stake. The prisoner's face glowed brightly like a saint's.

He called loudly, "Jesus!"

"Convert or die!" yelled the crowd.

Eva ran toward the bound man. Did she know him? It didn't matter. In her heart, she knew he was innocent of any wrongdoing.

"Stop!" she screamed.

No one listened. It was as if she wasn't even there. Someone lit a fire beneath him. Flames licked the bottom of his clothes. Eva must save him! She leapt forward, yanking his chains. They didn't budge. Smoke filled her nostrils. Then he began to sing.

"Jesus, Jesus, I will not deny You … I come to You."

A woman dressed in a black headdress shouted, "You must die, you infidel!"

Eva froze. Her heart failed within her. She knew what was coming. She couldn't breathe.

"Help him!" she cried.

Someone grabbed her arm and shook it.

"Eva! Are you all right? You were shouting in your sleep."

Her mind reeled. She opened her eyes to a darkened room.

"Where am I?"

"Honey, it's me." Scott touched her cheek. "You're warm. Were you dreaming?"

"It was horrible," she managed. "They burned a man alive. I couldn't stop them."

Tears stung her eyes and she started weeping.

"Sshh. I am here."

Scott soothed her with soft sounds until she dried her eyes.

"Why did I dream this?" She flung off the blanket. "What am I supposed to do?"

"I have no idea, but can you fall back asleep?"

"No. Dreaming of people being persecuted for Jesus, I want to finish the journal and find out if Pieter died for his faith."

"We're both awake," Scott sputtered. "And I'm hungry."

He shoved on his slippers. Eva did likewise. In the kitchen, she scrambled eggs and toasted cinnamon bread, fresh from the Wholly Ground. The wonderful aroma reminded her of Lisa Dawson, who owned the café, and that led to Eva dwelling on the hate-filled letter Mr. Badger sent to all the parents. Except she and Scott didn't receive one, because Kaley's teacher had been targeting Kaley.

Eva put food onto their plates, her spirits sagging. "We have to act against Badger's letter telling students to shun Kaley for her Christian faith. Or I'll have no peace."

"I think better on a full stomach," Scott replied.

She watched him eat. She nibbled a piece of bread, not relishing a confrontation with the despicable teacher. But, she reasoned, what better option did they have? A lawsuit?

# CHAPTER 23

Eva and Scott herded Kaley into the den when she came home from the youth retreat. Their daughter seemed reluctant to talk about Badger's letter.

"Lexi's mom gave me a copy at church last week," Eva told her gently. "Dad and I are concerned how you're holding up."

Kaley sighed and seemed to crumble before their eyes. "Yeah, Lexi showed it to me."

"He won't get away with it!" Scott barked, his eyes bulging. "That you can be sure of."

Kaley perched on the leather sofa, her lower lip trembling.

"Badger is a proud atheist. He rules class like some Roman general. He'd love to send us Christians to the coliseum. Everyone knows he's after me. Lexi is still my friend anyway."

Eva's heart lurched. Kaley looked so downcast. Eva went over and rubbed her back.

"This has gotten way out of hand. Dad and I are going to confront him."

Scott gazed at Eva with concern in his eyes. "I know what we decided, but hearing how other students are piling on, will we make things worse?"

Eva shut the door so Andy and Dutch wouldn't hear what she said next. Then she whirled on Scott. "So a bully wins? Just like Russia?"

"We're talking about Kaley's life, not Rome or Russia," Scott shot back.

"I'd love to meet the weasel in a dark alley some night and show him what I think, man to man."

"Oh sure, that will help," Eva declared.

Kaley raised her arms, her fists clenched. "Forget it! I'll finish his dumb class without making trouble. Next year, I'm transferring to the charter school. He won't ruin my senior year."

Scott and Eva traded intense looks. Eva draped an arm around her hurting daughter.

"If you are prepared to handle it, then fine."

Scott jumped in. "Just remember, we care for you. Other students may not have parents to back them. We have a chance to stop the guy in his tracks, and we should."

"Heather Pentu is a lawyer," Eva said. "I might call her and see what our options are."

Kaley shook her head and stomped from the room. Scott flashed Eva a thunderous look.

"Lawyers, private investigators, courts—we can do it all. But nothing restores Kaley's innocence, does it?"

"Oh, Scott."

Eva fell into his arms and clung to him. What could they do? At length, he convinced her to phone Heather, who proved to be a sympathetic ear. She understood Eva's parental concerns that Kaley not be censored.

"I'm no expert in this field," Heather admitted. "We need to find out how Virginia handles freedom of expression cases in public schools."

Eva took out a notepad. "Our question is, can a teacher silence Kaley's Christian beliefs in class? Doesn't she have a First Amendment right to voice her views?"

"It seems logical that she does. The teacher's caustic and harmful letter is over-the-top."

Eva said she'd appreciate hearing back soon. Heather agreed to start researching right away, and promised to set aside a buy-sell agreement she was drafting for a client.

"I have nothing going on this evening. Besides, I know how difficult waiting can be," she said, her voice frayed with tension.

Eva fiddled with her pen. She feared the answer, but asked anyway. "Has Raj gotten in touch with you?"

"Not a peep. I'm hoping he will come home any day."

Her voice fell away, prompting Eva to say, "You and he are in my many prayers."

"Thanks, Eva. And I'm always glad to help you."

"Tomorrow is the church craft fair. I'm looking forward to your cookies and raising funds for Transitions." Heather chuckled. "The local paper ran an article. I hope it generates more interest."

"Do I sense a story here?" Eva asked.

"A wealthy donor read about the church's fundraising and already made a sizable donation. It's a scholarship for needy girls. My prayer life has increased, Eva, and I thank you."

"Is that why you feel more content for Raj?"

"Yes. My faith is increasing too."

Heather agreed to meet Eva at the café after completing her research. Eva ended the call and briefed Scott on Heather's willingness to help. She restored the phone to its base.

Eva smiled at her husband. "God is at work when we're in the valley of despair, which reinforces how our faith must go deeper than a mere belief that He exists."

"You're right." Scott sighed. "Sorry I blew up. We don't face the enemy alone."

"To see Kaley hurting is painful. God wants to take away our hurts. We have to let Him."

MEANWHILE RAJ PENTU HUDDLED IN A SMALL WAREHOUSE. He'd been holed up in this warehouse for more than a week, with no idea when he'd be able to leave. He was still somewhere in Egypt, but didn't know exactly where. Yakov, the Russian arms-dealer-turned-informant, leaned against the wall.

He grumbled incessantly, about lack of food, and everything really. Tonight, it was the oppressive heat.

"When we get free?" he asked Raj.

He could only shrug and tune out Yakov's cursing. Without warning, the warehouse door burst open. There stood Hamadi Von Bilgon, smiling. The Coptic Christian had saved both Raj and Yakov from the Egyptian Brotherhood, who had every intention of killing them both. That was what made their escape from the warehouse so tricky.

Before Raj could react, an associate wasted no time backing up a van. He stopped with its rear door open. He plunged from the van carrying a semi-automatic pistol in his left hand. Raj flinched on instinct. Adrenaline pumped through him. His eyes sought the RPG they'd swiped recently from the Egyptian Brotherhood.

"Come." Hamadi motioned Raj over, and swiftly introduced Butrus. "He is named after the great Apostle Peter, and is like a brother to me."

Butrus pumped Raj's right hand with gusto. "Excuse my gun. Hamadi told me about you. I too am Christian. The Brotherhood burned my home, and killed my wife and children. I fight."

Raj relaxed his shoulders. Butrus pulled a photo from his pocket, which he thrust in Raj's hands. "My wife of twelve years and two daughters are gone."

Raj held the picture, envisioning Heather. She must be worried sick about him. Their first anniversary had blazed by with Raj stuck in Egypt and no way to make contact. He gave Butrus his photograph and placed a comforting hand on his arm.

"I am sorry. You bear a heavy burden, my friend." Raj turned to Yakov and said, "Butrus is also a Christian."

"Bah." Yakov spat. "It wastes time to believe in a god what never existed."

"Will you never learn? God is the One who saved us."

He refused to translate Yakov's diatribe in Arabic.

Butrus may have understood Yakov's lousy English as he briefly shut his eyes, and then pointed to another man sitting in the van.

"He is my brother, and was to marry a young woman from our church. The rebels killed her and her entire family because they refused to convert to Islam."

"The Brotherhood live to kill," Raj admitted, his heart weighted with their loss. "Will you go or stay in Egypt? It's dangerous for Christians throughout the Middle East."

Hamadi gestured to the van's open door, and urged them to hide in the back. "We transport you to a safe place."

"And where is that, exactly?" Raj asked.

"In Egypt. You will see. The IS in Iraq has all but wiped out the Christians. God is our strength and our shield. The Brotherhood did not destroy our church building, but they lock us out, at least they think they do."

Yakov folded his arms and stood his ground. "Where we go?"

"Someplace better than here," Raj replied. "Stay and face the Brotherhood alone."

He climbed into the rear with the RPG. Yakov flopped in behind him. Hamadi quietly folded a light tarp over them. With Butrus driving, they sped along in the van for maybe two hours. Raj was roasting, and struggled for breath. Exhaustion seeped into his bones. Despite the constant jarring, he kept nodding off, only to be awakened when the van jolted into a huge rut.

He sensed the van slowing, and nudged Yakov. "Wake up."

"I too hot," Yakov hissed. "De bumps, dey kill me."

"No, but the Brotherhood almost did." Raj's hand flew to the RPG, giving him some assurance. He told the Russian, "Listen, Yakov, escape beats the alternative. We could've been blown through that church wall. Thank God you're alive instead of spitting in His eye."

"Bah. You know nothing of what I live through."

That might be true, but Raj didn't care about Yakov's miserable childhood or whatever. His corruption and greed had plunged Raj into this mess. The van made a series of sharp turns, forcing him to reassess the situation. He and his mission were a failure. *If . . .* no! *When* he got home, he would rip into Bo Rider.

The van came to a halt. The front door banged shut. Odd sounds reached his ears, like someone opening steel doors. Of course, Raj couldn't see a thing crouched beneath this stifling tarp. Sweat pooled under his armpits. Yakov shouted obscenities in Russian.

"Pipe down!" Raj commanded. "I need to hear what's going on."

The van moved a few feet, and the engine shut off. Raj anticipated what might come next. His hands curled around the RPG. Though so far Hamadi and Butrus acted like Christians, they could easily be sabotaged again by the Brotherhood. Raj wasn't going down without a fight.

The rear doors flung open. The tarp was yanked off. Raj spun his head around. Hamadi gaped at him. Raj scurried from the van, gripping the RPG. Beyond the open garage door, he spotted a solid stone wall rising as high as he could see. Yakov gasped. Raj peered left and right.

The huge wall rose before him, an insurmountable obstacle. His mind tumbled.

"Hamadi, are we in prison?"

The Coptic held his stomach and laughed. "No. We are outside the walls of the ancient monastery of St. Catherine. We are in the mountains of the Sinai."

Raj coughed a sigh and told Yakov where they were. Hamadi led them outside, the ancient wall towering a good thirty feet above them.

"Are we safe here?" Raj wrapped his hands around the RPG. Would he need to use it?

Hamadi gestured with his hands. "Muslims surround us, yet leave us alone here. Pilgrims and tourists flock to St. Catherine's. It was built in the fourth century by the mother of Constantine the Great."

"If you have any kind of satellite phone, I can contact help," Raj said.

"No phones are necessary." Hamadi lowered his voice. "We have a better plan—to arrange your escape with a tour group."

Raj figured it could work, provided Yakov didn't act up. That was a pretty big "if." Raj told the Russian arms dealer they would be smuggled out with the tourists, adding, "You know all about smuggling and had better cooperate fully."

"Why dey help us?" Yakov looked puzzled.

Raj turned to their rescuer. "Why take such risks? You know little about us."

Hamadi touched a cross on his collar. "The enemy of my enemy is my friend."

"It is more than that for you, at least I think so," Raj insisted.

"In here, I know." Hamadi patted his shirt by his heart. "You are no enemy, but my brother in Christ. It is my honor to suffer for Him."

The Coptic's words penetrated Raj deeply. He didn't spend time thinking about God's purposes for his life, let alone suffering for another. Not until now.

He clapped Hamadi's shoulder with his free hand. "Yes, we are brothers."

"Tonight, you stay here in a special hideaway. Tomorrow, you explore the monastery and leave on a tour bus."

Raj was troubled by one obvious gap in the escape plan. If the Brotherhood discovered he and Yakov lived, wouldn't they find them in this ancient Christian haven?

# CHAPTER 24

**M**orning was sizzling hot for Raj. With one hand, he shaded his eyes from the intense sun while waiting in a curved line of tourists at St. Catherine's Monastery. In the other, he grasped a sack of bread sandwiches Hamadi gave him to eat later. His Coptic "brother" had found empty seats on a soon-departing bus. The guide reluctantly agreed to include the pair only after Raj paid for a complete tour, forking over a stack of Egyptian pounds.

Despite Yakov sulking at his side, and complaining of hunger pains, a kernel of hope flickered within Raj. Given the myriad of tourists speaking English, German, and French, escape seemed imminent. Then a snag loomed beyond the library complex. A thin man dressed in black suddenly appeared. He kept glancing at Yakov as if he knew him. Even odder was the folded umbrella he carried. It never rained in the desert.

Raj rejected his misgivings as paranoia. He'd been spending too much time around a slimeball named Yakov. Listening to the Orthodox monk who guided the tour, Raj stayed vigilant. The guide's long, heavy beard, black robe, and pillbox hat made him appear like a character from hundreds of years before, as if he'd been hewn from the very rock surrounding them. Raj couldn't believe this amazing oasis of Christianity in the Egyptian desert.

The monk addressed that very topic, telling visitors how many were shocked to find the aged Christian monastery. "While my country is largely Muslim, we have eight million Coptics and as many as sixty million worldwide. *Coptic* is the Arabic word for "Egyptian," and we are the native Christians of Egypt. Thus, we are known as Coptic Christians."

Raj faced Yakov with a shrug. "I guess you could call me a Coptic Christian."

Yakov didn't call him anything; he simply acted restless. His eyes scanned the others milling about. He plunged his hands in his pockets and then out again, before repeating the whole process. Perhaps Yakov had also seen the lean man with the umbrella. Raj concluded that a previous deal with him had likewise gone sour.

He set his jaw, regretting he'd gotten mixed up with such a shady character. Bo Rider and the CIA got him involved in this op. The goal—to cut off arms to the Brotherhood—was admirable. The EB smuggled weapons through tunnels into Gaza, fueling violent attacks against Israel. Well, Raj was all for stopping the bloodshed, even if it meant cozying up to the likes of Yakov. He just strove to get out of here in one piece.

Raj caught another snippet of the monk's lecture. He stepped closer, fascinated by what their guide revealed next. "Our first bishop was John Mark, the disciple who brought the teachings of Jesus Christ here from AD 42 to AD 62. You may know him as the author of Mark, in the New Testament."

"I never knew that," Raj muttered under his breath.

Yakov shuffled toward him. "You say something to me?"

"No, I listen."

Raj's eyes followed the monk's arm as he pointed to the rugged mountain behind the monastery walls.

"You stand on holy ground. Mount Sinai is where God gave Moses the Ten Commandments, and commissioned Moses to lead the Jewish people from their Egyptian captors."

Raj was spellbound. He wished Heather was here to see him enjoying spiritual matters. Another wild thought swirled in his mind. Maybe they could come here together. Raj longed for her; he longed for home. The monk gestured toward a cobblestone walk, and the tourists huddled around him. So did Raj.

"See the lush greenery ahead? We believe God spoke with fire to Moses through that very bush, which was not consumed by the fire. Eventually it was moved inside these walls."

Raj glanced back at Yakov, who lagged behind. Was he trying to make contact with Mr. Umbrella Man? The thin man veered away, toward the far side of the group. Raj focused his eyes on him, all the while trying to listen to the monk.

Their Coptic guide stopped near the entrance gate, explaining that in the fourth century, Saint Helena, the mother of Constantine the Great, had the Chapel of the Burning Bush constructed. Could this place be so ancient? Raj's parents had never brought him here before they left Egypt.

Apparently the stone walls, built in 527 AD, were some thirty-six feet high and eight feet thick. The monk said the name became Saint Catherine's in the tenth century, and the reason made Raj shudder. The head and hand of a third-century martyr, Saint Catherine of Alexandria, were brought here for safekeeping. Pilgrims had been arriving ever since.

Raj felt someone nudge his elbow. He spun around. Yakov fidgeted at his side.

"Calm down," Raj hissed. "We need to blend in."

"I need to be free of here," Yakov griped.

Raj understood, but they had to wait for the tour to end. They neared the chapel library, where the guide folded his hands. A smile lit his lined face.

"Here stands the oldest library in the Christian world. We have three thousand manuscripts and five thousand early religious books, second in rarity only to the Vatican library. It has two thousand icons of Christ."

Mr. Umbrella Man's hand shot up. "What about the bell tower? It looks newer."

"Very astute," the monk said. "It was built in 1871 by monk Gregorius. The nine bells were given by the Tsar of Russia. I pray God's blessing on your tour."

Raj was shocked to see Yakov's hand go up.

"Please, I have question," he yelled in fractured English.

The monk stopped walking and faced him. "Yes. What do you ask?"

Yakov seemed to relish the attention. "Why do Muslims not attack you?"

"Good question!" yelled Mr. Umbrella Man.

Raj wondered if he and Yakov were a tag team.

The monk dipped his head. "We live peaceably, thanks to God's protection."

Applause broke out.

He whirled a finger in the air. "You have five minutes to take photos. Then please follow me to our bus."

Raj leaned over to Yakov. "Snag a seat in the rear. I'm taking another look over there."

The NCIS agent rubbed his aching neck. He wanted to investigate the ancient burning bush. What must it have been like for Moses to see the back of God? If he had looked at God directly, the prophet would have died, just like the sun would burn your eyes if you looked right at it.

A peculiar noise made Raj turn, but he stood there alone. On this rock, God had called Moses to lead His people out of Egypt. An inner voice urged him to listen. He did, but heard nothing. Was God asking Raj to do something? Maybe He was telling Raj that he'd make it out of Egypt alive. Okay, he could live with that.

He darted to the bus, where Mr. Umbrella Man stood by the door. When Raj passed by and looked at him, the man shifted his eyes away. Raj did get his aisle seat as the bus door swished closed. Oddly, the guy with the umbrella put on his sunglasses and stayed outside. Yakov was still out there, banging on the door. The driver eventually let him in. Huffing, Yakov climbed over Raj, who closed his eyes and feigned sleep.

A friendly woman sitting ahead of them spoke to Yakov, "You just joined us. Where is your home?"

Yakov spewed a couple of sentences in Russian.

"Oh, too bad," she said, sounding dejected. "You don't speak English."

To Raj's chagrin, Yakov began a loud version of what sounded like a Russian beer drinking song. Heads turned their way.

Raj poked him and whispered, "We don't want people noticing us."

Yakov glared at Raj before turning to watch out the window. For much of the trip, it was as if Raj and Yakov had traded places. Yakov rested, and Raj couldn't settle down. His mind buzzed with a wretched scenario—the EB chasing them down, stopping the bus, and slaughtering innocent people. His pulse raced. What might happen? Yakov was the big unknown. So was the weirdo with the umbrella. Why hadn't he boarded the bus?

Raj's morbid thoughts intensified when the bus screeched to a halt.

"Remain in your seats," the driver shouted.

They were being stopped! Raj craned his head to see beyond Yakov out the window. He saw a sedan blocking the road. The tour driver opened the bus door. A man shouted in Arabic for him to get off. As he floundered down the steps, his cap flying off, two men brandishing automatic weapons stormed in and barged down the aisle.

An audible gasp rose from the tourists. Raj clenched his fists. He no longer had the RPG to fight a terrorist with an AK-47. Hamadi was the keeper of that formidable weapon.

A swarthy-looking man stopped by Raj. Towering over him, he commanded, "Show your passport. Him too."

The armed giant nodded at Yakov. Raj's mind whirled. What could he do but comply? He was unarmed with no authority in Egypt. What about the voice assuring Raj that he'd make it out? He must be hallucinating and losing his mind.

A very shaky Yakov handed over his passport. So did Raj. The gunman perused their passports, handing Yakov's back to him. If Raj bolted from his seat and tackled the guy, those automatic weapons would tear him apart. He seethed. The armed man remained silent. Without warning, with Raj's passport in hand, he flicked the muzzle of his weapon, indicating for Raj to exit the bus.

Steeling his insides, Raj stumbled to the front. How had the ideal escape plan gone so wrong? Outside the bus, Raj's captor gestured for him to get into the rear seat of the sedan. Raj got in and slid next to Mr. Umbrella Man. He took off his sunglasses.

All Raj could think of was Moses seeing God in a burning bush. And in the confines of the black sedan, he prayed like he'd never prayed in his life.

THE FOLLOWING NIGHT, EVA SWITCHED ON THE NEWS in the family room. Scott turned a page in the newspaper. Their kids were in their rooms, supposedly doing homework.

"Will this bother you or should I mute it?" Eva asked.

"Leave it on."

Eva was rereading Heather's legal memo about Kaley's free speech rights when Scott cried, "Uh oh!"

"What's going on?" She tossed down the papers and bolted over to him.

"It's Israel again. Listen."

Eva turned up the sound in time to hear the reporter announce, "Tourists were traveling to Israel from the Sinai. Rebels kidnapped an American right off the bus. Later, at a border crossing into Israel, his Russian companion was arrested. Our government refuses to comment. This is Norm Moon reporting from Tel Aviv."

"Another American in the hands of terrorists." Scott lurched to his feet. "I hope he won't be used as a pawn for ransom."

Eva's stomach turned. "The more who are taken, the more money kidnappers demand. They use the ransom to buy bigger weapons. I'm heartbroken by all the killing of Christians, Israelis, and Americans. We must act to stop these murderers."

"I'm glad you're not overseas. There's no end to the evildoers who want to kill us. What does Heather say about Badger?"

Eva picked up Heather's memo, torn by her conclusions.

"She thinks we should bypass the principal, and lodge a formal complaint with the school board. The problem is, Kaley wants to handle this herself. Should we let her?"

Scott raised his hands as though surrendering and called it a night. He had an early meeting with the speaker of the house. Eva locked the doors, set the alarm, and with mixed emotions, looked in on the children. Their sons' sweet faces in slumber made her want to weep.

Kaley had a night-light on, but was curled in her bed, breathing quietly. Eva tiptoed in, and as she reached to turn off the light, she spotted Kaley had the family journal open on her desk. Surprised, Eva's first instinct was to take it. Then she stopped.

It was all right if Kaley read about their ancestors who faced persecution with great courage. Maybe their lives would bring her much-needed hope.

Eva went to the den, realizing this was "knee time." In faith, she knelt by a chair and prayed with fervor for her country, for Coptic Christians, and for her family.

# CHAPTER 25

A week passed. On Thursday morning, Eva arrived first at the office, so she made the coffee. Things with Kaley had settled down, allowing Eva to immerse herself in the Chechen terrorist case. Russia's Foreign Intelligence Service (SVR), through its Washington embassy, referred them to Griff. He asked for her help in following them around the suburbs. They hadn't discovered them doing anything subversive or illegal. As a last resort, she and Griff planned to interview them.

A sneaking suspicion crossed her mind. Russia was probably using her group to spy on its political enemies. Eva assumed the National Security Agency (NSA) listened to the Chechens' phone calls, but NSA's missions were so super-secret, she'd never know for sure.

One good thing occurred last night. Heather had messaged Eva: *He's home!*

Thankful for the news, Eva slept more soundly than she had for weeks. She was also grateful Scott was comfortable with her undercover assignments and ability to take care of herself. Or was he? Hadn't he mentioned recently he didn't want her going overseas?

She rose for a coffee warm-up when Raj burst through the door.

"Our wanderer has returned." Eva clapped her hands together.

"It's fantastic to be on American soil, I tell you." He sped to her cubicle. "Heather bubbled over with how helpful you've been. Thanks for everything."

Touched by his generous words, Eva replied with emotion, "We're happy you made it back safe."

"So you heard of my capture?" Raj rubbed his scraggly beard. "I guess a story aired on the news."

Eva reeled. "Captured? No! What are you talking about?"

Raj looked around at the other agents arriving. "Let's meet in the conference room. I need plenty of coffee."

He went for hot java while Eva reached for a pad and pen. On second thought, Raj wouldn't want her taking notes. She grabbed her cup instead. After filling it to the brim, she went in and shut the conference room door.

Eva perched on a chair. "So tell me. Where have you been?"

Rather than answering, Raj dropped in a chair and guzzled his coffee. He wiped his forehead. "Heather saw nothing on TV. Eva, you must *never* tell her."

"Of course. Were you helping Bo Rider?"

"Yes, but never again." Raj shot out of his chair and paced the room. "He tasked me to supervise his asset, some insane Russian who sells weapons to the Egyptian Brotherhood. His language is as filthy as his arms dealings."

"Bo sent you into Egypt?"

"Yes and no. Apparently this arms nut dealt to the Brotherhood before. It's something the Agency cooked up with Mossad."

"Ah." Eva sipped her coffee. "Did you meet Judah Levitt?"

"How did you know?"

"I worked with him and Bo in the past."

"Neither he nor Bo mentioned a connection with you."

"Duh!" Eva declared. "Spooks never do."

"You're right. Unfortunately, posing as Yakov's interpreter, I was sucked into the clutches of the Egyptian Brotherhood."

"Yakov being the Russian arms dealer, I presume."

"Apparently he—" Raj slammed a fist into his other hand. "No, the CIA must have put the tracking device on the earlier shipment, and then stole the arms back before the EB killed anyone. The rebels blamed Yakov and tried to kill us."

"How did you escape?"

"That was a long, arduous ordeal."

Eva well understood the danger he was still in. "Enemies have been after me in the past. Did Bo brief you before you went in?"

"Very little. He said zero about stealing that first delivery, so I was unprepared for their intense hatred of Yakov. The rebels captured us. Then an amazing thing happened. We were rescued by daring Coptic Christians. Judah Levitt's associates staged my kidnapping to free me."

"Judah is one serious Mossad agent. What about Yakov?"

The corners of Raj's mouth twitched. "Mossad detained him the moment he entered Israel."

"That's it? End of story?"

Raj ran a hand through his thick hair. "Hardly. Mossad debriefed me for days. They know more than either I or Yakov do about the weapons' shipments. After that, the CIA took a crack at me. Eva, that's the last time I'm helping Bo. Yakov is a total jerk."

"Heather must be thrilled you're home," Eva said, deflecting criticism of Bo.

"Yeah. She's a real trooper. It's a good thing she missed the news on TV."

"The reporter never said who the American was."

Raj took a swig of his coffee, asking about the task force. Eva briefed him on the interviews she and Griff were conducting of Chechen nationals referred by the SVR.

She arched her brows. "Interested, or did you have enough Russian intrigue?"

"Thanks, but I'm taking annual leave and spending tomorrow with Heather."

"Good idea," Eva said, smiling. "Have you planned something fun to celebrate your anniversary?"

Raj's eyes became huge. "I completely forgot."

"Heather and I have enjoyed becoming friends while you've been away."

Raj yawned and checked his watch. "I have to meet Bo again at Langley. Another time I'll tell you about the Egyptian Christians and the persecution they're experiencing."

"I'm interested to hear it. My daughter is being hassled at school for being a Christian, which keeps me up nights. Heather is helping with the legal slant."

"Keep me in the loop, Eva."

She nodded. Though she returned to her cramped cubicle, thankful Raj was all right, she was eager to hear about the Christians who risked their lives saving his.

THAT NIGHT, EVA TURNED ON THE LIGHT NEXT TO HER BED. Having retrieved the journal from Kaley's room, she opened it, ready to pick up where she'd left off reading of Pieter Vander Goes and his family. Scott came in and sat by her on the bed, his eyes shining. His smug look told Eva that he was harboring a secret. She'd try to wheedle it out of him.

"What are you keeping from me?" She closed the journal.

Scott grinned. "Who, me?"

"You can run, but you can't hide. Your flickering eyes give you away every time."

"Well, you got me."

"I'm all ears."

He grabbed her hand. "The speaker is concerned about what's happening to Christians in the Middle East. Pressure is building to restore foreign aid to Egypt. I'm conducting deep background for a possible hearing."

"It sounds like the speaker is relying on you," Eva said, pleased for Scott. "And maybe expanding your duties?"

"Correct on both counts. He appreciates my time as a captain in the Air Force. I'm to coordinate with the House Select Committee on Intelligence."

Eva fluffed a pillow behind her head. "I understand you can't say more if it's classified. You should know Raj Pentu was the American taken from the tour bus. It was a ruse by Mossad and the CIA. Before that, he'd been captured and held hostage by the Egyptian Brotherhood while helping the Company. Some Coptic Christians saved his life."

"Wow. Would he talk to me?"

"He's off tomorrow, but I'll ask when he's back in the office."

Scott leaned over and kissed her cheek. He left to get a bowl of yogurt, whistling. Eva reclined on her pillow. If Raj's harrowing experience with the Brotherhood could aid suffering Egyptian Christians, she wanted to be part of it.

The next morning, before she and Griff started their interrogations, Eva called Raj, conveying Scott's question. The NCIS agent promised to assist with the hearing. On the following day, he briefed Scott about the persecution of Hamadi and his church members in Egypt. As press secretary to the house speaker, Scott then reached out to the chairman of the Intelligence Committee.

In the end, Eva benefitted from Scott's prodding. The following Thursday, she sat in a cramped staff area of a secret room, her cell phone turned off. The entire Intelligence Committee office and hearing room was one giant Sensitive Compartmented Information Facility (SCIF). No cell phones worked within their space. It was a miracle the CIA and NCIS even agreed to let Raj appear. The one caveat: The hearing would remain highly classified and closed to the public.

Eva waited anxiously for the proceedings to begin. Today would be unlike past hearings she'd attended on Capitol Hill. In those, each representative gave lengthy speeches before a single witness appeared, with cameras recording every word for broadcast on local stations back in their districts. This hearing had no spectators or cameras. The terrace seating area was limited to committee members only. A single row of tables up front was reserved for witnesses.

Chairman Whittier, a representative from North Carolina, stalked in. He shoved on a pair of reading glasses, and banged the gavel. His opening statement was a mini-lesson of America's and Egypt's partnership, dating back to the Camp David accords. Eva listened attentively. Taking no notes, she agreed with the chairman's opinion that for years, America sent aid to the military-led government of Egypt because it was a stabilizing force in the region.

His voice rose. "The Middle East is a tinderbox. Armed factions battle for control. Our country must make the hard decision. Who deserves our financial and military might? Before bringing in today's witness, let me provide a bit more background."

Eva sat forward, absorbing his every word. When the CIA discovered Russia selling weapons to terrorists in Egypt, the Agency turned to a Russian arms dealer, sending him to meet the Brotherhood. His mission was to discover what weapons they sought, learn where they stored the shipments, and uncover their ultimate target.

"One of our own, NCIS Special Agent Raj Pentu, a native-born Egyptian, went along to interpret for the informant." Whittier yanked off his glasses. "I'm sorry to say the Brotherhood kidnapped these men. Today's witness is the hero responsible for their escape. Hamadi Van Bilgon is a Coptic Christian, and will testify under oath how Coptic Christians are being attacked in Egypt. Special Agent Pentu will translate."

The chairman stood. Eva lifted her head, observing the witnesses emerging from a hidden door. Raj Pentu looked sharp, dressed in a dark suit, white shirt, and gold tie. He was followed by a priest wearing a small black pillbox hat and floor-length black robe. Around his neck dangled a chain with an affixed cross.

Whittier welcomed them both, after they found their seats down front. "Reverend Van Bilgon traveled a great distance to help us understand heightened threats to the Egyptian religious minority. We are thankful."

As he raised his right hand, so did the men. Raj spoke to Hamadi in Arabic, repeating what the chairman said: "Do you swear or affirm to tell the truth, the whole truth, so help you God? Signify by stating, 'I do.'"

Both men stated, "I do."

Whittier started off questioning Hamadi. "What recriminations do Egyptian Christians face these days?"

After Raj repeated the question in Arabic, Hamadi gestured with his hands, letting Raj speak his words, "Egypt is ten percent Christian. We eight million Coptics are brutally attacked by the Egyptian Brotherhood. They blame us for their loss of power. They come after Christian women, violating and enslaving them. They kill us without mercy."

Whittier urged him to "please continue."

Hamadi kept his tone grave. "Last week, forty churches were looted and burned. Fire and explosives damaged twenty-three others. The Brotherhood marks Christian businesses with a red X, while Muslim businesses receive a black X, signaling they are protected. More than one hundred and sixty Christian-owned buildings have been destroyed."

Eva's mind veered to the persecutions detailed in Aunt Deane's journal. Seven hundred years ago enemies of Christ killed His believers, only they were called by different names. It was all so horrendous. Jesus had warned His disciples they would face opposition by those who hated Him.

Eva stiffened as Anna Glinin, the ranking member and most senior of the minority party, said curtly, "I sympathize with your plight. Didn't your Christian church bring this on itself by criticizing the former government made up of the Brotherhood?"

The Coptic priest waited for Raj to interpret. Then he threw his arms up in the air. Raj answered for him, "Do you suggest moral people remain silent in the face of immorality to keep peace? Isn't that what happened in WWII?"

"We desire the truth," she snapped. "Is your cause just or to blame?"

Hamadi glared at Raj, waiting. Once Raj told him what Glinin said, he grew more agitated. There was no stopping Hamadi now, and Raj appeared to struggle to keep up.

"These rebels are ruthless killers. They use loudspeakers in local mosques, and shout lies that Christians attack Muslims. They inflame the people who take the lives of Christians in the streets. It happens over and over. Many Christians are injured and murdered in cold blood, and not just in Egypt.

Make no mistake. Islamic militants will stop at nothing until they rule the Middle East under their caliphate. If you fail to stop them, they will soon seize Saudi Arabia, Syria, and Jordan. They will control all of Africa and Europe, before moving to your White House and the entire world."

Glinin lifted her chin. "You exaggerate and slander a great religion. Let me tell you this. America no longer polices the world. You in the Middle East should stop these bullies yourselves."

Eva was astounded by Anna Glinin's callous attitude. Raj whispered to Hamadi, who simply shook his head as if he, too, couldn't believe her naïve views. A representative from Florida, whose family escaped Cuba years ago, leaned into the microphone.

Marino Flores asked kindly, "What can our nation do to help Christians who struggle against Islamic tyranny?"

Hamadi sat calmly as Raj translated the question, then folded his hands. "My family is all dead. My brother's wife and children were butchered by those who hate Christians with ferocity reminiscent of Genghis Khan and the Mongol hordes. Last week, we buried the bodies of four young men from our church. They were kidnapped and forced to dig a tunnel from Egypt into the Gaza of Israel, so the Brotherhood could smuggle weapons to Hamas. When the digging was complete, the youths were murdered so they wouldn't show the tunnel they'd dug. This is the Brotherhood some of you speak of supporting."

Hamadi blotted tears streaming down his face. "You and your government *must* act against Jihadists. They interpret your silence as approval. We wonder, does the United States sympathize with those who torment us?"

His incisive question filled Eva with dread. Hamadi was right. Evil was triumphing over good. It was the same wicked theology that killed her sister Jillie and so many other innocents on September 11, 2001. Hadn't the sane and good people of the world learned a thing?

Chairman Whittier thanked Hamadi and announced another CIA witness would be called. Raj and Hamadi scurried from the room via the secret door. Eva waited to see if Bo Rider would walk in and testify. Instead, a young woman with gigantic glasses sat at the witness table. Eva didn't recognize her, so she hurried out the back door.

She wanted to follow up on a lead from her interrogation of the Chechen suspects while it was fresh in her mind. Unfortunately, the clues turned out to be a dead end.

Eva spent a quiet evening with her family. Scott played chess with Andy. When their match ended, she told her husband she would be meeting Reverend Van Bilgon at lunch.

"He and other Coptics live knowing each day might be their last."

"What option do they have?" Scott asked.

"The world declares what's wrong is right, and what's right is wrong," Eva lamented. "I thought my stopping the bad guys was getting results. The thugs are winning."

"Speaking of thugs," Scott said, "as Raj and Hamadi walked off the garage elevator after the hearing, a *Washington Star* photographer snapped a picture of him in his robe."

"Oh no! How could that be?" Eva was incredulous.

Scott took out a half-empty carton of frozen yogurt from the freezer. Eva waved off the temptation, demanding he tell her everything.

"Apparently some minority staffer tipped off the press. They claim the committee wants to embarrass the President by blaming him for foreign policy failures."

"The hearing was secret." Eva fought rising anger. "If the *Star* publishes his picture, Hamadi's life will be in danger when he returns to Egypt."

"The garage isn't part of the secret hearing room," Scott said, shoving the carton back in the freezer. "We'll never find out who leaked his presence to the *Washington Star*."

"So you're doing nothing?" Eva raced after him as he went to the family room.

He faced her, concern clouding his eyes. "His photo will be published in tomorrow's paper. The editor blew off our request to pull the story. She said the public has a right to know."

"Have they no shame? A godly man is as good as dead. All to score political points."

"Chill out, Eva. I've scheduled an emergency meeting between Chairman Whittier and the Attorney General. If the article isn't pulled, the chairman will insist the AG grant Hamadi special refugee status so he doesn't have to return to Egypt."

He sat on the sofa, plunging his spoon into the bowl. Eva sat beside him and pinched his cheek.

"That's my honey. You make one terrific Boy Scout."

Eva watched five minutes of the news. The world was falling apart at the seams. An entire town of Iraqi Christians had been wiped out overnight. Tears stung her eyes. Scott shut off the TV and they stared at each other for several moments.

"I'm checking on the kids," she said, jumping to her feet.

"Wait."

He came over and hugged her. She cradled his face with her hands.

"Scott, do you know how much I love you? How much I need you?"

He kissed the palm of her hand, whispering, "Me too."

# CHAPTER 26

E va spun her tires while entering the parking lot in Tysons Corner, fuming. Not because Raj chose this Greek eatery. It was close to Dulles International Airport, and he thought Hamadi would enjoy the food. Rather, it was that Hamadi would catch a return flight back to Egypt later that tied her stomach in knots. The lot was full, so she wedged her Ford Fusion between two oversized trucks.

Seething with anger, she gathered her wits before storming inside. Eva scanned the lunch crowd for Raj and the priest. She hoped he wasn't wearing the black robe and pillbox hat that had shown up in the morning's paper. His photo being trumpeted on the front page was bad enough. But then Scott just phoned with worse news.

The Attorney General refused to intervene for Hamadi, claiming it would open the floodgates to every Middle Eastern Christian.

Scott could only remind Eva to pray for Hamadi's safety once he returned home. True, God's intervention was his only hope. The gentle Egyptian loved the Lord, giving her something in common with the Coptic Christian. They both worshipped the same Jesus. Anguish squeezed her heart. This might be the last time Eva or Raj would see him alive. It was their fault for bringing him here to testify before the U.S. Congress!

She spotted Raj standing and waving at a table. Hamadi was seated, dressed in a gray suit.

Eva came right over. "I'm glad he's not wearing his robe. I presume you saw the paper."

"Correct." Raj grimaced. "Here we want to blend in."

"The AG says he must return home," she whispered.

Raj widened his eyes and spoke to Hamadi in Arabic. Eva heard the Coptic say her name as he graciously shook her hand. They took their seats. The waiter arrived to take their orders, sea bass and vegetables for Raj and Hamadi. Eva stuck to safer fare, a meatball sandwich with chips.

"I told Hamadi that you're like me, a federal enforcement agent and a Christian," Raj said, his voice catching. "I owe him my life. How can we send him back?"

"If only we could ensure his safety," Eva replied through clenched teeth.

From there, conversation flowed with Raj interpreting. Their guest feared for those in his church being mistreated by the rebels. Eva recalled Grandpa Marty hiding Jews from the Gestapo in WWII. She gave Raj a vexed look. It was beyond the pale to think she could hide Hamadi in her basement, wasn't it?

The approaching waiter turned her mind to the food. Hamadi bowed his head, and gave the blessing in Arabic. His calm manner impressed Eva. Greatly admiring his boldness against his tormentors, she ached to help this man who had lost everything.

Raj ate his fish before saying how Hamadi wished his wife and family were here to enjoy his first visit to the U.S. "Unfortunately, the Brotherhood took their lives."

"Tell him I wish I had known his family," Eva replied softly.

She fought the urge to ask about Hamadi's prediction that the Brotherhood would soon control the entire Middle East and Europe. She avoided such a risky topic in a public setting, and instead ate her sandwich. The meatballs rolled in her stomach, the more she dwelt on Hamadi's suffering.

Would she be as strong if her family was killed for believing in Christ? Eva shuddered even thinking that. She wanted to see all her children and Scott live their lives to the fullest.

Eva waited for Hamadi to finish his lunch, then pushed her plate away. She touched Raj's sleeve. "Ask Hamadi how we and my church can pray for him and Christians in Egypt."

Hamadi nodded repeatedly as he responded in his native tongue. "Pray we will be resolute," Raj said for him. "Adversity strengthens our faith in

God's goodness. Without persecution, the joy of our faith might diminish. We suffer for Christ, who suffered for us."

His answer took Eva by surprise. He saw persecution as a good thing? Verses she'd read in her Bible earlier this morning flooded her mind. After Christ's death on the cross and resurrection, the Apostle Peter urged believers to rejoice in affliction for Christ, as the Spirit of God rested on the persecuted.

Eva tried wrapping her mind around this holy truth, coming up short. Respect for Hamadi blossomed into love for her Christian brother.

He raised a hand as he had more to say. Raj told Eva, "Our friend is concerned for the evildoers. Christ is coming to reclaim His church and judge those on earth who reject Him."

"Raj, tell him that I agree. With the wars and rumors of wars, Christ may be coming soon. He taught us to pray for His Kingdom to come." Eva smiled knowingly.

Raj interpreted what she had said, and Hamadi's vibrant smile made it harder for Eva to admit that the U.S. government wanted Hamadi's testimony, but were unwilling to protect him. The committee's leak to the press put him in the greatest possible danger in Egypt. Through Raj, Eva told this dear man that she and her family would be prayer warriors for him and the survivors of his church.

Hamadi thanked her profusely, then excused himself to go to the washroom. Raj directed him to meet them by the entrance, before facing Eva.

"I'm conflicted. Because he saved my life, Hamadi's is at risk."

Eva rubbed the back of her neck. "You'd better explain his picture was in the papers here, which will be seen in Egypt. He needs to be careful."

"I will," Raj agreed. "But this stinks. Why won't the AG grant asylum?"

"The administration is pressured to have no more battles in the Middle East. It makes me want to do something, but what?"

Raj nodded toward the front. "He's waiting by the hostess. I'll make sure he knows to take extra precautions."

They each left money for the bill. Outside the restaurant, Eva opted to hug the priest rather than shake his hand. She squeezed him, a lump forming in her throat. Had they made him an easy target?

Her heart filled with guilt as she slid into her car. Did she and Scott use Reverend Hamadi to advance their careers? Her mind searched for answers. This dear brother was as good as dead if he returned home after being heralded in the Washington newspaper as a secret witness against the Brotherhood. She decided to phone Scott and talk things over.

He answered right away, sounding tense. "How is Hamadi?"

"Scott, I'm bringing him to live with us. He can't return to Egypt."

"No, you can't. Your oath requires you to uphold the law."

"Everyone else in government takes the same oath. Yet my agency turns a blind eye to border security. Terrorists can flood in. We must protect Hamadi, no matter the personal cost."

Scott's tone turned sympathetic. "So you'll drive him home and what—hide him?"

"Yes. I'll call Raj before he gets to the airport, asking him to bring Hamadi to our house."

"Eva, we'll be prosecuted. They'll make a high-publicity example of us to deter others."

He made complete sense and Eva knew it. She surrendered with a sob.

"Okay. But what can we do? He isn't safe."

"Let it go, Eva. We already decided to pray for Hamadi. God has a better plan."

"I'll see you at home." She sniffled. "I've just convinced myself to quit ICE. God has a different plan for me too. Get my drift?"

DURING HER NOON LUNCH AT WASHING HIGH, Eva's daughter Kaley sat across from her friend Lexi at an otherwise empty table. Other students still avoided them. Kaley twirled the stem off her apple. She and Lexi were trying to figure out what the future held. "My mom's okay with me transferring in the fall." Kaley tried to sound cheerful.

Lexi shoved a straw in her milk box. "I'm thinking of the charter school too."

"That letter Mr. Badger mailed about me is wrong. Kids go along with him because they're afraid to step out of line, like sheep."

"Yeah. What other kids do, they do."

"Thanks for being my best friend, Lexi."

Lexi gazed at Kaley, her brown eyes no longer sparkling. "You and me are friends forever, Kaley. I know what it's like being left behind."

"Because of being my friend?" Kaley asked, holding her breath.

"It's more than that. You know I'm adopted, right?"

Kaley nodded. "That makes no difference to me."

"Yeah." Lexi giggled nervously. "My parents used to fight about me. We lived in a flat in Moscow."

"You're from Russia? I never knew that. You have no accent."

"That's because I came to America when I was six. I still remember the day my folks brought me to the orphanage. Neither one wanted me." Lexi's eyes filled with tears.

"Wow." Kaley wiped her eyes. "And I thought Mr. Badger was bad."

Lexi blew her nose on a napkin before saying, "He is terrible, and we shouldn't let him bully us. That's what my mom and dad, you know the Dawsons, taught me. They love me for me, even when I mess up."

"Mom says the same thing. She and Dad want me to stand up for myself."

"So do it," Lexi chimed. "I'll help."

Kaley's eyes widened. She tapped her chin. "What if we wore the same shirts with crosses on them?"

"I like it!" Lexi drank her milk and looked up. "Do you have one like that?"

"No, but we could check at the Christian bookstore."

"I'm off work at seven and they're open till eight. Will your mom take us? I'm not supposed to drive after dark."

The teens gave each other high-fives and finished their lunches. Kaley felt optimistic for the first time in weeks. Later, she and her mom returned home from the mall after dropping Lexi off. Kaley was excited about wearing identical shirts on Monday to Badger's class.

As she headed for her room to try on her shirt, she saw a blinking light on the answering machine. "Mom, we have a message. It might be Lexi."

"I'll get it." Her mom quickly pressed the button.

Kaley waited to hear. There was a scratching sound and a high-pitched voice said, "Mrs. Montanna. This is Dr. Wiles at the Smithsonian. I have more questions than answers about your Bible. Do you have family correspondence with further clues? If so, please call me on Monday."

Kaley rolled her eyes. "Does that mean our trip to Annapolis is off?"

"No, honey. You and Dad go with your brothers. I'll stay home and pretend I'm cramming for homework."

"Homework!" Kaley squealed.

She sped to her room. If she was going to the Naval Academy in the morning, she needed to get busy. Her calculus test was on Monday. On her computer, she found the tutorial her teacher had posted online. It wasn't too hard. She'd just finished when someone knocked at her door. Kaley reached over and pulled it open.

"Time for lights out," Eva said, holding her journal. "Me, I'll be up for a while."

"Why do you have to prove that's our Bible?"

"You said so yourself once. I never let go of an issue until I see it through."

"Oh, Mom, can't you forget what I said to you? I was upset."

Eva came over and patted the bed. Kaley hopped over.

"Sorry to bring up something that bothers you," her mom said, sounding sincere. "You told me how you felt about my pressuring you to stop Mr. Badger. But you're finding your own way of confronting him and I approve."

"You do?"

"Yes, and I approve of you."

Kaley let out a whoop. Life was getting better by the day. She was especially happy for Lexi's support, and now Mom's.

Eva rose, carrying her journal under her arm. "And more than finding proof for Dr. Wiles, this research is for me. You read some for yourself, how our ancestors faced persecution. Though they lived hundreds of years ago, they're helping me deal with my struggles."

Kaley's cell phone rang. She saw it was from Lexi. "Do you mind if I take this?"

Her mom left the room wearing a smile.

Kaley answered Lexi's call. "What's up? I'm almost ready for bed."

"Did you get my e-mail?" Lexi asked. "You won't like it."

"Oh great, someone's blistering me again?"

Kaley toggled to her e-mail account on her computer. There for the whole world to see was a picture of her stuffing a burger in her mouth. Ketchup dripped down her chin. It had been originally posted by someone named "Ivan the Terrible."

Her stomach plunged to her toes and she dropped into her chair.

"Who is he, Lexi?"

"I dunno. Alice McTavish sent it to me, and I forwarded it to you. I'll ask her who Ivan is."

Kaley stared at the gross photo of her, quelling the urge to sob. "Probably Badger made up the name. Wasn't I eating that juicy burger when he walked by me in the cafeteria today?"

"I can't wait to wear our shirts. That will teach him."

Lexi's words had a strange effect on Kaley. She brightened considerably.

"You know what, Lexi? That's exactly what we should be doing. Even though Badger takes the low road, we walk the high road. I won't let him destroy my faith."

"How can you be so calm? I mean, you look disgusting."

Kaley lifted her chin. "Thanks for that. My mom and I just had a great talk. She loves me, and reminded me that my great-great whatevers faced death by burning. They never relented, Lexi, and I won't either. I'll tell you about them on Monday."

The teens said goodnight. Kaley deleted the offending e-mail and shut off her computer. She went to the den and told her mom about Lexi's call.

"You do look shaken. What are you going to do?"

Kaley pocketed her hands. "Not let them get to me. Christ was spat on and rejected. Doesn't the Bible say if God is for me, what can man do to me?"

"Want to stay up with me for a while? I'll read Aunt Deane's journal aloud."

Kaley nodded, and mother and daughter both leaned back on the sofa. Eva shared what happened to Pieter when he came back from St. Barnabas. As with Kaley finding that horrid photo, life for the Vander Goes family did not go as expected, challenging their faith to the very core.

*Jesus said to His disciples, "Peace I leave with you; my peace I give you. I do not give to you as the world gives. Do not let your hearts be troubled and do not be afraid."*

John 14:27 (NIV)

# CHAPTER 27

## MIDDLEBURG, THE NETHERLANDS

Pieter Vander Goes returned from his trip to Saint Barnabas fairly bursting with news for Aneka. He struggled to stay mum while his family ate their dinner. With Justinus away with Angus at school studying Greek, and Dirck in Mainz printing Bibles, it was three of them gathering around the table. Jenny playfully slid a piece of eel around her trencher. Pieter drank his cider, growing antsy. Aneka slowly reached for a slice of bread.

Pieter erupted, "Can't you hurry? I have much to tell you."

"In your library?"

"Yes, now!"

Aneka gazed at Jenny. "Go ask Mollie to bring my dessert to Papa's book room."

"I won't." Jenny tossed her red curls. "He promised to take me riding."

A weary look darted across Aneka's pinched face. Pieter decided to end his daughter's stubbornness once and for all. He walked to her chair, and pulled it away from the table. He took her by the shoulders and set her on her feet.

"Young lady, mind your mama, or you will be confined to your room."

Jenny toyed with a ribbon on her gown. Her green eyes flashed. Then she curtsied and whirled from the room. Pieter propelled Aneka to the library to avoid any more delays. Mollie was there lighting a candle, but left the room. Pieter shut the door.

"I must tell you what I learned of the baby. Please, sit here on the settee."

He held her hands, explaining how he'd met the father of the woman who died giving birth. "Wolfgang Halsma's daughter was named Becca. She was taken advantage of by a priest named Father Gerard."

"Oh, the brute!" Aneka's hands flew to her face.

"Convinced she was with child, and to keep her father from scandal, Becca left home. Father Gerard gave her the silver chalice you found and perhaps money as a guilt offering."

"What did the wolf in sheep's clothing have to say?" she asked, gripping his fingers.

"The scoundrel guessed why we had come, and escaped before we laid eyes on him."

Aneka grew quiet as if reflecting on what should be done. With somber eyes, she asked if the babe's grandfather would travel to see his grandchild.

"Wolfgang is aged," Pieter explained. "His wife, too, died in childbirth. He raised Becca himself, and her death has taken the last bit of life."

"What about the baby?" Tears clung to her lashes.

"You and I are to care for him, if you'd like. You seem so tired and worn out."

Aneka clasped his hands in hers. "Oh, I was worried, but no longer. I love the wee bairn."

"Then you'll be happy Wolfgang signed adoption papers. Everything is settled."

"Not quite."

Aneka handed Pieter a letter from Dirck, who wanted to come home because Mollie had written to him, telling of a stranger lurking about their home.

"What happened while I was away?" Pieter demanded to know.

Aneka dropped his hands and leaned back against the settee. "Alphonso de Alvarado showed up several times. Mollie knows why. I was busy looking after Jenny and the baby."

"I'll write Dirck and inform him that I'm home. Do you agree he should stay with Gutenberg, if he chooses?"

"You decide."

Aneka yawned and went to lie down for a rest. Pieter took out his quill, but before writing a word, he considered Alphonso's peculiar and unwelcome visits. Pieter laid down his quill and found Mollie caring for the infant, who was wailing loudly. He let Mollie be.

Instead, he walked along the river, questioning if he and Aneka pursued the right course by adopting another child. Jenny was already a handful. A noisy crow cawing about his head only magnified his doubts.

Still perplexed, Pieter joined Aneka in their sleeping chamber. He lit a candle and sat by her, smoothing her long hair.

"I have let you down in many ways," he admitted.

"After Jenny's birth, I sensed you slipping away. The wee child heralds a new beginning for you and me."

Pieter cupped her face in his hands. "Are you sure? Promise to share your heart fully with me, and I will share mine with you."

She trilled a merry laugh. It had been years since his wife sounded so happy, and Pieter realized their marriage completed him far more than the farm ever did. Aneka was his life's partner, given to him as a blessing by God. He regretted time wasted on superfluous matters.

Before he could tell her of an idea that occurred to him journeying back from Saint Barnabas, she smiled.

"You ask about my heart's desire. I have longed to pray with you," she replied shyly. "May we do so now?"

For the first time in their marriage, husband and wife united their hearts before God in thanksgiving. Their tender moment was interrupted by the baby's piercing cry.

"I should see to the child. Are we to call him Wolfie? That's too harsh for a baby."

"What do you suggest?"

"Alexander Douglas, after your Scottish grandfather. Do you agree?"

Pieter did like the name. He held the lamp as they went down the hall. The moment they stepped into the baby's room, Mollie entered, breathing hard.

"Good. Yer seein' to the bairn."

Aneka picked up Alexander, while Mollie motioned for Pieter to follow her.

Out in the hall, her hands flew to her hips. "Ye best be lookin' fer the scoundrel Alphonso."

"Aneka mentioned he'd stopped by and talked to you, Mollie. Why are you worried?"

After wiping her lined face, she told how Justinus had found Alphonso and his horse on a far corner of Pieter's land, carrying a shovel, and saying he'd been trapping pelts. "Something or someone dragged away his trap," she sputtered.

"Justinus didn't tell me," Pieter said, then realized his mistake. His son was now away at school.

Mollie waved her hand as if it was of no matter. She had more to tell. During Pieter's absence, she'd caught Alphonso in the barn sharing whiskey with Fitch. Later, Pieter's groom had confided to her that Alphonso offered him a job.

"That one's up to no good," she concluded, struggling for breath after such a long speech.

"Mollie, thanks for being so alert. Maybe Aneka can use your help with the wee one."

The good woman that she was, Mollie went immediately to the baby's room. Pieter sprinted down the stairs. Was Alphonso spying on the family? If so, his treachery might be far-reaching. Even more troubling was Fitch colluding with him. Pieter vowed to keep a closer eye on his family.

PIETER FOUND TIME TO WORK ON HIS IDEA FOR A NEW SCHOOL. He and Maxim were inspecting the premises before it opened to students. Pieter gazed with satisfaction on the refurbished rooms. Soon, Steven and Father Cornelius would teach fifty boys from Middleburg and surrounding towns mathematics, history, and the Scriptures.

Pieter adjusted his cloak. "Angus will participate too, once he returns with Justinus."

"Will Gutenberg's Bible be ready for the dedication?" Maxim wondered aloud.

"Dirck's reply hasn't yet come from Mainz."

"Then we will use the abbey's Wycliffe Bible until the proper time."

Maxim locked the door behind them. On the way to the abbey, he said in a low tone, "The bishop is investigating Father Gerard, but I've heard nothing since."

"Gerard assaults a young woman, yet remains as priest? I will notify Duke Philip."

"The duchy's power supports the church's power. We at the abbey try to live honorably. However, corruption in the church is widespread, as you know."

"More reason for our school to teach of Christ's humility and compassion for the weak. Have you seen Count de Alvarado or his son in town in recent days?"

Maxim rubbed his chin. "Not that I recall. You sound concerned."

"You always could read my thoughts." Pieter looked over his shoulder. "Alphonso had the temerity to bribe my groom with whiskey to spy on me. He offered him a job."

"To what purpose? What does he hope to gain?"

"Information is power, and to that family, power is their lifeblood. His actions are not criminal, not yet. Still, I mean to stay alert for the danger they pose my family."

Maxim laid a hand on his arm. "Go with God, my friend. All will be well."

They parted and Pieter met with Captain Van Ritter, who was in between voyages. He agreed to bring Dirck home. "Perhaps two months from now," was Pieter's best guess.

He rode home on Willow, determined to protect his family at all costs. Without reservations, he wrote:

*To the Honorable Duke Philip:*

*I am your loyal servant and do not take lightly writing to you of troubling matters in the duchy. Consider the Bishop of Utrecht's investigation of Father Gerard at St. Barnabas. You should seek an immediate report of his conduct, which has brought stain upon the church. In addition, Count de Alvarado's son, Alphonso, has caused mischief with my staff. With this message, I am attaching a list of my past decisions and the results, as you requested.*

Pieter signed the note, and sealed it with his ring. After attaching his report, he rolled the parchment together and tied it with a string. He would find a messenger in town and not trust this to Fitch. With his daily agenda accomplished, Pieter looked forward to spending time with Aneka, and reading her some poetry.

# CHAPTER 28

T wo days later, Pieter was overseeing the rye harvest when Justinus came riding up with a burst of speed on the new mare. He finished his schooling and brought startling news.

"Papa, I just arrived home. Duke of Philip is waiting."

Pieter spun his head around. "You mean he sent me a message?"

"No! Mollie seated him in your library. Mama is all a twitter, trying to put a meal together. She says you'd best come quickly."

Pieter mounted Willow hastily. Why the duke was in his home with no warning, he couldn't fathom. He and Justinus raced on their mounts, passing a grand carriage with two beautiful horses waiting out front. Justinus jumped off the mare. Fitch snatched the reins. Pieter followed suit, wiping dust from his work clothes. He ran his fingers through his hair.

"Hurry, Papa," Justinus urged.

"I can't think of what he wants, unless he replies to my message in person."

Pieter strode into the manor house, going straight to the library. Duke Philip sat warming his hands by the fire. He looked elegant in a burgundy hat and cloak. The Order of the Golden Fleece was draped around his shoulders. Pieter straightened his sleeves, desperately trying to look presentable.

"Your Grace, I am sorry to keep you waiting. I never received word of your coming."

Duke Philip motioned Pieter to the fire. "That is because my trip to Middleburg is secret. I want no record made of our discussion. Close the door."

Pieter complied instantly. This sounded serious.

"Have you received my messages about Count de Alvarado and his son?" The duke's long and narrow face paled. "I did not! What has he done?"

What should Pieter tell him? The truth was best. He quickly explained his ruling when Count de Alvarado had sued Harmon Van Fleet. The count was an official for Duke Philip and Pieter was treading dangerous ground.

"Your Grace, I did not approve of his corrupt dealings in lending money to poor farmers, only to seize their lands when they were unable to pay. You seem to find it acceptable. As a result, I sent you a letter of resignation. When I never—"

Duke Philip snorted loudly. "I do nothing of the sort. Who spreads such lies?"

Pieter showed him two letters he had received from him.

Duke Philip raised a fist angrily and proclaimed, "These are forgeries."

"So that's why you never replied. I just assumed ... well, I don't know what I thought. Your Grace, why are you here?" Pieter asked in trepidation.

The duke pressed a finger to his lips. "You may know of your father's service to me years ago in my marriage to the duchess. He accompanied my delegation, along with the master painter, Jan Van Eyck, who is no longer with us. His services are greatly missed."

"Yes, I am aware my father assisted you in Portugal."

The duke dropped his voice to a bare whisper. "You were present last year at the grand feast when I vowed to fight the Turks."

"Yes, sire. You were greatly concerned with Mehmet II's Ottoman forces firing on Constantinople. That great Christian city has fallen to the Turks."

"Which is why I want you to sail to England and present my message, in person, to King Henry."

Duke Philip handed him a rolled parchment tied with black and burgundy ribbons.

"May I know its contents?"

"To rally support against the Turks and the Ottoman Empire."

Pieter held the parchment close to his heart. "It is my honor to serve you."

Duke Philip briefed Pieter on what strategy he was to convey, and Pieter told him of his last message regarding Father Gerard and Alphonso's conduct. The duke agreed to look into both matters. Pieter saw him to his carriage, leaving his Sovereign with a chivalrous bow.

If his sudden visit hadn't disturbed Pieter's inner calm, the message Aneka brought him thirty minutes later did. She rested a hand on his shoulder.

"This just arrived from Count de Alvarado. He and his son want to call for dinner."

Pieter flinched. What fast work by those two charlatans.

"He must have already heard of the duke being here. Instruct the staff to say nothing of his visit. I must hurry and find Van Ritter."

Pieter rode into town with a new proposal for the captain. He needed to reach England as soon as may be.

WHEN PIETER RETURNED HOME, HE FOUND Jenny sprawled on the kitchen floor. Her right arm was swollen and red. Mollie scooted over with a clean cloth. Justinus stood by the hearth with something akin to fear in his eyes.

Pieter pressed the cloth against her wound. "Jenny, what happened?"

She bit her lip as if trying not to cry. "It hurts, Papa."

"Justinus, how was your sister injured?"

"I do not know. She was in the barn with me yesterday and started scratching."

Aneka entered as fast as she could in her constricting gown, demanding, "What is wrong with my little girl?"

Tears plunged down Jenny's pink cheeks. "I was in the hay. Something bit my arm, Papa."

"But you don't know what animal?" Pieter asked, gazing closely at her reddening skin.

Jenny shook her head and began coughing. Mollie applied an herb poultice to her forearm, and covered it with a cloth. Pieter lifted her in his strong arms. He carried her to her chamber where Aneka arranged her bedclothes.

"I need to change into fresh garments before our dinner guests arrive," she said. "Jenny, try to sleep. We will return to check on you."

Jenny moaned as she shifted on her bed. Aneka cooed to her gently.

After Pieter changed his cloak, he opened the front door himself, ushering in Count de Alvarado and Alphonso. The three of them made small talk of crops until Aneka and Justinus joined their party. Count de Alvarado made a show of presenting a wrapped book.

"What do you bring us?" Pieter asked, doubting the count's sincerity.

Count de Alvarado bowed slightly. "I have the honor of returning the valuable Bible stolen from you."

"Pieter!" Aneka cried, tearing off the wrapping. "It's our Wycliffe Bible!"

"How did you find it?" Pieter narrowed his eyes to slits.

Just then, Mollie announced dinner. Everyone took their assigned seats according to cards Aneka had placed on the table. She carefully set the Bible on the sideboard.

Aneka smiled profusely. "You have blessed us with a wonderful surprise. I would love to read from the Bible after dinner, if I may."

Sitting at the head of the table, Pieter mulled over the sudden appearance of de Alvarado with Pieter's Bible. Surely, the scheming count hadn't simply stumbled upon it. He'd wait until the meal's end to press him for the truth.

Mollie came in, clucking her tongue. It wasn't too hard to figure out she was upset at Pieter for allowing these shifty characters into his home. But Count de Alvarado was a counselor to Duke Philip. Pieter owed him some courtesy, didn't he?

As Mollie held a large dish by his side, the count heaped some on his plate. "Creamed rabbit is my favorite, Lady Vander Goes. Such an excellent meal is hard to find here in the Low Countries. I apologize for short notice, yet I learned only yesterday of Duke Philip's desire for me to consult with your husband."

Aneka blushed at his continual compliments. She glanced sideways at Pieter before replying, "After dessert, you and my husband may confer in his library. Will Alphonso join you or does he want to hear me read aloud from our Bible you found for us?"

Pieter cast an icy stare at Alphonso. The black-haired young man watched everyone with raven-like eyes. He rarely smiled, which came as no surprise to Pieter, being raised by such a wily father.

"Although I am eager for Alphonso to be included in my business, he will attend your reading," the count said with a firm nod at his son.

Alphonso tightened his jaw. Pieter sought to lighten the mood.

"My son is close to Alphonso's age. Dirck learns the duties of this estate but is away at present on business."

"I will listen to you, Mama." Justinus squared his shoulders. "Our treasured Scriptures have been missing for too long."

The meal progressed until a local girl, hired to help with the party, brought in the final course—cheese custard tarts topped with sliced pears and almonds soaked in spices. Alphonso flashed his white teeth at the pretty maiden.

*Well, he knows how to smile after all,* Pieter mused, detecting something artificial in his smile. He cast off worries of the son to concentrate on the father's true motive in coming. Most likely Count de Alvarado had forged Duke Philip's prior letters to Pieter. He led the count into the library where a roaring fire blazed.

"Tell me how you found my Bible," Pieter began.

The count took his time selecting a soft, cushioned chair. "I understood you posted a reward. My son and I sent out word for the item to be found. Because I am the duke's councilor, I have power to compel people to confess the truth. One such source came to me last night. He heard a groom bragging how he'd purchased it from another groom."

"Was this Fitch, my groom?"

The count flicked his hand. "You have no concerns there. You know how stories circulate. Indeed, my source brought me the Wycliffe Bible before we had left for your home."

"Then I shall pay you the reward." Pieter was certain he faced the thief.

He went to his desk and counted out one thousand *veirlander.* The count's eyes glittered as Pieter laid the cash in his open palm, which rapidly folded over the money.

"Now, Pieter, I am interested in what cases you've decided since the unfortunate Van Fleet affair."

Pieter simply gave a vague account of his work, prompting the count to inquire how the widow Van Fleet fared.

"Not well." Pieter tossed a log on the fire. "Harmon's debts were enormous. Mrs. Van Fleet sells off a piece of land at a time to pay creditors."

"She still owes a large debt to the duchy. So she remains a widow?"

"When Aneka and I saw her a fortnight ago, she said nothing of finances."

The count fingered the gold chain dangling around his neck. "Duke Philip mentioned a large tract of land under obligation to him by a former knight. He wants this valuable land, which happens to be the Van Fleet property."

"I see," Pieter said, doubting the duke proposed the idea. "Perhaps you are vying to be awarded the Order of the Golden Fleece?"

The count raised his chin. "Duke Philip wants a signed deed placed into my hands. Will you help me obtain it?"

"I must consider what is to be done. Call back in the morning."

"That is your final word?"

"It has to be. I must see to my child who takes to her bed."

"You may regret putting family ahead of duty."

Count de Alvarado swirled from the room, leaving in a huff with his son. Pieter hurried to his daughter. Aneka sat by her side, placing a cloth on her forehead. Her eyes were shut. Jenny thrashed her head from side to side. A sharp cry escaped her cracked lips. In between violent coughs, she talked nonsense.

"She is extremely hot." Aneka looked terrified. "Will you send for the doctor?"

"Justinus can fetch you cool water from the spring. I will bring Dr. Van Kalk myself."

On the way to find his son, Pieter passed Mollie in the kitchen cooking over the fire.

"I'm makin' Jenny special herbs."

Mollie's eyes darted in fright and she stirred more vigorously. Pieter ran to ask Justinus to pull water from the spring, telling him Jenny was quite ill.

"After bringing water to your mama, you make her rest. I am off to the doctor's."

# CHAPTER 29

Pieter hurried into town where he conveyed the urgency to the doctor, who rode immediately to the manor house. The count's dubious conduct and threat he posed to Pieter's family compelled Pieter to call on Mrs. Van Fleet. The housekeeper showed him to a sitting room where the widow straightened a cap covering her white hair.

"Lord Vander Goes, I'm afraid I do not have long."

"Are you also ill?" Pieter asked with alarm.

"My financial ailments plague me every day."

Relieved she did not have Jenny's sickness, he said, "Forgive my bluntness. I offer you a loan to pay creditors. I meant to come earlier, but Jenny is ill. I rode first to Doctor Van Kalk's."

The woman burst into tears. "You are so kind."

"We just have to agree on the terms."

Pieter withdrew a blank parchment from his cloak. Seeing the many crates, he asked if she needed help.

She dabbed her eyes. "I sold all my property before you arrived."

"Did Count de Alvarado purchase your land?"

"How did you know?"

"I made an unfortunate guess. Will you have enough to pay your creditors?"

"The duchy and merchants are satisfied in full," she muttered, a faraway look in her eye. "I soon travel to my daughter's home in Friesland to care for my grandchildren."

Pieter returned the parchment to his cloak. "Why was the count so eager for your land?"

"He wants the salt flats." Tears welled in her eyes. "I tried to hold on, to keep a tiny bit of my father's inheritance for my daughter when I am gone."

Pieter suddenly grasped the import of the count's purchase.

"Salt! No wonder Harmon wanted to keep de Alvarado from getting your land. Burgundy's new agreement to sell salt to England and Portugal makes your land twice as valuable. The count is a clever fellow."

"You say Harmon wanted to keep the count from owning this land? Did I do wrong?"

"You had no choice," Pieter soothed, placing a bag of coins on the table. "This is a gift from Aneka. Perhaps it will help you retain the house-keeper. I regret not arriving in time."

Widow Van Fleet wiped away her tears. "Will your daughter be all right?"

Her question startled Pieter into reality. He must return home!

Willow made the return trip with great speed. Pieter watched the doctor make an incision in Jenny's arm. Bright red blood bubbled forth. A stream gathered in a ceramic bowl placed under her arm. After a suitable amount flowed from her swollen arm, the doctor pressed a white cloth on the cut to stop the blood. Jenny coughed during the entire procedure, yet never awakened.

Van Kalk lifted her arm, revealing an ugly, purple bloated lump. "This is how it begins. Her cough means the disease has spread deep into her body."

He stuffed materials in a case. "Everyone must leave this room at once."

Pieter and Aneka scurried out with him. Justinus went to wait beneath the oak tree. Once outside in the fresh air, the doctor ordered them to send Justinus away, along with the baby. He instructed Pieter to clean the house and barn. Whoever had contact with Jenny was in danger of the sickness.

Aneka pressed her hands to her cheeks. "Is our daughter strong enough to survive?"

"You must prepare yourselves. Years ago, the Great Pestilence—or the plague—killed thousands upon thousands." The doctor's shoulders contracted. "This outbreak spreads from Italy to England. A colleague wrote of several deaths here already. If you stay, light hot fires and sit by them. Burn incense throughout the house."

"Is there any hope?" Pieter's mouth felt so dry, he could hardly speak.

"Jenny's life hangs in the balance. There is no known cure. Some survive. More die in a short period of time. You may want Maxim to administer the last rites."

With that horrifying news, the doctor mounted his horse. Then he thrust in a final jab. "I won't return unless someone else is stricken. There's nothing I can do."

He rode away fast, like the wind. Pieter had difficulty absorbing the tragedy. His wife fell to pieces before his eyes.

She ran into the house shouting, "Our little girl! I won't leave her!"

"Papa, I have prayed for my sister," Justinus said. "I will ask Maxim to come." Justinus marched toward the barn. Pieter strode alongside him, urging him to stress the seriousness. "He can decide if he wants to take the risk. Hurry, my son."

"Maxim will come, Papa. And do not send me away!"

Pieter hustled to find Mollie, directing her to light fires and clean the house. Roos fled to the village with baby Alexander. Standing beneath the giant oak tree, Pieter wanted to trust. How could he simply wait for his daughter's life to end at any moment?

He cried aloud, "Almighty God, Holy One. I am Your poor servant. Please spare the life of my daughter!"

THE NEXT EVENING, the sun cast purple shadows through the windows of Pieter's home before vanishing from the sky. He tried in vain to convince Aneka to leave the sickroom. She refused.

"Dearest, then stay near the fire as the doctor ordered."

Mollie entered the room declaring, "I'm an old one, noo. The good Lord can take me as He will. My lord an' lady, stay alive fer Jenny when she's better. And the baby."

"Mollie is right." Pieter pressed his hand against Aneka's arm.

With reluctance, she agreed to leave long enough to eat some herbal pottage Mollie had cooked. Pieter saw to the barn being swept and cleaned. Justinus relocated animals to the field. Fitch had gone to stay with his mother. Maxim had come, and stayed to provide whatever comfort he could.

Jenny woke for mere seconds. Mollie boiled special herbs for her to sip when she revived. She stewed figs with aloe, spreading this paste on purple lumps growing on Jenny's arm. Aneka hovered over the child. At midnight, she joined Pieter and Maxim in the library. They gathered around a blazing fire.

Pieter grabbed her hand. "Is Jenny any better?"

Aneka shook her head and left immediately to check on her. The silence accompanying her absence nearly overpowered Pieter. He clasped his hands so tightly they hurt.

He flung his head toward Maxim. "When my mother was ill, my boy heart never believed she'd die. But she did, and my grief was profound. I cried for days and failed to understand my father's lack of emotion."

"God is love, Pieter. He cares for Jenny more than you do. We must cling to His perfect plan for her."

Aneka bustled into the room, and Pieter's heart leapt with fear. She soon set his mind at ease.

"She sleeps more quietly. Pieter, I have never been so afraid."

"Me either, not even when Dirck was injured in Mainz."

He wrapped his arms around her, and they held one another. Maxim slipped out.

Pieter wiped her tears. "We will get through this. We must."

"Please stay well," she whispered. "I could not bear living without you."

Pieter pressed his lips against her damp hair.

"I love you as much as life," he told her tenderly.

Without warning, Maxim appeared in front of them. He inhaled sharply.

"Jenny's eyes are open. She is asking for you both."

Aneka sped away. Pieter followed close behind. The sight of his lovely girl's green eyes looking at him moved Pieter deeply. Aneka stroked her daughter's hair and placed another cool cloth on her head.

"Love you, Mama," Jenny croaked between coughs.

She shut her eyes. Soon, the coughing stopped. Her breathing became regular. Aneka kissed her cheeks and hands. Pieter took his wife away to rest. She shivered. He helped her to their sleeping chamber where he placed a woolen blanket over her. He pled with her to sit by the fire. She did as he asked. Heaping on more logs, Pieter soon had the fire crackling with heat.

"Stay warm," he commanded. "I will fetch some hearty pottage."

Aneka seemed to sag by the fire. "I am worn to the bone, but rejoice at Jenny's loving words. I'll never forget them."

Pieter left her to rest and become warm. Returning with a steaming cup of Mollie's brew, Aneka had fallen asleep. He sat beside her, and drank the contents himself. In moments, he too went to sleep with an arm flung around his wife. In the middle of the night, Pieter awoke with a start. He saw Justinus adding wood to the fire. Pieter sat up, rubbing his face.

"Forgive me for waking you," Justinus said. "A message arrived earlier."

Pieter held out his hand. "Let me have it."

"It's in your library."

Pieter covered Aneka with the blanket, and motioned for Justinus to come along quietly. He ducked into his library. The message took him by surprise.

*Pieter, I write unfortunate news. Johann Fust took me to court and won. Though the Bible is nearly printed, I am forced to leave the entire shop, printing presses, and every Bible with him. Your son Dirck has my approval to stay with Fust and Schöffer to see the Bible completed.*

*Yours in Christ, Johann Gutenberg*

How could this have happened? Pieter's first desire was to have Van Ritter take him to Mainz. Then his mind righted itself. A trip was impossible. Jenny was improving, but just. To leave Aneka alone would be heartless. How could he travel to England next week on Duke Philip's secret mission? He wrote to Gutenberg and Dirck. Then Pieter dropped to his knees, pouring out his heart to his new best friend, Jesus.

# CHAPTER 30

## MAINZ, GERMANY

The city of Mainz was unusually quiet. However, the silent dawn amplified the tumultuous emotions churning inside of Dirck Vander Goes. Sadness filling his chest as he stood outside Gutenberg's former home, he gazed up at the cantilevered windows. Last year when he'd arrived here with his father, how thrilled he'd been to help with Gutenberg's printing device. Now the great inventor was departing, never to return.

Dirck turned, asking his mentor, "Herr Gutenberg, where will you go?"

"Friends urge me to continue printing the Bible and important manuscripts."

"Are you sure Wilhelm and I can't accompany you?"

"Wait here until I am settled." Gutenberg looked him squarely in the eye. "Promise me you will stay with Fust and see the Bibles, all three hundred and ten of them, are finished. You want to be a printer, so it is wise to complete your work here."

Dirck choked back a sob. "I promise, sir. The same goes for Wilhelm."

"Good. Then I am content my life's work is properly cared for."

Herr Gutenberg fastened his cloak about his neck. Dirck was surprised how gaunt the printer's face looked beneath his long beard. A rush of regret filled him. Dirck was powerless to help the man who had led him to his life's calling. Herr Gutenberg started down the street.

"There goes an honorable man," Dirck whispered. "I will see other people know it too."

*Click click click.*

The master printer's walking stick made its pitiful sound on the cobblestones long after Dirck lost sight of him. When all traces of Herr Gutenberg disappeared, Dirck returned to the shop. The place he'd called home for months belonged to another, one less worthy. He climbed the three floors to his garret room, taking several steps at a time. Wilhelm splashed water onto his face from a metal basin.

"Well, he's gone," Dirck said soberly.

Wilhelm toweled his face. "Who? Fust?"

"I wish. No, Herr Gutenberg has flown away like a grand bird to find a new nest."

"Nice poetry, Dirck, but I fail to understand you. Gutenberg is to hand the keys to Fust at breakfast along with a complete explanation of the printing operation."

"If that is Fust's plan, I am happy Gutenberg foiled it. I said good-bye to him minutes ago. Where he goes, I know not."

"And to think I slept through his departure," Wilhelm grumbled.

Dirck dropped to his unmade bed. "Two things I know. With Schöffer staying on, Fust doesn't need Gutenberg telling him anything. I suspect he hoped to humiliate Gutenberg."

Wilhelm tied his working apron around his waist, then tossed Dirck his leather apron. "What's the other thing?" he prodded.

"I promised Herr Gutenberg that you and I will make sure every Bible is printed. We have five chapters in The Revelation yet to go. All should be completed within weeks."

"This is a regrettable moment, but you are right. We soldier on," Wilhelm replied.

Dirck lightly punched Wilhelm's arm. "I want history to record it was Gutenberg, and not Fust, who printed the first Bible."

"My friend," Wilhelm quipped, lightly returning the punch. "To make your deadline, we must work night and day."

BACK IN MIDDLEBURG, Pieter returned from the far field where he'd taken oats to the horses. As he neared the barn, Mollie scampered up to him, gasping for breath.

"I dinna like the looks of yer wife!"

Pieter dropped the bucket where he stood. "Send for the doctor!"

He ran up the steps two at a time. Aneka lay on the bed, her hair matted to her forehead.

"My darling, can you hear me?"

"Oohh," she moaned, her eyelids fluttering.

Pieter's hand shook as he placed a cool cloth on her brow. He waited with a racing heart until Van Kalk arrived. The doctor looked at Aneka, cut her arm, and drained her blood. Some minutes later, he removed the bowl from her arm.

"Pieter, you recall, I urged her to leave. She is feverish."

"Yesterday, she went for fresh air and slept. I thought …"

Pieter's heart was breaking. He would do anything to save his beautiful wife.

"I will not command you to leave her. You all are in danger of the Great Pestilence."

In hushed tones, the doctor implored Pieter to bleed her again in an hour, and the next. He needed to stoke the fires, and get them blazing hot.

Van Kalk collected his instruments. "I understand how committed you are to God. Only He can save her now."

Mollie crept in quietly, carrying a clean bowl. She promised to help with the bleeding. Deep worry lines creased her face as she whispered, "I ken how."

Doctor Van Kalk went to bleed Jenny as well, before hurrying to call on other sick patients. Jenny slept peacefully, which allowed everyone to attend Aneka. Pieter watched, horrified as her skin turned purple. More lumps appeared.

"No more bleeding, Mollie," Pieter said. "It's not helping. Bring your cooked herbs. Light more incense to clear the foul air."

Pieter longed for his cousin to be here, but he did not know how to reach Angus, who was preaching in the north. In his stead, Justinus rode once again for Maxim, who had gone to the abbey after Jenny had rallied. Pieter sat by Aneka with his head in his hands, his faith in God a fleeting memory. Where was all his boasting about following God's plan?

Agony pierced his soul with each labored breath Aneka took. Her coughing and suffering nearly drove him mad. Such unbelief was wrong, he knew. God loved Aneka in ways Pieter could not understand. Something else was clear to him. He didn't want to live without her.

At a swishing sound, Pieter looked up to see Maxim entering without a word.

"She will take no broth," Pieter blurted.

He jumped up and paced by the blazing fire, his heart torn into pieces. Maxim urged him to come outside and walk with him. Pieter refused.

Maxim folded his hands. "Pieter, you and Aneka are unified in Christ as one body. You must care for yourself."

Pieter hastened to her side and stroked hair clinging to her forehead. Justinus came in asking how she was doing.

"Is she better like Jenny?" His youthful eyes were full of hope.

"She worsens, like my mother." Pieter sobbed. "Like my mother! Oh God, no."

Justinus wrung his hands. "I will ask Mollie to make another poultice."

He rushed out. Maxim knelt by the chair. Hands folded, he was silent in the room while Aneka moaned softly. Anguish pushed Pieter to his knees. He uttered prayers for the life of the woman he loved desperately and so wanted to be healed.

The night passed. Pieter rarely left her side. The only time she was alone was when he went for fresh water. At dawn's first light, he lifted his head and watched Aneka closely. Her eyes opened.

"Aneka, dear Aneka," Pieter said in tremendous relief. "You are getting well!"

Her lips moved, and he lunged forward, straining to hear.

She whispered softly, "Pieter, my love … my life. Jesus comes for me."

"Oh, my darling! Do not leave me!"

A bright light hovered about the room and quickly faded.

"Aneka, Aneka!" he cried.

Pieter kissed her cheeks, his lips wet with tears. She was beyond his reach.

Maxim touched her wrist, and gripped Pieter's shoulder. "Her soul joins her beloved Savior."

Pieter gaped at her peaceful face. She had left him then!

Never was he more alone than in that heart-wrenching moment. With her gone from the earth, it was as if life had fled his body too.

"What about my prayers? Did God turn His back on me?"

Maxim gently closed her eyelids. "Her Savior loves her, Pieter. Never forget that."

"You say that, but how can I go on without her?"

"For the children, you must."

Pieter groaned. "How will I ever tell them? Their mama is gone!"

He dropped his face into his hands and wept bitter tears.

# CHAPTER 31

Life dragged by for Pieter, his days passing in a thick fog. Jenny shrieked when she heard of her mama's death. She took to climbing the tall tree, and stared down the road as if Aneka would somehow appear. Mollie finally coaxed her down with a promise that Dirck would soon be home.

He did return on Van Ritter's vessel, the same one that took him to Mainz with such high hopes. Angus arrived the following day, full of sorrow for what the family suffered in his absence. When the steward walked off one morning, Angus was there for Pieter. He suggested in his firm Scottish way that Dirck take charge of the farm, with Justinus' help. Angus saw to the burial arrangements. He walked with Pieter along the river, saying nothing, but making it known he was there for him no matter what.

Seeing his three children together without Aneka brought stinging tears to Pieter's eyes. One afternoon, Mollie brought him a message from Duke Philip, expressing his condolences, but asking when Pieter would be able to fulfill his mission to England. Pieter had no idea.

He stalked to the river to think. Instead, the flowing water made him more bereft. He was a hollow man, with no purpose, no plan. How could Pieter undertake to do anything for the duke, when he had no interest in anything?

Sounds of footsteps caused him to turn. Angus came alongside him, carrying something.

"Yer Wycliffe Bible drew me at sunrise," was all he said.

Angus waited for Pieter to ask what he meant, and then told him how he'd gone into the study to prepare a lesson for Justinus. He picked up the Wycliffe Bible, spotting a parchment inside. Angus hadn't read this parchment, which he now handed to Pieter.

Puzzled, Pieter seized the note. He instantly recognized Aneka's fluid writing. Overcome with grief, he forced himself to read her words:

*Pieter,*

*Having our Wycliffe Bible returned is like dawn bursting forth. Clouds are rolled away. Just as you shared your deep and abiding love for me, I now understand the Father's love for me is real. He sent Jesus to die on a wooden cross, but He rose for me, for you. What do you think of my poem? I wrote it after reading the book of John:*

*God's love is powerful, eternal. He gave His Son, the one and only.*

*I believe in Jesus, the one and only Savior. Tho' I die, I will never perish.*

Pieter wanted to cry out in pain, but restrained himself with Angus there. His wife must have written this days before she'd become so ill. Without a word, he handed Angus the parchment and slumped against a tree trunk, wiping tears from his eyes.

At length, Angus came over, clapping a hand on his shoulder.

"Aneka was amazin'. She is with Jesus for eternity. What more can ye ask?"

Angus was right, but Pieter found it hard to absorb. He took Aneka's parchment back from Angus with a probing question, "Will you show me these verses in John? My wife had more interest in this Bible than I did, to my deep shame."

Beneath the tree, Angus read aloud chapter 3 of John, verse 16. Pieter traced the words, written by Wycliffe himself in dark ink more than seventy years ago.

Light began to dawn on Pieter. "Although Aneka and I are parted, will we be joined with Jesus for eternity? This is what it means, right?"

"Now ye ken why I preach God's Holy Word. He wants no one to be lost."

Relieved of a heavy burden, Pieter walked home with Angus. Jenny was back up in the tree. She refused to come down, which caused Pieter to believe a change would do both of them good. He would take her to England, where they could visit his aunt and uncle. So he quickly wrote to Lord and Lady Douglas. Two weeks later, father and daughter sailed for England where Pieter met with King Henry's ministers. He caught wind of a great rift between Richard, the Duke of York, who had ruled as the country's "Lord Protector," and King Henry VI, who most recently had regained his senses.

Talk of war was in the air. Pieter began to better understand Angus' warnings of treacherous times in England. He was grateful to leave Windsor Castle and King Henry's conflicted court. Having done his duty in conveying Philip's wishes, Pieter doubted anything would come of the duke's quest to stop the Turks from seizing lands east of the Netherlands.

Pieter and Jenny spent a few quiet days with his aunt and uncle. When it was time to leave, Jenny clung to Aunt Emilee.

"But I don't want to go, Papa," Jenny said, cuddling Emilee's small dog.

Pieter voiced another possibility. "Aunt Emilee and Uncle Douglas can visit us. When you're old enough, you can come here and stay with them for several months."

"Can Monty go home with us?"

Pieter glanced at his aunt. Emilee rose from the fire and rested a hand on Jenny's head. "I will sail to Middleburg soon, and bring you a puppy of your own. Would you like that?"

Jenny's lips curled into a smile. Her red curls bounced as she nodded her agreement. Emilee motioned for Pieter to join her and his uncle in an adjoining room. Emilee faced him with a tender look in her bright eyes.

"Aneka wrote me before her death, sharing how she had saved baby Alexander. Are you able to raise the infant alone?"

"I have not thought … What are you suggesting?"

Emilee took her husband's hands in her own. Douglas cleared his throat.

"Your mother, my sister, too died young. She left Scotland when I was a wee lad myself. God has not blessed me and my wife with children. If He leads you to be the child's father, we completely understand."

Emilee's dark eyes glistened. "Our hearts go with you, Pieter. You are not alone."

Pieter reflected on their hopes for the boy's future. Emilee and Douglas would be able to provide emotionally and financially for the baby. He closed his eyes briefly, seeking some sign as to what Aneka would want him to do. Then it hit him squarely between the eyes.

"Aneka chose his name, Alexander Douglas, after you, Uncle Douglas. I think she had you in mind all along."

And so it was arranged for them to come to Middleburg within the month. There were legalities to see to, and Pieter wanted to discuss the changes with Wolfgang Halsma, assuming the grandfather still lived. Pieter slept soundly that night, believing he was in the center of God's will. The next morning, he and Jenny boarded a vessel three times the size of Van Ritter's boat, and set sail on the English Channel.

While rough weather greeted them on the water, Pieter was unconcerned. He loved the sea.


Dirck was excited about his father's homecoming. Justinus and Angus were away for the afternoon, teaching at the Vander Goes School. Dirck and Mollie were deep into celebration plans when Justinus barged into the kitchen. The sight of his brother's blotchy face gave Dirck much concern. Angus' hearty Scottish face also looked stricken.

"Are you ill with the Great Pestilence?" Dirck challenged.

"Pirates captured Papa and Jenny!" Justinus cried. "They demand a ransom!"

Mollie collapsed onto a chair. Dirck's mind turned black. All he could think to say was, "How do you know?"

"Captain Van Ritter says so." Justinus gasped for air. "Pirates want one thousand gold florin."

Terror seized Dirck. He couldn't let anything happen to his father and sister. Not after his mother had just died. Angus wrapped an arm around both boys, asking how much cash Pieter had on hand. Dirck recalled the money he left them wasn't all spent. He rubbed his chin, doubting it was enough. Justinus snapped his head forward.

"Count de Alvarado arrived in town yesterday. Maybe he will help."

"Ye have horses," Angus offered.

Then he suggested the count might loan the balance using the rye harvest as security. Justinus ran to retrieve Pieter's jeweled treasure box, which he set on the table. He lifted out a parchment and several family heirlooms. He turned to Dirck.

"The count referred to this Bible as valuable when he returned it. It's nearly a century old."

Dirck shook his head fiercely. "Not the Bible. Wilhelm still hasn't brought the ones I printed for Herr Gutenberg. What about this?"

He opened a case with a sparkling necklace. Their papa had it made for their mama on their twentieth wedding anniversary. It would fetch a handsome price.

"Not Mama's necklace!" Justinus bellowed.

Dirck grabbed Justinus' upper arms. "Papa and Jenny's lives are worth more than rubies and diamonds."

"You don't care." Justinus pulled away. "You weren't even here when Mama died."

Dirck reeled back as if his brother had struck him.

"I care, more than you know," he said between clenched teeth.

Justinus blanched. "Dirck, I'm sorry."

"What did you say that I haven't thought myself? I should have been home."

Justinus gripped his brother's hand. "You and I must save them."

"I'll help ye," Angus said forcefully.

Within the hour, the trio stood before Count de Alvarado in his grand room at the inn. He addressed them from behind a desk, arms folded, with Alphonso glowering at his side.

"Son, you saw the horses," the count said to Alphonso. "What is their worth?"

"The gray mare is sturdy but much ridden. The black mare is spirited, I suppose. Forty gold florin for both is fair."

Dirck fought rising anger. "They are the pride of our stable. Each is worth at least two hundred gold florin."

"You came to me!" The count aimed a jeweled finger. "You're in no position to bargain."

Angus stepped forward, advising they'd already informed Maxim of their mission.

Dirck latched onto Maxim's position. "Surely the abbot will believe a man of your standing will justly treat the family of Duke Philip's magistrate."

"Perhaps my calculation was hasty." Alphonso shifted his dark eyes. "Father, go see the horses yourself."

The count wrapped his cloak about him and they left the room. Dirck balled his fists. "I refuse to show them the Bible or Mama's necklace. They're cheating us"

"Be patient. It may work right," Justinus urged.

Dirck pressed a finger to his lips as loud footsteps approached. The count swept in, the apologetic Alphonso in tow.

"My son was too quick. They are fine animals. Did you bring anything else?"

"First, tell us what you will pay for the horses," Dirck insisted.

"If you include the riding gear, two hundred florin for each."

"I thank you, but we need more."

Alphonso struck his hand on the desk. "We won't pay more for those animals."

"You misunderstand me," Dirck replied. "Besides the four hundred gold florin for the sale of the horses, we need a loan of six hundred gold florin. Look at these other items."

Count de Alvarado resumed his seat behind the ornate desk. His robe fluttered about him. Dirck lifted his father's case from his leather satchel. When he opened it, the count gaped at a silver necklace adorned with dazzling rubies and diamonds. His finger touched the old Bible he had recently returned to Pieter and for which he received the reward.

He took out a leather pouch asking, "What's in here?"

"It once held Judas' thirty pieces of silver," Justinus proclaimed.

"Where did you get such an ancient relic as the coin purse of Judas?"

Angus snatched the pouch with his large hands. "Nay, this isn't fer sale."

"What do you propose then?" Alphonso snapped, his fingers on the necklace.

Dirck glanced at Angus. "We offer the jeweled necklace and Bible as collateral. The relic has no part in our negotiations. When Papa is released, we repay the loan within sixty days. You give us back our Bible and necklace."

A knock startled Dirck into action. "We must conclude this business. Lives are at stake."

Maxim opened the door and peered inside. Angus motioned for him to enter.

"How do I know the necklace is genuine?" the count blubbered. "These gems look like rubies, but could be anything."

Maxim gathered his brown robe around him and lurched toward the count. "I was with Lord Vander Goes when he commissioned this fine piece for his wife. With so many rubies and diamonds, it is worth more than a thousand gold florin."

"Doesn't your mother object to parting with such exquisite jewels?" the count probed.

"Our mother has died," Dirck said with a biting glance.

The count cleared his throat. "I was unaware. You shall have your loan. Wait downstairs while we prepare a document for you to sign."

# CHAPTER 32

The decrepit ship holding Pieter and Jenny captive reeked of decaying fish. A hard storm would sink her like a stone to the bottom of the sea. They were lodged in the ship's cabin, sitting next to each other on a wooden bench. Their feet were secured with ropes to its wooden legs. Dirty rags tied over their mouths stifled any sounds they tried uttering.

A lone candle flickered in the cabin. At least the pirates hadn't covered their eyes. But two ruffians guarded the door. One gripped a glittering mace and the other a long, sharp knife. Pieter glanced at Jenny's terrified green eyes. How much longer would they be kept alive? The pirates wanted a ransom paid in gold. Pieter lifted up an ardent prayer.

*God in heaven, help us! My daughter needs Your protection!*

Over time his spirit calmed. For some inexplicable reason, Jenny began humming a lullaby. Pieter's strong fingers struggled against the knot holding his hands. He turned his smallest finger until he sensed it loosening. He kept working at it while Jenny hummed her lively tune.

The pirate pointed his steely knife at her face. "Quiet!"

Jenny stopped at once. The room grew oppressively still, except for the other guard's sniffling. Pieter dared not move his finger. The door flung open and in strode a burly man, the side of his deformed foot scraping along the floor planks.

The giant barked at the reed-thin pirate wielding the knife. "Get on deck."

"Who says?"

"I says."

"Well, I ain't moving. One-eyed Jack told me to guard 'em."

The big man lunged at the bony man. He jabbed a finger in his chest, and shook his massive shaggy head. "Get on deck. Be on the lookout for the gold."

Then he poked a finger at the young boy gripping the mace. "Guard 'em with your life. Once we have the gold, carve 'em up."

He cackled and shoved the pirate and his knife out the door. Pieter eyed the boy no older than Justinus watching over them. His mind whirled. One-eyed Jack! That man had stolen Pieter's horse when he and Maxim had been searching for Wolfgang Halsma. The guard's eyelids slammed shut, and he leaned against the timbered wall.

Pieter acted fast. His fingers flew against the knot. One last bit of cloth … he grunted out loud as his hands burst free!

The guard's head jerked upward. Pieter closed his eyes, feigning sleep. In reality, he again prayed to Almighty God for help. He peered from one eye. Their captor's chin fell to his chest. Time to move.

Pieter speedily unfastened his feet. Then he freed Jenny's hands and feet. He ripped off the filthy rags covering their mouths. He pounced, knocking the guard down with a thud. The pirate's head hit the floor. He lay limp. Pieter wasted no time securing a rag over his mouth. In a final act of defiance, Pieter kicked the mace a good distance from his body.

"Jenny, get the rope. Be quick!" Pieter hissed.

He straddled the guard, who had come to. Struggling to free himself, the pirate kicked savagely at Pieter with his skinny legs. Although Pieter was older, he was larger and stronger, and managed to pin his arms to the floor. The constant barrage of kicks against his back wore Pieter down in his weakened condition.

"Jenny, tie his feet. Stop him from kicking me!"

She wrapped rope around his feet. With force, the pirate flailed his legs, his hard boot landing on her cheek.

"You beast!" she cried, crashing her small body against his feet. This time she skillfully tied his feet before he kicked her again. She tossed Pieter another rope, and he instructed her to bind his wrists.

"I'll hold him down," he puffed.

"Justinus taught me to tie a seaman's knot." She worked the rope with her small fingers. "Like this, Papa?"

"Perfect."

Pieter tightened the knots, and dragged the belligerent pirate to the bench. He pushed him down hard. In a flash, he secured his hands and feet to the opposite ends.

He whispered to Jenny, "Do what I say. Hide behind my back."

Pieter cracked open the door and Jenny scooted behind him. They stepped out into the black night. He gripped her hand. Suddenly, she sneezed.

Pieter covered her with his arms and waited. He heard voices up toward the bow, so instead, he crept with her toward the stern. There, they ducked behind coiled ropes. Releasing Jenny's hand, Pieter tripped over a wooden chest. He yanked her to him, and protected her with his body. He listened breathlessly for a knife or weapon to be thrown at them.

Nothing happened. He dared open the chest. It was empty. A plan sprang to his mind. He lifted Jenny to the ship's railing.

"Jump, my daughter," he ordered, his heart racing in his chest.

"Follow me, Papa! Don't fight alone!"

"I'll jump after you. Pretend it's the river you swim in. We'll float on this chest until we reach land."

Jenny plugged her nose. As she perched on the railing, a voice rose from the bow, "See the light portside? Look alive there and watch."

Footsteps thumped on the port side of the ship.

He heaved the chest far from the ship, unsure where it landed in the darkness. She leapt into the air, wrapping her arms around her legs. Pieter made sure she rose to the top of the water before he too sailed off the ledge. He landed feet first in the swirling water.

"Papa, I'm cold!" She coughed loudly.

"Shush, or the pirates will dive in after us. I'm swimming to you. Hum your lullaby so I can find you."

Pieter began swimming to her, trying not to splash. He paused kicking his feet to listen. Her humming seemed further away. Pieter turned in the water and swam in another direction. It was too dark to see Jenny or the chest. He felt exhausted and gasped for air.

He pled, "Jenny, hum louder. I can't hear…"

His mouth filled with cold water, and he choked. The weight of his own body was pulling Pieter under when something seized his hair!

He thrashed with his arms in the water, calling softly, "Jenny, is that you?"

A deep voice growled, "What varmint do we have here?"

With his fist, Pieter smacked the firm hand yanking his hair. He struggled to free himself from a man in a small boat.

"Jenny, kick your way to shore," Pieter commanded, sucking in water.

The hand lifted him higher toward the boat.

"Man, could it be?"

The strong hand grabbed folds of Pieter's soggy shirt and lifted him out
of the water.

"Give me the lamp … It is you! Mate, help me get Lord Vander Goes
out of the water."

Four strong hands pulled Pieter into the boat. The lamp's bright glare
blinded him.

"Who is it? Who knows me here?"

The man thumped his back. "It's Van Ritter, going to pay those thieves
your ransom."

"Van Ritter! I feared you were one of them. Shine the light on the water. There's my daughter! Make haste, before they know we're gone. They
planned to kill us and probably you, after you paid the gold."

The captain plucked Jenny from the foaming sea. He blew out the
light. His mate rowed fiercely to reach shore before the pirates learned their
quarry evaded them under the cover of night.

AFTER SEEING JENNY SAFELY TO THE ABBEY, PIETER CONCOCTED A PLAN.
So at mid-morning he confronted the innkeeper where the count had
been staying. The surly man poured ale into a tankard. He had a reputation for using his beak-like nose to ferret out his customers' comings and
goings. Peering above the counter, he gazed up into Pieter's eyes with his
watery ones.

"When did Count de Alvarado leave town?" Pieter demanded.

"What difference does it make?" The tiny man shrugged. "He's gone."

"Are you certain he didn't say where he was going?"

"When I took wine to his room, I heard him tell Alphonso to call for
a carriage."

Pieter placed another *vierlander* in front of the tiny man. "Take your time."

The innkeeper licked his lips, reminding Pieter of a frog striking a bug
with its tongue.

"You want ale?" he asked Pieter while staring at the glittering *vierlander*.

"No." Pieter's eyes never left the innkeeper's.

The wee man touched the coin with his finger. Slowly sliding it, he flicked the coin into his hand, where it eventually found rest in his pocket.

"I did hear de Alvarado order his son to sell two horses."

The diminutive man whispered something else, causing Pieter to straighten.

"Dirck, Maxim, let's be on our way."

"But Papa," Dirck began.

"Make haste, son."

Dirck turned with obvious reluctance. Pieter dashed outside, and down a side street.

He soon realized Dirck and Maxim struggled to keep up with his fast pace, so he called over his shoulder, "Alphonso sold our horses to the blacksmith. I aim to buy them back. The count also hinted he had business with Duke Philip."

Maxim puffed out a breath. "The duke could shed light on the count's whereabouts."

"I'll write Duke Phillip as soon as I retrieve Justinus and Jenny from the abbey," Pieter replied, slowing his steps.

Dirck ran on ahead, and when they joined him, he was talking animatedly to the smithy. The rotund man's face glistened with sweat. When the smithy saw Pieter, he raised a blackened hand in greeting.

"Lord Vander Goes, you've come for your mounts. When Alphonso brought them here, I recognized Willow and your mare Raven straightaway."

"They're out back, Father," Dirck interrupted.

The smithy put down his hammer. "It's a funny business, them having your horses. I bought them all the same."

Pieter didn't want the whole town discovering pirates had captured him for ransom, so he told the smithy, "Though Count de Alvarado did purchase them, we decided we shouldn't have sold them. Name your price."

The smithy scratched his gleaming bald head. "I likes horses. You buy 'em back for what I paid, two hundred and fifty gold florin each."

"Father, that's more than—" Dirck started to say, but Pieter held up his hand.

"A fair price." Pieter counted out gold coin.

"You looks after us in town, I tells my wife. She's been wantin' a new copper kettle."

Dirck wasted no time retrieving the horses. As they walked to the abbey, he lamented, "It isn't right. The count charged the smithy fifty florins more for the horses than he gave me."

"A small price to pay for their return," Pieter said. "Go and find your sister and brother."

Dirck sped off. Maxim urged Pieter to swiftly notify Duke Philip.

"Tell him of your success in England. Mention the count's conduct, leaving the return of your Bible and Aneka's necklace in God's hands."

Pieter was struck by an incisive thought. "The count once had our family Bible, and does again. Perhaps God wants him to read it. I had hoped Jenny would cherish her mother's jewels one day."

Memories of Aneka brought waves of fresh grief tumbling over Pieter. He longed to hold her in his arms.

Maxim rested a firm hand on his shoulder. "Rubies won't bring her back. Her love remains in your heart. Pour that same love like water into Jenny s heart."

Pieter's children ran down the abbey's stone steps, laughing. He just didn't know how to go on. Wouldn't he dishonor Aneka's memory if happiness lived again in his heart?

# CHAPTER 33

Two months passed swiftly after Jenny and Pieter's release. Emilee and Douglas paid their promised visit. They loved baby Alexander, and the adoption was finalized before they returned to England. Wolfgang Halsma knew nothing of it; he'd died shortly after Pieter had met him.

Jenny played for all hours with her new little puppy. For his part, Pieter was stirred to begin afresh. Justinus and Maxim were teaching students at the Vander Goes School. Angus showed Jenny how to play chess. She even beat Dirck, to his chagrin.

One autumn morning, a knock sounded on Pieter's library door, turning his mind to the present.

"Mollie, I'm reviewing accounts," he called. "Come back in an hour."

Dirck peered in. "I need to talk with you."

Pieter motioned him in. Dirck set a package on the floor before taking a seat.

He moistened his lips. "Father, in Mainz I was knocked unconscious. Jenny fell ill, and then Mama died. Pirates captured you and Jenny. Why are such bad things happening?"

Sadness permeated Pieter. His son was too young to face such heartache. Of course, Pieter's own mother had died when he was a boy. He wanted to offer him succor.

"Life brings sorrow and pain," he said tenderly. "Our tears will not dry until the Lord Jesus returns. Storms may come, but we must hold fast to His love. Your mother's death has sharpened my faith, much like iron sharpens iron."

Dirck seized the package. "Hasn't God also used you to advance His Kingdom?"

"I don't see how."

"You financed Gutenberg's printing of the Bible. We can't yet know the impact of your involvement. See here!"

Dirck tore off some wrapping. "Wilhelm sent this by courier. I hold an illustrated Gutenberg Bible made by my own hands. Your other nine copies are in the front hall."

Awestruck, Pieter lovingly opened one of the two volumes. He could hardly believe he held Scriptures in his finite hands. Pieter imagined Aneka reading the sacred text. Tears stung his eyes.

"Son, you too have been God's instrument."

Dirck's face beamed. "Father, even though the German court ordered Gutenberg to repay Fust and everything was turned over to him, I was there, holding Fust to your God-inspired commitment."

A tap sounded, and his door swung open.

Angus plunged in, his hair a mess. "We must speak of somethin' noo."

"You've come at an opportune time." Pieter rose to greet his cousin. "This is the first Bible created by mechanical means. Dirck helped Johann Gutenberg to print this very copy."

Angus reverently drew the Bible to his lips and kissed it. "Angels in heaven must be singin'. More can read God's Holy Word."

"We should celebrate." Pieter's chest filled with joy. "But you needed to discuss an urgent matter."

Angus gently placed the Bible on Pieter's desk, and turned to Dirck with a serious expression. "Do ye remember the pouch?"

"Of course, you refused to let the leather pouch be used as collateral for the ransom," Dirck replied.

Pieter frowned. "Is that because it belonged to Judas?"

"No. It contains ashes," Angus whispered.

"My mother had ashes?" Pieter reared back his head. "Why?"

He gently tugged the pouch off the belt holding his robe. With tears glistening in his eyes, Angus told how the ashes had come into the Vander Goes family's possession decades before: Christian men had rescued the ashes and hidden them in the deerskin pouch.

Pieter recalled seeing Jenny pull the pouch from his mother's trunk.

"Aneka and Jenny took it out, but we never looked inside. I had hidden away my mother's things for years. When Aneka died ..." His voice broke.

"Ach, I ken yer grief." Angus clapped a hand on his shoulder. "Ye need to keep this secret, as yer mamma did before ye."

"But Papa," Dirck chimed. "From what Angus just told us, these ashes are precious, and will be for time to come. We should make a permanent record without delay."

Pieter looked at his son's gleaming eyes and decided he was right. "It's important that we hold this trust in secret. We'll devise a code and mark the new Bible so your children's children will always seek to protect the pouch lest it be used as collateral or sold one day."

He opened the cover, his hands smoothing the first page. Angus and Dirck silently gathered around as Pieter took his quill and ink in hand.

"Angus, help me think of what verses to use as clues."

He did offer one, which Pieter marked. They had trouble with any others until Justinus walked in. After being told all, he quickly gave his father several more verses to mark.

"What valor, what strength you have, Cousin Angus," Justinus said in his deepening voice. "It is my honor to serve God with you."

Pieter put down his quill on the blotter, commending Angus, Dirck, and Justinus for their work. "Having the Gutenberg Bible in our home gives me hope. God will not allow His Word to be defeated."

The edges of Dirck's mouth turned up. "You're right, Papa. But Count de Alvarado disappeared with Wycliffe's Bible and Mama's necklace. I have to wonder if he wasn't involved somehow with the pirates capturing you."

"That rascal roams the Netherlands, looking for his next victim," Justinus declared.

"He and his cunning son," Dirck said with venom. "They shouldn't get away with their crimes."

Pieter chose his words carefully. "A man of God seeks to do what is right, no matter how the other fellow treats him. Justice may yet be done. The most important thing is to steer our course away from evil."

AFTER THEIR HEART-TO-HEART DISCUSSION, Pieter instructed Dirck on all aspects of the estate. He liked his clever ideas and implemented many of them. In time, one cold and rainy morning, they were ensconced in the library. Dirck showed him a ledger book.

"See? By rotating spelt into the north field, we produced a larger yield than last year."

Pieter scanned the page. "Excellent. Your method of crop rotation works. When can you have plans ready for next season?"

"Will this evening be soon enough?"

Pieter chuckled at his son's enthusiasm and agreed to meet after dinner. Dirck closed the ledger with a snap. He strode from the room, whistling. Pieter stood looking out his library window. He didn't whistle. A steady breeze blew in from the north, rattling the glass pane with heavy rain. He was more tired than he could remember.

A pounding on the front door brought him to the front entryway looking for Mollie. She was probably in the kitchen seeing to the luncheon. Her hearing wasn't as acute as it once was. He opened the front door. There stood a tall man soaked to the skin.

"What can I do for you?" Pieter inquired.

"Direct me to Lord Vander Goes. I bring a message for him and no other."

"See here, man, I am he. Come inside and dry off."

The man shook his head, spraying water. "I must leave straightaway. Please sign this."

Pieter signed a piece of parchment, and stuffed a coin into the man's damp hand. He gave Pieter a thick packet, clicked his heels, and turned abruptly. The dripping man rode off on a tired-looking brown mare. Pieter went inside thinking he should have gotten his name.

He turned the packet over and saw the duke's seal. He feared its importance, as the messenger had delivered the package in the pouring rain with much urgency. Pieter scanned the duke's message with great speed. A chill tore through him at the duke's astonishing words:

*Lord Vander Goes:*

> *You bravely completed your service to us in England. Thankfully, you are safely in Middleburg after your ordeal and resuming your duchy duties. Reliable sources inform us that Count de Alvarado was robbed the very night he left Middleburg. Alas, the whereabouts of your Bible and wife's ruby necklace are unknown. The assailants have escaped, for now. We did hear it was a Wycliffe Bible. It is best you no longer possess it. Arrange to attend us at the duchy palace. You are to be awarded the Order of the Golden Fleece.*

*His Excellency, Duke Philip the Good*

Before Pieter could react to the stunning news, Jenny flew into his library with cheeks as red as her hair.

"Is that letter about getting me a new mother?"

Pieter's head snapped up. "What put that absurd notion into your head?"

"Mollie and I just returned from the street fair. I heard the fishmonger ask a woman if you would marry and find me a new mother."

Pieter patted her hand dismissively "It's mere gossip, but I see it worries you. Now you understand why I tell you never listen to others' conversations."

Jenny's nod in agreement touched Pieter deeply. She looked so much like Aneka.

"I never intend to remarry," he added. "My love for your mother goes beyond what I could ever have with another. I pray you find such happiness one day."

She bounced away humming, leaving Pieter to construct a reply to Duke Philip. The news he'd just received was bittersweet. Being awarded the Order of the Golden Fleece was high honor indeed. But he couldn't help believing Count de Alvarado was getting away with high crimes. How could Pieter stop his further corruption? He also wondered why Duke Philip condemned Wycliffe's Bible—his own wife's mother had studied under Wycliffe.

Maxim came for dinner. Justinus was talking at the table, but Pieter's mind was consumed by Duke Philip's curious message. Did the duke truly believe the count's robbery tale?

"Pieter, did you hear your son's announcement?" Maxim prodded.

Apparently he hadn't heard. "Sorry, what did he say?"

Justinus shook his head. "Never mind. You don't have time for me anymore."

"How can I, when you're always gone with Angus and Maxim?" Pieter snapped, his voice rising. Then he repented. He shouldn't treat any of his children with disdain.

He lowered his tone, saying evenly, "I am sorry, son. I received startling news, which I will explain later. Will someone please tell me what I missed?"

"Yer son's fit to preach." Angus wore a wide smile on his brawny face.

Maxim's eyes shone. "Time spent with God restored my soul. Has it yours, Justinus?"

"More than I ever imagined." Justinus eyed Pieter. "Around every bend, I saw a lost soul needing to know Jesus. I am eager to begin my calling."

"Son, you will make a fine preacher, of that I am sure," Pieter complimented.

He stood quickly. "There is something I want you all to know. The parchment is in my library."

Justinus jumped up. "Allow me, Papa. Is it on your desk?"

"Indeed, with the duke's seal on it."

As Justinus scurried away, Maxim informed Pieter he wanted to preach alongside Justinus and Angus. Before Pieter could react, Justinus ran into the room, his eyes bulging.

He waved the parchment in front of him. "Duke Philip writes Count de Alvarado was robbed of our goods. It's not true. He stole them!"

Pieter regretted the unsettling news being broken in this manner. He seized the parchment, crumpling it in his hands.

"Don't!" Justinus cried. "Dirck should read it."

Dirck thrust out his hand. "What causes such an outcry?"

Pieter changed his mind. He smoothed the crinkled parchment and read it aloud.

"Order of the Golden Fleece!" These words zestfully rolled off Maxim's tongue. He looked extremely pleased.

"Why is my brother upset?" Jenny's eyes danced. "The duke says nice things about Papa."

Justinus boiled over. "You simpleton. The count pilfered our mother's ruby necklace, and your pouch. I told Dirck not to trust him!"

"He stole my special pouch?" Jenny turned liquid eyes toward Pieter.

Angus held up his hand. "Nay, the pouch tis safe with me."

"Oh, I forgot!" Justinus cried. "My mind is too filled with anger."

Pieter rose and tried calming him, but Justinus was opposed to reason.

"Then you are unfit to preach God's word," Pieter scolded.

Justinus gestured wildly. "But Papa, God showed me that he was a scoundrel. I let him take Mama's necklace anyway. I was wrong!"

In a steadier voice, Dirck proclaimed, "We had no choice but to raise the ransom."

"Sons, Van Ritter was fearless in rowing to a pirate's ship," Pieter said. "If you hadn't raised a ransom and had him bring the gold, the captain wouldn't have been in place when Jenny and I floated in the water. You were part of God's plan to save us. So was Count de Alvarado."

"At least you won't have to repay him the loan," Justinus replied.

Pieter shook his head. "Read the loan document carefully. Return of the collateral is not guaranteed. The loan is due or we lose the collateral. Plus interest accrues."

"So the count planned to forfeit the collateral all along." Dirck's voice rang with defeat. "Why didn't I read that clause before I signed?"

Maxim added his viewpoint. "We were all anxious for your father and sister's safety. What matters is they are alive. Justinus, our Lord commands us to forgive our enemies."

"Ay, He does," Angus agreed.

Justinus stalked over to the window. "Of course," was all he said.

"Sons," Pieter intoned. "We will repay the loan on time."

"What if he's never punished?" Justinus asked.

"We leave it to God to enact justice and to return our property." Pieter picked up his quill. "Now, who is going with me to receive the Golden Fleece?"

Jenny was the first to run over. "Don't leave me behind, Papa. I'm not afraid of pirates."

Pieter chuckled, and the tension evaporated in the wake of his good news. The preaching trip was put on hold and plans made for them all to meet Duke Philip.

# CHAPTER 34

## MIDDLEBURG, THE NETHERLANDS
## JULY 1467

Pieter sat reading a prayer book in his library, listening to Jenny's lively melody on the harp, which floated in through his open window. He found it hard to believe his little girl would soon turn twenty-one. Much had happened in the preceding twelve years.

After graduating from the University at Cologne, Dirck started a printing business with his friend Fredrick. They printed important books, following in the steps of Johann Gutenberg, Dirck's mentor. Dirck managed the estates in Middleburg and Goes. He'd also built a house in town where Fredrick lived and ran their print shop.

Justinus and Angus preached throughout England, wherever they found open ears. Justinus came home last month to help Fredrick operate their press. While Jenny and Dirck seemed to have settled into life's routine, Pieter harbored concerns for the difficult road Justinus had chosen as a Lollard. His musings were interrupted by Justinus himself.

"Papa, the horses are ready," he said in his booming voice. "Are you?"

Pieter sprang to his feet with alacrity. He'd nearly forgotten what he'd promised his son.

"It is a fine day," he said. "And I have missed our rides and long talks."

Pieter changed quickly, shoving his feet into leather boots. Before long, he and Justinus were atop their mounts, meandering along the sparkling river. Pieter stopped his horse by the old, gnarled tree. This was a good place to ask Justinus a question that gnawed at Pieter's mind since his son's return.

"Are you well received by the English?"

Justinus nudged his horse so he could slap a ragged section of the tree's trunk.

"See this jagged split? Lightning nearly ripped this tree in half that terrible day of the great storm. I turned to the Lord then, Papa, and will never look back."

"Yes, you did, son, and I pray each day for your success. You are skillfully dodging my question. Preaching with Angus in England is more dangerous than the peaceful Low Countries."

The horse beneath Justinus stomped its hoof and whinnied. He struggled to gain the upper hand. Eventually, he quieted the new mare.

"She is lively," he said, grinning. "Which brings to mind two spirited English families vying for control. The House of York has beaten the House of Lancaster, and King Henry is off the throne, for now. King Edward consolidates his power. As I speak, he searches for an advantageous husband for his sister, Margaret of York."

Pieter loosened the reins, letting his horse nibble the long grass. All Justinus' talk of the English king was cover for the real issue.

"Son, I keep up with the intrigues. King Louis of France wants to align with England, and vies to have Margaret marry a Frenchman. Here's what I want to know. Does the political strife make life more difficult for you?"

Justinus shielded his eyes from the rising sun's rays. "Papa, you may as well know. Angus took me to Norwich, the town where he once saw William White being burned. Though it was forty years ago, we wept."

"Does the Church of England still burn Wycliffe followers, those they deem heretics?"

"Not for years." Justinus paused, his voice catching. "But Angus and I are chased from many towns for speaking Jesus' name."

Pieter had no desire to convince his son to leave what God had called him to do, but he saw trouble ahead. And what if God had a different plan for Justinus at this time in his life?

"You forsake home and family to bring Jesus' love to a hurting world.

I commend you," Pieter said fervently. "Are you ready for a rest? Dirck and Fredrick need your help printing the great works."

"Papa, your wisdom and prayers have guided me all these many years. I will talk to God about what you suggest."

"Good. We'll ride the long way back."

Pieter wouldn't stop praying for Justinus or any of his children. Still, he tried to enjoy the beauty of fields and trees along the route home. Justinus saw to the horses. Pieter returned to his library. Sitting in his comfy chair relieved his aching bones. Mollie entered with a cup of cider, which refreshed him after the ride.

Pieter thought of his benefactor, Duke Philip, who had died a month ago. At the service, in the presence of Philip's son Charles the Bold, Pieter had given a heartfelt eulogy, praising the good Philip had done for the region. A knock at the door startled Pieter back to the present.

Justinus came in, saying gruffly, "An older, stooped man with an enormous hat is here."

"You deal with him, son. I find myself rather tired."

"Papa." Justinus wiped his flushing face. "The sight of him makes past anger surge within me like a raging flood."

"Who incites you so?"

His son flung his hands in the air. "I thought my life as a preacher filled me with love and not hate. I'm wrong, Papa!"

"Then confess your sin to our Divine Lord. He is faithful to forgive."

"Yes, but Count de Alvarado and his son seek an audience with you."

Pieter wiped a strand of gray hair from his eyes. He could only imagine what his old nemesis wanted after all these years.

"I hope he's not after a loan," he said. "Take them to the sitting room. I will be along."

"They claim to have a message from Duke Charles, but I believe nothing they say."

"Perhaps the duke sends a thank-you note." Pieter's spirits brightened.

"We shouldn't let them in the house," Justinus said, hurrying to the door. "To protect our valuable family portrait in the hall, I thought they'd be more comfortable outside."

Pieter grabbed his arm, entreating him to show hospitality to all. "And find Dirck. I'd like you both present when we meet two wily men from our past."

It didn't take long for everyone to assemble in the sitting room.

Pieter greeted the count and Alphonso, then rang a silver bell. Mollie walked in slowly and stiff-legged, carrying a tray. He wasn't sure how much longer she should continue as housekeeper. Of course, she'd always remain on the estate. After pouring a light-colored liquid from a pewter carafe into five cups, she shuffled away.

Pieter handed a cup to the count, who had aged considerably. Deep lines etched his ever-darting eyes.

"This new drink mixes lemons, honey, and sugar with water," Pieter said. "Some find it pungent. I think it's an appropriate offering after so many years."

The count bowed slightly. After tasting the concoction, he declared it delightful. Then sitting with a flourish in a carved wood chair between Dirck and Pieter, he intoned, "We bring an important message from Charles the Bold, our new Duke of Burgundy."

Alphonso stood scowling behind his father's chair. He wore a sour expression without even tasting the lemony liquid. Justinus remained near the door, with his arms across his chest as if ready for whatever these enemies brought forth.

"Then you didn't come this distance to be sociable," Pieter said, a hint of challenge to his voice.

"On the contrary, Duke Charles requested I deliver this letter personally." The count pressed his thin lips together. "I do not know its contents."

Though Pieter extended his hand, the count clutched the parchment. "I have another purpose to my visit, if you will allow me."

"That's no surprise to me," Justinus muttered.

Ignoring the caustic remark, the count bellowed, "Alphonso, open the case."

Pieter eyed Alphonso. His sleek black hair and pointy beard gave him every appearance of a rogue capable of treachery. Pieter had qualms over letting the crafty pair into his house. Jenny waltzed in wearing a silver gown as Alphonso held up a velvet bag.

"I thought I heard the bell ring," she said lightly.

Alphonso extracted a glittering object from the bag. Jenny darted over to him, seizing the shiny object from his hands.

"Jenny, where are your manners?" Pieter chided.

"It's Mama's necklace!" she exclaimed. "Oh, I knew it couldn't be lost forever."

She quickly fastened it around her neck. The red rubies were striking against her rosy skin, highlighting the vibrant red in her hair. In the shimmering gown trimmed in black fur and black hennin gathering her red hair, Pieter saw her with new eyes. His daughter exuded the aura of a royal princess.

Jenny was also the mirror image of his mother, Lady Jane Vander Goes. He drew in his breath. No longer a child, she was a beautiful woman who would soon marry and leave him. After introducing Jenny, Pieter saw Alphonso's gaze upon her lasted longer than was fitting.

"Please enlighten me," Pieter said. "This necklace appears to be my late wife's."

The count twirled a finger around a crimson ribbon hanging from his neck. "Imagine my hesitancy at Duke Charles commissioning me to come here, especially after I searched so many years for your ruby necklace. On our way, Alphonso suggested we visit my former servant. Alphonso had heard he was acting strangely."

Alphonso nodded his groomed head. "As fate would have it, I found your beautiful necklace in his garret, hidden beneath his pillow. What a fool to think he could get away with something like this. Of course, he's been dealt with."

"You had him arrested then?" Justinus asked, guarding the door.

The count simply flashed an oily smile. "We restore the necklace to its rightful owner who, if I might add, is a lovely jewel herself."

"Alphonso." Jenny faced him with somber eyes. "Did you find our Bible?"

Dirck stepped forward. "Was John Wycliffe's work under your servant's pillow?"

"Too bad the fellow was out of his wits, or I'm sure he would have confessed to having it. We will never give up our search." Alphonso held his hand toward Jenny, as if hinting for hers.

Instead, she touched the necklace and kissed Pieter lightly on the cheek.

"Never mind," she quipped. "Having Mama's necklace returned is the most wonderful thing to happen to me. After being saved from pirates, of course."

She beamed a grateful smile, meeting Alphonso's gaze before dropping her eyes.

"What about the parchment from the duke?" Justinus asked.

"Dear me, I nearly forgot." With a flourish of his jeweled fingers, Count de Alvarado handed over the parchment.

Pieter's eyes scanned his first message from Duke Charles, who wrote in bold strokes:

*Lord Vander Goes,*

*My dear father relied on you in his court. Your friendship with the noble family of York is key to completing favorable treaties for Burgundy, which could finally end piracy in the channel. I would consider it a great service if you would confer with the royal court of Edward IV to further my hopes of marriage to his sister Margaret of York. Please leave without delay. Thanking you, I am, Charles the Bold, Duke of Burgundy.*

Reading between the lines, Pieter was astounded. Duke Charles wanted him to arrange his marriage to King Edward's sister, Margaret of York!

He looked up to see every eye upon him, except for Alphonso's. The rascal stared at Jenny from across the room. Surely she was unaware of his impertinent glances. She seemed uninterested in suitors. Recently, she'd spurned a young man's offer to go riding with him.

"What news from Duke Charles?" Dirck pressed.

"His curious proposal requires a written reply." Pieter managed a smile. "Children, join me in my library."

Jenny cast a shy smile at Alphonso. "I will stay here, Papa."

"No, your presence is especially required."

Pieter swung open the sitting room door, letting her sweep from the room. As Alphonso's keen eyes followed her movements, Pieter knew for certain Jenny, along with one of her brothers, would immediately go with him to England. He had one other critical matter on his mind. And that was for Duke Charles to guarantee their safety from marauding pirates.

Two days later, Dirck grunted aloud. Using all his strength, he tugged on the worm gear handle. He pressed the type onto the paper before lifting the gear. His associate, Fredrick Zylstra, snatched out the paper, holding it carefully to prevent smudges. "Well done, Dirck. Every letter is clear."

Dirck squared his shoulders, muscled from daily labors on the farm and operating the printing machine. Though they stood eye to eye, Fredrick appeared taller because of his thinner frame.

Dirck wiped his hands on a rag. "And you'll finish the Dutch Psalter without me?"

"Your father needs you in England for many reasons, the most important being your sister. She is ever conspiring intrigue."

"Too true. One day she will become embroiled in an adventure she'd be better off without."

Fredrick removed ink from the plate replying, "England is rife with danger. The Yorks are still fighting the Lancastrians."

"That's why Duke Charles sends my father to negotiate the marriage treaty, instead of going himself. Father's taking one of the Gutenberg Bibles I printed to the king. It will fulfill my mentor's long intended wish. Are you taking us to the boat docks?"

"Of course. And be assured the two hundred Psalters will be completed for the Vander Goes School by the end of next week."

The men set the pages to dry. Dirck secured the metal type into the upper and lower cases, pleased he was assisting in his father's mission. They went out to the well, and scrubbed their hands with linseed oil, salt, and warm water.

"The grime stays imbedded in my skin," Fredrick grumbled.

Dirck handed him a bowl. "Gutenberg taught me a trick. Vanilla bean paste takes away the smell."

"Thanks." Fredrick rubbed the paste into his fingers. "I hope she finds me acceptable."

"Oh? Are you courting a lady I know nothing about?"

Fredrick shrugged, and Dirck playfully sniffed the air.

"I imagine your special lady will think you've brought her an expensive tart."

Fredrick winced. "Is the vanilla smell too much?"

"Unfortunately, yes. However, we must leave. My father wants to speak with the captain about danger from pirates."

"Will you and your sister be away long?"

"However long these negotiations take," Dirck replied. "It's my first voyage across the channel."

"Let's hope you are all safe from pirates!"

Back in the shop, they changed from their work aprons. Fredrick donned a white linen overcoat, a perfect match to his long, white hair. He handed Dirck several copies of the Book of Prayer they printed in English, also for King Edward.

Dirck slapped his arm. "Fredrick, perhaps you should go in my place!" "I see your father by the litter. We'd best hurry."

He marched ahead of Dirck, giving Jenny a mock bow. "Your adventure begins. I, Fredrick Zylstra, am at your service."

Dirck realized his sister must be Fredrick's special lady. He wondered if she shared his interest, the way she gazed down the road. Fredrick helped her into the litter. She tilted her head and sniffed.

"Did Mollie bake almond tarts for our journey?" Jenny asked, crinkling her nose.

"Our dear Freddy exudes the heavenly aroma," Dirck replied in jest. "I fancy he's dining with a lady after seeing us off. Am I right?"

Jenny arched an eyebrow. Fredrick's pale skin glowed as he entered the litter.

Justinus tucked Fredrick's prayer books into his bag. He was also heading to England to help Angus with his preaching. Glad for his brother's company, Dirck hopped in beside Fredrick.

"I wish you wouldn't let Jenny think I'm courting anyone," Fredrick hissed.

Dirck wore an impish grin. "Will she object?"

"Oh, never mind. Just keep her safe on this trip and in the English court. There are many plots against the king, I understand."

"You scarcely leave the shop for a bowl of creamed herring. Frankly, I'm surprised you're interested in English political drama."

"Does your family see me as so singular?" Fredrick kept his eyes on the moving horses.

Dirck apologized for offending him, adding, "I enjoy our work too."

"I study so we know what to print. Truthfully, I rarely think of engaging with others."

"In my absence, why not challenge Maxim to a game of chess?"

"Did Angus really teach you to play blindfolded?"

"Yes, and he showed Jenny the same trick," Dirck said. "She thinks she's the greatest chess player to ever live."

"Please watch her closely on this trip," Fredrick again coaxed, as he maneuvered the litter to a seagoing vessel docked near Captain Van Ritter's.

They wouldn't have far to walk. Pieter and Justinus greeted the captain while Fredrick and Dirck loaded their belongings on their ship.

Van Ritter handed Jenny a single red rose, glancing sideways at Pieter. "Alphonso brought this for you earlier. He wishes you a safe journey."

Fredrick warned her, "He's not the kind of man you should spend time with."

Jenny sauntered away, admiring her flower.

Dirck turned to Van Ritter. "What do you know of him?"

"Alphonso inquired of another captain about passage to England." Captain Van Ritter nodded at a larger ship. "Is he goin' with your family? He's a bad 'un for your sister. I've seen him in the company of a lady of ill repute."

Dirck clenched his teeth. "You make me more determined to keep Jenny safely in my sight."

# CHAPTER 35

## WINDSOR CASTLE, ENGLAND

Jenny spent a restful hour in the most elegant room she'd ever seen. She rose from the massive bed and clasped the ruby necklace around her neck. The vibrant red gems reminded her of Alphonso's red rose. It was a kind gesture, but what did he mean by it? Should Jenny even be thinking of marriage? Papa still needed her special attention.

Besides, she was here to enjoy herself and make something of her budding friendship with Margaret, the king's sister. Although Jenny was a few years younger, she and Margaret shared much in common. They both loved music and reading. Margaret had been pleased to learn Jenny had a printed Bible from the renowned inventor, Johann Gutenberg.

Jenny laid her new gown on the bed. A maid entered and curtsied. She handed her a folded note, pressed together with a red, wax seal.

"Madam, this arrived for you. And Lady Margaret is ready for you to join her."

Jenny quickly tore off the seal and unfolded the note. She read the words scrawled across the page as if written in haste:

*My dear Jenny Grace,*

    *I trust you received my red rose from the captain, a reminder of how beautiful you look in your mother's necklace. It was my honor to recover it for you. I too am in England. Send word where we can meet. It is imperative you help me get to King Edward and his sister, Lady Margaret.*

*Your devoted servant,*
*Alphonso de Alvarado*

Jenny's cheeks burned. Alphonso found her beautiful! She should show this note to Papa.

Was such action really required? No doubt, this was simply Alphonso's way of speaking. Her brothers never addressed her so openly, but they were brothers, steeped in books and printer's ink. What did they know about the world? Not much, by her way of reckoning.

She looked up. The sight of the servant girl staring at her snapped Jenny back to reality.

"You say Lady Margaret wants to see me now?"

"Yes, madam."

Jenny slid Alphonso's note beneath her jewel case. The timid maid brought Jenny to Margaret's adjoining chamber, an even more elaborate room. Tapestries covered the walls and a fire blazed. Margaret rose from her dressing table, her hands outstretched.

"What a stunning necklace you wear," she exclaimed.

Jenny let her friend examine it, and then said wistfully, "This belonged to my mother."

She briefly explained it had been used as collateral for a loan when she and her father were taken by pirates years ago. She touched one of the gems.

"And this magnificent piece all but disappeared until days before we left Middleburg."

"How extraordinary!" Margaret declared, returning to sit at her dressing table.

She showed Jenny a gold necklace of carved white roses set with pearls.

"White roses proudly adorn my neck. They are symbols of the York family, and have been since before my father was born."

"Alphonso gave me a fragrant red rose before we sailed," Jenny boasted.

Margaret jolted in her seat. "For goodness sake, get rid of it!"

"Am I forbidden from liking red roses?"

Margaret gazed at Jenny with solemn gray eyes. She led her to a settee by the fire.

"Please, do not even smell one," Margaret said ominously. "Red roses symbolize the Lancastrians, who are my father's enemies. They killed him!"

Jenny was aghast. "Margaret, I'm sorry. I didn't know who killed your father."

"Our two families have been warring for twelve years."

Margaret dropped her eyes, regal-looking even in her sadness. "I will never forget that dreadful day, when the Lancastrian army stole his life at Wakefield. If you stay long enough, I will take you there."

Jenny shivered even though close to the fire. She'd seen enough death in her young life.

Not seeing Jenny's shiver, Margaret prattled on about her brother, King Edward. "After our father's death in battle, Edward rallied the knights and fought the Lancastrians at Mortimer's Cross. He was only eighteen years old."

"I am anxious to meet your brother," Jenny replied, striving to change the subject. "My father informed me of the king's desire to strengthen ties with our two countries, which should please everyone. You and I might visit often."

"Would you like to hear more of the king's decisive battle?"

Margaret's attachment to King Edward was commendable. Though Jenny was anxious to dash off a message to Alphonso, she nodded politely.

"Edward carried on where my father could not. On the 2nd of February, six years ago, he prepared his knights. At the break of dawn, three suns appeared in the heavens. Edward believes it was the Holy Trinity leading him to be crowned king."

"Oh, I have gooseflesh." Jenny rubbed her arms. "I hope he stays king for years and years. I should have known about your enemies and red roses. Please forgive me."

Margaret asked Jenny to fasten her necklace, then said, "For my brother's sake, I must marry well. Never mention red roses to my family, no matter who gives them to you."

Jenny was thoroughly chastised. What should she do with Alphonso's note—tear it up?

"What did you do with the rose?" Margaret inquired, scowling.

"It blew overboard on the crossing, so it won't be seen tonight." Jenny lightly touched Margaret's hand. "You must miss your father as I do my mother. And I do love Papa so."

They remained silent, with Jenny firmly deciding to show him the note at dinner.

For now, she was tired of death and political intrigue, so she asked lightly, "What color is your gown, Margaret?"

"A dull grey. My mother insists I wear the color matching my eyes."

"May I suggest something bolder? Something perfect for our duke, Charles the Bold."

Jenny hurried through the door to her adjoining room. The same nervous maid was busy straightening her dressing table.

"Don't bother with that," Jenny said. "And I will dress myself."

The servant dropped her hands, curtsied, and left. Jenny made a selection before speeding to Margaret's chamber where she displayed a deep burgundy gown with sleeves of black fur.

Jenny lifted her pert chin. "You may be unaware, as I was about the hidden meaning of red roses, that burgundy and black are royal colors for your Duke Charles."

"Is he my duke?"

"He will be, if my father has anything to say about it."

A bashful smile crept across Margaret's pale face. She held the rich-looking gown before the mirror. "Edward will be intrigued by my color choice. He may think I'm sending him a message about Duke Charles."

"And will you be?" Jenny asked, her nostrils flaring.

Margaret's shoulders fell. "My cousin, the Earl of Warwick, is in France trying to negotiate a different marriage treaty. I do wish to marry a man I respect. Duke Charles showed great bravery fighting the King of France."

"At least Charles is on the same side as Edward. You'd live closer to me if you move to Bruges, Margaret."

"Charles is widowed. His daughter Mary is ten years old."

"There is something you should know," Jenny whispered. "The brother to the King of France approached Charles, wanting to marry the heiress-presumptive, who may soon be your daughter."

"Mary won't marry for eight years or so. However, I must unite in marriage to unite a kingdom."

A noisy gong clanged. Margaret rose quickly.

"Hurry and dress. My brother's wife will be cross if we arrive at dinner after she does."

Jenny sped to her room, sad that Margaret had no choice in a husband. Donning a gown of spun gold, Jenny carefully tucked Alphonso's note into her sleeve. The English court lay before her. She'd forget Alphonso and enjoy herself even if Papa and her brother hovered nearby.

# CHAPTER 36

Jenny stepped into the lavish banquet hall at Windsor Castle with her papa, the pressure of his hand reminding her of something she needed to do. After dinner, she'd give him the note hidden up her sleeve. Her heart quickened at such lively music being played. She leaned closer to her father.

He said pleasantly, "You and Margaret seem to be fast friends already."

"Loyal to her brother, she does seem favorable to our duke. But I heard fear in her voice as she spoke of King Louis of France and his plans for her."

Pieter replied in such a whisper Jenny strained to hear him above the instruments. Did he say he hadn't been told when he would meet King Edward? Jenny was about to reinforce Margaret's preference for Duke Charles, when her friend entered the banquet hall.

She walked erect, her hand resting on Dirck's right arm. The king's jester danced ahead of them. The wiry man was costumed in black and white hosiery, matching cape, and floppy hat with a white rose pinned on its side.

As a herald led the procession, carrying a long stick entwined with white roses, Jenny told her father, "Margaret looks majestic. Remember, I told you how she praised the duke."

He nodded, his eyes twinkling. The Vander Goes family was shown to seats at Margaret's left. Jenny relished the festive atmosphere. Musicians decked in white outfits played soft melodies. At her father's prompting, she gazed upward. Jenny examined the family crest with a smile. Slung from the ceiling, it bore the three suns and the Mortimer rose.

Cheers abounded in the great hall as King Edward IV and Queen Elizabeth paraded in. Jenny was awestruck by their stately bearing. The queen seemed tiny compared to the ample-figured king. The royal couple settled into elaborate wooden chairs. Guests were introduced and directed to sit on cushioned chairs.

Jenny marveled at the intricate menu. The first course consisted of pickled lamprey, eels in sauce, large crabs, boar's meat with mustard, and a special sweet. A second course would follow. Her eyes widened, thinking of eating royal pork pies, minced chicken, lobster, fried smelt, and a swan-shaped confection. She couldn't even fathom having room for the third course of freshwater crayfish, mixed herbs, perch, steamed trout, and large shrimp.

"How can we consume so much food?" she asked a woman to her left.

The guest wrinkled her nose, scrutinizing the ruby necklace circling Jenny's neck. Was it Jenny's imagination or did the woman, whose title was Duchess Something or Other, tell her husband, Duke Nobody, the gems looked like paste? The scarf on the woman's hennin became a colorful barrier between the two women.

Had Jenny blundered? Margaret considered her a dear friend, so Jenny fluttered a menu in her direction. Securing her attention wasn't easy. Margaret sat two chairs down to her right.

"Margret, these delicacies are more than I eat in a week!"

"I promised you, Jenny, the king's banquet would be glorious."

The herald rang his bell announcing, "Hear ye, hear ye, the banquet given by His Majesty in honor of Lady Margaret of York begins."

Jenny applauded along with the other guests. The entire table quieted as costumed servants made the rounds with large platters of food. Pieter used the lull to speak in a low voice to Margaret. She smiled graciously, and Jenny heard her ask him, "Did your meeting with the king go well?"

Jenny didn't hear his reply. The duchess to her left coughed, forcing her scarf into Jenny's nose.

Dirck nudged Jenny's side. "She would lose if you challenged her to chess, sister."

Despite the chilly reception on her left, Jenny's cheeks grew warm. Her brother had actually complimented her. She ate the sweet dessert, content to watch Papa and Margaret discuss matters quite seriously.

Conversation buzzed all around her. Jenny leaned closer to better hear Margaret's answer to her father's inquiry if the Earl of Warwick was in attendance.

"My cousin is in France." She touched a white rose on her necklace. "He plants seeds of hope I will marry a Frenchman. I dare say he'll be unhappy if I marry your Duke Charles."

"Does King Edward favor you marrying Charles or does he seek to ally with France?"

Margaret's gray eyes clouded. "If only Edward would tell me. I had hoped he would tell you, Duke Charles' emissary."

She spooned a bit of confection into her mouth.

Pieter tried again. "Lady Margaret, do you have a say in the matter?"

"Do not let the steward hear us. My mother says what's best for England is best for me."

"Your mother isn't here tonight," Pieter replied. "What are her wishes?"

"Lord Vander Goes, please do not inform Duke Charles of my mother's absence. She has yet to accept my brother being married, or his choice of wife."

"My point exactly. Does your mother want you to marry Duke Charles and become Duchess of Burgundy? It would be a powerful alliance on both sides."

"She hasn't declared it to me. My future depends on keeping power from the Lancastrians, and the queen's family. Edward seeks to mollify France, so I await his decision."

"I await discussing this subject with the king. Is that possible before the night ends?"

She rose and grabbed hold of Jenny's hand. "Lord Vander Goes, please come with me."

Margaret led Jenny and Pieter to the dais. Here, she curtsied to her brother.

"My noble King, Lord Vander Goes tells me of the beauties of Zeeland, which I desire to see. His daughter, Lady Jenny Grace, is my valued friend. They invite me to visit. Lord Vander Goes is eager to discuss the particulars with you in private. Do you have time?"

Jenny curtsied, her heart skipping a beat. The queen looked at her with a friendly nod. But the king acted so stern Jenny dared not breathe. With his small dark eyes, King Edward gaped down at her papa, before extending a hand for him to kiss.

He remarked jovially, "We long have had friends in the Netherlands.

Margaret, recall I took our younger brothers there for safekeeping after Father was killed. Now that I am king, Richard and George are back in England brimming with stories of windmills and fishing."

The king smiled at Jenny, and then agreed to meet her father in his private chamber when the entertainment started.

Pieter bowed low from his waist, saying, "I am honored, Your Majesty."

The king rested his gaze upon Margaret. "Dear sister, you have never looked lovelier. Thoughts of a trip to Burgundy bring out your natural beauty. Your choice of gown is most becoming. Lord Vander Goes, surely burgundy and black are the colors of Duke Charles."

"Your sister does our country credit in displaying our colors," was Pieter's amiable reply.

Margaret kissed the king's proffered hand. "Dear brother, the banquet you hold in my honor does me more good than you will ever know. You show more kindness to a sister than she deserves. I thank you."

Jenny noticed a smile lit Edward's full face. She imagined he was touched by Margaret's thankful heart. Papa's mission for the duke might succeed after all. They returned to their seats, while Margaret stayed to chat with the queen. A servant pulled out Jenny's chair. She ate a spoonful of mixed herbs, when the hall doors burst open.

Uniformed palace guards charged in, swords drawn. They rushed toward King Edward, then forcefully turned to face the table of guests. Margaret edged sideways, looking fearful. The contingent formed a powerful barrier between King Edward and Queen Elizabeth and everyone else. Ten more guards marched in, surrounded the table, their eyes scanning the dukes, earls, lords, and ladies that were seated. Jenny decided Duchess Something was in trouble.

The next moment her heart collapsed in fear. Two enormous guards grabbed her father from behind, yanking him out of his chair. He struggled in vain. Dirck jumped to his feet, only to be subdued by three of the king's men.

Jenny leapt to her feet, finding her voice. "What have we done? I will find Margaret and make you stop!"

To her horror, Papa and Dirck were dragged away before her eyes. She whirled around. A burly guard seized her arms and hauled her from the table. Lady Margaret stepped to her defense, but a guard with a sword glistening at his side stepped between them.

"Do not interfere, Lady Margaret. The king requires your presence."

Soldiers wrenched Jenny's arms, pulling her away. Her feet collided with a rug in the hallway. There a hefty guard with a raw scar running down his cheek barked, "We know of your wicked plan!"

"I asked Margaret to visit me in Zeeland. The king approves! Ask him!" Jenny cried.

Towering over her, the guard twisted her arms behind her back. She cried out in pain. Another began grabbing and squeezing Jenny through her gown. One raised her skirt, exposing her ankles. Another pinched her arms, making a crinkling sound.

"Ah hah," he exclaimed. He rolled up her sleeve and snatched out Alphonso's note.

"That's from my suitor," Jenny protested.

"Oh, is it now?"

Scarface read her note, and then flung her a devilish look. With an open hand, he struck her face. Jenny's eyes tingled. She burst into tears. Why was this happening?

This vicious guard thrust the note into his commander's hands. He read it quickly.

"As we thought," he snapped. "It's from the same scoundrel. Confine her in the dungeon. Take the others as well. Spare nothing to make them talk."

Jenny's heart failed her. She wept uncontrollably as she was pushed and dragged down the dark and narrow steps into the putrid bowels of the grand and glorious castle. The foul air smelled of perspiration and body waste. Her stomach reeled.

As they passed a corridor, she heard a man screaming as though his arms were being torn from his body. Men shouted obscenities. Panic filled her senses. Deep into a dark pit she was cast. The cell had iron bars on the door. In front of her sat both her father and brother. As the door slammed, Jenny fell against Papa. He stood and embraced her.

"My dear heart, I can't believe you are enduring this. I have no explanation."

Dirck hugged her next. His tears brushed against her cheek. Jenny stepped back and tried to compose herself.

"This is Alphonso's wicked scheme!" she sobbed. "A guard found a note he sent. The commander recognized his name and ordered me to the dungeon."

Pieter led Jenny to a stone ledge and made her sit. "This isn't a time for accusations, but for prayer."

Before he could lead them in a prayer for justice and safety, a voice shrieked agonizing screams of a man in distress.

"Oh, Papa!" Jenny sobbed.

"Someone is being tortured," he said, pain in his voice.

Dirck put one hand on Jenny's shoulder and one on their father's. "Do you think the man could be a Wycliffe follower? They still burn Lollards here."

"What about Justinus?" Jenny asked wildly. "He and Angus are preaching near London."

"They are to the north, miles from here," Pieter assured.

Jenny's insides shook. Tears plunged from her eyes at the idea of her brother being tortured. She refused to believe it was him. With the background of inhumane cries, the three of them spent hours praying, weeping, and encouraging each other.

At last, Jenny rested her head on Papa's shoulder. Would they be lost down here forever? She realized Margaret would do whatever her brother ordered her to do. If Jenny and her family were his enemies, they would suffer the consequences. Surely God saw them here and would not let them die in a dirty prison cell.

Pains gnawed her empty stomach, but Jenny thought nothing of food. Her spirit was pierced through and through with what Jesus the Christ had done for her. Forsaken by friends, He was beaten and died a harrowing death on the cross for her sake. Jenny's face fell into her hands. She cried silently to the Lord of Hosts, from the utter depths of her heart.

*Oh, dear Lord, take my black sin from me. I have been willful and selfish. Make me white as snow, Jesus. You are the King of Kings. I care nothing for this court or earthly king. If we suffer for You, give us strength and courage. If we die, may our deaths bring You glory. If we live, may our lives bring You honor. Help me, Father, to be everything You want me to be.*

Papa wrapped an arm around her and started singing a hymn. It seemed quite late when the lock on their cell turned, and the door clanged open.

The captain of the guard entered with a lantern.

"I come with the king's apology," he said earnestly. "A crisis has passed. You are no longer considered a threat to the kingdom. Follow me to your rooms. Food will be brought. It is late now, but in the morning, you will meet with His Majesty King Edward."

# CHAPTER 37

After bathing and being refreshed by eating fruit, Jenny was escorted to a side room along with Pieter and Dirck. On the way in, her father grabbed her hand and squeezed it. She smiled at him with her eyes, but no words formed. She was exhausted from the ordeal. Life had changed forever. She would question everything and everyone.

The palace guard rested a hand on a sword hanging by his side before taking them into a small parlor. King Edward sat in a carved chair, flanked by two sullen officers of the guard. Though Jenny had been told "the crisis has passed," the dour look on the king's face made her wonder if they faced new difficulties.

She set her chin, prepared to be cast from England forever. Home called her. Jenny couldn't wait to sail the channel, so long as Papa and her brothers came too. Papa and Dirck bowed, drawing Jenny out of her immediate concern for Justinus' whereabouts.

She curtsied, with no fondness for the royal personage. In her heart, she knew she served the King eternal. Edward, King of England, motioned for them to be seated.

"I regret yesterday's horrid events," he began. "I was as surprised as you when the palace guard interrupted our meal. It was not for want of a good reason. My security forces discovered a scheme to assassinate Lady Margaret."

Jenny shrieked and nearly fell off her chair. Pieter started to reply, but the king put forth his hand in a gesture that he should not be interrupted.

"Alphonso de Alvarado has been arrested and detained in our prison chamber. He came to England, my home," Edward raised his voice and boomed, "and was recruiting an assassin to act when my family would be distracted by wedding plans of my sister to Duke Charles. That is the very union you come to proffer on the duke's behalf, Lord Vander Goes."

The king glared so fiercely at her papa that Jenny's cheeks blazed. Why had she encouraged Alphonso's attentions? And taken his ugly red rose? Oh, he was a wicked fiend. She began to comprehend what Margaret meant about her family having enemies. Jenny forced herself to listen to the king.

"We discovered that Duke Charles' message to you, Lord Vander Goes, was delivered by Alphonso's father, Count de Alvarado. My guards have persuasive ways. They applied certain techniques to Alphonso, and he confessed his father read the note before giving it to you. Alphonso and his father proceeded to inform my mortal enemy, King Louis XI of France, of Charles' hopes of marriage to Margaret. At the behest of the French, Alphonso hoped to arrange for an assassin here in England so Louis could promote a French bride for Charles."

King Edward paused, an ominous look erupting across his broad face. "The poor chap failed to realize my people love me and are the most loyal of subjects."

"Is your sister … is Margaret in good health?" Jenny stammered. "May I see her?"

The king's stern face burst into a rare smile. "She desires the same thing. My guard will take you and your brother to her. She is praying at St. George's Chapel. Lord Vander Goes, you and I have much to discuss."

Jenny rose to follow the guard. Dirck stayed at her side as they hurried down a hallway filled with animal skins and heads. She shuddered, and faced her older brother.

"In that rank cell, I saw my sin, Dirck. I didn't listen on the ship when you warned me of Alphonso and his true intentions. It was wise of you to throw his red rose into the sea. If I had brought that horrid flower into the castle, I might have lost my head."

"And I realized in our captivity that rather than printing Bibles, I might better teach of God's love and plan as Justinus is doing. It is a more urgent cause."

Jenny pulled on Dirck's sleeve. "Please don't think so lightly of what you are doing. Gutenberg's Bible and the Christian manuscripts you have printed will endure for years after we and Justinus leave the earth."

IN A LUXURIOUS EATING ROOM AN HOUR LATER, Pieter helped himself to a light meal. A servant stood silent and grave near a high table filled with grilled meats, bread and cheese, and small boiled eggs. Pieter asked the servant for pottage of oats, then took a seat at the table, mulling over Alphonso's duplicitous acts.

The scurrilous man had finally met his match. King Edward refused to tell Pieter what would be done with him. It must have been Alphonso they heard screaming in the dungeon. Would he be confined for a time and then let go? Or would he hang for his crimes?

The servant returned with a steaming bowl, only to disappear behind a door set into the wall. Dirck sped into the room. He sat down, his eyes watery and red.

"This was supposed to be a trip to remember for the ages. Instead, it has brought me quite low, Father. I never liked Alphonso or his father. But to be ensnared in their depraved schemes using Jenny is unthinkable. What should we do?"

"Vengeance is mine, says the Lord. We leave him to the King of England."

"Do you have a favorable report for Duke Charles?" Dirck put a tiny egg on his plate.

Pieter chewed a piece of bread, and then wiped his mouth.

"Son, the exact details are for the duke's ears only. King Edward thinks highly of our duke, especially since Charles invited him to join the prestigious Order of the Golden Fleece, held only by knights of the Burgundian realm."

"You were awarded the Order," Dirck reminded him.

Pieter nodded. "There is something else to perk your spirits. The king was impressed to receive the Gutenberg Bible. He will also share your Book of Prayers with the queen."

"That is good news. I don't imagine Alphonso will be on the ship when we sail home."

Pieter got up from the table and looked out the large window. Sheep grazed serenely on a far hill. Peace was far from Pieter's mind. What happened here went beyond his understanding.

At length he turned and said, "No, son. We may never hear his name spoken again."

"Would that be such a bad thing?" Dirck asked.

"I propose we visit Uncle Douglas and Aunt Emilee," Pieter remarked. "It's been years since we've seen them and the babe Alexander. From their letters, he grows into a strapping young man. Perhaps he is a good candidate for our school. "

Dirck agreed it was a fine idea. "They live north of London, do they not? I want to see Justinus, who is in their village of St. Albans. We don't know when we may see him again."

# CHAPTER 38

Their sleek trading ship, *The Worthy*, put into port, her sails trimmed in the harbor. A beautiful morning unfolded for Vander Goes' family homecoming. Before saying their good-byes to Justinus, he showed them the shrine honoring Alban. The first British martyr, Alban had sheltered a priest from the Romans by exchanging cloaks and giving him time to escape.

"He never wavered believing in Christ, even after his arrest," Justinus had told them. "He was beheaded for his faith. I do not want to forget his sacrifice."

Pieter had embraced his courageous son. "Nor do I. You are in my heart, though we live in distant lands. Remember how much I care for and respect you."

Justinus had hugged them all, and as they drove away in the litter, he'd waved brightly. Then he turned with a walking stick in his hand and cloth bag slung over his shoulder. Pieter had watched from the litter until he could no longer see his son's brown robe.

Seabirds searching for an unwary fish brought Pieter's eyes searching the docks for signs of home. He spotted Fredrick milling about the shoreline. Long wooden planks were eventually lowered from the ship onto a timbered dock. The crew ran down the plank and tied the ship's ropes to several posts. Another mate rolled a barrel down the planks, loaded it onto a cart, only to return with another barrel.

Fredrick hopped aboard and helped Jenny to dry land. Pieter was surprised to see Count de Alvarado holding out a single yellow rose to her, placing the bud between her fingers. What new scheme was this? Pieter hastened down the plank.

He arrived in time to hear Jenny cry, "Oh! A thorn stabbed my finger."

The count bowed deeply to Pieter. When he straightened, tears streamed down his cheeks.

"A disturbing message reached me. King Edward arrested my son. Will you help me?"

Pieter spied blood on the tip of Jenny's finger. She tossed him an intense look and spun on her heel. "Papa, I am tired and want to go home."

Pieter asked Fredrick to take Jenny to their litter, adding, "As soon as Dirck appears, we must all go home at once."

With Jenny out of hearing, Pieter whirled on the count. "Your son is in deep trouble. He sought the death of the king's sister. I pray for him, but there is nothing I can do for Alphonso."

Pieter sped away toward the sloop to find Dirck, never looking back.

THE NEXT DAY, JENNY FLOWED INTO THE KITCHEN. A tall hennin etched in black ribbon framed her rosy face. When she thought of her time spent this morning with Fredrick, her pulse raced. When she confided to him of her terror at being arrested and held in prison, his face had paled.

He'd snatched her hands with such vigor that she blushed to think of it.

"My dearest Jenny Grace, you could have been killed. I thought of no one but you the entire time you were gone."

"Did you?" she'd whispered. "I myself thought of you the closer we neared home. The sight of you on the dock, with your blond hair blowing in the wind, took my breath away."

Fredrick had lightly kissed her hand.

"Did you?" he'd said, his eyes glittering. "Will you … is it too much to ask … Jenny, will you do me the greatest honor and consent to be my wife? I have loved you these many years. I should ask your papa first I know."

"Jenny, I am famished. When do we eat?"

She turned from the kitchen window to see Dirck gawking at her. Her mind retreated from the beautiful memories of Fredrick's marriage proposal.

"Why do you stare so?" she chided. "Do I have breakfast pudding on my chin?"

"Are ye ready for yer dinner then, me lady?" Mollie asked.

The good woman struggled to stand, grabbing the chair to straighten her spine. Seeing it was difficult for her nurse and friend to remain standing, Jenny dashed to her side.

"Our guests are all here. Please sit Fredrick next to Papa and let maids serve the meal."

When Mollie protested, Jenny held up her hand. "No opposition. You said yourself that I am the lady of this house now. It is time I acted like it. We'll find another girl to help you. I need your help managing household accounts, planning menus, and ensuring Papa has enough creamed herring. Agreed?"

"The good Lord isna' givin' me a choice. I'll do as ye say. Now, help me sit."

"Good. I hope we have plenty of creamed herring. Papa loves it so."

The dinner passed with jovial conversation and delicious food. Jenny kept a loving eye on Fredrick as he entertained Pieter with stories of village happenings while they'd been away. The maid brought in the final course—poached pears swirled with a delicate almond sauce. This signaled Jenny's request for Dirck to fetch the surprise. He returned in short order and handed their father a square package wrapped in a striped satin cloth.

"What have you done, my children?" Pieter asked, his eyes shifting to their eyes.

Jenny smiled. "Dirck thought of it before we left. Fredrick completed the present while we were in England. Are you going to open it?"

Pieter removed the cloth and held up a framed picture.

"How wonderful! My mother sewed this scroll nearly forty years ago."

Maxim took hold of it. "And it's covered in glass. I see her Latin phrase, *Jesus amor meus*. The Lollards say this is their credo. In English it means 'Jesus is my forever love.'"

"Papa, do you like it?" Jenny's green eyes danced.

"More than I can express." Pieter admired the framed scroll. "Thank you, Fredrick."

Fredrick cast a furtive glance at Jenny. "Sir, now that you have opened your gift, would you meet with me alone in your study?"

"By all means, but is it another kind of surprise?" Pieter asked, his brows raised.

Jenny nodded and was about to tell all when Maxim interrupted. "Before you leave, I found out from Dirck what happened to Alphonso and that his father met you at the docks. What can I do?"

An ashen look struck Pieter's face. "The count is obsessed with power. Nothing surprises me about his schemes."

"So you think Alphonso acted at the behest of his father?"

"The baby skunk smells like its father. So it is with Alphonso and the count. If we don't avoid them, we too will stink."

Pieter stood, putting an end to questions. "I leave in the morning to meet Duke Charles and report on my trip to England."

Jenny rose and pulled out his chair. "Oh, Papa, you and Maxim can talk of intrigue and politics later. Please talk with Fredrick without delay!"

"Fredrick is like family. He's free to talk with the rest of the family."

Pieter looked again at the beautifully framed scroll with the embroidered names of family descendents. He studied it for a moment, and his eyes began sparkling.

"Jenny, I thank you for this perfect gift. However, we should remove it from the glass."

She drew back. "But that protects the scroll. This piece is precious to me as to you."

"You misunderstand me. We need to add the names of you children and eventually your mates."

Jenny smiled widely, her heart fluttering in anticipation.

Her papa glanced at Fredrick, and then flashed her an exaggerated wink. "Will you excuse me? I need to speak to Fredrick in private."

*"If your enemy is hungry, feed him; if he is thirsty, give him something to drink. In doing this, you will heap burning coals on his head."*

Romans 12: 19–20 (NIV)

# CHAPTER 39

## FAIRFAX COUNTY, VIRGINIA

E va closed the journal and placed it on the floor next to the sofa. She turned to Kaley.

"I'm sorry we became so engrossed in the past. You need to get to bed."

Kaley still held the tissue she used when they read of Aneka's sudden death from bubonic plague. "Mom, please always stay safe."

Eva hugged her. "You know, our lives are in God's hands. Something else, Kaley. Because we're Christians, we will meet Aneka and her whole family in heaven someday."

"Oh, I never thought of that. Cool!" Kaley pronounced before confiding how uneasy she was about wearing her cross t-shirt to Badger's class. "At least he can't have me burned at the stake. I can endure anything he does. Our family toughness goes way back."

"It certainly does. More than we ever knew."

As her daughter headed for bed, Eva put the marker in her page. The Vander Goes family had experienced much pain and trouble. She felt Pieter's great loss, and approved of his committed love for his wife even following her death. Eva loved Scott as deeply.

Through the generations, family names changed, but life and death remained the same. She rose, joy flooding her heart. God's Holy Word, the Bible first printed by Dirck Vander Goes, would live forever. A chill tore through her. She had found the evidence to convince Dr. Wiles that the Gutenberg Bible did indeed belong to Eva.

She brushed her teeth in the guest bath, reaching a decision. On Monday morning she'd schedule an appointment with the Smithsonian. Slipping into bed next to Scott, she slept well, dreaming of Jenny's beautiful wedding to Fredrick where she carried a bouquet of white roses. The beeping alarm startled her awake. She dragged herself into the shower and dressed quickly, anxious to enjoy the rest of the weekend.

Monday brought new concerns over terrorists targeting America. Later in her office, Eva checked the wall clock. Griff should be calling any moment. He and another task force officer were on surveillance after getting a disturbing lead on their Chechen suspects. Recalling someone in Boston had dropped the ball on Russia's tip about Chechens, Eva figured Griff would be preoccupied.

He missed his check-in time, so she phoned him, reaching his voice mail. After leaving a hurried message, Eva set down her phone when she heard Raj Pentu slam down his. She raised her head over her cubicle. Raj spotted her and jerked his head toward the conference room. He bolted from his chair. Eva rushed into the room. He shut the door with a snap.

"What has you so fired up?" she asked, taking a seat.

Raj flopped into the opposite chair. "Bo Rider called last night, asking me to come to his office. I drove to Langley with mixed feelings. Though acting secretive as usual, Bo admitted he's been in touch with Judah Levitt from Mossad."

"With terror spreading in the Middle East faster than the Ebola virus, that's hardly surprising. Does he want you back in Egypt?"

"Don't get ahead of me. Mossad discovered the Brotherhood raided the home, a small warehouse really, where Hamadi Van Bilgon lives. The locals thought everyone had been killed."

Eva's hand flew to her mouth. "Hamadi has been killed?" She tried grasping what he'd said. "Wait. You say 'thought' like things may have changed."

"I just hung up with Bo," Raj said, jumping to his feet. "He hinted, using coded phrases, that Hamadi may be alive and hiding in a tunnel."

"But that's wonderful!"

"Wait." Raj raised a big hand. "There's more. I've been in that tunnel.

Hamadi rescued me and Yakov through an underground passage running between his church and warehouse."

"What are you planning?" Eva asked.

"I want to take in a rescue party."

"Going into Egypt is even riskier than when you were there last. We Americans all have a price on our heads."

"Yes, I know there's renewed fighting on Egypt's volatile border with Israel. The Islamic State—IS—now trains the Brotherhood, but Eva, the man saved *my* life!"

She relented. "I don't minimize his sacrifice. We should talk things through."

Eva urged Raj to sit while they hashed over the recent caliphate declared by IS in Iraq and Syria. Raj looked at her with dark piercing eyes.

"A Jordanian diplomat to the United Nations says IS wants to annihilate all of humanity that doesn't agree with their violent beliefs. They want to build a 'house of blood.'"

"Such evil must be stopped, but can we find Hamadi below the earth, let alone rescue him in time?" Eva arched her brows. "How long can he live down there? Does the Brotherhood already know of this tunnel?"

"You're instincts are spot-on. I'll take your questions to Bo; we're working up an action plan. Pray NCIS lets me return to Egypt. If the Agency requests it, they might agree."

Eva followed Raj out of the conference room. "I'll lock my desk and come with you."

"Uh, that's not a good idea, Eva."

"Yes it is. You need me. Bo and I go way back. I've also worked with Judah."

Raj swiped at his chin. "It's no good, Eva."

"Why on earth not?"

"I know you and Bo are friends. When I started the arms caper with him, he ordered me to tell you nothing about it."

Astounded, Eva stopped in her tracks. "Why would he say such a thing?"

"I have no idea. You know better than I how guarded he is."

Eva did some fast thinking. Her daughter was keeping important matters from her, and now Bo. What wasn't she seeing? She tried calming her anxious thoughts.

"Listen, Raj, ask Bo if he still feels that way about me."

"Okay, I will." Raj headed for the exit. "And keep praying for Hamadi."

"Absolutely."

Eva returned to her desk. Thoughts of Kaley reminded her to call Heather, which she did, scheduling a time to meet at the Wholly Ground. In the ensuing quiet, she pondered all sides to a possible op to free the Coptic Christian. Doubts assailed her.

She imagined Scott's fierce objection to her going to Egypt, where a raging firefight blazed all around. But Hamadi was no faceless hero—she'd met him and heard firsthand of his bravery. Raj owed his life to Hamadi. Moreover, while the *Washington Star* reporter had much to answer for, Eva and Scott were partly to blame for exposing him to the press by bringing him before Congress to testify.

Eva couldn't help believing God was directing her on this mission. If so, He would give her and Raj all the courage and wisdom they needed.

MEANWHILE, KALEY AND HER FRIEND LEXI wore their edgy t-shirts with the cross on the front to school. Several kids gave them high-fives. Everything was going swimmingly until lunch hour when Mr. Badger sauntered by their table. He spun around with an icy glare.

"You can't wear those in my class," he insisted.

Lexi put down her tuna sandwich and folded her arms. "Oh, yes we can."

"We'll see about that."

He sped away, mumbling threats to stop their "religious propaganda." When they went to his class, he was lying in wait for them at the door like an ugly black spider in its web.

"Girls, you go into the washroom and turn those shirts inside out. I will not allow you to wear t-shirts with the Christian cross in my class. It's too disruptive."

"Disruptive for you, maybe," Lexi fired back. "We have a First Amendment right to free speech."

Kaley pushed her way into the classroom. "Other kids think our shirts are cool. You like them, don't you?"

She stopped a lanky teen. He shrugged, taking off his backpack to slide past them. Badger's eyes blazed with contempt.

"It's irrelevant what he thinks. I, your teacher, demand you turn your shirts inside out. Or I will call security and have you removed."

"Last week, Dante South wore his 'Black Death' shirt," Kaley said. "You did nothing."

Badger adjusted his horn-rimmed glasses. "For good reason. The plague was a natural occurrence."

"For one thing, his shirt honors a drug gang called Black Death," Kaley replied hotly. "Even so, his shirt *disrupted* my ability to concentrate in class. My great-great-great-great-grandmother died from the Black Death. All I could think about was her terrible pain."

"Don't be ridiculous. The Great Pestilence was a historical event. How can you deny what really happened in history?"

Kaley thrust her hand on her hip and inched closer to her antagonist. "My point exactly. Jesus Christ died on the cross. Not a single historian doubts that. You didn't object to Dante South's historical event, but you discriminate against us because our historical event is religious. A lawyer told us you can't do that. No one is upset but you, Mr. Badger. Your stand will be defeated one day, I tell you that."

Badger folded his arms. "This is my class. I make the rules."

Not knowing what else to do, Kaley turned around. Lexi followed her down the hall. Reaching the outer yard, they plunked beneath a blossoming tree.

"Who's the lawyer?" Lexi asked.

"A lady my mom knows. She looked up Supreme Court cases and said we students can voice our religious beliefs in school so long as we don't interrupt learning."

Lexi flexed her painted toes in her sandals. "Badger prob'ly belongs to some anarchist group. Hey, wait," she chirped, sitting up. "Let's follow him after school."

Kaley balked at the idea, but eventually Lexi won the argument.

"I don't want any trouble," Kaley said. "But I guess you're right. I will be doing what my mom does on surveillance."

Lexi bobbed her head. "Sure. We stay out of his sight, and see what we can see."

"Whatever we find, tomorrow I'm wearing my cross necklace. He won't dare take a chain off my neck."

"Yeah," Lexi chimed.

Kaley narrowed her eyes. "And our cross earrings. I dare him to rip them from our ears!"

The two girls stayed outside, missing Badger's class. They attended their last-hour English class, but Kaley could hardly concentrate as she formulated her plans. After class ended, she and Lexi waited in Kaley's green Bug for Badger to leave the school grounds.

She drove behind his blue Jeep, staying back at a good distance, and nearly lost him when he ran a yellow light. Kaley slammed on her brakes.

"Don't lose sight of him," she hissed at Lexi.

Lexi turned her head. "He's at the red light around the corner. Hurry."

"I refuse to run a red light and get a ticket." Kaley tapped her fingertips on the steering wheel.

The instant the red light changed to green, she rammed the accelerator with her foot and made a left turn before oncoming traffic moved an inch. Lexi burst into giggles.

"Wow, Kaley. You could drive racecars. He's merging on the highway. Quick, he's passing that white truck!"

They trailed their teacher, staying behind him as he exited the highway a few miles later. They bumped along a country road until he pulled into the gravel drive of a rickety farmhouse. Plastic tricycles, toys, and junk littered the yard, which was dead and brown. A broken front window was covered with wood. Badger climbed out of his car and traipsed inside, his shoulders sagging.

"Does he live here?" Kaley slowly went by the rutted driveway.

Lexi rolled down her window. "What a dump."

"It's strange. I pictured him living in a large house with a swimming pool and three-stall garage. Let's see if he comes out."

Kaley waited in the turnaround at the dead-end street. Ten minutes later, she spied his car leaving. She eased her foot onto the gas, and passing the farmhouse, glimpsed a sign out front. Keeping her eyes on the road, she asked Lexi to read the sign.

Lexi ducked her head. Turning in her seat, she strained against the seatbelt. "I can't see exactly. Something like 'Green Acres Home.'"

"Badger lives in a rest home? Go figure."

Lexi straightened in her seat. "Stay on him to see where he goes, to be on the safe side."

"Tailing our teacher to his house and the store is hardly being on 'the safe side.'"

Lexi giggled. "Yeah."

Kaley buzzed around the corner. When they merged back on the highway, Badger wove his Jeep in and out of traffic before abruptly veering off the exit.

"He's spotted us," Lexi sputtered.

Kaley silently exited. After a few more turns, she saw Badger turn in the lot for Alley and Gutter's bowling alley, not far from her house.

"He brags about his bowling team," Lexi grumbled. "He'll be here for hours."

"We should rush home and change. Maybe he won't recognize us."

Thirty minutes later, dressed in caps, jeans, jean jackets, and sunglasses, the teens returned to the bowling alley. Kaley caught her breath as she spotted his blue car.

"He's still here. Ready?"

Lexi drew her chestnut-colored hair under her cap. "I called my mom and told her that we've a project to finish. She's not expecting me to work at Wholly Ground."

"I left my mom a note. Lexi, I saw a stakeout on TV," Kaley said, tugging her cap close to her eyes. "Federal agents pull their caps down. You're showing too much of your face."

Lexi yanked her cap down and Kaley approved. They spilled from the green Bug, and ambled into the bowling alley. The air smelled gross, like stale cigarette smoke and spilled beer. The bouncing of bowling balls and banging of pins were a strange sensation for Kaley's memory bank. They wandered behind a couple of the league bowlers, hoping to spot their mean teacher.

"He isn't here," Lexi complained.

Kaley nudged her toward a rack of bowling balls. "His car is, so he's gotta be here, somewhere."

They pretended to pick out a ball and then walked to the rental counter for bowling shoes. Kaley had a momentary stab of guilt over deceiving her folks, but it couldn't be helped. She rationalized her fib this way: Mom and Dad would try talking her out of her plan. Since she didn't really have a plan, there was no need to concern them. Not yet.

She saw Badger by the far lane, laughing with other bowlers. Anger seethed within her. How could he be so friendly away from school? She knew one thing. Her mom was right. He acted like a bully in class and she must stand up to him.

"Check it out, Lexi. He's probably bragging how he harassed us outside class today."

Lexi touched her phone on her waistband. "We could tape him."

"I'm not sure."

"Okay." Lexi pointed to the café. "We'll order burgers and see what he does."

Their burgers came with fries and large colas. The girls ate their food, chatting about camp. They were both planning to be junior camp counselors for primary school kids.

Kaley slathered ketchup on the last bite of her burger. "Did you hear Mitchell O'Connell will be there again this year?"

"Sweet! He lives in Maryland, not far from camp. He and I made that video about poison ivy. Did you see it?"

"How could I forget? Your video won the talent show, and beat my drawing of Civil War soldiers."

"Hey. I got an idea."

"For what?" Kaley wanted to know.

"Sshh! He's coming."

Kaley slumped in her seat and put a hand by her face. Badger sat a few tables over with his friends.

"He's ordering a pitcher of beer," Kaley observed.

When the beer came, she was shocked to see him drink an entire glass in one gulp, and then order another pitcher. Badger drank one beer after another as he talked animatedly with the bowlers.

Lexi pulled out her cell phone. "My, he is thirsty."

"I think it's sad, don't you?"

"Not really."

"We should head home. I wish we weren't seeing him smashed like this."

"Wait."

Lexi's eyes shifted to Badger's friend who went to the bar and bought two more beers. He carried them to the table. After placing them in front of Badger, he clapped him on the shoulder.

In an Irish accent he chimed, "May the road rise up to greet 'ye. Forget yer troubles. Yer daughter is safe where she is."

Then Mr. Irish and another guy left. Badger began drinking the fresh beer.

"Him sitting there drinking alone gives me the creeps," Kaley whispered.

Lexi turned on the video of her smart phone and leaned it against the condiment holder. She watched the filming as Badger kept drinking. Finally, he stood up, knocking over a chair. He stumbled to the door. Lexi continued making the video even though Kaley pulled on her other sleeve. Lexi ended the shoot, pocketing her phone.

She and Kaley followed at a distance while Badger staggered out to his car. Uneasy playing private detective, Kaley bustled into the restroom to wash her hands. When she rejoined Lexi by the green Bug, she saw Badger's Jeep had left.

"What happened?" Kaley asked, yanking keys from her pocket.

Lexi waved her smart phone in the air. "He dropped his keys. It took him two tries to pick them up, then he squealed off."

"If he's drunk, we should call someone."

"Well, he's gone now."

Lexi proudly showed Kaley the video. "After tomorrow, Mr. Karl Badger won't bother us ever again."

"Did you know Badger has a daughter?" Kaley asked, getting into the car.

"Nope." Lexi darted in and tore off her cap. "I'd hate to be her, anyway."

Kaley dropped Lexi off at her house. All the way home, she nursed a sickening sensation she'd been part of the underworld. Mom would understand. Still, Kaley couldn't decide if she should admit what she'd done.

She parked out front and went inside, calling, "I'm home!"

Kaley zoomed straight to her room, glimpsing the cross t-shirt she'd flung over the chair. Then she set out her cross earrings and necklace to have them ready for tomorrow. Footsteps lingered by her bedroom door. She snapped off the light and plunged beneath the covers. Whoever it was went away.

A compelling thought rattled around in her brain, keeping her awake.

# CHAPTER 40

Moments later, Kaley crawled out of bed and turned on her computer to check out Badger's daughter. On a social media site she entered "Karl Badger." Several popped up with his name. One was employed at her high school, and she clicked onto that account. A blank silhouette stared back at her. So her teacher was one of those coy subscribers, which was no surprise.

She clicked through a few photos. None were at the school or of Badger. One picture showed a little girl wearing a party hat, preparing to blow out three candles on a birthday cake. The caption beneath the picture said, "Happy Birthday, Olivia." Could she be the daughter Kaley had heard the bowler mention?

Kaley navigated to a list of sporting teams and businesses Badger had liked. One was Angel's Haven. Switching screens, she typed in "Angel's Haven," stunned to see an upscale home in a residential neighborhood in nearby Oakton. Their website indicated it was a Christian residence for special needs kids.

Maybe Olivia lived there. Something didn't add up with Badger stopping at that Green Acres Home. Kaley could see why he was such a crab. Everybody he cared about seemed infirmed. She copied down the phone number for Angel's Haven and concocted a plan.

Then she hesitated. It was ten minutes after nine. Was it too late to phone? Kaley decided she would try. Because of her mother's sensitive job, at least their home phone number was blocked from caller ID. So she took her notes and crept to the extension phone in the basement.

The phone for Angel's Haven rang three times before a soft-spoken woman answered, "Angel's Haven for children. Can I help you?"

Kaley was afraid her quivering voice would reveal her fear. Instead of banging down the receiver, she coughed slightly.

"Sorry to bother you so late. I keep forgetting to call during the day. The stuffed toy I sent my niece came back in the mail as 'return to sender.'"

"Oh, that's too bad," the lady said in soothing tones. "Who is your niece?"

"Olivia Badger," Kaley fibbed.

"Sweet little Olivia?"

"I missed her birthday," Kaley fibbed again.

"Well, dear, Olivia was removed from the Haven last week. We hated to see her leave."

"Do you know where I can mail her package?"

"Your uncle wouldn't say where he placed her. We didn't want her to leave, but we're a Christian organization. He couldn't abide by our rules. You should ask him."

"My uncle might not tell me either," Kaley said, keeping her voice low. "I'm a Christian. Sometimes he can't abide me either."

The lady chuckled and Kaley hung up, certain she'd done everything to investigate Mr. Badger the way her mom would have done. She tiptoed up the stairs, worry filling her heart about a little girl living in a dreary farmhouse called Green Acres. Maybe she should tell Mom everything. But then again, she'd order Kaley to mind her own business.

Kaley wasn't ready to do that just yet. So she spent most of the night plotting and planning.

THE FOLLOWING DAY AFTER SCHOOL, Kaley put Plan B into motion. She drove toward Green Acres, keeping under the speed limit and telling Lexi, "I'm only guessing Olivia is here."

"From her picture you showed me online, she's looks like a sweetie."

They rolled into the drive, tires crunching on the gravel. Kaley parked the green Bug and exhaled slowly.

"Lexi, is your phone set to shoot video?"

"I'm ready."

They got out quietly and climbed the steps, with Kaley carrying a gift bag. She was about to knock on the wooden storm door streaked with dirt, when a wide-eyed boy about five years old pushed it open. He eyed Kaley's colorful bag. They walked right past him and into the sparsely furnished house. The scuffed wooden floor had no rugs. Three folding cribs dotted the room, along with five high chairs and a stained rocking horse.

Kaley looked for an adult. Not seeing one, she leaned over and said to the boy, "We have a gift for Olivia. Is she here?"

He hopped on one foot toward a girl of about four. She sat with matted hair in a high chair against the wall. Her head drooped, and she appeared to be asleep, though she was sitting up. The boy pointed with a food-crusted hand toward the tiny girl.

"Olivia," he chirped, gazing at Kaley's gift bag.

Kaley raised her eyebrows, exclaiming, "Bull's-eye!"

Lexi activated the video feature on her phone and both teens bolted toward Olivia.

"Excuse me! Where do you think you're going?"

A heavyset woman stomped into the room wiping her hands on a towel.

Lexi stammered, "Ah … that small boy invited us in. We brought Olivia a gift."

The woman raised her chin, surveying both teens. "How do you know Olivia?"

"We know Mr. Badger from school," Kaley answered, holding up the bag. "When we found out about Olivia, we decided to surprise her by bringing her a gift."

The woman tossed down her towel and snatched the bag. "I don't permit gifts for the children. If I did, some would have plenty and others none."

"Sorry, we didn't know." Kaley reached for her bag.

"I'm Beverly Green and own this place." The woman pulled a stuffed Pooh bear from the bag. "We'll consider this cute little creature a gift for all the children."

Mrs. Green handed Pooh to the dirty boy. He clutched it to his chest as he ran through the room, disappearing around a corner. The woman nodded at Olivia with a shrug.

"As you see, her needs are too great to enjoy your gift."

"Hi, sweetie." Kaley stepped closer to the child. "Jesus loves you and all little girls."

Lexi held her camera nonchalantly, aiming it right at Olivia. She knelt by the poor girl's high chair and touched her arm. Olivia opened her eyes.

Without raising her head, she watched Lexi and Kaley from the corner of one eye.

Mrs. Green interrupted, "I must say, your visit flabbergasts me. I didn't think Karl had any friends. He's such a sad soul."

"Oh?" Lexi rose as if surprised.

Mrs. Green secured Olivia's hair with a clip. "Poor dear, you don't belong here."

"If you let Olivia have Pooh, it might help her," Kaley offered.

"I agreed to keep her until Karl finds a more suitable place." Mrs. Green fidgeted with her apron. "I quickly learned her needs are beyond what I can handle. That no-good wife of his up and ran off. She cares nothing for Olivia. What kind of mother does that?"

"She abandoned her baby?" Kaley whined.

Mrs. Green called to the small boy, "Jordan, bring Pooh back here."

Jordan skidded around the corner, the bear jammed under his arm. Mrs. Green told him to return the bear to Kaley. His eyes wide and lip trembling, he raised the stuffed animal into the air. Kaley took hold of it. She cuddled Pooh against her face, and knelt down by Olivia's high chair.

"Look, Olivia. Do you know Pooh? Would you like to hold him?"

The quiet little tot gazed at Pooh and the girls. Her expression never changed.

"That's our Olivia," exclaimed Mrs. Green.

Kaley didn't understand what was wrong with Olivia. She had looked so normal in the online photo. It seemed as if she'd heard what Kaley said. But Olivia didn't utter a peep.

Mrs. Green shook her head. "She doesn't emote or relate to us. I hope her daddy has better luck in finding her a proper home."

"I guess we should leave." Lexi tapped Kaley on the back. "We have homework."

Still holding Pooh, Kaley asked Mrs. Green if any homes in the area could treat Olivia.

"They're expensive. Karl provides for her on a teacher's salary. The mother is gone."

Kaley drove home, wondering how she could ever help that poor little girl.

# CHAPTER 41

Eva was in the middle of a discussion with Raj after his strategy meeting with Bo when her cell phone rang. The LED screen said it was her daughter. Eva instantly answered.

"Kaley, what's wrong?"

Her groan on the other end echoed into Eva's ear.

"Kaley, I'm at work. Please tell me what's happened."

"Mom, it's a long story. Do you have time?"

"For you, yes," Eva assured, waving Raj out of her cubicle.

Kaley told her in an excited voice about finding Mr. Badger's daughter, a special needs girl. "Olivia's languishing in a decrepit place called Green Acres."

"How did you 'find' this child, Kaley? What more aren't you telling me?"

"Lexi helped me. We did nothing sinister, but Mr. Badger refused to let us wear our shirts with the Christian cross. So we may have … ah … followed him."

Eva had a thousand words for Kaley, none positive. She counted to ten and tried to sound calm. "Do you think he approves of you stalking his sick child without his permission? I can see his lawsuit now, for breach of privacy or some such nonsense."

"Oh, Mom," Kaley squealed. "Mr. Badger won't bother us again."

"Your dad and I want to hear the whole story," Eva replied hotly.

Kaley puffed out a ragged sigh. "Sure, but later. I wondered if you'd call the lawyer you talked to about Mr. Badger's harassing letter. Doesn't she help out at a group home for kids? Olivia is so tiny, Mom, and looks scared."

Raj laid a white sheet of paper next to Eva and walked away. Eva didn't want to quell Kaley's concerns, even if she had gone about things in the wrong way. She agreed to contact Heather and ask her to come over later.

"We'll have a proper chat. Young lady, where are you now?"

"At the Wholly Ground, helping Lexi serve. Could Heather meet us here?"

Eva's eyes flew to the clock. "Okay. See you there around 5:30. I've gotta go."

She looked down at Raj's note:

*Eva, I have to run. Be prepared to discuss an ops plan in the morning.*

AT THE WHOLLY GROUND, EVA spotted Heather chatting with Kaley and Lexi at a table near the kitchen. Heather's eagerness to meet on short notice had surprised Eva, but she did say she owed Eva "big-time."

"Hi, Mom," Kaley called. "I've already briefed Mrs. Pentu about Olivia and answered most of her questions."

Kaley's maturity made Eva smile as she took the empty seat. Lexi offered to bring her coffee. "You like it hot and black, right?"

Eva nodded and Lexi headed to the coffee pot.

"Kaley and Lexi are two wonderful girls," Heather said, admiration in her voice. "They've shared Olivia's distressing story, but they know nothing of her true medical condition."

Lexi brought Eva coffee and Heather a tall glass of lemonade. Kaley looked on anxiously as Eva sipped the brew before saying, "I was hoping to hear more of the story."

Both girls shrugged their shoulders. Eva zeroed in on Kaley, who shifted in her seat. Eva wasn't too happy with her daughter's behavior.

"I can't believe you kids put a tail on your teacher," she said. "Kaley, I raised you better than that."

Kaley flashed a grin. "Would you say that if I told you I'm seeing if I want a career like yours, Mom?"

"I see," Eva said curtly. "The investigation is the easy part. You have my permission to give me a verbal report rather than a lengthy written one."

"You go first." Lexi jumped up. "I'd better serve that hungry family their dinner."

She sped to the kitchen, leaving Kaley to repeat the blow-by-blow account, ending with Lexi shooting a video of Mr. Badger being drunk. "We have something juicy on him, and can get him fired if he picks on us again for being Christians."

"You did what?" Eva was aghast. She stared at her smiling daughter whose lopsided grin vanished.

"Ah … we did it because Olivia, his special needs angel, lives in such a dump."

Heather interceded, "Kaley was saying the tot's mother abandoned her and Karl Badger can't afford a proper group home on his teacher's salary."

Lexi stalked up, wiping her hands on an apron. "She doesn't talk. Watch this, Mrs. Montanna."

She played the one-minute video on her cell phone. Eva watched Olivia sitting mutely in her high chair staring at Pooh. Both teens seemed visibly shaken when the video ended. How could Eva criticize their actions in wanting to help this girl? Heather's look of grim determination as she took out a handheld computer prompted Eva to put their minds at ease.

"Mrs. Pentu is on the board for Transitions, a faith-based home and school for special needs girls. I think she has some ideas for Olivia."

"Yes, one minute." Heather began searching on her small computer.

Eva drank her coffee, and then faced Kaley. "I understand your dilemma."

"What dilemma, Mom?"

"I see it like this. On one hand, you think you have ammo to black-mail Mr. Badger into leaving you alone. On the other hand, you want to help him by helping Olivia. They're mutually exclusive. If you blackmail him, he'll dislike you and your faith even more. He'll never accept your help with Olivia."

Kaley shot an "uh-oh" glance at Lexi, who shrugged again.

"So you girls must decide on the right strategy," Eva insisted.

Kaley shook her head, sending her long blond hair trembling. "Mr. Badger is beyond help. He took his daughter out of Angel's Haven because he didn't like their rules."

"Couldn't we try to do something?" Lexi asked. "For Olivia's sake?"

Dynamics changed when Heather looked up from her computer and said, "Transitions is designed for severe cases. Olivia may be perfect for our specialized services."

When Heather smiled, the dimples in her cheeks showed.

Kaley wiped tears from her eyes. "Olivia looks severe to me. You saw she couldn't even reach for the Pooh bear." "I noticed her motor skills are absent," Heather replied. "This is excellent timing, because we received funding from a Christian chain of stores and have completed a new wing. We're reviewing applications."

Looking relieved, Kaley went to clear a nearby table and Lexi scrambled to greet two ladies. Heather leaned toward Eva, promising to see what she could learn from Mrs. Green and Angel's Haven.

"Do you want to contact Karl Badger or should I?" Heather asked, putting away her computer.

That was a good question. Who could best encourage him? Scott's opinion mattered in this delicate situation, and so did Kaley's.

Eva decided to punt, telling her lawyer friend, "Let's see what you find out first."

When Eva walked in the house, Scott wasn't there; he was working late on the Hill. So she was spared having to tell him of their daughter's spying techniques. Rather, Eva spent time after a quick supper with the kids sketching a possible rescue plan for Hamadi. This wouldn't be Eva's first rodeo.

In the morning, she drove to the office with heightened anxiety. Should she even be planning to assist on a mission to Egypt? She knew that delay spelled tragedy for Hamadi. Raj wasn't in yet, so she made coffee and turned on her computer. It was time for her monthly report on the fugitive Andrei Enescu. The Romanian terrorist's cold, menacing eyes stared back at her from a photograph on her computer screen.

The vulgar threats he'd shouted after the federal jury convicted him of supporting terrorism resounded in her mind. As the U.S. Marshals cuffed him, he'd yelled at Eva and Griff, "I'll get you lousy maggots! See if I don't!"

Within a month, he'd escaped while being moved by the marshals to federal prison. That happened two years ago. While Griff pretty much ignored his being on the loose, Eva's antenna stayed on high alert. She worried even more about her family's safety after last year's events with Brittany Condover.

She considered the "threatening" letter mailed to her recently. Had Enescu sent it? He might try intimidating her. Her fingers flew across the keyboard, updating law enforcement of Enescu's status as an escapee and that she was tracking his whereabouts.

Failure gnawed at her insides. She'd documented Enescu in Bulgaria and Paris using various bogus passports. Last year he'd entered the U.S. posing as Robert Shields, an American from Chicago. Somehow, and Eva didn't know how, he'd gotten a fake U.S. passport. If Enescu the terrorist could sneak into Chicago, he could find her and her family in the DC suburbs.

After all, hadn't he slipped through her and Griff's fingers at the mall using the name Francois Petit? Eva was so engrossed in writing her summary she failed to hear Raj Pentu step behind her chair.

"What's your interest in Yakov Gusev?" he asked crisply.

Eva spun around in her chair so fast her head became dizzy.

"Raj, hello. I didn't hear your question."

"Yakov Gusev." He pointed at the man staring from Eva's computer monitor. "Why are you interested in him?"

Eva's cell phone buzzed on the desk. But she ignored it. This was too important.

"No, he is Andrei Enescu, my one and only fugitive."

Raj squinted his eyes and leaned closer to the screen.

"Well, he must have a split personality. That's the guy who was with me when Hamadi rescued us from the Coptic church in Egypt. His name is Yakov Gusev, the flamboyant Russian arms dealer who almost got me killed."

Eva bolted to her feet. She jabbed both her fists into Raj's shoulders.

"Get out of here! Are you sure?"

Raj stepped back as if shocked. "Eva, the guy's a total jerk. I can't stand his arrogance and bad temper. How could I ever forget him?"

"We need to talk in the conference room. Now!"

Eva grabbed her coffee cup, her mind in a tumult. For the next twenty minutes, her emotions soared and dipped on a roller-coaster ride. Still, she pressed Raj for answers. The two agents finally discovered the single denominator bringing them to the stifling conference room. And his name was Bo Rider, agent for the CIA.

At last she slumped back in her chair. "Though it makes sense now, I still can't believe it. Griff and I get Enescu convicted for aiding terrorists. Then Bo, the Agency, and the U.S. Marshals fake his escape. They use him to pose as a weapons dealer in the Middle East. Bo slips him fake passports and inserts my fugitive into the Egyptian Brotherhood. After the first weapons sale, Bo realized he couldn't trust Enescu so he sends you along as his interpreter."

"Bo must have brought Enescu back to the U.S. after the first arms deal failed." Raj rapped his knuckles on the table. "You and Griff almost nailed him. Was Bo involved in his slipping away?"

"He posed as an FBI agent and sprung Enescu before Griff and I could arrest him."

Eva downed the last of her stale coffee, the acrid taste driving in the bitter truth: She should have figured out Bo's charade.

"Raj, a few years back, I took Bo along on a smuggled art delivery. We raided a house and because he wasn't armed or trained, I made him stay out in the yard. Later, I came out to find he'd convinced a local cop he was an IRS agent. He has pockets full of fake federal IDs."

Raj shook his head. "I figured Yakov was no Boy Scout, but I had no idea he was a wanted fugitive or connected to our task force."

Eva picked up her cup. Should she make her final point? Well, Raj needed to hear it.

"Here's where I come unglued, Raj. Bo knew Enescu or Yakov—or whatever his current alias is—was untrustworthy when he let you enter that snake pit in Egypt. He failed to warn you."

Then Eva realized something more troubling. She stuck her finger into Raj's chest.

"Now I know why he warned you not to tell me about your op. He knew I would tumble onto Yakov's real identity."

She marched out to her cubicle with Raj on her heels. Eva slammed her desk drawer and locked it. "I'm going to confront him."

"Yeah, me too," Raj said. "He skipped our meeting yesterday and hasn't even called back about Hamadi."

Eva held up her hand. "I was so wrapped up with being fooled by him about Enescu, I completely forgot about Hamadi. I am sorry, but we have to keep you clean for that mission. No reason for you to burn your bridges with Bo or the CIA."

She stormed out to her car, tossing her purse on the passenger seat. After jamming the car into drive, she called Bo on her cell. It went to his voice mail. She hung up and drove up to the gate, the security barcode on her rear passenger window triggering it open. Roaring out of the task force compound, within minutes Eva was speeding toward CIA headquarters at Langley. As she exited the highway, Eva tried again, leaving him a message to call the gate and let her in.

"I don't need much time, Bo. It's important."

She slowed at the entrance and waited behind several other cars, which were all waved in. Eva gave the guard her name. He consulted a handheld computer.

"Sorry, ma'am. No Special Agent Eva Montanna is on my list."

"It was a last-minute meeting," she said. "Probably a computer snag. Let me see if I have a text."

"Back away from the gate, ma'am. Others are coming in behind you."

Eva turned her G-car in the small turnaround area and left, defeat dogging her on the trip back to the task force. It would be better talking with Bo when she wasn't so fired up about his deception. Losing control of her case, any case, didn't sit well. Yet, she'd worked with him long enough to realize national security trumped their friendship every time. They both lived by the same hard and fast rules.

The rest of her afternoon passed in relative peace. Raj tried calling Bo for some word on Hamadi. Griff never surfaced, being entrenched with his Chechen suspects. Eva went home early, stopping at a local store to pick up groceries for supper. Home cooking would make a nice change instead of takeout. She'd try convincing Scott to grill the chicken.

They did enjoy his tender barbeque chicken with sweet corn on the cob. He ate his with a contented smile until Kaley threw a bombshell.

"Well, Dad, I suppose Mom told you what Lexi and I did."

He shook his head. "No, but you'd better tell me."

Kaley's eyes searched Eva's, who said nothing. Kaley blew out a long breath.

"Okay, we tracked Mr. Badger and found his daughter Olivia. She's a high needs little girl living in a fleabag home. It's no big deal; I was practicing to be a federal agent."

"You did what?" Scott's eyes bulged. "You tailed your teacher, pretending you were Mom?"

Andy and Dutch fled the table without a word, leaving their pie behind. Kaley looked sullen, toying with her dessert. Eva came to her rescue and told Scott the rest, about the teens videotaping their teacher getting drunk.

"She meant well, Scott. Heather's working on finding the child a placement at Transitions. We should wait for her results."

"Sounds good to me, Mom."

"While I agree you acted strongly to get Badger to back off," Eva added, "I don't approve of you letting him drive away intoxicated."

"He could have killed someone!" Scott barked.

Kaley blushed. "Sorry, Dad. We should have told the bowling manager. It all went fast."

She picked up her dish and scurried out of the dining room.

Scott reached for Eva's hand. "Sorry I blew up. My day fell apart. I shouldn't take it out on Kaley."

"Want to tell me about it?"

"Maybe later. I'm too steamed."

Eva stood up and kissed the top of his head. "How about another slice of pie? I'll warm it and put ice cream on top."

"Sounds good." He grabbed her hand and smiled.

When Eva served him the pie, they went into their home office to talk. Scott shared about his disastrous hearing, where the featured witness testified differently under oath than in their press release. Eva listened, encouraged, and then complained about Bo.

"I can't tell you why, honey, but I'm having a hard time forgiving him."

"Don't let your anger fester. Call and give Bo a chance to explain. You and he are good friends."

Scott's opinion made sense. Eva put aside the CIA agent because another issue was bothering her. She walked down the hall to Kaley's room, finding her daughter listening to music on her bed. Eva peered around the door, and Kaley waved her in, removing her earbuds.

"You'll make a first-class federal agent, Kaley. I didn't do everything right when I was a probie. I still don't."

Kaley flopped back against her pillow. "Mom, the most important thing is for me to show my concern for Olivia. In the end, it might cause Mr. Badger to think differently about our faith."

"And then maybe not, but it's the right thing to do," Eva said. "You have devised a better strategy. Concentrate on helping Mr. Badger, by helping Olivia."

Kaley jumped off her bed and hugged her with genuine love. Eva said goodnight, grateful her daughter was at last talking openly about life's pressures. However, Eva couldn't say the same about her work relationship with Bo. His secretive attitude toward her was troubling.

They'd fought side by side in the most dangerous of times, and Eva had never done anything to cause him to mistrust her. Had she?

# CHAPTER 42

Eva arrived early at her office. She still hadn't told Scott about a possible Egypt trip. Everything was too much up in the air. Besides, last night he'd been pretty low. Griff surprised her by bringing her a cup of fresh coffee. Eva took a big swig before telling him of the struggle involving Kaley's teacher. He brought her up to speed on the Chechen case.

When Griff went to take a phone call from an FBI contact, Eva called Bo, ready to have it out with him, *if* he answered. She listened to his cell phone ringing in her ear when Raj entered the squad bay at a fast clip. Eva looked up, astonished to see Bo right behind him.

Raj stuffed his weapon in his desk drawer, and nodding at Eva, shifted his eyes toward the conference room. She strode in, leaving her coffee behind. The moment Raj shut the door, she let Bo have it full force.

"Are we together helping Hamadi, or are you using us so you can redeem Enescu again? Or do you call him Yakov?"

Bo dropped into a seat. "Sorry. I couldn't admit Enescu was working for us. I was under strict orders."

"Why didn't you create a fake incident, showing him as dead? I've been fearful of him coming after my family ever since he escaped."

"Eva, think about that," Bo said, smirking. "If I made up some pretend record of his death, you'd simply keep digging to prove it was phony."

"I guess so. Where is he now?" she demanded.

"Judah Levitt has him, and Enescu's so afraid of Mossad that he won't be a problem to your family. Besides, he was angry you sent him to prison and he's no longer in prison."

"Okay, I'm glad we have that behind us." Eva grinned.

Raj plunked in a chair and leaned forward. "Bo has a strategy to rescue Hamadi, but he's forbidden to implement it. So he's here for our help."

"Let's hear your plan," Eva said, perching on the edge of a chair.

"What I'm about to say, I've scrubbed to an unclassified version," Bo said. "Though Judah is arranging certain matters, Mossad is delaying retrieving Hamadi because they have another op in Egypt."

"What kind of op?" Eva asked.

Bo shrugged. "He can't tell me more. Everything's political, which I stay out of. Frankly, I think it's because Israel receives little support from our government. When the State Department insisted Israel negotiate peace with neighbors seeking to destroy them, they have no reason to help us."

Sadly, Eva couldn't deny Bo's take on things. Their discussion of the political problems and possible course of action continued through the morning. Even the Egyptian government was helping Israel more than the U.S., cracking down on militants and destroying tunnels the Brotherhood built to smuggle weapons into Gaza. The Brotherhood was aligned with Hamas, which in turn smuggled their fighters into Israel through those tunnels.

Bo ran a hand through his curly hair. "Judah knows Hamadi protected Raj when he tried helping Mossad and me at the Agency. He's also aware of the CIA's assistance to Israel using other back channels."

"By back channels, he means ferreting out weapons going to radical groups in Egypt," Raj explained, "and getting funds to Israel to replace their depleted Iron Dome missiles."

"Then we cut off the missile shipments." Eva took a long sip of her coffee.

Bo went on to discuss Egypt's efforts to reach peace between Israel and Gaza. "Israel's military is far superior to Egypt's. The new Egyptian president's peace efforts are creating problems for him. The Brotherhood still wields power."

He hesitated, looking at Eva and Raj. Then he admitted the current U.S. administration was paralyzed by public opinion polls showing Americans were tired of war in the Middle East.

"Forget polls," Eva snapped. "We should do what's right to protect our national security, and save Hamadi."

"Yeah, I agree. But it's complicated," Bo replied.

He spread his hands as if powerless to stop global violence by himself. Iran, comprised of mostly Shia Muslims, provoked terror against the Sunni-Muslim governments of Jordan, Saudi Arabia, Syria, and Egypt. The purely evil terrorist cabal called IS had blossomed like a ferocious cancer, spreading from Syria, into Iraq, and elsewhere.

"They're decapitating Christians and many children," Bo said. "Their horrid motto is that Christians and Jews must convert to Islam or die. They're deeply connected to the Brotherhood. So any venture into Egypt is at our peril."

Bo's direct gaze didn't make Eva flinch. She understood the risks.

"It sounds overwhelming, but I tell you both that God is our shield." Eva clenched her fists. "We waited to stop IS and look what's happened. Civilization as we know it is about to vanish, unless God Almighty intervenes. I've prayed and I am certain He's directing me to help Raj go in and take Hamadi out."

Bo rubbed a hand against his chin stubble. "The countries I mentioned all hope Israel's battles with Hamas, which is really the Brotherhood, will beat the Brotherhood down so there's a greater chance of peace, even short-term. Certain officials fear a wrong move on our part will set the region aflame."

"It's already aflame," Eva said, puncturing that argument. "People are dying and the State Department is paranoid about getting involved in Egypt."

Bo's eyes clouded with trouble. "It's a fact and their paranoia bleeds over to the CIA. The Agency insists if we achieve a credible ops plan, State must approve it. Nothing can be traced to our government's involvement. It takes weeks of review. Blah, blah, blah."

Eva leapt to her feet. "So they'll let Hamadi die! He saved Raj's life."

"I'm furious," Bo insisted. "That's why I'm here."

"We could go and do it ourselves," Raj offered.

Bo stood, pocketing his hands. "Are you serious or just nuts?"

"That's it!" Eva cried. "We go as tourists on vacation and rescue Hamadi."

An uneven smile crept to Bo's face. "I'd hoped you would say so, Eva."

"What? You agree? Earlier you didn't want me knowing anything."

"I didn't want you clued in to classified arms shipments. It would breach national security."

Eva erupted into laughter. "That old excuse again. Never mind."

"Are you in?" Bo asked. "It means going to Egypt without official cover."

"I'm in," Raj said.

"Me too," Eva chimed. She hoped Scott would understand. He knew all about Hamadi's courage under fire.

Bo bumped their fists with his. "Okay, get ready to pull an all-nighter."

Raj immediately went to pick up a large order of burgers and fries. Eva left as Bo had calls to make in the conference room. She approached Griff.

"Raj and I are going with Bo to pluck Hamadi from Egypt."

As she filled in the details, Griff palmed his moustache in apparent frustration.

"I'm away a few hours on surveillance and you pick up a new case. What gives?"

She told him to sit down. "Let me pick your brain. I need some kind of plan."

"How come you kept me out of the loop?" Griff demanded.

"I just was put in the loop myself. Bo's breaking the news to Julia. Our trip is unofficial, at our expense as tourists. You have your Chechens to babysit. Besides, we need you here in case we run into trouble. We're desperate to rescue Hamadi."

"I suppose you need to develop a ruse," he interjected.

Both agents were quiet, thinking of what might be possible.

Then Griff arched his eyebrows. "What about your college friend in Israel?"

"She teaches there at the International Christian College. So?"

Griff laughed. "So, case solved. You hook up with her and go into Egypt as international studies students."

"Haven't I always said you are a genius?"

Eva grinned and started scanning contacts in her smart phone. What better time to call her friend Charlotte Tate in Tel Aviv?

EVA, RAJ, AND BO DIVIDED RESPONSIBILITIES. If Hamadi was still hiding in the tunnel beneath his house, he may have limited food and water. His life was at risk the longer they waited to go in. The next twenty-four hours passed in a flurry with Eva getting tickets, annual leave approved, and finalizing arrangements with Scott.

Raj was due at Eva's house in thirty minutes after he collected Bo. She still had to pack her duffel bag. As Eva scurried around her bedroom, Kaley ambled in.

"It will be hard, but I'll try keeping my brothers in line." Kaley's lower lip quivered. "We need you around here, Mom."

"I love you, honey."

At Kaley's forlorn look, Eva pushed aside her packing. She patted for Kaley to sit next to her on the bed, reinforcing the love she had for Kaley and the family.

Kaley gripped her hand tightly. "I'm kinda used to the drill; you go away and come home. But Mom, seeing Olivia in that high chair all alone makes me realize something."

"Heather Pentu will let you know if she can help Olivia and Mr. Badger."

"That's not what I mean."

Eva patted her hand affectionately. "I'm listening."

Soon her daughter would be a senior and then college … Eva forced herself to hear what Kaley was saying.

"You and Dad are always here for me. I mean *always*. Never for one second have I been adrift or uncared for."

Eva was filled with such joy, she thought she would burst.

"That's my heart's desire for you and the boys," she said softly. "Your father's too."

Kaley sniffled. "I don't want you to go. I'm afraid something might happen to you."

"While you and I are apart, we'll pray for God's protection, right?"

Kaley nodded, then she said, "Last night, Lexi and I watched a movie called *Constantine and the Cross*. Romans fed Christians to the lions. But on screen, the Christians loved Jesus so much they went to their deaths singing about Him. I feel silly letting Mr. Badger upset me. He can criticize my faith, but he can't stop me from loving Jesus."

"You're getting so wise." Eva gave her a squeeze. "This is my chance to help Christians in a danger zone who are persecuted for believing in Christ."

"Mom, will you wear my cross?"

Eva wiped away a tear as Kaley fastened the chain around Eva's neck. She embraced her daughter.

Releasing her, she said, "Your necklace being close to my heart reminds me of you."

"And remember Jesus' shed blood, Mom. He wants everyone to know of His sacrifice, even the ones who persecute Him."

Out of the mouths of an innocent came truth. Eva regretted leaving, then steeled herself, knowing she did not go alone.

Kaley whispered, "I love you, Mom," and dashed from the room. Eva jammed her stuff in the duffel bag and hustled to find Scott before Bo came to whisk her off to the land where Christians were dying. Scott acted unusually tense saying good-bye.

"Having you go across the ocean is almost unbearable," he said, drawing her to him.

Eva clung to him. "Are you saying you don't want me to go?"

"No, but you'd better come back to me, to us!"

"Kaley said something similar, which makes me uneasy. You and I talked it over, and prayed for a chance to free Hamadi. I can't let Raj go alone. He lacks experience and training."

"The longer we're together," he said in a bare whisper, "the more I want to be with you, always."

A car door slammed. It was now or never.

She touched his lips with hers, telling Scott, "You are my forever love."

He helped her into Raj's backseat and waved as they pulled out from the driveway. On the way to Dulles, powerful emotions washed over Eva. Was she being rash?

Bo twisted slightly in the front passenger seat. "Is your annual leave approved?"

His practical question burst her internal struggle. Their boss had signed both leave slips. Raj exited the freeway, and sped toward the airport with Bo barking orders.

"No badges, no guns. Nothing on your person connecting you to our government."

"Wait," Eva objected. "We're traveling on U.S. passports."

"Yes, but as tourists and nothing more. Got it?"

She gazed out the back window, her stomach queasy from too much caffeine. A jet roared overhead. The loud rumble drowned out Raj. He had to repeat every word, how the naval attaché at the U.S. embassy in Tel Aviv was a personal friend. He and Raj were once assigned together at the NCIS office in Italy.

"He's reserved rooms and arranged transport," Raj went on. "I did it all on my personal e-mail account."

"Did you take care of our signage?" Bo fired back.

Raj chuckled. "He's taking care of that too."

"What about your friend, Eva?" Bo turned and smiled. "Did she come through?"

"Everything is arranged."

Eva had graduated from Wheaton College with Charlotte Tate, now the Dean of Women at the International Christian College. Her husband taught journalism at the college in Tel Aviv. Eva stopped talking as Raj turned onto a service road. They would park near the Airport Task Force office, and have an agent drive them to the departure area.

Eva leaned forward, asking Bo, "Do you know if Hamadi is still in the tunnel?"

"We assume so, but there's little intel."

Eva didn't need reminding of the scarcity of hard evidence about his proof of life. Neither did Bo's final warning, "If caught as tourists, we're strictly on our own," come as a surprise.

Still, she grumbled, "Thanks for that."

Raj wheeled into such a tight parking spot that Eva had to squeeze from the backseat, her fanny pack clamped around her middle. When they unloaded all the bags, Eva did a double take. They really did look like tourists.

She fought skepticism to the Jetway, but the moment she entered the giant plane, her misgivings vanished. She was a federal agent on a quest to free a dear man who loved the Lord. If she had to lay down her life … no, she must focus on the op that spanned before her across the ocean. Eva longed to find Hamadi and embrace him once again.

# CHAPTER 43

Forty-eight hours later Eva fought being tired. No—she was literally exhausted. After her long flight to Israel, she awoke at four a.m. and trudged onto the bus for a tedious six-hour ride to Egypt. Now she was touring Saint Catherine's Monastery in the Sinai. The sun was sweltering.

Eva wiped the back of her neck. Besides struggling to breathe in such high temperatures, the time lapse dampened her enthusiasm. Was it possible she and the other agents could find Hamadi? Would he be alive?

Before she signed on for this op, she'd never heard of this monastery commissioned by Constantine the Great. Professor Tate had hastily scheduled a tour to legitimize their student "field trip." The chapel lay before her and she wandered over, thinking of the movie Kaley had just seen about Constantine. He stopped all persecution of Christians by Rome. The amazing thing was that her daughter had no idea Eva would be here. Eva fingered Kaley's cross beneath her t-shirt and noticed a sign.

As she walked closer, her breath caught. Was this truly the ancient site where God talked to Moses through a flaming bush? Apparently this rose plant had survived thousands of years. Eva looked for Bo to ask his opinion. He wasn't in sight. Neither was Raj.

She turned her attention to the scraggly leaves. Then she recalled hearing of giant redwood trees in the U.S.'s northwest that had first germinated thousands of years before Christ's birth. Eva looked over her shoulder. A hush enveloped her. The blue sky above sparkled with iridescence. A seed of faith sprouted within her.

Why couldn't this remnant belong to the same bush? Almighty God had plans for His people, including her. He revealed those plans through Christ's death and resurrection. And the Apostles had witnessed everything as recorded in the New Testament. Heroes like Constantine had saved and protected Christians through the ages. In the same way, God had used Eva's ancestors to come alongside Johann Gutenberg and print hundreds of Bibles.

Why couldn't God task Eva to help save the Coptic Christian named Hamadi? What else might He want her or her family to do?

A thrill shot through her. Though God's voice hadn't spoken in the bush, Eva's faith came alive. She must trust He would carry her through, helping her to tackle any and all obstacles. Though she flinched upon hearing the guide announce the tour was over, Eva turned with renewed purpose. This morning's revival of her spirit was etched forever in her memory.

Still, she boarded the bus with tension mounting. Had the Brotherhood already found Hamadi in the tunnel?

With a hand on her fanny pack holding her passport, Eva went down the aisle. The students buzzed with laughter. They looked professional in crisp white shirts and black slacks. Eva slipped into an empty seat across the aisle from Raj and Bo. The bus pulled away from Saint Catherine's with a jerk.

"What did you enjoy most about visiting the monastery?" Eva asked the young man sitting next to her. A year or two older than Kaley, here he was ready to begin undercover work.

"I'll show you."

He stopped typing notes on his mini-computer and switched to photos he'd taken. The first one to pop on the screen showed the monastery's high outer walls, which had been built long before modern machinery lifted the stones.

"This one's my favorite." The journalism student flipped to another photo. "Christ's crucifixion was painted in the thirteenth century. I never knew this place existed."

"Ditto," Eva quipped. "The vast numbers of ancient art astonish me."

He turned to her with a grin. "Based on what Professor Tate said, this tour was a ruse for our true assignment. Will we really get to interview the Brotherhood militia?"

"That's the plan." Eva chose her next words carefully. "They may be shy about being questioned."

Her seatmate returned to typing his notes. From the corner of Eva's eye, she saw Raj and Bo consulting a map. She leaned back against the seat and shut her eyes. She dropped off to sleep, only to be startled awake by the air brakes chirping. The bus stopped and the door swished open.

A gush of hot air swept into the coach. Eva looked out the window. They were at a rest area. No other vehicles were around. Raj and Bo barreled out the door. Brandon Tate, the journalism professor, strode to the front of the bus.

He spoke into a microphone, telling the students, "We are about to embark on our interviews." Eva slipped past him and plunged down the steps.

The door closed behind her. Pumped to begin, she joined Bo and Raj by the baggage compartment where the CIA and NCIS agents were yanking out two large canvas bags.

"Eva, you distribute these," Bo ordered. "Raj and I will tape on our banner."

She pulled the canvas bags a few feet before rapping on the bus' door. When it opened, she dragged them up the steps. Professor Tate blocked her seat, so she angled past him, hauling her bags to the rear as he continued giving instructions.

"Remain in small groups of at least two. Stay in view of the bus. If you wander too far into the neighborhood, you could be taken hostage and held for an exorbitant ransom. To give you a shield of protection, we're all representing the U.N. Commission on Human Rights."

Adrenalin burst through Eva's body. With great speed, she removed stacks of blue U.N. helmets, handing them out as she hurried down the aisle. Some young women giggled. Their helmets were too big. Eva adjusted the liner to make them fit snugly.

Professor Tate directed Arabic speakers, who had assigned videographers with microphones, how to approach village residents. "Interview them using sample questions you received yesterday. We want to know if any Coptic Christians remain in the community, so ask where you might find some to interview."

Not wanting to stand out, Eva pulled her blond hair atop her head, and plunked on her helmet. She sped outside to give Raj and Bo their headgear. They stood admiring their banners.

"Will they do?" Raj asked her.

Eva stalked around the bus. Each banner stretched the length of both sides, and written in both Arabic and English, they proclaimed: "United Nations Commission of Human Rights." They were festooned with the U.N.'s blue global logo.

She returned up front. "We're official. Let's get rescuing."

After storing extra helmets in the baggage area, they boarded the bus and departed. She snagged her seat across from Bo and Raj. Raj pointed to their location on the map. He spoke in hushed tones, explaining they were traveling along the Gulf of Aqaba, a large body of water separating parts of Israel and Egypt.

"We're heading to a mountain village above the coastal town of Dahab, which means 'gold' in Arabic," he said. "Only, we're hunting for another type of treasure. In twenty minutes, we'll connect with our police escort, such as it is. Sit back and relax."

Unwinding was the opposite of what Eva did. She mentally reviewed their plan, trying to punch holes in it. She could picture Hamadi's face, but she had never been in his tunnel. She liked visuals. And although Raj had drawn an exact map of the area, Eva wished she had a webcam in the tunnel so she could see what was happening in real time.

But she didn't. She pressed her sweaty hands together, and glanced at Bo and Raj. They both stared out the large window. Eva wondered if Bo was keeping important facts about the Brotherhood from her. She'd better not meet up with Yakov or Enescu or whatever his name was these days. She moistened her lips.

That couldn't happen, could it? But would Bo sacrifice his source for Hamadi? She had to admit, that had a nice ring to it.

They approached a waiting police car on the roadside. A uniformed officer stepped out and raised a hand, commanding they stop. The bus pulled over and Raj charged down the steps. He and the officer exchanged words and animated gestures. Eva rose in her seat to better hear their Arabic dialogue, which she barely knew.

She had to be content watching the policeman point. The dangerous part of the mission lay right around the next corner. She and the other two agents were responsible for the students' safety. Bo had unique abilities in the field and Raj had survived Dahab once before, which provided a small measure of confidence. These students, chosen for their language skills and academic achievement, were the wild card. Could they be trusted to follow the game plan?

Raj hopped aboard, and Eva sat down. The young student stored his computer in a leather case. With lights flashing, the police car escorted them into Dahab and up a bumpy road. Bo issued final orders via the microphone while they kept moving.

"We will stop by a burned church. Spread out quickly to locate neighbors for interviews. If you encounter hostility, return to the bus ASAP. Don't lose sight of the bus or police escort."

Moments later, the bus rolled to a stop next to the hollowed-out remains of the Coptic church. Though the escort pulled in front of the bus with its lights flashing, the policeman never budged from his car.

In seconds, Raj bolted off the bus, followed by Bo and Eva. Three armed men stood ahead of the police car. Eva instantly spotted AK-47 rifles slung over their shoulders. She was weaponless and longed for her Glock. Professor Tate, who had lived in Israel for ten years, acted unconcerned. He ambled along, supervising the students in their blue U.N. helmets and walking in pairs up and down the street.

A student news crew approached the armed men. Eva steeled herself for the worst. The militiamen raised the AK-47s, aiming them directly at the youths. Her pulse racing, before she could react, the students withdrew.

Raj wore sunglasses and had shorn his hair into a buzz cut. Eva knew he didn't want to be recognized by his earlier captors. He looked much like the students anyway in his blue helmet.

He stopped one of the students, took his microphone, and instructed, "Come with me."

Eva uttered a silent prayer. Phase One was about to begin.

Raj beckoned the videographer to follow, and the trio stepped toward the automatic rifles aimed right at them. Eva tensed. She slowly walked their way. Raj barked questions in Arabic, while the videographer filmed the encounter. Close enough to touch the armed men, Raj lobbed another question, extending his microphone. The gunmen stepped back.

Raj and his videographer advanced, with Raj firing the same question. A second team filmed the scene as Raj and the two students marched forward. This backward dance continued until Raj had backed up the men by about seventy-five yards. Eva realized his question wouldn't be answered.

He gave the other student back his microphone, telling him to take over the interview. "Keep asking if they destroyed the church and where are the Coptics that lived here."

Eva and Raj walked backwards toward the bus in the midst of students interviewing locals on the street. People streamed toward the cameras from every direction, some with rifles over their shoulders. Mainly, the crowd seemed curious.

The three agents grabbed a duffel bag from beneath the bus and sprinted to the charred remains of the once-thriving Christian church. A pair of students filmed the destruction. Rancid odor of burned wood and fabric stung Eva's nostrils. She walked among the rubble, stirring up piles of dust and ashes. She sneezed loudly. Raj motioned them forward behind the broken altar.

He pointed to a faded outline of an oasis painted on the blackened wall. "The trap door is behind there."

They sped around the altar. Eva's heart fell at the horrific sight of rafters and charred beams covering the entire area. Had the tunnel collapsed? She kept this concern to herself, and began tossing aside debris. Raj and Bo pitched in.

"We need heavy equipment to move such a gigantic pile," Eva huffed.

Bo straightened. "Raj, you sure the trap door is beneath this rubble?"

"Yeah, quite sure. It can't be anywhere else."

Raj gazed toward the rear of the church and pointed. "The tunnel runs that way and exits inside a home. See the burned building back there? That's possibly the other end."

Eva ducked her head to get a better look. So did Bo.

Then Raj announced, "Quick! Get the teams on the bus. We'll drive over there. They can conduct interviews on that street too."

As they ran toward the bus, the team was successfully interviewing the armed men.

"Our dogged reporters wore them down," Raj said, sounding pleased.

He and Bo raced to retrieve the teams and Eva herded everyone on the bus. Students clamored with colorful stories. The ones who'd interviewed the gunmen gave a blow-by-blow account to Professor Tate. Eva could only think of Hamadi's life perishing with each second they delayed pulling him out of the tunnel.

Raj boarded last and stayed up front. Reaching around Eva, he snagged the microphone from Tate. "Our escort's taking us around the block to another burned-out building."

This was their final chance to find Hamadi. Had they crossed the ocean and faced down armed gunmen only to fail? Such a disastrous outcome Eva refused to believe.

# CHAPTER 44

When the bus halted by the destroyed home, Raj hissed at Eva, "I think this is Hamadi's home. I should recognize the interior when I see it."

After Bo and the professor conferred, Tate grabbed the microphone.

"Okay, listen up," he said. "You've had relatively good experiences under adverse conditions. For those of you who feel you didn't learn much, this is a second chance. You can all go out and try again. Same rules apply. Stay within view of the bus."

The door opened and the "human rights" interviewers went forth. Raj and Bo made their way toward the second gutted building. Eva trailed behind looking for anyone who might give them trouble. Her seatmate with the computer asked if he could come along.

She agreed, telling him to bring a video crew. "You must follow my orders."

He nodded and grabbed a videographer. The blue helmets bounded toward the house. This time, no gunmen prevented their access. Raj walked to the center of the slab floor. He spun around as if searching for familiar features. He gestured toward a huge pile of scorched wood that once had been glowing embers.

Eva surveyed the ruins of Hamadi's life. She exhaled sharply, thinking people had cooked here, slept here, and sang praises to the King of Kings.

She wondered if Raj could find the tunnel below. She saw no signs of one while he continued poking around.

Suddenly he pointed dramatically. "I think the concrete lid is under here. Start digging."

The three of them dug by hand, tearing away charred wood and roofing. Eva wished she had thought to bring gloves. Of course, she had no way of knowing she'd be knee-deep in debris.

"Ouch!"

She picked up a painful splinter. But there was nothing to be done about it now. Impatient to find Hamadi, she shrugged off the small cut and threw junk off to the side. Bo spotted it first.

"I found it! Raj, help me lift this beam."

As they moved a heavy section of wood, Eva saw a square cement lid. She and Raj grabbed opposite sides and heaved, eventually sliding off the solid top. She stared down into an opening that dropped straight into darkness. Bo handed her a flashlight to hold while they had a look. Raj launched down a ladder. Bo climbed after him.

Eva told the students where to stand. "Shout at us if anyone shows up. Don't let *any* other team members come in here."

She peered into blackness and prepared herself.

Phase Two was about to begin.

She called, "Bo, catch my light," before dropping the flashlight. Then Eva rushed into the dank void. At the bottom, about ten feet below, she squeezed past Bo. Bending over slightly, she removed a small pocket light. This she turned on and followed Raj as he walked on ahead with his tiny light.

He called out in Arabic sporadically, saying Hamadi's name.

A hand grabbed her shoulder. Eva jumped and spun around in the darkness.

"Eva."

It was Bo.

"I'm going up top to act as lookout," he said. "In case armed Brothers show up."

"Okay, but I'm losing hope."

Eva couldn't stand erect without hitting her helmet on the tunnel's curved ceiling. It seemed like she'd been walking stooped over for a good city block when a high-pitched voice began speaking in Arabic. Sounds of whispered excitement echoed in the dim tunnel. Eva tried to see what was ahead. Raj shone his light at her, blinding her. She cringed and blinked rapidly.

"What's happening? Raj, are you safe?"

More Arabic, and then he cried, "He's alive! There are two of them."

Eva lurched a few steps, shining her light forward. Hamadi crouched on the tunnel floor, his back resting against the wall. Her heart skipped a beat.

"Raj, is he well enough to go with us?" she asked.

"He's extremely weak, but ready to leave."

"I'll get the bag from Bo and be right back."

Eva lurched toward the ladder, using the flickering light to gauge the distance. When she reached the ladder, she called up at Bo, who was peering down.

"We found him and one other. Snatch the bag from the bus."

"Are they healthy? Mobile?"

"Yes!"

"I will, but hurry," Bo urged. "Students see armed men swarming the burned-out church."

"Don't tell *me* to hurry. You hurry!" Eva shouted back.

After what seemed like an eternity, Bo's unshaven face appeared at last by the opening. "Step aside, Eva. I'm dropping your supplies."

She jumped back just in time as a duffel bag landed with a thud at her feet. Eva snatched the handles and whirled around to re-enter the tunnel.

"Make it snappy," Bo called. "They're moving timbers in the church, and could find the other tunnel entrance any minute."

Stooping, Eva yanked the bag behind her, all the while holding the flashlight. Sweat poured from beneath the helmet into her eyes. The tunnel was hotter than any sauna she'd ever been in. It was amazing Hamadi had survived down here at all.

Raj shone his light on her and then on Hamadi. Eva ripped open the bag, jerking out two pairs of black slacks, white shirts, and blue helmets.

"Put these on," she ordered.

Raj told her, "After hiding here so long, even this scrap of light is searing their eyes."

"They should get used to the light, because outside—"

A loud boom erupted behind Hamadi. Eva jumped up, banging her head. Hamadi's arms flew up to cover his face. Raj spoke to him in Arabic, and then told Eva, "I hear them removing debris from above the other entrance."

"Get a move on," she barked. "They'll have to walk and get dressed at the same time. Pretty soon they'll start shooting down at us."

Raj urged the two Coptics to go faster. Adrenalin drove Eva to the entrance. Footsteps crunched behind her as she hustled to the ladder. In the opening above, Bo whirled his arms furiously.

"Get up here, Eva. The Brotherhood is making serious progress back at the church."

From the veiled light coming down the shaft, Eva could see Raj squeezing against the wall and pushing Hamadi forward. Eva grabbed him, enfolding the Coptic in a bear hug.

"Hamadi, our prayers are answered."

She checked him over as he tucked his white shirt into his new trousers. She straightened his helmet. "Bo, here he comes. Take him right to the bus."

Hamadi started up the ladder. In the obscure light, Eva noticed Raj pushing another man. "This is Butrus. I met him the first time I came here."

Another awful boom swept through the tunnel. Blood pounded against her ears. She fought to still her fear. Eva had to think. She heard distinct sounds of concrete being scraped. On impulse, she straightened Butrus' helmet and hauled him toward the ladder. As he disappeared out the top, bright lights flared at the far end of the tunnel.

She elbowed Raj. "Go! They found us."

She scampered up the ladder, her mind spinning. She was barely out when Raj crawled right behind her. Bo scurried to the bus with Hamadi and Butrus in tow. Student videographers recorded the mad dash. Eva didn't like being filmed, but she had no time to debate with them.

"You'd best run to the bus," she snapped at them.

Eva heard motorcycles revving nearby. The students' eyes rounded and they dashed away. Raj bent over the concrete lid. So did Eva, grunting as she helped him snap the lid back in place, which should buy them some time. They escaped to the bus, and she reached her seat, panting for breath.

"We managed to close the lid in time, I think. Before the Brotherhood realized their discovery led to a tunnel."

From the bus window Eva observed two motorcycles pull up to Hamadi's charred house. Each one carried a passenger on the back. The riders approached the house, with AK-47s at the ready. As the bus pulled away, Eva reached across the aisle and poked Bo.

Pointing at the cycles she warned, "They may start digging for a tunnel. We'd better hurry if we're going to make it out of Egypt alive."

THEY TRAVELED ON THE bus for thirty minutes, shooting straight for the Israeli border crossing. Without warning, the driver swerved into a parking lot. He stopped. Eva had to think what was happening. She peered from the window. Thankfully, she didn't see or hear any motorcycles. As Raj and Bo hastened out, she realized they had to remove all U.N. signs.

Phase Three was about to begin.

Bo threw Eva the duffel from beneath and she collected the blue helmets. She dashed into the hot sun, and jammed the bulging bag beneath the rumbling bus. The three agents swiftly made it back inside. The bus driver veered onto the road. Raj seized the microphone.

"Attention please!" he said in an amplified voice. "Professor Tate informs me of speculation about our trip. For the record, this expedition is sanctioned by the International Christian University with help from private U.S. citizens."

Raj gestured with his free hand to Bo and Eva. "That's all you may know. That's all you may report. Include your interviews of residents in Dahab, but do *not* claim you posed as U. N. human rights investigators. If you're foolish enough to make such a claim, you might deserve the consequences."

Murmurs swept through the bus. Eva glanced at Butrus, who sat across the aisle. Hamadi rested in the seat next to Eva, his head against the window. Both escapees had been fed granola bars, apples, and water. Her smile at Hamadi brought one in return. He must be relieved to be safe at last. Because he'd testified before Congress, Hamadi could no longer live in Egypt. He must flee and find a new home.

"Although I doubt you would have been as safe without the blue helmets, you wouldn't have gotten a single interview," Raj told the students.

A smattering of nervous chuckles spread throughout the bus. Eva hoped everyone on board could be trusted with Hamadi's rescue.

Raj tackled this very sensitive subject next. "Some of you observed our finding two bearded U.N. investigators in a tunnel beneath the burned-out house."

His exaggerated wink prompted the students to laugh boisterously.

"They travel with us to Israel," Raj went on to explain. "They will be turned over to Israeli officials in hopes of being granted refugee status. Do not mention them in a single report you make. To answer the question you asked Professor Tate, if they are willing, you may interview them for background. If you remain orderly, I will act as interpreter. I have a final condition: Report what you learn as coming from persons interviewed in Dahab."

Eva was thrilled to know Hamadi and Butrus would find asylum in Israel, the one safe country in the Middle East for Christians to flee. It was an answer to all their prayers. Raj hung the microphone in its holder before nudging Bo and Hamadi to the rear of the bus. A pretty blue-eyed student swung into the aisle from her seat behind Eva. She followed Bo, then returned to Eva.

"Excuse me. I am Fiona," she said in a clipped British accent. "Some are whispering you three are really CIA agents on a mission to spring a couple of spies. Care to comment?"

"If that's true," Eva said, arching her brows, "would we let you interview the spies?"

The girl blushed. "I suppose not."

Eva rose, placing one knee on her seat, facing the student. "We are three American Christians trying to help persecuted Coptics. You should join the interview."

The British student bobbed her head before traipsing to the rear. Eva caught Butrus' eye. Gesturing toward Hamadi, she wondered if he would join the interview. He shook his head and remained in his seat.

Eva sat down, a searing question battering her mind. Had this mission been a ruse to rescue Butrus, one of Bo's assets in Egypt? She might ask him later, but maybe not. She wouldn't force Bo to lie to her.

Time passed with the students asking Hamadi questions and Raj interpreting. Convinced all was well, Eva's shoulders melted against the seat. Her eyes closed. She felt her body tremble and she breathed in deeply. Thoughts of freeing Hamadi and his friend flooded her with tremendous happiness.

Eva jolted awake. Her last memory had been of Raj giving Hamadi's answers to the students. Now he and Bo sat across from her, their seats in the resting position. She peered behind her seat. Hamadi and Butrus were asleep in two backseats. She sensed they must be getting near the Israeli border. From behind her, Eva heard Fiona dictating her news scripts.

Eva perked her ears for any forbidden material.

"In Egypt," Fiona said, "two hundred and forty Coptic Christians were killed in this last week. Two thousand were injured. Today, this correspondent roamed the streets of Dahab, Egypt, looking for evidence of claimed persecution. A Copt is an Egyptian word meaning 'Christian.' There are eleven million Christians, or Copts, in Egypt. Their theology is similar to Roman Catholicism and Eastern Orthodoxy. Copts I spoke with today fear for their lives. They are literally hiding underground."

Fiona paused as if checking notes, then continued, "The Christian's church in this town was burned to rubble. Their homes have been destroyed, lost among the ashes. Christian business owners are threatened. Many attempt to flee, but there's nowhere for them to go. Eighty-five percent of Egyptians are Muslim, and the militants blame Christians for ousting the former president who favored their jihad. Christians endure persecution as a result."

Eva approved of Fiona's report so far. When her voice dropped, Eva could barely hear her tell what she'd learned from armed rebels in Dahab.

"Egyptian Brotherhood men carry AK-47s everywhere. They claim Christians spread lies about them and create dissention. They aim to drive Copts from the land. Many Christians are kidnapped, only to be held for steep ransoms, which these poor people can't afford to pay. Their loved ones are slaughtered."

Fiona's voice trembled as she said, "One young girl was brutally beaten and killed for hanging a cross in her car. Lawyers are swamped with calls from Copts desperate to leave Egypt. In a remarkable twist in this cauldron of terror, one Coptic may find refuge in Israel where they are welcomed to live in freedom. Fiona Billingham, reporting from the streets of Dahab, Egypt."

Eva kneeled again on her seat, giving Fiona a look of respect. "You deserve an A grade. What do you think of the experience?"

"I was scared out of my wits," she replied, her blue eyes flashing. "Is that the Israeli border ahead? If we all leave Egypt alive, my prayers will be answered."

"Mine too," Eva said, deeply emotional at helping Hamadi.

Suddenly, Bo and Raj stood and gaped out their window. At the racket of roaring motorcycles, Eva plunged into the aisle. It was those two motorcycles from Hamadi's house! One driver zoomed past the bus, his rider gawking closely at the bus' windows. The bike swerved in front of the bus and jammed on its brakes. The bus jerked and slowed.

The second cycle pulled abreast of the first. The drivers could be seen yelling at each other. Both cycle drivers progressed slowly to a side road, pulled over, and watched the bus go by.

Bo turned to smile at Eva. "They are looking for us. With our signs removed, they must think we're a different bus."

Eva's shoulders sagged in relief. She was eager to climb off the bus and board an airplane. Since their rescue of Hamadi, the bus driver kept them abreast of reports of rocket fire into Israel from Lebanon. Eva briefly shut her eyes. She knew Hezbollah colluded with militants in Gaza. Enemies of the Jewish people squeezed Israel from both borders. Things were heating to a boiling point in the Middle East. Flying for home across the Atlantic couldn't happen too soon.

The bus approached the heavily fortified border. Eva arched her back, lifting her head. Armed soldiers guarded the gates in both directions. She caught her breath and said a silent prayer for safety. A ramrod-straight soldier checked the driver's papers and let the bus pass through the Egypt border without any hassle.

Israel's checkpoint was just ahead. The bus rolled to the Israeli line with Eva crouched in the aisle. She looked out the large front window, and couldn't believe her eyes. Was it really him? She stepped up front to be sure. Yes, it was!

Judah Levitt leaned casually against a small building. All three federal agents had worked with the courageous Israeli Mossad agent. Apparently, Bo had made contact with him. Judah must have greased not only their arrival, but Hamadi and Butrus' asylum as well.

She came back and whispered to Bo, "Your friend's waiting."

"Who ... oh, right." He grinned sheepishly.

"Can I assume Andrei Enescu is somewhere nearby working for Judah?"

Bo's lips twitched. "I won't be working with him again, and you won't see him again."

"Fine by me."

Two Israeli border officials boarded the bus, striding one by one down the narrow aisle, checking everyone's passports. Bo eased past them, and left the bus. Eva watched him stroll right by Judah. He disappeared behind the building. Judah swiveled his head and darted behind the building too. Eva hoped to talk with him, but would never compromise his identity.

The Israeli officials took Hamadi and Butrus by the arms. Eva shook their hands, as did Raj. When the two Coptic Christians left the bus, the rest were cleared to leave. Outside, Hamadi and Butrus looked ready and willing to assimilate into Israeli society. For her part, Eva was anxious for Bo.

He was going to miss the bus. She plunged up the aisle, glimpsing him rushing toward the door. Then to her surprise, he bolted beyond the door. The cargo door beneath their seats opened and closed. The driver put the bus in gear.

They rolled forward. Instead of climbing onto the bus, Bo sauntered away with a canvas bag slung over his shoulder. He joined Judah and the two Coptic Christians. The four of them scrambled into a waiting SUV. Eva glanced at Raj, whose mouth hung open.

He shrugged. "Bo must have some other op we don't know about. Good for him. Me, I am taking a trip with Heather when I get home."

"I suppose you're right."

Eva leaned over and whispered in Raj's ear, "You rest easy. Hamadi is safe. I just hope our friend who just left us doesn't have some other plan for him."

Raj dropped his jaw again. "Would he do that?"

"That's his job," Eva said with a shrug.

# CHAPTER 45

## NORTHERN VIRGINIA

eanwhile, Kaley trained her eye on the speedometer as she drove back to Green Acres. Thoughts of her mom flooded her mind. Dad had spoken to her somewhere in the world and she was due home this evening.

"Come home safe, Mom," Kaley mouthed.

No one was in the car to hear. Kaley was handling this mission alone, which she hoped to successfully complete before Mom returned. She so wanted to give her good news. Kaley cranked the final turn toward Olivia's hideous abode. Even now, the nasty smells of cooking grease and musty rooms assailed her senses.

Kaley rehearsed what she'd tell Mrs. Green. Heather Pentu had promised Kaley everything was in place. All Mr. Badger had to do was contact Transitions. But would he?

She rolled her Bug to a stop in the driveway, sighing at the sight of the filthy windows. The screen door still boasted a ragged hole. A tricycle was sprawled upside down by a tree with no leaves. Spring rains had greened her yard, so that scraggly tree was probably a goner. Kaley hoped Olivia's dad would get her out of this forlorn place by tomorrow.

Turning off the car, she grabbed her keys and climbed the steps. The door swung open unexpectedly. This time it wasn't opened by a small boy. Mrs. Green plunged both hands on her hips. She wore her usual frown above her purple half-glasses.

"If you've come to see Olivia, she's napping. She's had a bad morning."

Mrs. Green flung her arm across the open door. Kaley wasn't going to be invited in.

She jangled her keys. "I'm not here to see Olivia."

"Oh. What brings you here then? Shouldn't you be in school?"

"My first hour went on a field trip. I chose to come here. You said Olivia needs more than you can provide and the cost of her care is great."

"So?" Mrs. Green demanded. "Get a move on. I have kids to attend to."

Kaley pulled a paper from her jean's pocket. "A lady we know sits on the board for a group home called Transitions."

"Oh?" Mrs. Green's smile was fleeting. "Transitions is the best in the area. Karl can't afford to place his daughter there."

Kaley's mind turned in different directions. How to convince Mrs. Green this was a terrific option for Mr. Badger and Olivia? She fluttered the paper in her hands.

"We told this lady about Olivia. She's excited 'cause Transitions opened a new wing. Mrs. Green, there's an opening. Olivia may qualify for a grant made available by a wealthy benefactor who lost a child. She can enter with whatever aid she's receiving."

She handed Mrs. Green the note. "Please give this to Mr. Badger right away. The admissions lady's name is on there. She's expecting his call."

Mrs. Green dropped her arms to her side, and glared over her half-glasses. "Why not give him the note yourself?"

"Simple. I don't want him to think I'm looking for brownie points." Kaley grinned. "I study hard and don't need anything from him."

She turned with a heavy heart. At least she'd done what she came for.

"Wait!" Mrs. Green shook the note in the air. "I'll call Karl and tell him to contact Transitions. I can use some brownie points."

Kaley twirled around and gave the woman a quick hug.

"Thank you, thank you," she chirped.

Mrs. Green stepped back. "My, my, you do come on strong. But you seem like a good girl. Run along. We'll hope for the best in a sorry situation."

Kaley tossed a wave and ran to her car. An interesting thought entered her brain. Would Mrs. Green let Kaley, her brother Andy, and the youth group clean up around Green Acres? She couldn't wait to find out. But first she had school.

During every class, Kaley hoped Mr. Badger would contact Transitions. At the end of his government class, she and Lexi grabbed their book bags. They joined the throng of students heading out the door.

"Kaley! Lexi!" Badger barked. "I need to see you both!"

Fear washed over Kaley. How angry he sounded!

She and Lexi trudged to his desk. He tilted his head. His intense glare spoke volumes. Kaley swallowed, waiting for the worst.

He let them have it with double barrels. "I understand you two have been sticking your noses into my personal business."

He stared from behind his metal-framed glasses. Neither Kaley nor Lexi said a word. Tightness crawled up Kaley's throat.

"Come now," he bellowed. "Don't act like you don't know what I'm talking about. Mrs. Green said two girls came to the home where my daughter Olivia is being cared for. I recall her exact words, 'Both teens wore chain necklaces with crosses.'"

He jammed a finger against his temple. "Duh! It's not too hard to figure out."

Kaley shrugged her shoulders, afraid to say anything. Lexi also stood mute. He heaved his shoulders. Kaley shot a glance at Lexi, whose eyes stayed glued to her shiny flat shoes. Their teacher fled to the side of his desk to perch on the edge. The corners of his mouth turned into a kind of pathetic smile.

"She also called me this morning to say one of you came back suggesting I contact a woman at Transitions."

"That was me," Kaley finally admitted. "We're sorry to offend you by being interested in Olivia. I'm considering a career in special ed. When we heard about your daughter, we thought we could at least bring her a stuffed toy. Lexi and I brought her a Pooh bear."

"Mrs. Green told me. I'm okay with that."

Kaley released her tension by sighing and Lexi broke out in a nervous giggle.

He clasped his hands. "God knows, Olivia needs more love than I can give her."

Kaley was shocked to hear Mr. Badger invoke God's name when he objected to His Son Jesus so publicly.

She was about to ask him about the contradiction when he asked, "How did you find out about Olivia?"

He cast his eyes upon Kaley and then Lexi. Again, neither teen responded.

"Since you're kind to help her, I'll bring you up-to-date. I contacted Transitions during lunch. Once I sign the papers today, Olivia moves in next week."

"Sweet!" Kaley clapped her hands. A great burden lifted from her shoulders.

Lexi giggled and clapped her hands too.

"You must have real clout," Mr. Badger said. "When I first inquired at Transitions, I was told they had no slots. The cost was more than I could afford. Now Olivia is being admitted and *all* her costs are covered."

A lump formed in Kaley's throat. Tears gathered in her eyes. She struggled to find the words she wanted to say. "Mr. Badger, you mentioned the answer earlier. You said God knew Olivia needed love."

His rugged face grew pale.

"I mean it." Kaley smiled at him and Lexi. "God intervened for Olivia. Since we took her the Pooh bear, we've been praying God would provide a special home to care for her."

Mr. Badger took off his glasses and wiped his eyes. "Well, I'm the last person to admit it, but it worked. Your kindness to Olivia means more to me than Jesus shirts or crosses you wear."

"We're glad that you're glad," Lexi offered.

Kaley wanted to tell Mr. Badger something more, to explain the love Jesus had for him too. Maybe their helping Olivia would begin softening his heart. The very next words out of his mouth encouraged her that his barriers to Jesus were falling down.

The teacher collected his papers. "I also called you up here to say you have my permission to write your final paper on Christ's crucifixion by the Romans. They were an ancient government that did use crucifixion as punishment."

"Thank you, Mr. Badger."

Kaley wanted to, but didn't hug him as she had Mrs. Green. She pulled her backpack over her shoulder, and with Lexi, turned to leave.

"One more thing," Mr. Badger called after them.

Kaley stopped and walked over to him. Lexi didn't budge from the doorway.

He rubbed his hands together. "When Olivia is moved, it's all right if you want to visit her."

"You can count on us," Kaley promised.

"I think I can," Mr. Badger said softly. "Now hurry up, or you'll miss your next class."

Kaley couldn't be happier. Then she remembered one thing. She'd better ask Lexi ASAP. As they dashed down the hall, she pulled her friend aside.

"Do you still have the video we took of Mr. Badger at the bowling alley?"

"Yeah, but I should erase it, don't you agree?"

Kaley shifted her backpack. "Yes, but we also need to pray he quits drinking."

"My mom tells me to take one pill at a time." Lexi shrugged. "Are you really thinking about going into special ed?"

"I'm not sure. You love accounting, but I know numbers aren't for me. We'd better hurry or we'll be late for our next class."

Kaley kept her true thoughts to herself. When Mom came home from overseas, would she approve?


EVA'S TRIP HOME FROM EGYPT LEFT HER DEPLETED OF ENERGY. She'd arrived home late last night, and after hugging her family, she dropped into bed. Too tired for an early day at the task force, she brought a cup of coffee to her home office. Eva checked her messages. Her office voice mailbox was full. She listened to each one, deleting some and returning a few calls.

The last was from Wednesday. Eva could hardly hear Dr. Gretchen Wiles' husky voice. She played it a second time. "Mrs. Montanna, this is Gretchen Wiles at the Preservation Center. When we last talked, you said you wanted to come to the Center and study Gutenberg's Bible. My time's winding down. I'd hoped to meet before returning to my university. Please call."

Eva sat in silence. How could she have totally forgotten about her family's Bible? She called Dr. Wiles, who didn't answer. At the prompt, Eva left a message explaining she'd just returned from being out of the country.

"Dr. Wiles, I'll stop in tomorrow morning. If I hear nothing to the contrary, I'll assume you agree to that time. Looking forward to seeing you then."

Eva made a note to submit a request for annual leave. After going to the Smithsonian, she planned to come home and rest. Kaley walked in and set down her backpack. She stopped by the office door, her face aglow.

"Good news, Mom. Mr. Badger is getting Olivia into Transitions. He's letting me write the paper I want."

Eva stood and gave Kaley a hug. "God heard our prayers. He is so good."

"I have something else to tell you." Kaley gazed at her with wide eyes.

Eva's heart skipped a beat. "Your face tells me it's bad news. What happened?"

"No, it's good news, I think. I plan to study criminal justice in college and be a federal agent like you."

Eva let out a whoop. "Your investigation of Mr. Badger and Olivia has given you a taste for justice."

Kaley smiled, showing all her teeth. Her eyes sparkled.

"Keep your options open." Eva advised her to study business just in case, adding, "One reward for my hard work is when you apply for a job as a special agent, you'll be given preferential consideration."

"Isn't that unfair to other applicants?"

"You question the ethics, however it is fair. You and other children of agents already know how demanding the job is and have realistic expectations. Plus, it's easier getting you through a security clearance."

Eva paused to grin. "Because parents like me are so demanding of our kids."

"Yeah, and your kids know about all the exotic places you travel to."

"There you go with unrealistic assumptions." Eva laughed. "I just returned from a trip to Egypt. I saw no pyramids and no sphinx. I came home exhausted."

"Can I bring you a nice, hot cup of tea?" Kaley asked. "Or maybe one of your green smoothies?"

"You know, tea sounds good. I don't really like those smoothies, do you?"

Kaley chuckled, heading for the kitchen.

*What a beautiful family I'm blessed with.* Eva leaned in her chair, thinking of heading to see Grandpa Marty and Michigan's sandy beaches. Summer vacation wasn't too far away.

# CHAPTER 46

Early the next morning, Eva slid out of bed and prepared to shower. She picked up her cell phone only to discover it was on silent mode. Her parents had left a message. Eva listened to their voice mail saying they loved Windsor Castle, but the dungeon at Lambeth Palace brought tears.

That seemed an odd coincidence. Their ancestors, Pieter, Dirck, and Jenny Vander Goes, had spent a difficult time in Windsor Castle's dungeon. Eva figured with the time difference, her folks might be eating lunch. Eva had not yet eaten breakfast. Picturing crispy fish and chips on a plate, her stomach growled. She punched in her folk's number. Mom answered, sounding out of breath.

Eva spoke softly to keep from waking Scott or the kids. "It sounds like you and Dad are enjoying England."

"We drove the entire length of Scotland and found direct links to my ancestors, which I'll share when we see you. Dad and I are about to jump aboard a double-decker tour bus for St. Paul's Cathedral."

"Give him my love. We miss you."

"So do we. Oh wait, before I hang up, at Lambeth Palace, we visited a tower where Christian Lollards were imprisoned. John Wycliffe was tried there for heresy."

"My early ancestors committed their lives to preaching with the Lollards."

Marcia spoke quickly. "Yikes, they're boarding the bus. I know you're researching our Gutenberg Bible. We saw one at Lambeth's library. Ours is more pristine."

Eva mentioned she'd be meeting Dr. Wiles at the Smithsonian in a few hours. "I'm convinced the Bible has been in our family since Gutenberg's printing. Wiles doesn't agree and may cause trouble."

"The truth will come out. Your dad took photos of the prison's wooden walls. Iron rings that bound Believers are still on the walls. Guess whose name is scratched on the wall?"

"John Wycliffe?" Eva guessed, thinking of the English reformer who started the Lollard movement.

"Clifford, wait a sec. Eva, I'd better go. Your dad is antsy about being late. But the name carved on the wall is Justinus Vander Goes. We wonder if he's related."

Eva gasped. "He's Pieter's son. He preached in the English countryside of Christ's love. He was in Albans, north of London, when I last closed the journal. Can Dad send me a picture?"

"I'm getting on the bus, so I may lose our connection."

"Mom, have Dad e-mail me a copy of the photo."

"Okay—"

Loud static buzzed in Eva's ear. She stepped into the shower, her mind churning about why Justinus' name was on that prison wall.

EVA BOUNDED UP THE STEPS TO THE SMITHSONIAN carrying her journal, and mulling over Bo's call this morning. He'd cryptically told her to submit a travel voucher for the Egypt trip and cancel her vacation request. Since their op went off without any snags, his "Company" found money to pay for the expenses.

Eva wondered if Bo had made it home or was still in Egypt. He didn't say. She entered the Preservation Center's reception area and asked for Dr. Wiles. The receptionist frowned.

"She's no longer here. Her appointment ended last Friday."

"You're kidding!" Eva's pulse quickened. "I'm Eva Montanna who owns the Gutenberg Bible she was working on. I left her a message I'd be coming in today for research."

"No problem. I'll have someone on staff retrieve your Bible." The woman consulted a ledger. "The conference room isn't scheduled to be used. You may sit in there and do your research. Please take a seat."

Eva found a comfy upholstered chair. She considered their success in

Egypt. Once again, God had been involved in every detail. Along with Raj and Bo, she helped save two men from certain death. They avoided injury and an international incident, which was nothing short of miraculous.

Her mind returned to the present when a technician stalked into the reception room from the laboratory area. He whispered to the receptionist before scooting away. The receptionist smiled at Eva, assuring her the wait wouldn't take much longer. Despite being anxious to open the Gutenberg Bible, Eva nodded in return.

She gazed around, marveling at how a facility with old wooden floors, high ceilings, and glass walls facing public corridors could be kept secure without any visible security apparatus. The Center maintained valuable paintings, jewels, and ancient books, Eva's Bible being one of the rarest. The more she thought, the more her worry mounted over the delay.

Eva strode to the receptionist with all the authority of her badge, although it remained tucked in her fanny pack. "Please check and see what's wrong."

"Well …" The young woman blushed and stammered. "I'm told the staff can't locate the Gutenberg Bible. They're still searching."

"What?" Eva growled. "You tell me Dr. Wiles is no longer here. Now you discover my family treasure is missing!"

"But they are looking," the flustered woman interrupted.

"They've had long enough. Ask Director Prescott to get out here now! Don't tell me he's no longer employed here."

A lady in a gray suit walked past and stopped to peer at Eva. The receptionist was already talking on her phone. "Mr. Prescott will be right out, Mrs. Montanna."

Ms. Gray Suit took Eva by the arm. "I will seat you in the conference room."

"Oh no! You're not sticking me in some conference room." She shook off the interloper's arm. "I'm staying put until Cecil shows up. He'd better have a good explanation."

With a burst of energy, Cecil Prescott entered the area from the double doors, stuffing his arms into his suit jacket. He lunged at Eva with a thousand apologies.

"Eva, sorry Dr. Wiles is late this morning. Her car won't start."

She pointed at the trembling receptionist. "She said Dr. Wiles is no longer here."

"Au contraire." He stepped toward the conference room. "Please come along and I will tell you about developments."

Eva walked beside Cecil, saying loudly, "You mean about how you've lost my Bible?"

They spilled into the conference room where he adjusted his bow tie.

"Be seated and be comfortable," he soothed.

Eva refused. "How can I when you have lost a treasured family artifact, let alone an extremely valuable one? Cecil, I trusted you."

She folded her arms and waited. Cecil ran a finger around his inside shirt collar.

"Dr. Wiles was scheduled to return to her university last Friday. She told me last week she discovered something interesting about our Bible, I mean your Bible, to be precise."

"Go on." Eva didn't move an inch.

"Yes, of course." He cleared his throat. "She asked for permission to remain another week to finalize her research. All our systems show her as having left. Even the receptionist thought she was gone."

"Okay, but how do you explain my missing Bible?"

"I suspect Gretchen locked it in her working safe. She's due any moment, Eva. I'm sure all is well."

He fumbled with his collar before gesturing to a chair. "Please take a seat. I seem to remember you like coffee. May I get you a cup?"

Eva's blood pressure began subsiding. She even smiled. "All right. Black coffee, please."

Cecil hadn't been gone long when the door opened. Gretchen Wiles stuck her head in.

"Ms. Montanna, I apologize." She smiled profusely. "I have interesting news for you. Let me retrieve the Bible from my safe, and I shall return pronto."

"Fine. I'm going nowhere without my Bible," Eva shot back.

She was far from being placated by polite words. She drummed her fingertips on the mahogany table and waited and fumed. Finally, Cecil bustled in with a tray of coffee and three cups. Dr. Wiles entered moments later, pulling Eva's little suitcase behind her. She also had a laptop computer. They were all smiles.

Cecil handed her a cup, which she accepted gratefully, needing something to help calm her. She sipped the steaming brew. Cecil acted contrite, which she hoped meant a positive report. He pulled out the chair for her by the head of the table. Then he and Dr. Wiles sat on opposite sides, closest to her. He glanced at Eva's journal, grinning broadly.

"Have you authenticated my Bible?" she pressed. "Dr. Wiles seemed unsure if my family truly owned a Gutenberg."

Cecil gestured to Eva graciously. "Once again you have given us a real treat."

"I have not *given* you the Bible, Director Prescott," Eva objected.

He fussed with his bow tie. "No. Rather, you've brought us a spectacular artifact. Dr. Wiles will share her observations."

The scholar opened her laptop computer before removing Eva's two leather-bound volumes from the tote. These she pushed to the center of the table.

"Ms. Montanna, I will explain my doubts. First, let me say you have a previously unknown original Gutenberg Bible."

Eva's jaw dropped. "And to think it sat unloved for generations. I am so sorry."

"Not to worry." Cecil fluttered his fingers. "Your valuable piece survived extremely well."

Dr. Wiles flipped to an ornate page in Genesis. She explained Eva's Bible was authentic because it was printed on vellum, the skin of a young calf or lamb, which Gutenberg used for his early works. Also, this Bible contained his signature 42 lines of print.

She concluded, "We were aware of forty-eight copies of Gutenberg's Bible. Of those, only twenty-one are complete."

"Yours is rare." Cecil lightly tapped the leather cover. "It's the tenth one here in North America, and only the third complete one on vellum. One is in a private collection in California, while the other is safely at the Library of Congress."

Eva struggled to absorb the facts. She was pleased to have God's Word, for which her family and Gutenberg had sacrificed. A question loomed, for which Eva had no answer.

She let out a sigh. "I need to confer with my husband about what to do next."

"You must insure it immediately," Cecil cautioned. "Thirty years ago, the last sale of a complete Gutenberg Bible sold for more than two million dollars. Today a complete Gutenberg on vellum would sell for between twenty-five and thirty-five million dollars."

Eva's entire body throbbed in disbelief. Adrenaline surged through her like electricity. Was it possible she possessed such a magnificent Bible?

Dr. Wiles cleared her throat. "Director Prescott and I would love to display it here at the Smithsonian. In fact, you are welcome to come any time and examine it further."

"I have no idea what I'm going to do," Eva insisted.

Dr. Wiles confirmed Gutenberg had printed the Bible in Latin. Then she scowled.

"Someone made notes and underlines." Her finger rested on a page. "See here, in Daniel 9 verse 3."

"Do such marks devalue my Bible?"

"It depends on the reason and who did the marking," Dr. Wiles replied crisply.

Eva took out her smart phone, which had a Bible app. She looked up and quickly read the verse. "It says Daniel turned to the Lord, pleading with him with prayer and in sackcloth and ashes. What other verses are underlined?"

"There's one in Job."

Dr. Wiles carefully turned many pages, reaching Job 2, verse 8. Eva looked this up on her phone. "Job sat in ashes after the suffering he faced."

While the scholar furiously took notes, Eva reread the verses. A memory broke forth. Cousin Angus and Pieter had inserted a secret code into their Gutenberg Bible. She reached for the Bible asking if other marked verses were found.

"Yes, sorry to say," Cecil muttered. "Most collectors consider them blemishes."

Dr. Wiles returned to the first volume, revealing an underlined verse in Proverbs 1, verse 14, which Eva read aloud:

"'Throw in your lot with us; and we will share a common purse.'"

A final underlined verse in Matthew 11:21 dealt with people repenting in sackcloth and ashes. Eva wiped her hands on her slacks, not knowing what to say. She imagined the ashes on her mantel. Was she about to learn their origin?

Dr. Wiles looked up from her notes. "All these verses deal with ashes and a purse, which could be some kind of container for ashes. Look what else I found."

She returned to the second volume, where in bold ink someone had written the name "John Wycliffe" and the year 1428. Dr. Wiles smoothed the page. "I thought the date was in error because Wycliffe died in 1384. The mistake led to my asking you to bring in more evidence."

Eva craned her neck to see. "Is it an error?"

"I don't think so," Dr. Wiles replied. "I knew of Wycliffe's English Bible, as ancient manuscripts are my specialty. The Church of Rome objected to Wycliffe's bold calls for reforms in the church. Pope Martin V ordered his body to be exhumed and then burned in that year—1428. These verses about ashes, a purse, along with the reformer's name could signify your family knew of his being burned. They may even have had his ashes."

Eva's mind tumbled. Before she could say anything, Dr. Wiles toggled to a site on her computer.

"After the Pope declared Wycliffe a heretic, he ordered his ashes scattered so they could never be traced. He wanted Wycliffe's name and teachings utterly extinguished."

Eva blew out a hot breath. "I have a pouch of ashes at home. Wycliffe's weren't scattered."

"You own a pouch of ashes from the Middle Ages?" Cecil slid a finger under his bow tie as if it was strangling him.

"Yes." She tapped the etched cover of the journal. "Cecil, you met my Grandpa Martin Vander Goes last year. You recall the other items you evaluated for me?"

"My dear, how could I ever forget those pieces?"

"Well, the pouch Grandpa Marty gave me, which I thought held silver dust or mineral ore, was analyzed and the FBI lab concluded it to be human remains. I had no idea they belonged to John Wycliffe, but I think my Bible and what's written in this journal prove they are his."

"If you leave your journal with us, we can authenticate his remains," Dr. Wiles offered.

Eva turned to her page marker. "Recently, I was reading how Justinus Vander Goes followed Wycliffe as a preaching Lollard. My family also possessed one of his Bibles."

"You have a Wycliffe Bible too?" Cecil hissed. His face turned crimson.

Eva shrugged. It was all so confusing. "Not that I know of."

Dr. Wiles drew her attention to the inside Bible cover with family names. Eva squinted at the handwritten entry: *A Dutch hero who died for Jesus, Justinus Vander Goes 1467.*

She lifted her gaze and held up the journal. "In here it reveals how Justinus' brother Dirck helped Gutenberg print the Bibles, and their father Pieter financed the project, receiving ten copies of Gutenberg's Bibles."

"Does it say what happened to the other nine, or their Wycliffe Bible?" Cecil fidgeted with his bow tie.

"Can we stop right here?" Eva cried. "My parents found Justinus' name carved in a prison for Lollards."

She quickly scanned through pages detailing Jenny's wedding to Fredrick. The guest list didn't contain Justinus' name, so he must have stayed in England. With her finger moving line by line, she perused the next section with her fingertip until she found his name.

"Oh, no!" She clapped a hand over her mouth.

Dr. Wiles leaned forward expectantly, and Cecil blurted, "Did you find the Wycliffe Bible?"

Eva tried focusing on Aunt Deane's tiny letters that suddenly grew blurry. She blinked back tears. "Pieter gave Duke Charles a favorable report about his possible marriage to Margaret of York."

"What else?" Dr. Wiles snapped.

"Okay, Pieter walked Jenny down the aisle in the abbey and she wed Fredrick Zylstra. After the newlyweds left for a honeymoon in Bruges, Cousin Angus brought Pieter terrible news."

Eva swallowed raw emotion and the whole sordid story gushed forth.

Justinus had been snatched from Albans days after Pieter sailed with Dirck and Jenny for the Netherlands. Alphonso blurted out Justinus' name to his guards in exchange for his freedom. Because Justinus was a Wycliffe follower, owned a Wycliffe Bible, and preached its truth, he was arrested and burned with no trial.

Witnesses testified to him singing bravely of Jesus as flames licked his feet. Angus had buried Justinus' remains near the church in Albans, close to the site of the first British martyr.

"You have an extremely important journal," Dr. Wiles said softly.

Eva dashed away her tears. "There's a bit more to tell you about Wycliffe."

The journal recounted Angus compelling Pieter to record Justinus' death in volume one of the Gutenberg Bible and Pieter wrote: *A Dutch Hero who died for Jesus, Justinus Vander Goes 1467.* Then he had written John Wycliffe's name along the top of volume two.

Pieter locked the great reformer's ashes, hidden in the deerskin pouch, into his mother's trunk, forever after wearing the key around his neck. King Edward IV was so distraught over Justinus' death that he gave Jenny and Fredrick an enormous estate in Thetford, England, for a wedding present.

"This is amazing," Eva quipped. "Listen to what else Cousin Angus told Pieter after they safely hid Wycliff's ashes."

In the year 1428, when Angus had been a Lollard for several years, he watched King Henry's men gather along the River Swift, where they were supposed to scatter Wycliffe's ashes. One official was a secret Lollard.

"He switched pouches, scattering instead some burned ashes of his deceased dog," Eva said. "The official secreted Wycliffe's ashes to Angus, which he sent to the Netherlands for safekeeping along with his Wycliffe Bible."

"What about your Wycliffe Bible?" Cecil asked for the umpteenth time.

Eva could not tell him. These discoveries had exhausted her. The truth pierced her soul like a sharp arrow. Her thoughts were mired in Justinus being burned alive for his faith in Christ. He would wear a martyr's crown in heaven. She was in awe that the ashes on her mantel were John Wycliffe's, who had changed the world by wanting the common man to read the Bible in English.

Dr. Wiles touched Eva's hand. "Are your ashes stored in a deerskin pouch?"

"I thought it was leather. It does match the deerskin mentioned in the journal."

"There's no doubt in my mind," Dr. Wiles announced, her voice determined. "Pieter wrote the year 1428 by Wycliffe's name to let others know, based on his biblical markings, that the ashes in his deerskin pouch are from Wycliffe's exhumation in 1428."

Cecil tented his hands. "Eva, I am practically speechless. Your journal, with Wycliffe's ashes and the Gutenberg Bible, are the most important discoveries in Christendom here in the U.S. The value for the collection … we're talking somewhere in the range—" He stopped.

"I won't pretend to estimate the value. Taken all together, there's no limit on what the right wealthy person will pay."

Eva didn't know whether to laugh or cry. Her "collection" had come about by the martyrdom of Justinus Vander Goes and countless other Christians who lost their lives for believing in Jesus. She touched the sacred text.

No one could place a monetary value on the embers of courage rising from their persecution.

# CHAPTER 47

Eva rushed to her office, her heart racing and her mind a tangle. The meeting at the Smithsonian took longer than she'd anticipated. Griff and Raj were both away, and her boss was ensconced with upper management in meetings. Congress had called for urgent hearings about Eva's agency—ICE—releasing detainees with felony records into the community. It was a mess. She wanted no part of that fiasco, and so she gave her boss a wide berth.

Instead, she caught up on work-related e-mails, phone calls, and reports. Nothing sensational happened for a change. That suited her fine, after the exhilarating morning she'd had with Cecil. The family journal sat on her desk, reminding her of the Gutenberg Bible and pouch of Wycliffe's ashes. Experts considered them priceless. Would Scott approve of her decisions?

Eva shut off her computer, replaying the parting discussion with Cecil. In his grandiose style, he'd confronted her before letting her out of the conference room.

"So, Eva, are you walking out of here with a thirty-million-dollar Bible in your suitcase, or do we safeguard it until you decide?"

"Putting it that way," she'd fired back, "I'd be a simpleton not to display it here for the time being. I want a written agreement allowing me to return and read it anytime."

Cecil had gushed, "Excellent! Excellent! Thanks for sharing this treasure with us and our global visitors."

Both Cecil and Dr. Wiles had agreed. The Bible vouched for the ashes and the two artifacts offered together would attract huge attention at auction. Eva's journal wasn't left out, as Dr. Wiles pressured her to leave that also. Eva refused, citing her desire to finish reading it first. Cecil promised to arrange for Eva to conduct private research whenever she or her family desired.

When she had pondered the possibilities a bit longer, both scholars exchanged anxious looks. Eva had taken time to snap photos of her Bible, both open and closed. Having the pictures in her camera gave her some measure of peace. And so they had signed an agreement in triplicate allowing the Smithsonian to display the Gutenberg Bible until Eva made a final decision.

She first wanted to discuss things with Scott and see what he thought about their responsibility for the future. Eva picked up the phone to call him at his congressional office, and hesitated. She had failed to consider what God wanted her to do.

The answer to that question was the most important of all.

ALL THE WAY HOME, EVA'S MIND revolved around John Wycliffe. She hurried inside, desperate to secure his ashes. She passed Kaley studying at the dining room table.

"Guess what, Mom?" Kaley chimed. "Lexi and I are visiting Olivia on Saturday. We bought her a lamb that sings 'Jesus Loves Me.'"

"Will Mr. Badger let her keep it?"

"We asked him first." Kaley twirled the pen in her hands. "Know what else?"

Eva pushed aside retrieving the ashes from the mantel and guessed, "You've changed your mind about being a federal agent and will study special education instead."

"No way, Mom. I'm like you. When I make up my mind, there's no turning back."

Intrigued, Eva said, "I'm glad, honey, but I am no good at guessing. Just tell me."

"Remember Mr. Badger's letter saying a girl in class was a threat?" Kaley asked with serious eyes.

"I'll never forget it." Eva's mind burned, recalling his dastardly deed. But Kaley had moved so far from revenge. "Did he finally apologize?"

"Lexi's mom received a new letter in the mail today saying it was all a big mistake. He apologized for being wrong."

Kaley beamed. Eva went over and kissed the top of her head.

Sounds of yelling reached her ears. She peered around the corner and saw Dutch sitting in front of the TV playing a video game in the living room. She was surprised Scott could sit there reading the paper without being bothered by the racket.

"Dutch, turn that off," Eva said. "You're not supposed to be gaming on school days."

She headed over to secure the priceless pouch of Wycliffe's ashes from the mantel. It was gone!

Eva spun around in a circle. Had she moved it to a more advantageous display? Dread peppered her mind. His ashes had been safe for hundreds of years and she'd lost them?

The Egyptian hot sun must have fried her brain. She couldn't even concentrate.

"Kaley, have you seen the pretty can from the mantel?"

"Nope," came her speedy reply.

Eva sped toward the family room calling, "Andy!"

When he failed to respond, she asked Kaley, "Where's your brother?"

"Probably in his room admiring his airsoft gun." She shrugged. "He's organizing a battle at the park on Saturday."

Eva sprinted into Andy's messy room. Her fourteen-year-old son was flopped on his unmade bed, eyes closed and earbuds in place, listening to music. She tiptoed over and quietly took hold of one of the wires leading to the small speaker in Andy's ear. She pulled it with a snap. When it popped from his ear, Andy jumped and opened his eyes.

"You scared me," he protested.

He stood by his bed scowling and removed the other bud. Eva looked around his room, which was a complete disaster. Clothes were draped over the end board of his bed and littered the floor. His realistic-looking airsoft assault rifle hung from a sling on his chair. This was one of those times when she had to pick her battles.

She lifted her chin. "I assume your homework's done."

"Mostly. I've got time."

"Get it done, then you can listen to music. And another thing."

Eva smoothed the blankets on his bed. "I'm looking for the metal can from the fireplace. Have you seen it?"

"You mean the one that had a sack full of dirt?" Andy tossed down his earbuds.

Eva glared in disbelief. "What do you mean *had* a sack?"

"Yeah, I found it. The pouch is a perfect size for my airsoft BBs. It's in my closet."

"What?" she blurted. "Where are the ashes?"

Andy looked startled. "Ashes? Wasn't it dirt? I flushed it down the toilet."

The horror in Eva's soul flashed through her eyes. Before she could calm herself enough to say more, she noted a slight curl to Andy's mouth.

"You'd better be fibbing, or so help me, you're grounded until you turn eighteen, and I'm not kidding."

Andy doubled over laughing. He pointed to his open bedroom window.

"I used the can to prop open my window. I told Dad to fix it. It won't stay open and it's hot in here."

Eva stared at the open window, but there was no can. Her heart started hammering in her chest. John Wycliffe's ashes had been destroyed in one fell swoop.

"Andy," she said harshly. "Look for yourself. It's been stolen."

"Stolen? Who would steal a cheap can?"

Andy walked to the window and pulled back the curtain hanging on the side.

"See, it's here. It's not worth stealing."

Eva raised the window far enough to free the can. Furious at Andy's constant pranks, she lowered and locked the window. This trick of his was over-the-top.

"Dad can work on the window this weekend. In the meantime, turn on your fan."

She slipped the lid off the can, gingerly lifting out the pouch. The weight in her hands restored her trust in her son. Eva threw an arm around his shoulder.

"Andy, I love you."

# CHAPTER 48

Eva and her family scrambled into the house after a meaningful church service. Their congregation spent much time praying for persecuted Christians around the world. They ate a delicious lunch afterwards with Raj and Heather. Raj had hinted he needed to talk to Eva and would phone her later. Though curious, Eva let it pass. He probably wanted to avoid discussing a case in front of their families.

Scott settled into the family room with the Sunday paper. Kaley hurried to put the finishing touches on her paper about Christ's crucifixion. Andy and Dutch dashed outside to test-drive Dutch's recently-fixed remote control race car. A flashing light on the telephone alerted Eva to a voice mail message. She pressed the button.

"Eva, it's Julia Rider. Bo left recently, saying he'd be traveling with you. I saw you in church this morning and didn't want to ask there, but I haven't heard from Bo. Do you know when we might expect him? If you can't say, I understand. Please call if you can."

Eva deleted the message and strolled into the family room. Not long ago Heather Pentu had phoned looking for her husband, Raj. Eva considered the tumultuous events Raj's escapade had spawned. She hoped Bo's absence wasn't the beginning of some new drama.

What should she say to Julia? To help her decide, Eva walked up and snapped the backside of the newspaper hiding her husband. He lowered the paper.

"Are you trying to get my attention?"

"Yes, honey."

"What's up?"

"When I'm gone on assignments, do you phone anyone to see when I'm coming back?"

Scott looked puzzled. "What?"

"Answer my question," she demanded.

"Certainly not! Why?"

"Julia wants to know where Bo is. A while back, Heather asked about Raj's whereabouts. I wonder, is it a gender thing?"

Scott folded up his newspaper. "Just so you know, when you were in Egypt, I did reach out to someone."

"My boss?"

He rose and grabbed her hands. "No, sweetheart. You and I both call Him Friend. He is the one I've learned to rely on."

"That's good to know then. What about my leaving Gutenberg's Bible at the Smithsonian? I was so rattled, I couldn't think."

"Funny you should ask. I just saw an article about a new Bible museum being built by a Christian businessman, right here in DC. Meanwhile, we could consider the Scriptorium in Florida. I was reading it has a wonderful collection of Bibles."

Eva squeezed his hands, thankful for his input. Almighty God had used her ancestral family to preserve His Holy Word through the ages. He would show them in time what was best.

She returned Julia's call and gave her the unsettling news. Eva had no idea where in the world Bo Rider was.

TWO WEEKS PASSED AND SCHOOL WAS OUT FOR THE SUMMER. Eva received a call from Julia, inviting the Montannas over for a fun night of burgers and volleyball in the Riders' backyard. Bo was home and well. Eva felt a twinge of guilt having to decline.

"Sorry, we're visiting Grandpa Marty and playing along Lake Michigan's beach."

Julia sighed into the phone. "Too bad for us, but good for you. We haven't even planned summer vacation yet."

"That's not easy with your husband's traveling. Let's plan something when we're home."

"Our kids love seeing yours. Have fun, Eva. Oh, here's Bo. He wants to talk to you."

Eva heard voices in the background before he came on the phone. The CIA agent sounded cool as usual, as he said, "We'll talk more when you're back from vacation."

"I know you can't say now, but what transpired after you left me on the bus?"

"That's classified. On another note, you should watch today's news."

With that, Bo hung up. Eva stared at her phone. It would be hard to find any news since they were lakeside, flying the racing kites Scott had bought the kids. She forced Bo's curious hint from her mind, and turned her eyes to her family.

"Mom, watch my loops," Dutch yelled.

She laughed at his antics, snapped pictures, and joined in their fun. Later at Marty's farmhouse, he was napping so she surfed websites for news channels. It took a while, but finally she stumbled on what Bo might have referred to. Eva enlarged her screen and turned up the volume.

"This is Fiona Billingham, reporting from Dahab, Egypt, for BBC."

The camera focused on angry-looking Egyptian Brotherhood militiamen. They stood by the burned-out church in Dahab, where Eva had gone with Bo and Raj searching for Hamadi. Fiona, the British student from International Christian University, was reciting verbatim the script Eva heard her read on their frantic bus trip out of Egypt.

Fiona certainly had managed to nab a cushy job with the British Broadcasting Company. Eva drummed her fingers on the small desk. From past cases with Bo, she knew his undercover documents identified him as Skip Pierce, an international corporate recruiter. Could it be? Had Bo already recruited Fiona as a CIA asset?

"The Agency" might recruit credentialed reporters as spies. They had perfect cover to travel anywhere in the world. How or when he'd inserted her into the BBC remained a mystery.

Eva's mind leapt to Brewster Miles, her friend and colleague with British MI5. Brewster might have helped the BBC take on Fiona. Perhaps she was an asset for Brewster and Bo. It wouldn't be a first. After all, the Agency and Mossad had both used Enescu aka Yakov to spy on the Brotherhood.

A sickening thought occurred to Eva. Hadn't she thought Fiona quite mature and accomplished? Maybe the Brit already worked for Bo, and he included her on the rescue op to Egypt without Eva and Raj's knowledge. Maybe Professor Brandon Tate also wondered who Fiona Billingham was.

Then again, Professor Tate might be a spy. Eva's mind spun in circles until she reached a stunning conclusion—she and Raj may have been the only non-spies on the trip.

Her cell phone vibrated. Raj was calling, and she quickly related her suspicions about Bo and his spies.

"I've discovered our buddy Bo is an ideal spymaster," Raj agreed. "When you meet him, he exudes confidence and charm. You never know what he's doing or who he's recruiting."

"What about Hamadi? Is he in Bo's clutches by now?"

Raj chuckled in her ear. "That's one reason I phoned you. I just spoke to Bo. He inferred, through some of his secret means, that he arranged for Hamadi to be granted asylum in the U.S."

"How wonderful," Eva exclaimed, happiness filling her heart.

"You and I would think so, but Hamadi isn't convinced. He might stay in Israel."

Eva dropped in a chair. "At least our government made the offer. God will guide Hamadi and show him what to do. He may have an unusual outreach in Israel. And Raj, I haven't congratulated you on rescuing Hamadi and his friend. I hope you'll stay on the task force."

"Ah," he cleared his throat. "I may be going back to the Agency."

"Back to NCIS?"

"No, the 'Company.'"

Eva leaned back, dumbfounded. "You truly work for the CIA? So I really was the only non-company person in Egypt?"

"No, I couldn't resist." Raj laughed gleefully. "In truth, NCIS is looking to hire special agents with experience. Are you interested? You'd be a perfect fit."

"Watching the waves roll in, I did think about my future. Recently, I hinted to Scott that I might leave ICE. If I join NCIS, could I stay in DC?"

Raj thought so. "We have openings at the Joint Base Anacostia, and one at Quantico."

"I shoot there on the range." Eva tried to imagine working cases for the Navy.

She paused to consider his tempting proposal, and then said, "You know I'm not pleased with the way political factions in our government are destroying ICE. Raj, my gut reaction is to stay on the Terrorism Task Force, so long as I'm doing real law enforcement work."

"But Eva, if and when they send you chasing down criminal illegals, NCIS may have no openings."

"True enough, Raj. I'll have to trust in God's timing. He hasn't failed me yet."

Eva told him to greet Heather and ended the call. As she pocketed her cell phone, Grandpa Marty walked into the cramped office room. He wore a splendid smile, but held his hands behind his back.

"Eva Marie, your visiting with the family brings me much happiness. The art show is tomorrow."

"We wouldn't miss your exhibition," she said, rising to her feet. "What pictures you are showing?"

"This and that from my time in WWII. One of Aunt Deane, and this new one."

He swung his arms around to display a stunning acrylic of Lake Michigan. A family sat around a campfire. Eva drew closer to his painting.

Her hands flew to her face. "You and Dad are toasting marshmallows. So is Mom."

"Who else do you see?"

She giggled. "Scott and our three kiddos. And me. Oh, Aunt Deane and Grandma Joanne are by the poplar tree. Why are they looking on?"

"That's meant to show them in heaven. Keep looking."

Grandpa Marty set down the painting and they gathered around the desk. He pointed at Kaley wearing a jeweled cross. "I'm giving her an early graduation gift."

"What a stunning necklace. She will love it with the many gems. You are generous."

Grandpa Marty drew Eva's attention to her lap. "See, you have our family's Gutenberg Bible opened to Romans."

"It's small lettering. I need a magnifier," Eva said, squinting.

"I used a miro-brush to paint the letters. Kaley told me how she helped the teacher's daughter Olivia after he'd criticized her faith. The verse in Romans twelve seems appropriate."

"Let me look it up." Eva toggled to her cell phone Bible app. "It says we shouldn't repay evil for evil, but we are to help our enemies."

A tear stung her eye. She hugged her grandfather, feeling his bones. She straightened.

"You're not through yet," he said.

There was Andy gripping two drumsticks from his drum set. Decked out in his Air Force uniform, Scott had captain's wings pinned on his shirt. And Dutch wore his soccer outfit, his tiny hands clutching a kite.

"Grandpa, I will treasure this always."

He traced his finger along the leaves. "I painted in a few faces on our 'family tree.' Can you spot Pieter Vander Goes and his family?"

Eva was stunned by the intricate detail. Grandpa Marty had included so much of their family history. She kissed his cheek tenderly, and then touched the Gutenberg Bible on the canvas.

"What are these tiny letters along the shoreline?"

"Good eye, Eva. In the foam, I've written in white paint the names of John Wycliffe and Johann Gutenberg. Their enemies meant to stop them, but failed."

"It's pure genius," Eva said in awe. "They showed courage by saving God's Holy Word for the ages to come. We'll add a prologue to your memoirs making sure they aren't forgotten."

With her cell phone camera, Eva snapped several shots of his exquisite painting. Just then, Scott called up the stairs.

"Eva, the mail is here. I see a weird-looking letter addressed to you."

She shot Grandpa Marty a pained look and rushed down the steps. Before taking the envelope, she ran to the kitchen, grabbing sheets of paper towel and a sharp knife. Griff had recently informed her that the last "threatening" letter contained no fingerprints except hers.

Eva slid the knife beneath the flap while Grandpa Marty and Scott looked on. With the paper towel, she pulled out a single sheet of paper. On it was written in slanted writing, *Join us for a celebration of the life of Martin Vander Goes.*

Relief spread into her bones. She smiled at Grandpa Marty. "It's an invite to your art exhibit and the open house following."

Eva hugged him and started laughing. Once she started, she couldn't stop. She seriously needed to chill out and enjoy the precious family God had given her.

She snatched Scott's hand. "Come on, love. I'll race ya to Grandpa's tree swing."

Without thinking about terrorists or her next case, Eva ran out the door with Scott close behind. Their future was secure, in God's omnipotent hands.

# A NOTE FROM THE AUTHORS:

## ON FACT AND FICTION

We write fiction to entertain. We also conduct research and weave in historical facts to enlighten as it fits the story. In *Embers of Courage,* a cast of characters is included where historic persons are identified with an asterisk. We've been careful to report their contributions to history. The Reverend William White is a Christian martyr whose death is recorded in history. John Wycliffe did translate the first Bible into English, and his followers, the Lollards, were greatly persecuted. History records that his ashes were thrown into the River Swift. The historical account of Johann Gutenberg's development of movable type and printing press are true, as are accounts of his legal and financial woes. While he had investors, they didn't include Pieter Vander Goes, our fictional character. Unfortunately, Johann lost everything to Johann Fust when he ran into financial problems. At least he is still credited with his great contribution as the inventor of the printing press. The marriages and wars of the Dutch, French, and British royal families are mostly true. Margaret of York, who did marry to unite Burgundy with England, was a "bibliophile" who loved the written word and commissioned many manuscripts. She was a patron of William Caxton, who introduced printing to England.

We refer to our novels as "factional fiction" because each one contains some historical facts, noted above, or are influenced by cases we worked or witnessed in our careers in the justice system. While the methods (sometimes pretext) used by Eva Montanna, Bo Rider, Griff Topping, and Raj Pentu are realistic, the undercover and rescue operations written about in *Embers of Courage* are fictional. In the following pages, you will see our earlier books, of which *The Camelot Conspiracy* and *Stolen Legacy* also include a mix of history and fiction.

May you be blessed by this story of courage and faith,

Diane and David Munson

## The Joshua Covenant

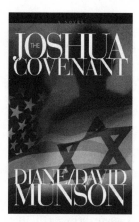

ISBN-13: 978-0-983559009
336 Pages, trade paper
Fiction / Mystery and Suspense
14.99

CIA agent Bo Rider moves to Israel after years of clandestine spying around the world. He takes his family—wife Julia, and teens, Glenna and Gregg—and serves in America's Embassy using his real name. Glenna and Gregg face danger while exploring Israel's treasures, and their father is shocked to uncover a menacing plot jeopardizing them all. A Bible scholar helps Bo in amazing ways. He discovers the truth about the Joshua Covenant and battles evil forces that challenge his true identity. Will Bo survive the greatest threat ever to his career, his family, and his life? Bo risks it all to stop an enemy spy.

## Night Flight

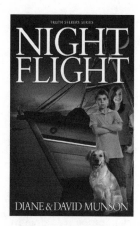

ISBN-13: 978-0983559023
224 Pages, trade paper
Fiction / Mystery and Suspense
14.99

In *Night Flight* the Munsons crank out a high velocity thriller for the young and young at heart. When CIA agent Bo Rider's kids ask for a dog, Bo adopts Blaze a mature dog for Glenna and Gregg. The teens are shocked when Blaze confronts shady criminals making counterfeit money. They discover what their parents never told them: Blaze is a retired law enforcement dog. When the crooks are arrested, Glenna and Gregg become witnesses and take refuge with their grandparents in Treasure Island, Florida. When Grandpa Buck learns what Blaze can do, he permits the kids to put Blaze to work solving crimes. Glenna and Gregg use the reward money to help a friend with an urgent need. Danger follows them from Skeleton Key in the dark of night as Blaze reveals a surprising twist.

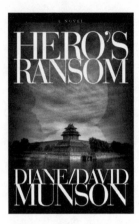

ISBN-13: 978-0982535530
320 pages, trade paper
Fiction / Mystery and Suspense
14.99

## Hero's Ransom

CIA Agent Bo Rider (*The Camelot Conspiracy*) and Federal Agents Eva Montanna and Griff Topping (*Facing Justice, Confirming Justice, The Camelot Conspiracy*) return in Hero's Ransom, the Munsons' fourth family-friendly adventure. When archeologist Amber Worthing uncovers a two-thousand-year-old mummy and witnesses a secret rocket launch at a Chinese missile base, she is arrested for espionage. Her imprisonment sparks a custody battle between grandparents over her young son, Lucas. Caught between sinister world powers, Amber's faith is tested in ways she never dreamed possible. Danger escalates as Bo races to stop China's killer satellite from destroying America and, with Eva and Griff's help, to rescue Amber using an unexpected ransom.

ISBN-13: 978-0982535547
320 Pages, trade paper
Fiction / Mystery and Suspense
14.99

## Redeeming Liberty

In this timely thriller by ExFeds Diane and David Munson (former Federal Prosecutor and Federal Agent), parole officer Dawn Ahern is shocked to witness her friend Liberty, the chosen bride of Wally (former "lost boy" from Sudan) being kidnapped by modern-day African slave traders. Dawn tackles overwhelming danger head-on in her quest to redeem Liberty. When she reaches out to FBI agent Griff Topping and CIA agent Bo Rider, her life is changed forever. Suspense soars as Bo launches a clandestine rescue effort for Liberty only to discover a deadly Iranian secret threatening the lives of millions of Americans and Israelis. Glimpse tomorrow's startling headlines in this captivating story of faith and freedom under fire.

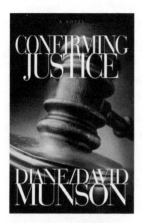

ISBN-13: 978-0982535516
352 pages, trade paper
Fiction / Mystery and Suspense
14.99

## Confirming Justice

In *Confirming Justice*, all eyes are on Federal Judge Dwight Pendergast, secretly in line for nomination to the Supreme Court, who is presiding over a bribery case involving a cabinet secretary's son. When the key prosecution witness disappears, FBI agent Griff Topping risks everything to save the case while Pendergast's enemies seek to embroil the judge in a web of corruption and deceit. The whole world watches as events threaten the powerful position and those who covet it. Diane and David Munson masterfully create plot twists, legal intrigue and fast-paced suspense, in their realistic portrayal of what transpires behind the scenes at the center of power.

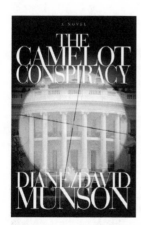

ISBN-13: 978-0982535523
352 pages, trade paper
Fiction / Mystery and Suspense
14.99

## The Camelot Conspiracy

The *Camelot Conspiracy* rocks with a sinister plot even more menacing than the headlines. Former D.C. insiders Diane and David Munson feature a brash TV reporter, Kat Kowicki, who receives an ominous email that throws her into the high stakes conspiracy of John F. Kennedy's assassination. When Kat uncovers evidence Lee Harvey Oswald did not act alone, she turns for help to Federal Special Agents Eva Montanna and Griff Topping who uncover the chilling truth: A shadow government threatens to tear down the very foundations of the American justice system.

# THE MUNSONS' THRILLERS MAY BE READ IN ANY ORDER.

ISBN-13: 978-0983559047
336 pages, trade paper
Fiction / Mystery and Suspense
14.99

## Stolen Legacy

*Stolen Legacy*, by Diane and David Munson, tells the daunting tale of Germany invading Holland, and the heroes who dare to resist by hiding Jews. Federal agent Eva Montanna stops protecting America long enough to visit her grandfather's farm and help write a memoir of his dangerous time under Nazi control. Eva is shocked to uncover a plot to harm Grandpa Marty. Memories are tested as secrets from Marty's time in the Dutch resistance and later service in the Monuments Men of the U.S. Army fuel this betrayal. The Munsons' eighth thriller unveils priceless relics and a stolen legacy, forever changing Eva's life and her faith.

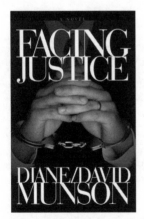

ISBN-13: 978-0982535509
352 pages, trade paper
Fiction / Mystery and Suspense
14.99

## Facing Justice

Diane and David Munson draw on their true-life experiences in this suspense novel about Special Agent Eva Montanna, whose twin sister died at the Pentagon on 9/11. Eva dedicates her career to avenge her death while investigating Emile Jubayl, a member of Eva's church and CEO of Helpers International, who is accused of using his aid organization to funnel money to El Samoud, head of the Armed Revolutionary Cause, and successor to Al Qaeda. Family relationships are tested in this fast-paced, true-to-life legal thriller about the men and women who are racing to defuse the ticking time bomb of international terrorism.